As the Crow Flies

By the Author

Meeting Ms. Roman

The Feeding

Nightshade

Love Spell

As the Crow Flies

by

Karen F. Williams

2018

ISBN 13: 978-1-63555-285-0

This Trade Paperback Original Is Published By
Bold Strokes Books, Inc.
P.O. Box 249
Valley Falls, NY 12185

First Edition: November 2018

Credits
Editor: Shelley Thrasher
Production Design: Stacia Seaman
Cover Design by Melody Pond

Acknowledgments

I wish to express gratitude to the incredible staff of professionals at Bold Strokes; to my editor, Shelley Thrasher, for her sharp eye and insights; and to a fine group of friends and beta readers for their respective contributions: Judith Portnoy, Donna Ramirez, Jean Giunta, Charlotte Demescko, Marie Monterosso, and Francie McMahon. Heartfelt thanks go out to Carryl Cole for keeping me and my story on point; Michelle Lisper for her support and technical expertise; and Dr. Kelly Wacker, my dear friend and on-call luminary. I'm blessed to have you all in my life.

This book is dedicated to Carryl

And to the memory of an extraordinary junkyard dog
whose life I changed, and who changed mine.
I'd give anything to rewrite her story.

And to my readers.

Life is like a game of connect the dots.
Never underestimate the unseen forces that draw those lines
and link us in mysterious and purposeful ways.
The ink may be invisible, but the connections are indelible.

Chapter One

For almost five years now, since the eve of her forty-second birthday, Samantha Weller lived on borrowed time. She didn't mind it, though; in fact, she rather enjoyed the notion. There was a strange pleasure, an odd sense of liberation, in knowing you'd defied death, beat the forces—outlived yourself, so to speak.

Of course, a taxi ride around Manhattan was a sure way to further tempt the Fates. Samantha braced herself in the back seat of a yellow cab as the driver cut off two cars and a bus. "Hold on, *mami*," she warned Samantha in broken English, a wad of pink gum muffling her words and obstructing her vision as she blew a bubble so big it touched the brim of her purple baseball cap.

The only thing left for Samantha to hold was her breath, and she did just that as the taxi crossed two lanes and careened to the corner of Hudson and West 10th Street. Stunned, Samantha looked at the giant pink bubble and two dark eyes staring at her in the rearview mirror. For a moment they regarded one another blankly, and then the cabbie began slowly inhaling, deflating the bubble until half of it collapsed on her chin. Samantha watched, amazed, as a tongue darted out and, in one quick swipe, gathered up the whole pink mess and retreated into her mouth.

"*Mami*, you gettin' out or what?" the cabbie asked. And when Samantha didn't respond, she cracked her gum so loud Samantha thought someone had fired a gun, and she jumped.

Forcing a polite smile, Samantha took a deep breath, paid, and climbed out.

The cabbie gave her the once-over with a crooked smile, her elbow propped and sticking out of the open window. "Thanks," she said, acknowledging the generous tip.

"Oh, no, thank *you*, Ms. Ramos!" Samantha bowed with an exaggerated sweep of her arm. "A roller-coaster ride couldn't have been this exhilarating."

Ms. Ramos stopped chewing, her eyes narrowing. "How you know my name, *mami*?"

"It is Ramos, yes? *Myra* Ramos?"

Squinting suspiciously, she gestured at Samantha with her chin. "Me and you…we slept together?"

Samantha laughed. "No, we did not! And it's a good thing for me. I barely survived a taxi ride with you." She pointed to the displayed photo ID. "Nice picture, too."

Smirking, Ms. Ramos stared her up and down, then cracked her gum again and sped away.

Samantha shook her head as the cab veered back into traffic and took a moment to collect herself. It was June and unseasonably cool in New York City this week—mid-seventies, expected to dip into the fifties tonight—but the late-afternoon sun was strong, and the reckless taxi ride had her sweating. Samantha slipped out of her blazer, checking the street signs as she rolled up the sleeves of a white shirt. Then she hiked the strap of a messenger bag over her shoulder and tightened her grip on a canvas bag in which she carried an old bookend.

The bookend itself was a ceramic sculpture of an open book, a nearly life-size crow perched upon its pages—unless the crow was meant to be a raven. Samantha couldn't be sure. She'd bought the thing at an estate sale only last week. But it was heavy, a good few pounds, and after carrying it around the city all day, she felt like it had doubled in weight.

Strolling down Hudson Street, she craned her neck to note the names of shops along the way. She was searching for her sister-in-law's sister—the gay sister of her brother's new wife, to be exact. Liz Bowes owned an antique shop somewhere in the vicinity. At least that's what she'd told Samantha at the wedding four months ago. Liz had named the shop after a movie, she remembered her saying, although just what movie she couldn't for the life of her recall.

Samantha could have had the bookend appraised elsewhere, but she preferred to deal with someone who, by moral reason of them being related by marriage, wouldn't take advantage of her ignorance. Not that Samantha intended to part with the piece. It wasn't every day one stumbled upon art in the form of a raven or crow. The ill-reputed birds had certainly made a permanent nest in the branches of literature and folklore, but definitely not in the visual arts. People didn't seem to care for the likes of them in their homes—a raven figurine on a shelf, say, or a crow on canvas over the sofa. People preferred ducks, roosters, flamingoes, whimsical birds with less threatening aspects. It was an unfortunate fact, especially for Samantha, who happened to be the proud owner of a real crow. Never mind finding a painting of a crow to hang over her sofa—finding a woman to sit on the sofa with a *live* crow proved a more difficult task these days.

Time and again Samantha's dates outright insulted the bird. From mistaken remarks such as "crows carry disease," to the more superstitious "crows and ravens are bad omens," right on down to the more sophisticated "that bird gives me the freaking creeps," Samantha had heard it all. And so it came to pass, as it always did, that Samantha was forced to choose between a woman and her bird, which didn't leave much choice at all. For, contrary to superstitions surrounding the black birds and bad luck, Bertha the crow brought only good luck.

Hurricane Bertha was sweeping the East Coast on the night Samantha and the bird made one another's unlikely acquaintance. Driving home from a friend's birthday dinner in the city, she was stopped at a red light in White Plains when, amidst whirling branches and wind-driven debris, something black and very much alive tumbled to the ground. What with the drag created by the bird's panicked flapping and fluttering, the fledgling survived the fall, but to Samantha's left and right, where the traffic light was green, oncoming cars approached in the distance. In the middle of the road the helpless crow hobbled in dizzy circles, cawing, summoning Samantha to its rescue.

Without taking time to think, she threw her car into park and jumped out. Using a forearm to shield her face against the windswept rain, she dashed into the intersection, scooped up the huge baby with both hands, and backed away from oncoming traffic just in time. But as she did, a thunderous *crash* and a *boom* came from behind, followed by shouts and screams and the honking of horns. Squinting against the pelting downpour, Samantha spun around to see her car—what little she could find of it—buried beneath the canopy of a fallen tree.

The windshield was mashed, the roof crushed clear to the steering wheel. And at that moment Samantha realized she had been meant to die that night—right there, at a red light, an inadvertent victim of Hurricane Bertha. Or maybe she wasn't meant to die.

Soaked and in shock, Samantha and the baby crow shared a ride home in the tow truck that evening, and for the rest of the night she sat in her kitchen, alternately feeding the fledgling and trying to decide whether she'd saved the crow's life or the crow had saved hers. By morning she concluded, in no uncertain terms, that she and the bird had simultaneously saved each other. The whole event, Samantha was sure, was a fine example of cosmic intervention. Synchronicity, perhaps. Maybe synchronicity had saved them both. And so Samantha and Bertha, as the crow was aptly named, went about conducting their lives on borrowed time. And the living only got better with the bird around.

Before Bertha, Samantha's would-be career as a mystery writer had been bereft of good luck. She'd spent the past fifteen years as a forensic investigator working for a crime lab, which is to say she worked long hours in unsafe and unsanitary conditions, tolerating offensive smells and disturbing scenes. Sometimes those scenes included dead people in various stages of decomposition—in basements, in pieces, in dilapidated buildings, wooded lots, sometimes in two feet of mosquito-infested pond water. In accordance with strict chain-of-evidence procedures, Samantha wrote her highly detailed reports, one after the next, year after year, until one day she decided she wanted to write something else. Forensic investigation wasn't as glamorous as it appeared on television, but it had given her plenty of ideas for writing glamorous murder mysteries.

Over the course of a year, Samantha spent her days off creating a fictional counterpart and completing a manuscript, but her hopeful agent couldn't find an interested publisher. And then on the night of her first Halloween with Bertha, Samantha got a new and even better idea for a would-be sleuth.

She had just carried a lighted jack-o'-lantern in from the porch and set it by the hearth for Bertha to see. "Do you remember when we met?" Samantha asked, stretching out on the floor beside the crow and the pumpkin and affectionately recounting their fateful meeting. "Come on, Bertha...speak for Mommy, speak for Sam-Sam. Say it. It was a dark and stormy night," Samantha began, as all good stories do. "Come on," she coaxed the crow, ruffling the shiny black feathers on its neck. "It was a *dark* and—"

"*Daak!*" the crow yelled, visibly mesmerized by the orange glow. She inspected the pumpkin's nose and peeked through its triangular eyes, fixated on the flame of the burning candle inside. "*Daak-daak!*" Bertha squawked when Samantha tickled her under the wing.

"That's right, Sam-Sam's brilliant little birdbrain. It was a dark—or *daak*, if you prefer—and stormy night. A *daak* and stormy—"

Without warning, the idea struck Samantha as hard as the tree had struck her car, and she found herself caught up in another storm: a brainstorm this time, about a nocturnal sleuth who travels the world, solving paranormal crimes under the guidance of her familiar, a psychic crow. She'd call her sleuth Detective Candice Crowley. Bertha would become her avian Watson.

Samantha wrote it. Her agent liked it. The publisher loved it. Mystery readers couldn't read the stuff fast enough. In less than four years Samantha had become the acclaimed author of the best-selling Detective Crowley mystery series, her fifth book coming off the press in two weeks. No small thanks to Bertha. And no small thanks to the cosmic principle of synchronicity that had brought them together.

Looking up at the signs around Christopher Street, Samantha wiped her brow with the back of her hand and was just turning to backtrack when a shop across the street caught her eye. Tiny pink lights twinkled in the window, and on a green awning above the door were pink letters reading "Somewhere in Time." That was it! *Somewhere in Time*. She'd known it was around here…somewhere.

Samantha waited for cars and a limousine to pass, then sprinted across the street and peeked in the window. Two customers stood at the counter with their backs to her, but between them she recognized Liz standing in front of an old brass register. It looked like a scene from a bygone era. She knew Liz was only thirty-two, but with sparkling earrings, knotted beads, and wavy auburn hair slicked back, she looked like a 1920s flapper who'd just stepped out of…well…*somewhere in time*. Of course, at the wedding she'd been more formally dressed, both she and her female companion, as it were. According to Samantha's brother, Jason, Liz was quite the ladies' woman: charming, decadent, rarely seen twice with the same one. Samantha remembered Liz's older sister, Lisa, telling her over dinner one night that her sister's promiscuity was attributable to what she suspected was untreated *attention-deficit disorder*. "Liz can't focus on anything or anyone for too long. She's always been the wild child," Lisa had said.

Wild or not, sitting at Liz's table at the wedding had been a lot of fun, and Samantha wondered if perhaps Lisa was secretly envious of her sister's charisma.

Samantha turned the handle of the glass door and went in, bells jingling overhead. As much as Liz appeared to step out of the past, Samantha felt herself stepping into it. The door seemed to be a vortex to the Roaring Twenties. She attempted to close it quietly, but the bells jingled again. Liz looked up from the counter, acknowledging her with an impersonal glance at first. But then her big green eyes widened in recognition. "Sam?"

"Liz!" she said with a nod of greeting. The two women at the counter turned, looking Samantha up and down, and then turned back and whispered to each other.

"Sam—oh my God!" She beamed. "What are you doing here?"

"I was in the city having lunch with my editor, and, well," she gestured at the bag in her hand, "I need something appraised."

"I can't believe it. Are you in a hurry?"

"No, no." Samantha held up a hand. "Take your time."

"Good. Have a look around."

Samantha didn't care how long she waited. She had found the place and was glad she'd decided to come. Glad, too, that Liz was so happy to see her.

Chapter Two

Samantha hated antique shops. Such dank, dreary, depressing places they were. Everything for sale was old, used, somehow expired—like the original owners, she speculated—and if forced to work in one, she'd require antidepressants by payday. That and nasal spray to combat the stuffiness.

But not this place. Liz's shop was different—colorful and very much alive. Ragtime music wafted from hidden speakers, glass lamps casting seductive glows, and the scent of potpourri masked any would-be mustiness. Overhead, a ceiling fan fit for a saloon spun in rhythm with the music, stirring together sounds and scents and collective memories so that, all in all, the shop had an enchanted feel.

In one panoramic glance, Samantha surveyed everything. She felt like a kid who had discovered the treasure-filled attic of some abandoned mansion. Each aisle was loaded with a hodgepodge of curiosities, an *expensive* hodgepodge, and she suddenly grew uneasy about breaking something. Setting her belongings down beside a Chippendale chair, she slipped her hands into her pockets and headed down the nearest aisle to browse. But just as she turned, she bumped into her own reflection in a cheval mirror and almost pardoned herself.

Feathery boas and sequined hats were draped over the top of the mirror, and seeing her image framed by it all made Samantha think that, like Liz, she wouldn't have looked so out of place in the nineteen twenties or thirties. She stood in front of it, thinking that she seemed strange to herself—a bit taller than she remembered, brown eyes darker, lips fuller, jaw more pronounced. Maybe this was an old trick mirror, some antique recovered from a Coney Island carnival and—

"Yoo-hoo! Where's the mistress-of-mystery hiding?" Liz called, both her voice and the jingle of bells ringing out as the customers left the shop.

"Nice mirror," Samantha said with a sheepish shrug when Liz came up from behind.

She put her hands on Samantha's shoulders, but Liz was slightly shorter and had to lean out to the side to see their reflections side by side. "So nice you lost yourself in it, huh?"

Liz was the first redhead she'd ever met who didn't have freckles. Her skin was fair and flawless, her short wavy hair a dark russet, her eyes green as emeralds. Really, she was quite beautiful, and so young, Samantha thought. She looked at Liz's roaring-twenties outfit in the mirror, smiling at the low-cut, sleeveless top, the loose and breezy skirt with its fringed hemline. "I could get lost in this whole store," Samantha answered her.

"And find lots of ideas while you're getting lost, I bet. I've always thought antique shops would be great places for writers to get ideas, you know?"

"I already have one," Samantha said, "about a mystery writer who finds herself mesmerized by an old mirror…except the mirror isn't really a mirror, but a portal."

"Ah…" Liz twisted her lips. "Sort of like a C.S. Lewis grows up. I like it. Just remember to mention that you got the idea in my store. It'll be good for business. And then you can do a book signing here, and I'll have lines out the door." She grinned and rubbed Samantha's arms affectionately before letting go and stepping aside. "My customers thought you were Rachel Maddow when you first walked in."

Samantha shrugged. "I get that a lot…even though I don't wear glasses," she said. "It must be my haircut."

"Could be. Either way, you're very attractive."

"Why, thank you." Samantha lowered her eyes bashfully. "And if you ever want me to do a signing here, I will."

"Really?" Liz put a hand to her chest. "You'd do that? I'll hold you to it, you know." She turned and motioned for Samantha to follow her.

Samantha walked to the front of the shop and set her canvas bag on the counter, immediately drawn to the purple glow of a black light coming from a small curio cabinet mounted on the wall behind Liz. The small shelves held an assortment of green shot glasses and little glass animals that were brilliantly phosphorescent. "What is all that?"

"Uranium glass. Also called Vaseline glass. It's radioactive." She turned off the light. "See? Without the black light it looks like plain green and yellow Depression glass, but with the black light on," she flipped the switch again, "it fluoresces. Is that cool or what?"

"Very cool. Is it safe?"

"Pretty harmless. The uranium is contained in the glass, and it's just a tiny amount, although some pieces will register radiation on a Geiger counter. Sometimes I think of having a dinner party with uranium-glass table settings and replacing all the lightbulbs in the dining room with black lights so that the whole table glows green."

"That's a dinner party I don't want to miss."

"Then I'll put you on the guest list." Liz bit her bottom lip and gazed thoughtfully at her. "So the writing's going well, huh?"

"Very well."

"You're one of my favorite authors, you know."

"I didn't know."

"I tell my sister that all the time."

"No one tells me anything."

"I've read all your books, Sam. Do you remember my date at the wedding?"

"Sure. I danced with her. Lori, wasn't it?"

"Good memory. After meeting you, she ran out and bought all your books. Then I started reading and," she shrugged, "what can I say? I'm hooked."

"Well, thank you. Thank Lori for me, too, for the compliment and all."

Liz waved a hand. "She's history. They all go down in history."

"I'm sorry."

"Don't be. It's me. I don't do relationships," she said with a roll of her eyes. "And speaking of all the dear and dispensable people in my life, have you seen our siblings?"

"Once since the wedding," Samantha confessed. "Have you?"

"Twice since the wedding. We talk, though."

Samantha narrowed her eyes. "Do we unconsciously avoid them?"

"Personally? I make a conscious effort to do so."

"I guess it's wrong to dodge our kin like that."

"They leave us no choice, Sam. I mean, all they do is talk incessantly about their life, their work, their plans, their friends. There's never any conversation, just boring monologues about people I don't even know.

No offense, but neither one ever shuts up long enough to say, 'Hey, Liz. How's the interior-design and antique-furniture business? What's new? What's up with *you*?' "

Samantha frowned. "Don't feel too bad. When I sent them my last book, they never even called to thank me."

Her lips curled in something of a snarl. "Are you serious? How rude!"

"I don't know whether they liked it, hated it, or even bothered to read it at all."

"What socially inept little shits."

"*Shits?* You mean *siblings*."

"Face it, Sam. We've got shits for siblings."

"Maybe they're just too busy."

"They're busy being shits! Don't excuse that narcissistic behavior. If you ask me, they suffer from the same personality disorder, and if they're busy doing anything it's bumping into each other's ego."

Samantha grinned. "I guess that's why they bought that enormous house in the Hamptons. So their egos would have enough space."

"Oh, *please* don't get me started on the East Hampton house. I have fantasies about that house floating into the Atlantic Ocean while they're asleep in their Ralph Lauren pajamas under their Ralph Lauren sheets."

Samantha smiled. "Maybe we should start an in-law support group."

"Yeah. Let's see…" Liz thought for a moment. "We'll call ourselves…the *Out-laws*."

"I love it. Sign me up." They stared at one another, eyes twinkling with mischief, until they both laughed aloud.

When they'd regained their composure, Liz turned her attention to the object in front of her. "So. Now that we've vented and validated one another…what's in the bag, mystery writer?"

"Your sister's head."

"Ha! You're lying. You know how I know you're lying? Because my sister's *mouth* wouldn't fit in that bag."

Samantha chuckled as she fiddled with the zipper. "Actually, I've got a bookend from a yard sale."

"Yeah? Just one?"

"I think it's old, probably not worth anything, but I was hoping you might—"

"Well? Let me see," she said, flailing her hand at the bag to hurry her along.

Samantha had covered it in a ridiculous amount of bubble wrap to ensure a safe and padded journey.

Liz tapped her polished nails on the counter as Samantha carefully unrolled several feet of the plastic stuff. But once she freed the sculpture and set it in front of Liz, her eyes widened with the intrigue of an antiquarian. "Oh, wow…this is Rookwood," she said.

The moving blades of the ceiling fan caused the lights to shift and play upon the high-gloss finish of the crow's dark-blue body and the yellow book on which it stood. The piece was ornate but eye-catching, especially here, where it complemented the other antiques.

Liz turned it upside down for careful inspection, then set it down again and stroked the ceramic crow as though petting a real bird. "What did you say you bought it for?"

Samantha shrugged. People collected all sorts of animals, didn't they? Cats, frogs, bears, Scotty dogs, penguins. "I bought it because it was a crow."

"I meant, what did you pay for it?"

"Three dollars."

"Three—? Do you have any idea what you have here, Sam?" She shook her head, waiting expectantly. "Rookwood is a highly desirable American art pottery."

"So, then the bird is a rook, not a crow?" Samantha asked.

"They list their birds as rooks, but I wouldn't know a rook from a crow."

"They're all in the same family—ravens, crows, rooks, magpies."

"Well, this one bookend is worth several hundred dollars. What made you bring it here if you thought it was worthless?" she asked, talking to Samantha as she picked it up and inspected the piece.

"I only bought it because it looked like my bird. One person's junk is another's treasure, I guess. But when I got it home and started looking at it—*really* looking at it—it seemed too perfect, somehow special."

Liz gave her a sideways glance. "So you've got an eye for valuable pieces. I should start dragging you along to estate sales and letting you sniff out the treasures. It's every dealer's dream, you know, to buy a piece of furniture for—oh, a few hundred dollars, say—and discover it's worth thousands."

"That happens?"

"Sure it happens. Of course, now that tag sales and antique flea markets have become a favorite pastime, people are paying more attention to what they have."

Samantha nodded. "How do you know it's *Rookwood*?"

"Come around here and I'll show you," Liz said, turning the bookend over again and picking up a pencil.

Making her way behind the counter, Samantha came up alongside her to view the incised mark on the bottom of the bookend.

"See the backward *R* and the *P*? They stand for Rookwood Pottery." She pointed with her pencil. "Anyway, see the circle of flames around the letters?"

Samantha squinted to see the little squiggly lines.

"Each one represents a year," Liz said. "This particular mark was first used in eighteen eighty-six. So, starting from the left, the first flame stands for that year. A full set of fifteen flames brings it to the year nineteen hundred. After that, roman numerals were added. See if you can figure out the date."

Samantha counted fifteen flames. "Nineteen hundred," she said.

"And…?"

There were two *X*'s and a *V*. "Plus twenty-five, so that's 1925?"

"Exactly," Liz said. They stood shoulder to shoulder. "Rookwood is one of the most expensive potteries. Some pieces command thousands of dollars, especially the earlier, artist-signed pieces. The pottery went commercial during the art deco period in America, and this rook bookend is one example of that fact.

"To give you an idea of how it compares with other pottery," Liz said, "take a look at a few pieces around here. There's McCoy, which, like Fiesta, was only dime-store stuff at the time. Of course, now it sells for a lot more—especially since Martha Stewart plugged it on her show. Then there's Roseville and others, which you would have purchased in finer department stores. But Rookwood is top-shelf, so to speak."

Samantha turned over the piece and examined the mark again. "I'm impressed with your knowledge."

"Nah," Liz said, straightening up and waving a hand. "This is all general stuff. I'm not a pottery expert. I deal in furniture, mostly—but

I do know a few dealers who specialize in art pottery." Liz looked up at an antique clock hanging on the opposite wall. It was five past five.

"I'm sorry to keep you," Samantha said.

"Don't be. It's not like I have a wife to get home to or anything. In fact, let me make a quick call." And with that she disappeared behind a curtain-covered doorway. A moment later Samantha heard her exchanging pleasantries with someone, and not long after that Liz peeked out from behind the curtain, her hand held over the receiver.

"Sam? You're not looking to sell it, are you?"

"No. Ideally, I'd like to find a match."

"How romantic," Liz whispered. "That's what we call a marriage… finding a cup to match a saucer, or a salt shaker to match a pepper shaker." She extended her arm, motioning for Samantha to hand her the pad and pencil on the counter, and then disappeared behind the curtain again.

"Yeah, Ed," Samantha heard her say. "Uh-huh…well, my sister in-law would like to make a marriage if possible. What do you think the chances are of…uh-huh…uh-huh…should I contact her directly?" Liz was silent for a moment, then, "That'd be great, Ed. Laraway? Where's she located?"

Another minute and Liz was back, scribbling something on one of her business cards and handing it to her.

Samantha looked at it. "Gwen Laraway?"

"She's up in the Berkshires, western Massachusetts, just east of the Hudson Valley. Ed says she has an enormous Rookwood collection, some of which are museum-quality pieces. He says she does sell on occasion but doesn't do third-party dealings unless it's at auction."

"You think she might have something for me?"

"Call her. It's worth a try. If you don't have any luck, Ed suggested you look on eBay, or even call the Cincinnati Art Society. That's where the Rookwood auctions are held every year." Liz stared at her, a satisfied gleam in her emerald-green eyes. "Isn't this exciting? I feel like a matchmaker."

"On the phone you referred to me as your sister in-law."

"Yeah, well, it's easier that way," Liz said.

"I wish I *were* your sister in-law."

"No, you don't. That would make you married to my sister."

"Or you to my brother."

"Don't even go there, Sam."

"You're right. I guess it's better this way."

"Much better," Liz said.

"Hey, do you have to be somewhere?"

"Not particularly. Why?"

"Let me take you to dinner," Samantha said.

"You mean like a date?"

"Well, not a date-date…you know, just a dinner date."

"Good," Liz said and took a deep breath, "because I think you're hot, and if I didn't know you I'd sleep with you in a heartbeat, but, well, we're out-laws now. It would be a little strange."

Samantha smiled in amusement. "Number one, as hot as *you* are, you're too young for me, and number two, yes, sleeping with my out-law would feel incestuous. So how about grabbing a bite with me…and then I have to hurry home to my crow by sundown."

"Okay." Liz laughed. "I forget that Bertha, the psychic crow, is a real bird. I want to meet her one day. And you know what?" she said, her eyes darting around the shop. "Now that I know you collect crows, I might have something for you." Sidestepping Samantha, she moved around the counter and went down an aisle. Samantha heard the clinking of glass and pottery and watched her return with a whimsical crow sporting a tuxedo, red vest, and top hat.

"It's an old bourbon decanter," she said, pulling off the hat to expose the cork, "from the Old Crow distillery in Kentucky."

"Wow…he's wonderful!"

"A dapper fellow, isn't he?"

"I'll say…" Samantha inspected the bottle, deciding she must add it to her new crow and rook collection. "Sold," she said.

"Hey, we're family. I can't take money from an out-law. He's yours. Consider it a gift from a fan and relative…or relative fan." And with that she took the bottle, wrapped it in newspaper, and handed it back to Samantha.

"Thanks. This is very generous."

"Don't mention it." She turned off the fan and the lights in the shop. "I picked it up at an estate sale. You know, Sam," she added, as she disappeared down another aisle, "I really am glad you came today."

"Me, too…" she said, carefully packing both her bookend and the Old Crow bottle into the canvas bag she'd transported it in. "Me, too," she said again to herself.

Chapter Three

Cappuccino, please," Liz told the waiter. They'd found a busy café on Christopher Street and tucked themselves away at a corner table on the outdoor patio.

"Make it two." Samantha pointed to their leftover mussels and calamari. "And a doggy bag, please."

"A *bird* bag." Liz corrected her. "It's for her pet crow."

"A crow?" The ponytailed waiter's eyes lit up. "For real?"

Samantha nodded.

"That's so cool. I'd love to have a crow," he said. "Do you like mysteries?"

"Sure. Doesn't everybody love a good mystery?"

"Oh, man, then you should definitely check out Samantha Weller. She writes the Detective Crowley series. It's like…you never really know if Crowley is human or supernatural, but she has this pet crow who flies between this life and the afterlife to help her solve crimes."

Samantha winked at her as they listened to the waiter. He couldn't have been more than twenty. A college student, Liz guessed.

When the waiter cleared the table, Liz inclined her head toward Samantha and whispered, "Why didn't you tell him you're the author?"

"I don't know…I'm shy that way." Samantha shrugged. "But it certainly is nice to encounter a young person—anyone under the age of twenty-five, actually—who reads for pleasure."

Liz nodded, regarding her thoughtfully before she spoke. "So… you live alone with that crow?" she asked, just as the waiter came back with Bertha's bird bag and the check.

Samantha snatched the check as Liz reached for it and handed it back to the waiter with a credit card. "Just the two of us," she answered.

"So Bertha isn't just her fictional name?"

"Nope. She's Bertha all the time—on and off the pages."

"And she really eats this stuff?" Liz circled a finger at the bag of leftover seafood. Having read Samantha's books and grown so familiar with Bertha's fictional counterpart, she felt as though she knew the bird. "What's it like living with a crow?"

"A challenge," Samantha admitted. "She's beyond inquisitive, hopelessly curious, constantly seeking stimulation."

"Geez, Sam. That's me to a T."

"If she were a woman she'd have exhausted me by now." Samantha laughed. "But she does retrieve my car keys when I can't find them."

"What…you mean she's really psychic, like in your novels?"

"No, she's a thief. She steals and hides them, then retrieves them when I lose patience. She likes to steal and hoard any shiny object she can carry."

"Wow…just like a dragon," Liz said.

"A dragon?"

"Yeah. In mythology dragons hoard treasures—like in *Beowulf* and *The Lord of the Rings*, remember?"

"Then I guess she is like a dragon…or a pirate, for that matter. Her favorite pastimes are hoarding, listening to music, and staring at candlelight."

Liz raised her brow. "Quite the thieving hedonist, huh? Reminds me of the woman I was with last weekend."

Samantha smiled. "You can't trust her alone with a burning candle, though, because she becomes mesmerized and stands too close. An ornithologist over at the zoo told me crows have been known to carry burning material to empty nests, just to watch the flames…the same way people enjoy bonfires, I suppose."

Elbows propped on the table, Liz folded her hands and rested her chin on them. "Bertha sounds like the sweetest little sociopath. I can see the headline now: MYSTERY WRITER GOES UP IN SMOKE: FEATHERED PYROMANIAC HELD SUSPECT IN AUTHOR'S DEATH."

Samantha laughed as she drank her cappuccino, and it suddenly occurred to Liz that Samantha herself exhibited all the behaviors she attributed to her crow. While Liz was closing the shop, Samantha had stood by the door, clearly captivated by the pink twinkling lights in the window. And when they'd reached the restaurant, Samantha had asked for a corner table by a potted arborvitae tree covered in tiny white lights. She'd even asked the waiter to light the candle on the table, even though it wasn't yet dark.

Liz looked at Samantha's upper lip, which was now replete with a cappuccino mustache. She thought to tell her to wipe her mouth, but then decided it looked cute for the moment and neglected to mention it. "Don't you feel bad keeping a wild bird caged?" she said instead.

"I don't. She's outside all day long—that's why I have to get home. Around dusk she looks to come in. She even knows the sound of my car, and unless it's dark she sometimes waits up the block and flies home alongside me."

"Really?"

"Yep. And I really shouldn't call her a thief, because half the time she actually brings me gifts."

"Like what?"

"Shiny things she finds in the street—bottle tops, buttons, pieces of metal, broken glass. I know it's stupid, but those gifts mean the world to me. I have a jar full." Samantha smiled. "It may not be as pretty as beach glass, but it's an interesting collection."

"That's incredible. I'd say a complex thought process is at work, not to mention the feelings of affection involved in gift-giving."

Samantha nodded like a proud parent. "Anyway, when she comes inside she has a few parrot-size perches scattered throughout the house. If she's not on a perch, she's usually walking around following me."

"What does she do all day outdoors? Fly with a flock of other crows?"

"That would be a *murder* of crows, not a flock. And I don't know. I can't very well spy on her without wings. I thought she'd grow up and leave me for a crow, but we don't have any in the area. People tell me the West Nile virus wiped them all out there."

"Why don't you just clip her wings? Wouldn't that be safer than having her outdoors?"

"It supposedly changes their personalities—makes them nervous and nasty."

"Nervous and nasty…sounds like another one of my recent dates."

"Geez." Samantha frowned. "It doesn't sound like you're too good at picking women. Maybe you should get a bird instead."

Liz pondered the idea. Maybe she would do well to give up on the prospect of a long-term relationship and get a pet bird instead. Maybe a lovebird. A lone, unpaired lovebird, sort of like Samantha's bookend.

Then she and her lonely, lovesick lovebird could pine over their shared state of *lovelessness*. Of course, Samantha and *her* bird could always visit, and the four of them could pine together.

Liz leaned back in her seat as the waiter returned with Samantha's credit card.

"Oh, man," the waiter said. "This is embarrassing…*you're* Samantha Weller? *The* Ms. Weller?"

Liz tapped Samantha's arm. "Wipe your mouth," she said in a low voice.

"Huh?"

"Froth." She pointed to her own upper lip.

Samantha quickly patted her mouth with her napkin and turned back to the waiter. "Ah, you caught my name on the card. Good detective work. I will confess, I am her."

"I'm sorry for not recognizing you, Ms. Weller. I—"

"Don't be. No one recognizes writers. We work behind the scenes. But thanks for plugging my books to your customers."

"Yeah, but still…you always have a picture on your jacket covers. Is the bird bag really for Bertha, the psychic crow?"

"It is. And I'm sure she'd want me to extend her thanks."

"Awesome. Um…could I ask you for an autograph?" He offered a pen and paper.

Samantha took the pen but refused the pad. "I have something better," she said, reaching into her messenger bag and pulling out a black-and-white glossy of Bertha and herself. "I happen to have a few copies of the photo that will appear on the jacket of my new book."

Liz reached across the table. "Oh, Sam, what a *wonderful* picture." In it, Samantha wore a black turtleneck and a houndstooth jacket. Bertha sat perched on her forearm. "Can I have an autographed one, too—to hang in the shop?"

"Sure." Samantha asked the waiter, "What's your name?"

"Charlie. Could you make it out to Charlie and the Count? Count's my black cat."

To Charlie and the Count, Samantha wrote. *May you never solve the mystery!* She signed it, *Sam Weller and Bertha the crow.*

Charlie read the inscription. "That's so cool…*never solve the mystery*…that's deep. Thanks very much, Ms. Weller."

Liz looked between them, puzzled as she tried to figure out what was so "deep" about Samantha's inscription. She forced an understanding smile, feigning comprehension until Charlie the waiter left and they were alone again.

"I don't get it," she said flatly. "What does that mean? Why would you never want to solve a mystery?"

"Because once you solve a mystery, the mystery's gone."

"Yeah…so?"

"So the fun of a mystery is that it *is* a mystery."

"You solve them in your books…"

"And see what happens? I have to create another mystery, because it's the intrigue of the mystery that attracts us. Of course, what I wrote to Charlie refers to the cosmic enigma—you know, life's *bigger mystery*."

"Hmm." Liz nodded in consideration of the idea. "I think I get it. I could use the same argument for why affairs are preferable to relationships."

"Oh, I have to hear this," Samantha said, sitting back with her arms folded. "Go ahead."

"Well, it's like you say, Sam." She paused to finish her cappuccino. "A new lover, an unknown woman, is a mystery. You have to admit there's nothing like the physical rush of being naked with someone for the first time. But in time—usually between twenty-four and seventy-two hours, in my case—the novelty wears off, the unfamiliar becomes familiar, the mystery unravels, and then," she threw her hands up, "I have to find another. So solving a mystery is like squelching desire. Once you squelch it, it's no longer desire."

"Agreed." Samantha smiled. "But in real relationships, that intensity of desire you're talking about just isn't sustainable. Compatibility, comfort, and contentment figure into the equation…and they can be just as nice, you know?"

"No, Sam. I don't."

"You're still young." Samantha picked up her cup and drained it. "When the right one comes along, you'll understand that a healthy, long-term relationship can hope for a ratio of maybe seventy percent to thirty percent."

"What, thirty percent contentment and seventy percent desire?"

"No. The other way around. If desire held at seventy percent, we'd all end up consumed by lust, staying home from work to have sex and losing our jobs. Long-term, that level of constant desire would distract us from accomplishing other goals." Samantha studied her. "Where do you meet all these crazy women anyway, online?"

"Never online. I'm a very physical person, Sam. I need an immediate visual. I like to watch, interact, mingle—in real time, not through social media." She shrugged. "I hang out here in the West Village…the Cubbyhole, Henrietta Hudson. And then there are always private parties, women I meet through business…and during the summer there's Cherry Grove and the Pines on Fire Island."

"Hmm. I haven't been to the Grove in a few years. Maybe I'll pull myself away from the computer and tag along this summer."

"You should. I'd love to spend more time with you."

Samantha checked her watch. "Right now, I should be catching the Metro-North," she said. "I didn't leave the porch light on, and Bertha gets spooked sitting alone in the dark."

"You mean Detective Crowley's psychic crow is afraid of the dark? I'm shocked."

Samantha held a finger to her lips. "*Shh.* Please don't tell her fans. It'll ruin her public image, you understand."

"My lips—I mean, my *beak*—is sealed."

It was seven thirty when Samantha stepped off the curb to hail a taxi. And when one pulled up, she opened the door for Liz. "Get in," she demanded with a crooked smile. "I always see my dates home."

"It's out of your way, Sam. I'm on the East Side."

"Hop in. I'm on my way to Grand Central Station."

"Thanks," she said and got in. "You're very accommodating, very generous, too."

"Yeah, well, I'm trying to do everything right so you don't bad-mouth me like you do your other dates." Samantha grinned.

They traveled uptown together, and when they reached Liz's building, Samantha got out to say good-bye. "Would you go with me?" she asked.

"Where?"

"To *marry* my bookend—providing Ms. Laraway can find me a mate."

"Of course I would. I'd be happy to, Sam. You know that. Just give me a day's notice."

"Thanks." Samantha kissed her cheek. "Thank you for everything."

"Thank *you*, my dearest out-law." She opened her arms, inviting Samantha in for a tight hug. "And don't worry about me bad-mouthing you," Liz whispered against her ear. "This grab-a-bite thing was the most stimulating date I've been on in a while."

"I could say the same."

"And I'm so happy you went to that estate sale and bought that bookend. If you hadn't, it might have taken another family disaster—namely, the inevitable birth of *their* firstborn, our niece or nephew—before we found out how well we'd get along."

"I believe fate is at play here, Ms. Bowes."

"I couldn't agree more, Ms. Weller. Something tells me it's part of that *bigger mystery* of yours."

CHAPTER FOUR

The yellow porch light cast an amber glow on the tiny Tudor but did little to illuminate the front door. Samantha fumbled with her keys, but before she could get the key in the lock, she heard the sudden *whoosh* of wings. She shuddered as the sharp claws of crow feet gripped her shoulder like the gnarled fingers of a witch's hand.

"Jesus, Bertha!" Samantha muttered.

No matter how many times Bertha spooked her, no matter that Samantha always expected it, the crow's surprise landing from the roof still shocked her. Somewhere, in the recesses of her colorful imagination, Samantha feared that one night it wouldn't be Bertha but the hand of a malevolent entity. Maybe she'd been writing too many paranormal stories. Or maybe she'd just worked in forensics too long.

"*Kaa-kaa!*" The black bird cackled, balancing on her shoulder and pecking at her scalp.

"Hey, quit foraging. I don't have any nits to pick."

Bertha squawked as Samantha pushed the door open. The black crow flew to the ground and rushed in ahead of her.

Samantha dropped her messenger bag in the foyer, then took the canvas bag to the living room and emptied its contents on the coffee table. Later, when she was comfortable, she'd want to sit back and admire her Old Crow bottle and her Rookwood bookend—especially now that it was worth a few hundred dollars. From the pocket of her jacket she retrieved Ms. Laraway's number, studied it for a moment, then placed it beside the pile.

"*Ung-ung.*" Bertha was complaining.

"You're hungry. I know. I'm sorry. But guess what Sam-Sam has for you," she cooed, shaking the doggy bag at the crow and heading for the kitchen. "Fish—I got *fishies*!"

Bertha bobbed her head, hopping in place and flapping her wings so that she appeared to be jumping rope. Excitedly, she jabbered and kept hopping, and after Samantha left the living room, she raced on foot to catch up with her. Samantha put fresh water in her bowl, kibble in another, then opened the round tin and placed it on the floor. "Mussels, calamari, rice. Have I redeemed myself for being late?"

The black bird tiptoed gingerly toward the seafood, first turning her head to the left to inspect the offering with one eye, then to the right to examine it with the other one. She paused as if weighing the two perspectives, then helped herself to a mussel.

Samantha opened the refrigerator and decided to pour herself a glass of Yellow Tail sangria. She needed to unwind. A day in Manhattan, her reunion with Liz, news about the bookend, cappuccino—all of it had left her overstimulated. In a good sort of way.

She left the glass in the living room, opened the windows, quickly showered, and by nine o'clock was settled on the sofa with everything of immediate interest. But Ms. Laraway's number interested her most. Sipping her wine, she wondered if it was too late to call.

Nocturnal by nature, Samantha was aware that her writing habits often made it difficult to estimate the bedtimes of respectable people. She'd have to remember to consult a site on etiquette for updated rules on the matter. For now, though, she decided to dispense with etiquette and chance a quick phone call.

Samantha dialed the number and waited. If no one answered after three rings, she'd assume Ms. Laraway was in bed and hang up, but on the second ring someone answered.

"Hello?" a woman said.

"Yes, hi…Ms. Laraway?"

"Speaking."

"Hi. My name is Samantha." The woman sounded very young. "I'm calling about a piece of Rookwood. Ed Greenbarn referred me to—"

"I'm sorry, Samantha, but I think you want Dr. Laraway. Is it Gwen you're trying to reach?"

"Gwen, yes."

"If you'll hold just a moment I'll get my aunt."

"Sure. Thank you." Samantha heard music in the background—classical tunes like the ones Liz played in her store—but then the volume diminished to an almost inaudible level, and she heard the sound of muffled voices. Samantha waited, the light from a nearby lamp playing on the glaze of the rook's blue body and giving its face an intelligent, lifelike glint.

"This is Dr. Laraway," came a second voice.

"Yes, hello, Dr. Laraway. My name is Samantha Weller."

"Yes, Ms. Weller. How can I help you?"

This voice was more mature, resonant, deeper than the first. It made Samantha nervous. "Well," she said, "my sister-in-law, Liz Bowes, is an antiquarian and good friend of Ed Greenbarn. He gave us your number hoping you could help with a marriage."

"Ed's getting married—*again*?"

Samantha cringed. Here she was mimicking Liz, using antique-world jargon, all for the purpose of, what, impressing the woman? Dr. Laraway hadn't the slightest idea what she was talking about. "No, no. I'm the one looking to marry."

"And…? Where do I come in?"

Samantha rubbed her face. "I'm sorry…Please. Let me start over."

"Take your time," Dr. Laraway said good-naturedly.

Samantha took a deep breath. "I recently purchased a single Rookwood bookend at a yard sale and would like to find a mate for it. My sister-in-law said this would be considered a *marriage*."

"Ah…so you want to marry two *bookends*."

"I do."

"What is it you have, Ms. Weller? An Oriental figure?"

"No, a crow. A rook, actually."

"You have a *rook*?" she inquired, her tone losing its frivolity. "Hmm…which one?"

"Uh, let me see. The right one, I think."

"The design," Dr. Laraway said. "Rookwood produced several."

"Oh." Samantha looked at the bookend, thinking how best to describe it. "Well…it's a rather ornate piece. The bookend itself is a book standing open like the letter *L*. The outside is a dark purple, I'd say, the pages yellow, and the rook is a midnight blue, which—"

"That yellow would be *mustard* and *ming* blue," Dr. Laraway said.

Cradling the phone in her neck, Samantha lifted the piece in two hands and held its glossy finish to the light. "Ming blue," she said, then set the piece down again. "And there's a floral branch, too. A blooming sprig of pink flowers that—"

"That pink was known as Persian rose."

"I see."

"Go on, Ms. Weller."

"Well, the flowers, the *Persian-rose* flowers," she was careful to repeat the exact words for Dr. Laraway's benefit, "cascade over the top of the book and onto the rook's feet."

"Cascade, you say?"

"Yes. Beautifully so." Samantha reached out and ran a finger along the flowers. "They flow down to tangle themselves around the rook's feet."

"Tangle? Hmm…how interesting," Dr. Laraway commented, although she was beginning to sound more amused than interested.

"Should I tell you more?" Samantha asked.

"Tell me where you're from."

"Pardon?"

"Your accent. I'm getting visions of cowboy hats and horses."

Samantha laughed. "You have a good ear. I was actually born in Texas, but we moved to New York when I was twelve. I thought I'd lost the accent."

"Oh, don't ever lose it. It's very subtle…*very* sweet."

Samantha grinned. "Why, thank you," she said, unable to remember what she was saying before Dr. Laraway interrupted her.

"So…?" Dr. Laraway waited. "You were saying?"

"I don't remember."

"Something about cascading tangles of Persian-rose flowers."

"Right…" Samantha hesitated. "Is this description helping at all?"

"Absolutely. Your observations are quite astute."

"I'm trying my best."

"Your effort is quite commendable, Ms. Weller."

Samantha suddenly felt like a college student taking an oral exam with a professor. In fact, Ms. Laraway sounded like a professor. Her manner was eloquent yet very relaxed, self-assured. It was sexy, too, in a scholarly sort of way. "Would a description of the rook itself help?"

"Oh, by all means."

Samantha tilted her head this way and that way, inspecting the rook as Bertha had inspected the mussel shells.

"Its body is facing into the book, but its head is turned so that it's gazing back."

"*Gazing?* At whom is it gazing?"

"At the observer."

"Are you observing it right now?"

"Yes. It's right in front of me…looking back at me."

"Hmm…and what of its countenance?"

"It's count—? Geez, I don't know." Samantha cradled the phone again, studying the rook closely. "I guess I'd say its countenance is one of omniscience, if you want to know the truth."

"Nothing but the truth."

"It almost seems like a sentinel," Samantha said.

"A sentinel!" Dr. Laraway said, a note of surprise in her voice. "As though it's guarding, what, the book on which it is perched?"

"Yes. Or more precisely, the *knowledge* contained in the book."

"Guarding knowledge…" She paused, evidently pondering Samantha's assessment. "I like the way you think, Ms. Weller. I've never quite considered—"

"Don't get me wrong, Dr. Laraway. It's not a malevolent bird. It's definitely a sentinel, but in a peaceful, affable sort of way."

"Affable?" Her tone rose with amused disbelief. "I dare say, Ms. Weller, have its eyes blinked yet?"

Samantha chuckled. "Dr. Laraway, if this sculpture blinks it will spend the night on the front lawn. It's dark and I'm all alone. If you spook me, I might not be able to sleep with it in the house," she said, poking fun at herself.

With that, Dr. Laraway broke into a soft and sultry laughter that seemed to signal the end of her game. "Two-two-seven-four," she said with resignation.

"What?"

"Turn the bookend over, Ms. Weller. You'll find an identification number incised beneath the Rookwood mark."

Samantha turned the piece upside down and grimaced. There it was, two-two-seven-four, incised below the Rookwood mark. Dr. Laraway had let her ramble on and on about cascading Persian-rose flowers and sentinels with affable countenances, when all she needed to do was instruct Samantha to flip the bookend over. "You could have spared yourself, Dr. Laraway."

"I didn't have the heart…or the inclination, particularly. I'm thoroughly enjoying your enthusiasm, and as long as we're telling the truth, I must say I've never listened to a more beautifully detailed description—critique, I should say—of that particular rook. It's a commercial piece from the nineteen twenties, inexpensive by comparison to other Rookwood pottery, but it's always been one of my favorites. In hearing you describe it, I find myself falling in love with it all over again."

Samantha didn't respond. She held the receiver and waited.

"I take it you're not a dealer," Dr. Laraway said, her words more a statement than a question.

"Me? No. Not a dealer. Just a writer."

"Given your descriptive narrative, I should have guessed. And what kind of just-a-writer might you be?"

"Mysteries"

"Ah, a *mystery* writer. There's nothing like a good mystery… except for a good romance."

"Is there a difference?" Samantha joked.

"Between mysteries and romances?" She chuckled. "Is that to say matters of the heart mystify the mystery writer?"

Samantha could almost feel Dr. Laraway smiling. "Thoroughly," she admitted.

"Well, I can't very well argue your point. Love is its own existential mystery."

"Spoken like a philosopher."

Dr. Laraway laughed. "I *am* a philosopher."

Samantha hesitated, not sure if she was being teased again. "Seriously?"

"Seriously. I taught metaphysics for twenty-five years."

"I had that feeling," Samantha said.

"That I was a philosopher?"

"That you were a professor. You sound like one."

"So we both have a good ear—me for accents, you for professions." She paused for a second and then spoke again. "So what interest does a mystery writer mystified by love have in American art pottery?"

"I don't. I mean, I didn't until now. The bookend caught my eye at a yard sale because it looked like my pet crow."

"A crow? How fitting. Every mystery writer should have a crow."

"Except that I didn't get a crow because I'm a mystery writer. I'm a mystery writer because of the crow. It's a long story—a long *metaphysical* story."

"Well then, I will look forward to enjoying that long story when we meet."

Samantha hesitated. "Meet…?"

"At the wedding."

"The wed—?"

"I thought you wanted to marry off your single bookend?"

Samantha couldn't help but smile. "You mean…you can make a match?"

"Presently, I have five bookends from that particular mold, one pair in solid matte turquoise, the other solid brown. The fifth, my odd one, is a mate to yours. Some fifteen years ago, *its* mate was accidentally knocked over during an indoor Frisbee game between my dog and my niece. Many bookends were made from that one mold—as I said, it's a commercial piece from the twenties—but I've never seen an unpaired one surface, at auction or otherwise."

"And you're willing to sell?"

"When you reach my age, Ms. Weller, collections become clutter, and the impulse is to subtract rather than add to the clutter. Culling one's possessions creates the illusion of freedom."

Samantha remembered her grandparents saying something like that years ago when she had wanted to give them a kitten. Of course, they hadn't phrased it quite as eloquently as Dr. Laraway. *No more pets to tie us down* was what they'd said. *We don't want anything. We're getting rid of everything. So we can travel!* Not that they ever went anywhere.

"In answer to your question," Dr. Laraway said, "I'm willing to part with my rook…as long as you promise to cherish it as I have."

"I do. I will love and cherish it…to death do us part."

"Then I think we can do business and arrange a marriage," Dr. Laraway said with satisfaction."

"As I said," Samantha added, intent on proving her worthiness, "the fact that I own a real crow makes having the bookends extra special."

"I'm quite familiar with crows and ravens. I once had the privilege of raising two orphans. And if there's anything I learned, it's that they cannot be *owned*. Dogs allow themselves to be owned, but crows are like cats. You never *own* them. You simply *live* with them."

Bertha came running out of the kitchen just then, heading for the staircase with a mussel in her beak. Samantha cupped her hand over the receiver. "Bertha? Drop it! I said drop that right now," she demanded in a hushed whisper. The crow regarded her with a mixture of defiance and indifference, then turned and dashed up the stairs with the mussel, half hopping, half flying. A second later came the pitter-patter of long-nailed feet running across the bedroom floor. "I'm sorry, Dr. Laraway. Let me retract that last statement and say that I *cohabitate* with a crow."

Dr. Laraway was silent for a moment, and then she asked, "Does your husband mind a crow in the house?"

Something about that question, something about the way Dr.

Laraway asked it, gave Samantha the feeling she was fishing for personal information. They seemed to have an immediate chemistry, and unless Samantha was completely misinterpreting their exchange, Dr. Laraway was flirting.

Samantha decided to take the bait. "I almost had a wife once, but never a husband."

"Huh! I might have had a wife, too," she offered, "if a woman could have legally had one fifteen years ago. In retrospect, it's better we couldn't marry, because it would only have ended in divorce."

"Mine, too," Samantha answered. "In fact, I'm curious to see what the divorce statistics will be over the next couple of years."

Dr. Laraway laughed. "I'm glad you bring that up, because I keep wondering the same thing. With gay marriage legalized, I think many couples are joyously running out to marry simply because they can… and with little regard for true love and compatibility."

"I wholeheartedly agree. Having been denied the right to marry for so long, we're easily swept away by the romantic notion of proposing, marrying, playing house…but it hasn't yet sunk in that if the marriage fails, we can't pack our bags and leave like we used to."

Dr. Laraway chuckled. "It's so nice to discuss the subject with another pessimist."

"I think we're more realists than pessimists. At any rate, it will be interesting to see how the numbers play out."

"I take it you're not the marrying kind."

Samantha laughed. "I actually am, but if it ever comes to that, I won't make a frivolous decision."

Regardless of Dr. Laraway's unknown current status, she'd at least made it clear that she'd been with a woman. For argument's sake, they'd just come out to each other, hadn't they? Samantha wanted desperately to ask Dr. Laraway's age, but she didn't dare. If Dr. Laraway—*Professor* Laraway—had taught college for twenty-five years, that would make her, what, fifty-four, fifty-five? Not so bad. Age differences were commonplace in the gay community.

"Where are you, Ms. Weller?"

"I'm sorry, I was just thinking…"

"I was referring to your location. Where do you live?"

"Oh. I'm in New York. Westchester County."

"I'm in the Berkshires, in Stockbridge…probably a hundred miles or so from you. We could arrange to meet next time I'm in the city, possibly next week…unless I can interest you in coming here. If you do, I'll give you a crash course in American art pottery. I have a substantial collection."

"I'd love that. My schedule is flexible and I don't mind driving."

"Well, then…how about here, the day after tomorrow?"

"Thursday's fine. Would you mind if I brought along my sister-in-law, Liz?"

"The antiquarian who found me? I'd be delighted to meet her, and so would my niece. Isabel is a collector of ephemera, books mostly. In fact, why don't the two of you join me for a late lunch."

"I don't want to impose."

"No imposition. One o'clock, say? That way Isabel can arrange to be here."

Samantha grabbed a pen and paper to jot down the address.

"And bring the bird, why don't you," Dr. Laraway added.

"I will."

"I'll see you Thursday, then."

"Uh…" Samantha hesitated, "not that it matters, but…what's your asking price on the bookend?"

"My asking price? Hmm…that all depends."

"On?"

"On how much I like you, Ms. Weller."

Samantha opened her mouth to speak, but when nothing came out, she closed it. She could only hope Dr. Laraway would like her as much as she was liking *her* right now.

With a simple good-bye, and before Samantha could even think to speak, Dr. Laraway hung up, leaving her mentally suspended for the moment.

She sat there, lost in thought, although it wasn't exactly a *thought* she was having. It was more a *feeling*, that rare and inexplicable sense of intrigue that follows a stimulating conversation with a new acquaintance. All of it, all of Dr. Laraway, left her somehow affected, enough, at least, that she was oblivious to the fact of holding the receiver in her hand until the recording sounded: *If you'd like to make a call, please hang up and try again…if you need help, hang up and dial the operator…*

"I need help," she mumbled, "but it's not an operator I need."

Chapter Five

Library walls covered half the interior of the Laraway gallery. Several shelves held Gwen's books, but mostly they belonged to her niece: rare books, out-of-print books, favorites, first editions. By the age of four, Isabel went about opening a new book the way a connoisseur tastes wine. Child eyes wide as plums, she inspected every detail of a new book—cover, binding, title page—before pulling the book to the tip of her nose and inhaling deeply as she thumbed through the pages. Gwen suspected it was the scent of fresh ink and new paper that appealed to little Isabel's olfactory sense.

"What do you smell?" Gwen would always ask.

Considering the Laraways had made their fortune in the paper business, Isabel knew at an early age that paper comes from trees. Gwen had repeatedly explained the steps involved in making paper, never mind that she had added the part about elves having a hand in the process.

"I smell the trees," Isabel would say, her smile tiny, her nose upturned, so that she herself resembled an elf. "I can smell the whole forest. Here, Aunt Gwen, you smell!"

On cue, Gwen would open the book, take an exaggerated whiff, and agree that, yes, she could indeed smell the bark and blossoms of the trees from which the elves had made the paper.

Accepting her aunt's agreement as a confirmation of magical workings in the *paper forest*, Isabel would then giggle and scrunch her shoulders as though overcome by the sudden chill that magic brings. After she handed Gwen the book, she'd climb into her lap, and together they'd open to the first, crisp page and begin a new story.

So many, many stories ago.

To this day, her niece would never begin reading a new book

without first poking her nose in the pages. Only twenty-eight years old, Isabel already had expertise in ephemera. If it was made of paper, she could tell you everything about it, whether it was printed yesterday or during the seventeenth century. But when she wasn't poking her nose in a book, managing her feral-cat colony, or helping her father run the company, she was busy poking her nose in Gwen's business.

Isabel was kind and loving, but her caretaking, worrywart ways annoyed Gwen. Knowing her niece meant well, Gwen managed to mask her annoyance, but she did often wonder where those worrywart genes came from—certainly not from the carefree Laraway side of the family.

Gwen only wished that Isabel would fall in love one day soon and have someone else to worry about. Of course, Isabel hadn't had a date since her high school prom.

Throughout college and graduate school, Gwen had never observed her taking an interest in anyone of the opposite sex. When Isabel was born, Gwen had been with Jean, and it wasn't until Isabel was fourteen that they split up. During those years they'd never hidden their relationship from Isabel, and Isabel had grown up perfectly comfortable with same-sex couples. Still, Isabel obviously wasn't comfortable with herself. Not once had she ever hinted at being straight or gay, and Gwen never pushed the subject. She could only hope that an appropriate suitor would happen along in the near future, male or female, to awaken desire in this sleeping beauty and sweep her off her feet.

Gwen flipped a switch on the wall, adjusted the dimmers, which controlled the showcases, and folded her arms beneath a white sweater draped loosely over her shoulders. Lighted showcases stood everywhere, the warm glow accentuating the artful treasures they contained. Strolling through the cool gallery, she made her way around the mahogany table and opposing love seat in the center of the room, and then over to a lit wall unit containing her prized Rookwood pieces.

"Aunt Gwen?" A voice echoed in the hallway.

Gwen heard approaching footsteps and the jingling of dog collars. She rolled her eyes. "In here, Isabel."

With a five-bedroom house, two guest cottages, and six acres of land, the Laraway estate was large enough that, theoretically, the two of them—more, if you counted Rosa, the resident housekeeper, and the indoor pets—should have gone about their respective business without seeing each other for days at a time. But wherever Gwen was, there was Isabel, nearly bumping into her at every turn. And wherever Isabel was, the animals weren't far behind so that, all in all, they lived in relatively cramped conditions. Even Rosa, who occupied a cottage in back, had become so much like a sister that she'd lost all boundaries and didn't think twice about dusting right across Gwen's face when the urge to clean struck. Only late at night did Gwen find the solitude she so enjoyed.

"You're off the phone?" Isabel asked.

"Mm-hmm," Gwen said, peering into the showcase with her back to her niece.

"Were you able to help her?"

"I was. Would you believe she has my blue seated rook?"

"Really? Wherever did she find one?"

"A yard sale, of all places. She wants to make a match."

"Oh, I don't know, Aunt Gwen. It's always been one of your favorite pieces."

"True," she said, turning to face her niece, "but perhaps it's time someone else enjoyed it."

Despite her small stature, Isabel had a commanding presence. Her dark hair was straight, parted on the side and cropped stylishly above her shoulders to frame perfect features and light-brown, almond-shaped eyes—another gene that didn't come from the tall, blond, blue-eyed Laraways, but from a Latina mother born in Brazil.

A red-nose pit bull and a black Scottish terrier appeared alongside her, Loosey Goosey and Blue. They peeked in the doorway, smiling their dog smiles, wagging their tails, waiting for an invitation.

"Hi, girls," Gwen called, inviting them in.

Loosey Goosey, fondly known as the Goose, was Isabel's constant companion of five years, a happy-go-lucky dog who carried around stuffed animals the way children carry teddy bears. She loved everyone and everything, especially if it included hiking, swimming, or going to the office with Isabel every day.

And then there was Blue, who had been hit by a car on the bitter cold night of a blue moon. With broken teeth and a concussion, she'd been left for dead until a Good Samaritan called animal control. But the Scottie had been vicious—pain-aggressive, as Isabel called it—and when her owners never claimed her, Isabel received a call from a friend at the shelter who knew too well that aggressive dogs could not be put up for adoption. It had taken two weeks before Gwen or Isabel could touch her, but she was now an affectionate and loyal dog with an over-inflated image of herself and a highly evolved sense of humor to match. A poker-face comedian she was, sometimes to the point of silliness. But Blue was as discerning as she was silly; her sensory perceptions were extraordinary. As Rosa the housekeeper put it, Blue had *the sight*, and that was cause for an immediate bond between Gwen and the dog, a bond that extended beyond intelligence and into the realm of spiritualism.

Isabel looked around and sighed. "Remember when I broke the other rook playing Frisbee with Alley in the living room?"

Gwen frowned halfheartedly as she straightened up and adjusted her sweater. "How could I forget?"

"I almost ran away from home that day."

"I know…I caught you and Alley leaving the grounds with your pajamas and dog biscuits in a paper bag."

Isabel smiled wistfully. "What was I—eleven at the time? And when you discovered the broken rook you didn't even yell."

Gwen sighed and looked around the gallery…the art…the memories. "My beloved niece and beloved dog. How could I have stayed mad at either one of you? It was an accident, after all." She gazed around the room. "Every piece of pottery in here is exquisite, but…in the end it's only clay."

"Half a million dollars' worth of clay."

"Mmm…" Gwen smiled dreamily, but then her smile dissipated and her thoughts went astray. "Have you heard of her?"

"Who?"

"Ms. Weller. She's a writer."

"Weller?" Isabel mused. "*Samantha* Weller, the mystery writer?"

"Yes, Samantha. She writes mysteries."

"That was Samantha Weller on the phone?"

"You've heard of her?"

"Don't you read *The New York Times* book reviews? She's gained considerable popularity with fans of the mystery genre. She writes the Detective Crowley series. I think I saw an ad for a new book coming out."

"Have you read anything of hers?" Gwen asked.

"Only the first book. She's a good writer, but you know me…I'm not big on paranormal themes and all that dark fantasy. I thought I recommended it to you when I was done, though."

"I don't recall…" Arms still folded beneath her sweater, Gwen brought her fingers to her chin and nodded to herself. "I'd like to read some of her work before I meet her. How many books does she have out?"

"Several, I'm sure. I might still have that first one in my library."

"If not, I'll get them on my Kindle." Gwen bent down, rubbing Blue's back. "She's coming for lunch Thursday and bringing her sister-in-law, Liz…an antique dealer. I'd like it if you could arrange to join us."

"Sure. I'd love to meet them." Isabel wrapped her hair behind her ear and smiled at her. "Can I get you anything before bed?"

"No, darling."

"Are you going to bed now?"

"No. I think I'll stay up a while with a cup of tea."

"I'll make it for you."

"Thank you, darling, but I'll do it."

"I don't mind."

Gwen fought the urge to clench her teeth. "You know what? On second thought, I think I'll have a drink."

"A drink?" A perplexed crease appeared between Isabel's eyes. "Since when do you drink before bed?"

"Never. But I might tonight…if it's okay with you."

Isabel just stared at her.

"Is there something else?" Gwen asked. It was hard to get snippy with someone who meant well, but right now Gwen wanted to be alone, to think about her conversation with Samantha Weller.

"No…I guess I'll say good night, then."

"Good night, darling."

Isabel stared oddly at her for a moment, but finally took the hint and patted her thigh. "Come on, girls—let's go to sleep."

Goose nudged Gwen, and Gwen bent to kiss her on her heavily muscled head. And then Blue, who would not be left out, punched Gwen's leg with her nose, and Gwen kissed her, too. "Good night, girls," she said as they both raced ahead to follow Isabel. In the doorway, Blue stopped to glance back at Gwen with a twinkle in her eyes, then trotted off to catch up with the others.

Gwen was glad to be alone again, but here came Isabel again, handing her a book. "Sorry to disturb you," she apologized with a hint of sarcasm, "but if you're hoping to read one of Weller's books before Thursday, you better get started."

"Oh! Why thank you, sweetheart." Gwen looked at the cover and then turned the book over, smoothing her hand over the photo of

Samantha Weller and her crow. "She looks like Rachel Maddow," she remarked.

Isabel leaned in to have a look. "Maybe a little bit…I don't know. It might just be her dark eyes and the haircut. She's attractive, though."

"Hmm…she is." After Isabel left again, Gwen laid the book on the library table in the center of the room, the back cover faceup, then removed the rook from its showcase and placed it beside the book. Walking slowly around the table, admiring the rook from different angles, she smiled to herself as she recalled the mystery writer's description of the bird's countenance. She had never thought of the bird as a sentinel.

But now, upon closer inspection, it did appear to be guarding something…in an *affable* sort of way, of course. Ms. Weller's oh-so-serious description made her smile broaden, but as she thoughtfully circled the rook, her smile faded, and she began wondering just what the rook might be protecting. She wished the bookend were real, wished she could shoo the bird from its esoteric treasure, brush away the tangles of Persian-rose flowers, and possess the secrets inscribed on those imaginary pages made from clay.

The more she gazed at the rook, the more it seemed to gaze back at her, and it occurred to Gwen that Ms. Weller had been right; the rook knew something they didn't. Gwen left the rook on the table, tucked the book under her arm, and shut off the lights. She made her way down the hallway, into the formal dining room and over to sliding doors that opened to her ballroom. Everyone in the Laraway family knew how to dance. Gwen loved ballroom dancing, Isabel loved to salsa, and both enjoyed house music when DJs were hired for their seasonal parties. A crystal chandelier hung from the ceiling, and aside from a bar at one end and sound equipment at the other, there was nothing but polished floors. From a small refrigerator behind the bar she took out a jar of olives and a bottle of brine, and made herself a dirty gin martini.

Carrying her cocktail and book into the living room, she slid out of her sandals and settled into a comfortable chair, crossing her ankles on the ottoman in front of her. She smiled at the back cover again. What a lovely photograph. What an interesting woman. And what an unexpected evening it had turned out to be.

Chapter Six

Samantha had offered to drive into the city, but with rush-hour traffic, Liz insisted on saving her the aggravation. She hopped a cab to Grand Central Station and from there took Metro-North to the Goldens Bridge station. Driving a black Range Rover, Samantha pulled up at ten o'clock and was waiting when the train pulled in.

They swung by Samantha's rented Tudor for bagels and coffee, and a proper introduction to Bertha, and by eleven were finally on the road.

"Is that the Laraway address in your GPS?" Liz asked.

"It is."

"Let it recalculate. Ed gave me better directions," she said, taking out a folded paper from her bag. "Instead of taking 684 to 84 west to the Taconic, we'll take 84 east to Route 8 and cut through Connecticut. It'll save us ten miles."

"Good. That shortens the trip." Samantha turned onto 684, and before long they were resuming their conversation from dinner the other night.

Samantha was amazed to learn about collectibles from the sixties and seventies—everything from toys to cereal boxes—and she wondered, nostalgically, about all the old toys and comic books she'd discarded over the years.

"I recently sold a huge Barbie collection," Liz said.

"Your *personal* Barbie collection?"

"Yeah, why? Does that surprise you?"

Samantha shrugged as she glanced in her mirror and switched lanes. "It just strikes me as unusual that you played with Barbie dolls."

"You mean because I'm a lesbian?"

"Yeah, I guess."

"I'll have you know that Barbie, Ken, Midge, Skipper, and all the rest had a tremendous impact on my interpersonal skills and social development."

"Barbie and *Ken*? The epitome of heterosexuality?" Samantha looked over at her and snickered. "What the heck went wrong?"

Liz pursed her lips. "Well, everything was fine in the straight world until, one day, while Ken was away on a business trip and Skipper was at camp, Midge came over for a swim and found Barbie by the pool. Midge made margaritas, Barbie put on music, one thing led to another and—what can I say?—the whole Mattel household went to hell."

Samantha shook her head and laughed. "I will confess that I had a G.I. Joe doll that I sort of permanently borrowed from the boy next door. And I did have a Barbie doll, just the one, but she was more like my imaginary friend. We camped out in the backyard together a lot. My dad even built her a spaceship out of Styrofoam so we could go on great space adventures. I remember making her a space suit out of aluminum foil and Saran Wrap, and a space pack out of a matchbox covered in foil that was attached to her suit with rubber bands."

"Wow, how clever…and what fun. We would have played well together. But just so you know, my Barbie would have seduced your Barbie in outer space."

Samantha chuckled. "You mean something like, *let me help you with your suit*?"

"More like, *let me help you out of your suit*. And hopefully you'd have had some wine and cheese in that space pack of yours."

"Plenty of wine and cheese. NASA believes in redundant backup systems."

Samantha glanced at Liz as they laughed together. She was wearing a flirty floral skirt that popped her auburn hair, a green blouse to match her eyes, and silver jewelry that complemented and gave her outfit a casual, summery feel. She looked as if she should have been traveling into the city, not away from it. "You look very pretty," she said.

"Thanks. You look very nice, too, Sam, but why are you so dressed up?"

"I don't know," she said, feigning nonchalance. "I'm no more dressed up than you. We're going there on business, really…so I figured I should look presentable…worthy of her rook!"

But that was a lie. Samantha had spent the whole morning agonizing over what to wear, trying on so many different slacks and blouses that by the time she finished there were more clothes on the bed than in the closet. In the end she wore white pants, a red gingham shirt, navy blazer, and low red pumps.

"You look like you belong on a yacht, Sam…if not the *Minnow*."

"The *Minnow*?"

"Yeah, remember *Gilligan's Island*? When I first saw you at the train station, I thought Thurston Howell the Third had come to pick me up."

"You're bad," Samantha said. "You're so bad that I'm going to make a U-turn now and go home to change my outfit."

"Oh, stop." Liz smacked Samantha's arm. "I'm just teasing. You're too young and pretty to be Thurston."

"Really, though, do I look too…nautical?"

"What's going on with you? Why are you so self-conscious?"

"Gwen is gay."

"How can you know that? You were supposed to call her about a bookend. What kind of conversation did you have with the woman?"

"A very interesting one…flirtatious at times, in a reserved sort of way." Samantha told her all about their conversation.

"And now you're crushing on her? Geez, Sam, not for nothing, but…I think the woman might be in her late seventies."

"Impossible. She didn't sound that old."

"I'm not saying she's old-old. People stay young these days. Seventy is the new sixty, right? I've met plenty of very attractive women in their seventies, let me tell you. I tried to sleep with one or two of them, but neither had any interest in me." Liz sighed. "But in terms of having a long-term relationship? I'm just saying…"

"I think you're wrong about her age."

"Aye, aye, Captain. We'll find out soon enough."

"Don't start," Samantha warned her, forcing a frown to hide her smile. Liz was funny, fun to be with, she had to admit, and she liked their inexplicable closeness, despite the fact that they were really just getting acquainted. "And just so you know, I do have a white captain's hat to match my outfit, and I did bring it with me. I just can't wear it while I'm driving because it sits too high," she said, putting her hand between the top of her head and the roof of the car.

Liz snorted at her. "I so hope you're kidding."

Samantha laughed. "Yeah. I'm kidding."

"Good, because if you showed up to claim your Rookwood bookend wearing a captain's hat, I think it would be a deal breaker."

She looked over, her smile fading. "So what about you, Sam? What's your story?" she asked as they turned onto 84.

"My *story*?"

"Yeah. The other night you asked me about my love life. What about yours? How come you're not in a relationship?"

"I was for almost ten years. I ended it several years ago and let her buy me out of our house. That's why I'm renting one right now. I feel like, now that I'm writing full-time and not tied to a job location, I can live anywhere, really. I'm just too busy writing to figure out where I want to live."

"What went wrong?"

"With the relationship? Whatever usually goes wrong…people change, grow apart, fall out of love…I don't know. My ex was very controlling. Even when we were first dating, our mutual friends used to jokingly refer to her as 'the boss' and a 'complainer,' but I was so crazy about her those first few years I didn't see it. Sometimes things just slowly chip away at you, and then, one day, your eyes open and you see things you should have seen in the beginning. My advice to myself at this point in life is to pay close attention to the red flags."

"Meaning?"

"Meaning that the things you end up hating about a person are all right there on the first date—the red flags—but we choose to ignore them."

"Yeah, well, we overlook a lot of things when we're getting pussy."

Samantha laughed. "I suppose."

"So you're not getting any now?"

"What, pussy?" Samantha blushed.

"Am I embarrassing you?"

"You are," Samantha said, shaking her head. "I'm not in the habit of discussing my sex life in those terms."

"Well, you should be. Even lesbians need besties, you know, someone to confide in and—quick, Sam, get over. Route 8 is coming up on your left."

Samantha moved to the left as the road split. "Okay, if you must know, I'm not 'getting any' at the moment."

"At the moment meaning…since you left your ex?"

"There was one after that. We were together—not living together, although exclusive—for about a year, but then she wanted to take it further, and my heart wasn't in it. After that I dated several women... just dated. It's hard to find a woman who likes big, black birds."

"Poor Bertha. And poor you. That's a long time to go without sex. How do you do it?"

"It hasn't been *that* long," Samantha defended herself.

"Yeah, it has. Don't you ever like to just...you know...hook up, fuck around?"

"Sure. I'd love to fuck around. With a girlfriend or a partner."

Liz looked surprised. "I didn't realize 'the captain' was so conservative."

"Sorry, but I have little interest in sex with someone I don't know and don't care about. Sex for the sake of sex doesn't appeal to me the way it does to you."

"Hey, don't judge," Liz said.

"I'm not judging. But I do have almost fifteen years on you. Perspectives change. You'll see when you meet the right one." Samantha glanced at her. "Unless, of course, your intimacy issues go unresolved."

Liz raised her brow as though insulted. "I don't have intimacy issues. I really don't. There's nothing in my childhood that would have caused them. I had loving parents and grandparents, all of them happily married, and aside from having to share a bedroom with an egocentric, pain-in-the-ass sister from hell, my childhood was good. I don't know what it is, Sam. I just haven't met a woman I can tolerate being in the same room with for more than twenty-four—" Suddenly her mouth dropped open, and she looked over at Samantha as though she'd just had an epiphany. "Shit, Sam, maybe my sister did cause me intimacy issues. Maybe she's the reason I can't stand the idea of having to share a bedroom with someone. Damn," she said and stared out the window.

"You can make that check out to cash," Samantha teased her, "and we'll schedule another therapy session for next week."

"I'm surprised your brother doesn't need one. I don't know how he lives with her. She never shuts up."

They stayed on Route 8 for twenty-five miles until the highway ended and continued as a two-lane road that would take them into Lee and Stockbridge. Sun shone in the open roof of the Range Rover as they drove, the landscape opening up as the road cut through woodlands and rocky cliffs and led them around winding bends. Homes became sparse, and the few houses were large and sprawling.

"Well, if I ever do settle down," Liz commented every time they passed a big Colonial or old Victorian with gingerbread trim, "I'll want it to be in an old house I can restore."

"You'd leave Manhattan?"

"I could easily live between the city and country."

"You don't look like you'd adapt too well to rural life."

"Adapt? In case you've forgotten, I was raised in Maine. You've been to my parents' house. I spent my summers on the lake. Frogs and snapping turtles were my friends. Besides, I wouldn't exactly consider this rural. It's country, but with a lot to offer in terms of culture."

"I forget you and Lisa were raised in Maine. Still, it's hard to imagine you living outside the city."

"See? Even *you* have the wrong impression of me. Maybe that's why I attract the wrong women. I end up with too much quantity and not enough quality." She looked down at herself, smoothed her skirt with a hand. "People perceive me as some sort of party-loving bohemian and…well, maybe I am, but…"

"I can understand people thinking that of you. Jason tells me your social skills are what have landed you an impressive list of clients. He also told me you're a chick magnet."

"A chick mag—" She waved a hand in the air. "Jason's just jealous because he knows I get more pussy than he *ever* will. And trust me—I know my sister—he's not getting a lot!"

"Hey, even I've had more pussy than my kid brother." Samantha chuckled. "He was always too busy working out and admiring himself in the mirror to get any dates. Girls thought he was an arrogant jerk. Seriously, I think he only slept with one woman before he met your sister."

"That's one more than I would have guessed. But I can't blame Jason for the things that come out of his mouth because he only knows what my sister tells him. And it would *kill* Lisa to attribute my 'list of clients' to talent. Do you know she tells people that I have untreated *attention-deficit disorder*?"

"I know," Samantha confided. "My brother told me that, too."

"What?" Liz's eyes narrowed and her lips curled in a snarl. "What a *biatch*! Do you see why I can't stand her? She tells that to everyone. And you know why? Because growing up I was the popular one with lots of friends. Granted, my extracurricular activities and busy social schedule distracted me from being a great student in high school, but she had nothing better to do than lock herself in the bedroom and study because no one liked her." Her face contorted into a look of disgust. "I can't believe she goes around telling people things like that."

"Please don't say I said anything. It'll just start a fight."

"Oh, don't worry, Sam. I don't bring anything up anymore because it doesn't make a difference. I never win with her." She waved her hand in the air as if to shoo away thoughts of her big sister until she spotted signs for Route 102. "Turn left up here, Sam, and we'll take it four miles into Stockbridge."

A few miles later she pointed. "Hey, is that an apple orchard?" She looked down at the directions in her lap. "That's our landmark. Turn at the end of it, and the driveway should be on our right, about half a mile."

Samantha slowed down as they drove past the orchard and continued along a wooded area until they reached a break in the trees. A mailbox was half hidden in lilacs, and a sign said Laraway. Samantha's stomach flip-flopped as she turned in and stopped. White birch trees lined the winding driveway, and for a good hundred feet all she could see were their white trunks and a gravel incline.

She adjusted the rearview mirror to look at herself, then leaned over and reached for the glove box in front of Liz's knees. "Nice legs. Excuse me," she said, retrieving a can of mints.

"Getting ready for a blind date?"

"Care for an Altoid?"

"Thanks." Liz shook her head and plucked a peppermint from the open tin. "I see no reason why she wouldn't want to sell you the bookend. And if it turns out she wants to have sex with you as partial payment for the bookend…feel free to take your time. I'll nap in the car."

"Behave."

"Relax, Sam, I won't embarrass you. And I'm sure you'll make a good impression."

"I hope I can interest her in conversation."

"You said you two already had a great conversation and that it got somewhat personal."

"It did…but I don't know anything about art pottery or antiques…or academia, for that matter. She's a philosophy professor. Did I tell you that?"

"No. You forgot to mention that detail, but stop worrying. If you run out of things to say and start feeling stupid, you'll make something up. You're a writer, for God's sake."

"Artifice, not spontaneity, is the writer's genius."

"So? You'll use artifice to create the illusion of spontaneity. How hard can that be?"

Samantha rolled her eyes and puffed her cheeks as she continued, tires crunching the gravel as they drove up the winding driveway. As the SUV climbed higher, the Laraway estate came slowly into view. First several chimneys, a black roof, and then a grand white house, all of it resting on a grassy knoll. A large covered porch, replete with ceiling fans and lots of white wicker furniture, ran the length of the house.

To their left sprawled a meadow, lush green grasses splashed with colors of wildflowers. They bloomed for acres, all the way down to the sparkling water of a pond that seemed to begin on the left side of the house and continued around to the back of it. To the right of the house was a scattering of smaller structures: a three-door garage, a gray barn, and two stone cottages. Samantha pulled up behind a white Mercedes.

"Wow…interesting architecture. I could live in a place like this," Liz remarked.

"You and me both," Samantha whispered. They climbed out of the truck, Samantha straightening her jacket and taking her canvas bag from the back seat while Liz lifted the box of pastries she'd picked up in the city.

Side by side they paused, the sights and sounds of the country in season assaulting Samantha's senses. The songs of birds carried on the cool breeze, their chirping and chattering harmonizing with a collection of chimes on the porch—the biggest collection she'd ever seen. And from far away, high up in the locust trees edging the meadow, came the familiar cawing of crows.

"Crows…" Samantha said.

"What a place."

"Mmm…" Samantha looked at the land, breathing deeply to calm herself. Head tilted back, she shut her eyes against the soft wind, until the creaking and sudden snap of a screen door caught her attention. She swiveled around, only to have the sight of Dr. Laraway assault her senses all over again.

Samantha felt her lips part in awe as Dr. Laraway strolled out to the porch railing with an easy smile and looked down at them.

She was as charming as she had sounded over the telephone, and much younger than Liz had suggested. Mid-fifties, Samantha guessed, and stunning. Samantha shot Liz a quick I-told-you-so glance, then returned her eyes to their hostess.

Blond hair fell about her shoulders in a loose arrangement of waves that caught the sunlight, and her eyes were blue, so blue the sky seemed to pass right through them. For a moment, her face seemed part of the landscape.

Wearing a white blouse and black slacks that sat low on her waist, she moved with the graceful stride of a dancer as she descended the porch steps and graciously extended her hand in greeting.

"Ms. Weller, Ms. Bowes…how do you do?"

"Please, call me Samantha…Sam, if you like," she said, taking both Dr. Laraway's hand and a deep breath. "It's a pleasure."

"The pleasure is mine, Sam. And please, call me Gwen."

Samantha stood there, thinking that Dr. Laraway was holding her hand a little too long. But then she realized she was the one not letting go. Quickly, she released her grip and slipped her hand into a pocket.

"Where's Bertha the crow?" Gwen asked, sounding almost disappointed.

"You told me to bring the bird—I thought you meant the rook," she said, raising the bag in her hand.

"That was a given, but I thought your crow—Bertha, is it?"

"Yes, Bertha."

"I thought Bertha would enjoy the visit as well." Gwen gestured toward the trees beyond the meadow.

Now it was Samantha's turn to be disappointed. Bertha, too, would be disappointed if she knew she'd missed an invitation to meet other crows in the country. "I'm sorry. I misunderstood. She would have loved it here." Samantha looked out into the distance and heard the cawing of crows and the loud squawking and babbling of at least one baby being fed. Bertha had sounded that way at feeding time when she was a fledgling. "Sounds like you have yourself a full rookery out there."

"Ah, yes…aren't they magnificent? They nest up in the locust trees." She looked up, using a hand to shield her eyes from the sun, then passed Samantha to greet and exchange pleasantries with Liz, who delighted in conversation.

Samantha stood between them, trying not to stare, but staring nonetheless as Liz asked questions and the two chatted about the century-old estate. Dr. Laraway reminded her of a movie star, a

Hitchcock actress. Janet Leigh, was it? No. Tippi Hedren. That was the one.

Suddenly, as though both women could feel Samantha's eyes, Gwen and Liz stopped talking and regarded her expectantly.

"Sorry," she said, embarrassed at being caught. She looked at Dr. Laraway. "I, uh…I was just thinking that you remind me of an actress."

"How flattering," Gwen said. "Which one?"

"Tippi Hedren."

Gwen regarded her quizzically. "Really? The star of Hitchcock's *The Birds*?"

"Yes, her."

Dr. Laraway gave a thoughtful nod. "Well then, Sam, perhaps it's better that you left your crow at home." She winked at Liz, then motioned for them to follow her. "Perhaps we should hurry inside."

Liz played along. "Yeah, before the birds attack!"

Samantha smiled crookedly as Dr. Laraway led them up the porch steps and held the screen door open for them.

"My niece, Isabel, is expected to join us for lunch. Aside from helping run the family business, she is an avid book collector. She's eager to meet you both. And I'm sure," she added, as they went in, "that Samantha's rook is even more eager to meet its mate."

Chapter Seven

Black and white tiles covered the floor of the spacious foyer, and from the vaulted ceiling hung a lantern-like chandelier. A grandfather clock and floor jardinière filled with eucalyptus stood against one wall, and against the other were a hall table and grouping of framed Black and White Scotch Whiskey prints featuring the famous pair of Scottish dogs.

Beyond the checkered tiles, Samantha glimpsed a grand staircase and the beginning of floral carpeting: vines of black, green and pink flowers tangled on a yellow background that crept and climbed and wound its way up the stairs like a magical garden path. She felt as though the outdoors had trailed them inside.

As Samantha stared ahead at the yellow carpeting, imagining the exquisite rooms to which its vines led, a shadow flickered in her peripheral vision and drew her attention back to the tiles on which they stood. On a large white square, a few diagonal squares ahead of her, appeared a sitting Scottish terrier. Black as night and as still as a piece on a chessboard, it stared intently, the whites of its eyes showing like half-moons beneath black bangs. Though the animal seemed neither threatening nor welcoming, its indifference intimidated Samantha. "Did this dog just jump out of those whiskey ads, or has he been sitting here all along?"

"Meet Blue," Gwen said. "The beard throws everyone off, but he's a *she*—and yes, she's been here assessing you all along. We've never quite figured it out, but when strangers first come she tends to make herself invisible on a black tile. Once she decides the situation is amicable and wishes to be announced, she moves to a white one."

"Oh my God, I can't believe you have a Scottie! I grew up with them." Liz beamed. "You are so cute, Blue!" She crouched down. "Can you say *ahroo*? Come on. Let me hear that Scottie voice I miss so much."

"*Ahroo!*" Blue's tail wagged as she bucked Liz's hand and rolled it back so that it came to rest on the dog's head.

"Hmm…she camouflages herself," Samantha commented. "That's tactical deception…a fairly advanced thought process." She crouched alongside Liz and extended her hand. "Hi, Blue. You certainly are a clever little—"

But Blue had no time for small talk and no time for Samantha. Like a person who rudely refuses to shake an outstretched hand, Blue turned her back on Samantha, kissed Liz's hand, and then trotted down the hall toward the sounds of someone cooking—pots clanging, pans sizzling, something steaming.

"I suspect she's off to beg Rosa for chicken. Don't take her aloofness personally," Gwen said. "She's a true Scot—unpretentious and slow to warm up. But once she decides she likes you, you'll have a friend for life."

Samantha knew Gwen was just trying to make her feel better. It had taken the Scottie all of thirty seconds to warm up to Liz. And Samantha suspected it didn't take much longer for women to warm up to her either. Liz was gregarious, casually affectionate, and a talker who loved also to listen. All in all, the easiness about her made people—and the dog—feel instantly comfortable.

As they moved on, Samantha's redheaded bohemian out-law oohed and aahed at everything in sight, while she herself absorbed Dr. Laraway's treasures in silent wonder. To their right, double doors revealed a portion of a huge living room. Classical guitar music played softly, sunshine and a sweet breeze streaming in from sparkling floor-to-ceiling windows that gave the house a cheerful and most romantic aspect. The ambience, Samantha suspected, was a mere extension of its owner's personality; Gwen was as light and breezy and cheerful as her surroundings.

Just then a clash in the kitchen interrupted the ambience, and a frantic Scottie passed them, running for cover. She bolted right through Gwen's legs as a woman yelled in a foreign language. Spanish, she guessed.

"Rosa?" Dr. Laraway called out in alarm. She rushed toward the kitchen, Samantha and Liz following her. A short, dark, buxom woman appeared in the doorway of the kitchen, wiping one hand on an apron and holding a sponge in the other. Her silver hair was pulled back in a bun, and her dark, expressive eyes animated her whole face when she spoke. "Oh, where my poor baby go? I drop a spoon on her head and she run. Blue? *Aquí!*" she called, turning back to wipe a white sauce from the floor.

Something punched Samantha's calf just then, and she looked down to see that Blue had returned. With her big nose she punched again, then pushed herself between Samantha's legs and peeked into the kitchen to search the floor for whatever had assaulted her. The coast clear, she trotted over and sat by the stove, obviously pretending the whole disturbance had never occurred, except that she had a glob of white sauce on her head.

"Is everything okay in here?" Gwen asked.

"*Sí, señora.*" Rosa dampened a paper towel, wiped the dog's head, handed her a piece of chicken, and then washed her own hands.

"Do you need help?"

"*No, señora.*"

"Well then, if you're sure…I'd like you to meet our guests. This is Samantha Weller…"

"*Hola, Señora Weller,*" Rosa said, drying her hands on her apron. She smiled, then turned to Gwen and said something in Spanish.

"No, no relation to *that* Weller…why are you speaking Spanish?"

Rosa just shrugged.

Gwendolyn rolled her eyes and turned to Samantha. "Rosa asked if you were related to the Weller of Weller pottery. Remind me to show you some examples of your namesake after lunch. And this young lady," she introduced Liz, "is Ms. Weller's sister-in-law…Liz Bowes."

"*Hola, Señorita Lesbos.*"

"That's *Liz.*" Gwen corrected her. "Liz *Bowes*. Bowes is her last name."

Rosa had it right the first time, Samantha thought, and pursed her lips to keep from laughing out loud, avoiding eye contact with Liz for fear she would lose composure.

Rosa put her hand to her mouth. "Oh, *lo siento.*"

"No need to apologize. *Hola.*" Liz greeted her without missing a beat.

Rosa's face brightened. "*Hola! Habla español?*"

"*Un poquito.*"

"Ah! Like me with *inglés—un poquito,*" Rosa said.

Liz commented that whatever was cooking smelled wonderful and then in Spanish must have asked Rosa something, because suddenly the housekeeper took her by the hand and pulled her into the kitchen. "Come, señorita…I show you," she said.

Gwen gestured to Samantha. "Perhaps you'd like a tour instead." With that she locked her arm through Samantha's and led her back across the hall.

"Are you bilingual?" Samantha asked Gwen.

"Not really. I can manage a very simple conversation. My niece and my brother, William, are both fluent. His first wife, who would be Isabel's mother, died when Isabel was a child, but William encouraged her to speak both languages. Background conversations served me well. I learned subliminally, I suppose, although I can understand much better than I can speak. And pay no mind to Rosa. She understands English perfectly well. She only pretends she doesn't when it's convenient or when she becomes self-conscious about her grammar."

"She's been with you a long time?"

"She's been with our family, part of our family, since my niece and her son were quite small. Her son, Carlos, is graduating from veterinary school at Purdue next year, and we're hoping he'll want to come back and join a practice in the area. It'll be nice to have a veterinarian in the family, and of course Rosa would love to have him nearby."

Laughter sounded from the kitchen. Samantha heard hushed chattering—broken English from Rosa, broken Spanish from Liz—and then the two women began laughing their heads off.

"Oh dear," Gwen said. "Rosa must have Liz's ear."

"I think it's the other way around. I had no idea Liz even spoke Spanish until now."

"How is that?"

"Her sister married my brother less than a year ago, and since neither of us sees our siblings much, we had limited contact…until I took the bookend to her for an appraisal."

"So the rook was the intermediary?"

"Yes."

"Then it's a good thing you found that bookend. The two of you seem close."

"I was thinking the same thing on the way here," Samantha said, positively enjoying the way Dr. Laraway was hugging her arm as they strolled through the double doors to the living room.

"What were you thinking, Sam?"

"How sometimes life seems like one big game of connect the dots."

"Hmm…it does, doesn't it? And I'm glad *our* dots have connected."

Gwen's touch, her rich and textured voice, even her heady fragrance seemed oddly familiar to Samantha. Like a déjà vu, it set her mind in a whirl of irretrievable memories. And when Gwen's perfume caught her nose again, she inhaled deeply and shut her eyes. "Jasmine… neroli…tuberose," she murmured.

Dr. Laraway stopped and looked at her. "Flowers?"

"Your perfume." Samantha smiled at her. "You're wearing Chanel, aren't you?"

"Why, yes…I am." Gwen seemed amazed. "You can distinguish all those floral notes?"

"I can."

"I'm drawing a blank on neroli," Gwen said.

"It's from the bitter-orange tree. The blossoms are very sweet, honey-like. I'm smelling gardenia, too," Samantha said, lifting her nose to the air, "but it's not coming from you."

"I've never known anyone with such a sharp olfactory sense. You have an extraordinary nose, Sam."

"Maybe I'm just a woman who knows her flowers."

"Is that *knows* or *nose*?"

"Both." Samantha grinned. "I have a good nose, and I *knows* my flowers."

Gwen chuckled, her eyes playing curiously on Samantha's face. "You know, a perfumer is often referred to as *le nez*—French for *the nose*—because of his or her acute sense of smell and ability to translate moods and emotions into fragrance compositions."

"Huh. I didn't know that." She glanced at Gwen. "Well, if ever I lose the ability to translate moods and emotions into language, and people stop buying my books, perhaps I can apply for work as *le nez*."

Gwen played along. "Feel free to use me as a reference."

Samantha smiled as they continued, unable to shake the uncanny sensation that she hadn't just met Gwen but had simply returned to her after too long an absence.

CHAPTER EIGHT

Rosa wasn't the only one Liz befriended. By the time Samantha turned to see Liz catching up with them, the slow-to-warm-up Scottie already had Liz engaged in a game. A punctured soccer ball in her mouth, the Scottie bounded into the living room with Liz chasing her. She ran toward the opposing sofas situated on either side of a fireplace, then jumped up on one where a black cat lay curled asleep. The cat opened one glaring eye, clearly disgusted with the Scottie for disturbing its nap.

"Oh, for heaven's sake." Gwen waved a hand in defeat. "You'll have to excuse them. I know they shouldn't be on the furniture, and we do keep things covered when company isn't here, but…well…what can I say? If they can't make themselves at home in their own house, it really isn't home, is it?"

"No, it's not." Samantha wholeheartedly agreed. "And I'm sure cats and dogs are a lot neater than one crow."

Samantha liked Gwen's down-to-earth style. Everything about this place exuded refinement, opulence, but there was nothing haughty or pretentious about her.

Liz petted the cat. "And who might you be?" The cat stretched, both yellow eyes wide open now.

"That's Salem, Isabel's beloved *familiar*. I've lost count of how many more live outside. My niece has a habit of bringing home death-row animals from various rescue groups we support. I prefer to give money, but Isabel prefers to give them homes. She's had the barn out back heated, completely winterized, and insists that as long as they're spayed and neutered they should be allowed to live out their natural lives. A *managed colony* is what she calls it."

Liz scratched the cat's chin. "What a kind heart your niece has."

Gwen rolled her eyes. "Oh, yes, Isabel's kind. Too kind. But it's her nature—and a virtue, I suppose—so I can't fault her for it," she said, leading her guests past the archway of a formal dining room.

Liz stopped unexpectedly, Samantha almost bumping into her. "Gwen, oh my God!" She stood there, hands on her cheeks, stunned by the sight of the art deco furniture. "Can I have a look in here?"

"Why, of course." Gwen turned on the dining room lights for her, and they all went in.

In the background, the sound of a door opening, followed by the thump of Blue jumping off the sofa, signaled to Samantha that someone had arrived. Liz appeared oblivious to the noise. She was too busy inspecting a large hutch, excitedly identifying the year and maker for all to hear.

As she did, a young woman conservatively dressed in a straight navy-blue skirt and sleeveless white shirt suddenly appeared in the archway. Petite and very pretty, she was either deeply tanned or just happened to have a beautiful bronze complexion. She smiled politely, acknowledging Samantha with golden-brown eyes a shade lighter than her skin, then curled a strand of silky dark hair behind an ear and waited quietly in the archway.

"And *this* piece, Gwen," Liz went on, unaware of the newcomer, "was featured at the 1925 Paris exposition."

"Your expertise is impressive," the newcomer remarked in the background. "What's your field?"

"Art hist—" Liz started to say, her back to everyone, but she stopped speaking and spun around when she realized the questioning voice wasn't Gwen's.

The black cat was awake now, rubbing up against Isabel's legs in greeting, and a pit bull with a squeaky toy rushed in the dining room to see the visitors.

"You're here," Gwen said. "Wonderful."

"I'm so sorry." Liz put a hand to her chest as Gwen's niece approached her. "I was totally lost in this furniture. You must be Isabel...mistress of dogs, savior of cats...keeper of books."

Isabel smiled, softly, shyly. "I see my aunt has told you everything there is to know about me," she said, then apologized for the pit bull's excited entrance. "This is Loosey Goosey, better known as the Goose. She's been at work with me."

Loosey dropped her toy, panted a smile, and raised her chin at Gwen, as if to say, "Hey, what's for lunch?" then greeted Samantha with an exuberance that made up for Blue's apathy. Next she went to Liz and leaned against her thigh.

"Hey, Goose! Rough day at the office?" Liz bent over to rub and pat the dog's side. Samantha smiled to herself as Liz's eyes slyly roamed the length of Isabel's legs, from the tip of her low-heel navy pumps all the way up to the hemline of her skirt.

More reserved than her aunt, but with as much social grace, Isabel congratulated Samantha on her upcoming book and the acquisition of her very first piece of Rookwood. And then she extended her hand to Liz. "I didn't mean to interrupt," she said as they shook hands. "You were saying…?"

"Saying?"

"About your background being in…?"

"Oh." Liz laughed. "Art history and interior design. My primary interest is in art nouveau and art deco."

"American?"

"French and American."

"Lucky for us. We actually have a couple of mysterious nouveau pieces in a guest room upstairs. Maybe you could take a look after lunch."

"If I can wait that long!"

Being with Liz, getting to know her personality, watching her operate in social settings—at the wedding, and now here with Gwen and Isabel, with Rosa and the dogs—Samantha was observing firsthand how warm and charming Liz was, how easily she could light up a room. It confirmed her suspicion that Lisa's derogatory comments were rooted in secret envy.

The four of them, caught up in separate conversations now, made their way down a wide hallway to the back porch where homemade crepes and a wonderful salad were to be served.

"So Isabel lives here, too?" Samantha asked Gwen as they dropped a few feet behind the other two.

"As always," Gwen answered with a halfhearted frown, implying that marrying off Isabel and keeping animals off the furniture were in the same category of lost battles.

The enclosed porch at the back of the house seemed like something out of *The Great Gatsby*—furnished in yellow wicker, with cotton rugs and pillows strewn about in an appetizing array of fruity colors. Even the dinnerware was appetizing. A corn-shaped pitcher sat on the table, with plates resembling water lilies and bowls shaped like cabbage leaves.

Liz gasped at the place settings. "Majolica? Oh, Gwen. I can't take much more. This is delightful—priceless!"

"Gee, thanks for saying that," Samantha commented. "Now I'll be sure to break something."

Taking a box of matches from a drawer, Gwen smiled at her. "We can't have you nervous, Sam, so rest assured that the more you break, the happier Isabel will be. She hates majolica."

Isabel shrugged. "I'm not particularly fond of the Victorian period—way too ornate for my taste."

"But in here," Liz said, "in spring or summer, nothing could be more perfect. It's exquisite!"

"Whimsical, too…sort of magical," Samantha added. "It seems like something you'd find in the kitchen of a hobbit's house or the cupboard of a rabbit's warren."

Gwen smiled as she struck a wooden match and held Samantha's gaze over the flame. "What a cozy notion," she said, lowering the match and lighting the floating candles in a bowl of fresh gardenias.

"Mmm…I knew I smelled gardenias." Samantha took a deep breath. "They make a beautiful centerpiece."

"I hope the fragrance isn't bothersome."

"Not at all. Gardenias are one of my favorite flowers, right up there with wisteria and lily of the valley."

Gwen looked puzzled, staring at Samantha as she blew out the match, smoke swirling between their faces. "How, exactly, did you come to know your flowers so well?"

"My mother was a florist."

"Ah…that answers the many questions I've been accumulating since you identified the notes in my perfume."

"Well, my brother Jason had the same mother, and he wouldn't be able to distinguish a gardenia from a garden hose."

"If you love flowers, Sam, just wait until you see my floral vases," she said, excitement sparkling in her eyes. "You're going to fall in love."

I'm already falling in love, Samantha wanted to say, but she smiled instead and asked to use the bathroom before sitting down to lunch. Liz had just returned from it and pointed Samantha in the direction she needed to go, but she ended up losing her way and getting lost.

Wandering down an unfamiliar hallway, Samantha went back and forth, then left and right, until the main floor of the large house became a labyrinth and she ended up entering the spacious kitchen through a back door. Rosa was nowhere in sight.

The commercial stove, Samantha speculated, was used to cook for the many guests Gwen undoubtedly entertained. In the center of the room stood an oval island, countless steel and copper pots dangling from an iron rack overhead.

Thinking it best to wait for Rosa to put her back on course, Samantha wandered over to a large breakfast nook at the far end of the kitchen and surveyed the breathtaking property through a bay window. More flowers, cherry trees, and way down at the water's edge she caught sight of another brown animal. At first, Samantha thought it was a small deer, but upon closer inspection she realized it was another dog—a German shepherd, if she had to guess. It stood motionless in the distance, staring up at the window, looking straight at Samantha.

"You get lost, señora?"

Rosa's voice startled her. She turned and regarded the housekeeper over her shoulder. "Yes. I was looking for the bathroom, but…is that another dog out there?"

Samantha heard only the busy sound of spoons against glass bowls, and when Rosa failed to answer her, she raised her voice a notch and tried again. "Rosa?"

"*Sí?*"

"That brown dog out there…is that another one of Isabel's?"

"I no see no dog."

Samantha didn't expect her to see it from the stove. "Not here, it's outside." She pointed. "Down there by the water. It looks like it's waiting for someone."

Rosa wouldn't even look. "Like I say," she repeated, her voice turning cold. "I no see a dog."

Shuffling utensils, she began mumbling in Spanish under her breath, and out of the corner of her eye Samantha saw her make the sign of the cross.

"Rosa…?"

"*Venga conmigo por favor*, Señora Weller." She picked up a large tray of food and waited.

"Huh? *No habla español.*"

"Come with me," she said in English, gesturing with her head for Samantha to follow. "This way."

Samantha glanced down at the dog once more, about to inquire again, but Rosa's stern expression made Samantha think better of it. Obediently she followed the housekeeper. Warm and welcoming a short time ago, Rosa no longer seemed so friendly.

CHAPTER NINE

Sometime between finishing lunch and beginning their tour of the gallery, Dr. Laraway slipped on a pair of half glasses that transformed her into the professor she was. Every time she lowered her face to peer over them, Samantha either breathed too deeply or forgot to breathe at all.

Isabel had already given Liz a quick tour of the gallery, but it was cut short by Liz carrying on over a rare nineteenth-century book on furniture design. Now the fast friends had retreated upstairs, Liz having offered to appraise several pieces of furniture.

Alone together, Gwen and Samantha began a leisurely tour. Decorating the walls in between the floor-to-ceiling bookcases were framed posters: one advertising Rookwood as the "Premiere Art Pottery of America and Perfect Attainment in Artistic Ceramics," another boasting awards, notably the Grand Prix at Paris in 1900.

"If nothing else, you should remember Rookwood's historical significance for America and for women," Gwen told her. "For one, it changed the world's perception of American art. Before the turn of the last century, American art, especially ceramics, was considered inferior and centuries behind the rest of the world in artistic attainment. Also, Rookwood was the very first female manufacturing company in the United States."

"So all this was happening along the timeline of the suffrage movement?"

"During the Progressive Era, yes."

Hands clasped behind her back, Samantha followed her to the lighted showcases, the hollow clicking of their heels reverberating throughout the beautifully lighted room.

"Do you know much about the pottery itself?" Gwen asked.

Samantha shook her head. "Educate me."

"Maria Storer Longworth started the pottery. Her fa considerable wealth. A patron of both the Cincinnati A Association and the Cincinnati Art Academy, he funded her venture. Maria, in turn, named the Ohio pottery after his countryside estate, Rookwood."

"I've been wondering about that," Samantha mused, "because rooks are native to Europe and Asia, not Ohio."

"As far as I know, the estate was named for the unusual number of crows inhabiting the grounds. Crows, rooks, and ravens all belong to the same family—corvids, if I'm not mistaken?"

"Yes, corvids. Blue jays and magpies belong to it, too."

"Well, I suppose Mr. Longworth took the liberty of generalizing when he named it Rookwood. In any event," she said, "the first kiln was drawn in eighteen eighty. Maria employed the finest artists, chemists, and potters of the time. She even brought in a Japanese artist noted for his perfection of a particular pottery technique she so admired. In fact, Rookwood pieces signed by him are highly desirable. I consigned one of his vases with the Cincinnati Art Gallery last year, and it brought in a hundred and fifty thousand dollars."

Gwen pointed to her left. "Van Briggle was another potter who worked for Rookwood before leaving Ohio and establishing his own pottery in Colorado Springs. His life was cut short, but the pottery is in operation to this day, so make a point of stopping in if your book signings ever take you there."

"I'll do that," she said, admiring a turquoise vase. It was a beautiful art nouveau piece named Lorelei, after the legendary siren known to lure sailors to their deaths. The arms of the nude and sensuous siren-of-a-woman hugged the turquoise rim, her flowing hair becoming the water and ultimately the vase itself.

In addition to Van Briggle, Gwen introduced her to Roseville and, of course, Weller pottery. But Rookwood enchanted Samantha most. She stood in awe before the first mirrored showcase filled with floral vases, some with high-gloss finishes, others with a transparent matte glaze that gave the flowers a three-dimensional quality.

Samantha feasted her eyes as Gwen schooled her in the various glazes popular at that time: vellum, sea-green, and iris glazes. Against mostly dark backgrounds, the life-size flowers seemed hauntingly real—as though they'd just been plucked and picked from the Laraway garden: white poppies, red poppies, orchids, and yellow jonquils.

Some featured apple blossoms, magnolias, and wild roses, and others contained thistle, hyacinth, wisteria, and lily of the valley. Her voice reduced to a mesmerized whisper, Samantha sounded out the names of every flower on every vase.

"You certainly *do* know your botanicals."

"Like I said—"

"Your mother was a florist."

"My father," Samantha said, fixated on the floral vases and only half paying attention to what she herself was saying, "was both an attorney and avid hunter—which is to say, when he wasn't preying on people, he preyed on animals. He always took my brother, against his protests, but I refused." She crouched to examine a vase on a lower shelf. "Instead, I spent my free time working in my mom's greenhouses with Arthur, one of my father's *reject* scent hounds. He had a bad nose," she said, looking up at Gwen from where she squatted. "Arthur was a Weimaraner, often called the gray ghost. But he was also what hunters call a ghost runner."

This term seemed to pique Gwen's interest. "A *ghost* runner?"

"Dogs who track imaginary scents. They take off, hot on the trail of something that turns out to be nothing at all. My mother always said Arthur wasn't imagining anything, that he simply preferred the scent of flowers. I think he just preferred to be with my mother and me. She would have loved these floral vases."

"Does she still have her business?"

"Unfortunately, we lost her fifteen years ago to breast cancer. She was only fifty-eight."

"What a devastating loss…I'm sorry to hear that. I myself was diagnosed several years ago."

Samantha's breath caught in her throat, and she stood up, regarding her with concern. "And? Are you okay?"

"I am. A mastectomy and reconstructive surgery all in one and… so far, so good."

"That's *really* good to hear. Diagnosis and treatment options are so much better for women than they were fifteen years ago. My mother might have survived if it had happened now instead of then."

Gwen nodded, her smile sad, and followed Samantha's eyes back to the vases.

"Incredible," Samantha said.

"Magnificent, aren't they?"

"These flowers look like they're alive and blooming beneath the glaze. I feel as if I'm seeing a garden through a magnifying glass."

"You say such beautiful things, Sam. Perhaps you'd do well to produce a book of poetry in between all those mysteries you write."

"If you let me come here for the inspiration, I just might."

"You have an open invitation."

Gwen drew in a deep breath, delighting in the pleasure Samantha took as she strolled from piece to piece. And while her guest made a study of the art pottery, Gwen studied Samantha: her stature, mannerisms, and the short hair that showed off her contoured jawline. She was as tall as Gwen and just as slim, and something in the way she moved, the way she stood with her hands clasped behind her back and bestowed her undivided attention intrigued Gwen in a way so new, yet so familiar.

Gwen hadn't been yet fourteen when she developed her first maddening crush on Margot, the daughter of the owner of a Cape Cod yacht club to which the Laraways had belonged. Margot had just finished high school and was on her way to Harvard. Gwen adored her. Her salty skin was always sun-kissed, short hair tousled from the sea breeze, and in her dark and dreamy eyes was an ever-present spark of mischief. Unconventional, adventurous, rebellious, Margot would have qualified as an adrenaline junkie by today's standards. She belonged to a cigarette boat racing team, and when she wasn't zipping around in her daddy's boat, she was ocean-kayaking or participating in nighttime sailboat races.

An instant chemistry between them had ignited, and Gwen, being lanky and tall for her age, had professed to be sixteen to encourage a friendship. Margot probably knew Gwen was lying, but when she wasn't with her older friends she indulged Gwen, sometimes inviting her out on the water for a joy ride or into her parents' cabin cruiser to sneak a drag of a cigarette or a swig of a cold beer she'd snatched from the club's bar. Just putting her lips on something that Margot's lips had touched excited Gwen in a way she couldn't explain. And when Margot was out of sight, Gwen thought of nothing else but seeing her again.

One night while a party was on at the yacht club, Gwen watched as Margot dragged an older girl off the dance floor and ran outside with her. When they didn't return, Gwen wandered down to the dock to see a light burning in the cabin cruiser. Beyond the sound of buoy bells and water lapping the side of the boat, she heard the muffled sound of rock music coming from inside. When no one answered her call, she climbed aboard and went down to find the two young ladies topless and engaged in a passionate kiss that shocked and changed her life that night.

Quietly, she crept away. Oh, how she desperately longed to be that girl in Margot's arms. She was jealous, yes, but more than jealousy she felt joy—a joy that instantly clarified her confused adolescence and gave definition to the same-sex attraction she'd been unable to put into words. Suddenly she understood why she never got excited over boys the way other schoolgirls did. It was wonderful to know others like her existed and, best of all, that Margot was one of them.

Toward the end of that summer, during a sunset walk on the beach with Margot, Gwen worked up the nerve to profess her adolescent love with a sudden and nervous and quite sloppy kiss. Obviously caught off guard, Margot waited a moment before taking hold of Gwen's wrists and stepping back in gentle rejection. "Whoa, kiddo, what are you doing?"

"Kissing you…" young Gwen had said. "I know you like girls."

Margot laughed. "I do, but you're a little too young for me."

"I'm sixteen," Gwen lied.

"Well, even if *that's* true, it still makes you a minor. I'm eighteen now." Without warning she grabbed Gwen's rib cage, tickling her until Gwen squirmed and struggled to free herself. And then Margot took off, water splashing and wetting her shorts as she ran along the shoreline.

Gwen ran after her, hurt by the rejection, humiliated by Margot's making a joke of her kiss. When Gwen had nearly caught up, Margot slowed down and turned, walking backward and laughing as she caught her breath. "So pretty little Gwen likes girls, huh?" she said between taking heavy breaths. "Your parents would send you to a shrink if they knew. Mine did. They think I'm cured now."

"I don't care what they do! And it's not funny!" Gwen bent down, forcefully scooping a handful of water in Margot's direction.

"Hey!" Margot hollered as the spray of cold water hit her chest. She looked down at her wet shirt. "You did that just to see my nipples get hard, didn't you?" But when tears filled Gwen's eyes she stopped. "Aww, come here…I'm sorry." She opened her arms.

Gwen rushed into them and cried.

"You are so sweet and so pretty," Margot said. "And you're going to be gorgeous by the time you turn eighteen. So when you do, come up to Cambridge and visit me at Harvard. I promise to let you kiss me then…for as long as you want." Margot broke the hug and pulled back to look at her. "Maybe I'll even kiss you back."

But Margot never made it to Harvard. She was killed in a boating accident a few days later.

Gwen had never experienced death before, and when her parents broke the devastating news, she fainted. It took her months and months to accept the fact that Margot was no more. How could someone so alive suddenly stop living? How could Margot exist one day and stop existing the next? Questions like these sometimes kept her up all night, eventually leading her to study philosophy and theology in college and ultimately pushing her toward academia to teach metaphysics: the study of being and the nature of existence.

Not until graduate school did Gwen meet her first lover and become involved with other lesbians and gay clubs. Prior to that time, she had unenthusiastically dated a few young men at her parents' encouragement. She had some pleasant dates, friendly courtships, plenty of potential suitors who'd tried desperately to win her love—and her family's money, she suspected—but none possessed the power to touch her heart or stir in her a sexual desire. Not the way women did, and certainly not like Margot had. Gwen never forgot her, and throughout the years she often wondered what Margot might have looked like at the age of thirty, forty, fifty. Probably a lot like Sam did now.

For a moment Gwen closed her eyes, thinking that if she were ten years younger, or Sam ten years older, she could easily fall for her, love her madly. But timing was everything, wasn't it? And in the larger scheme of things, their timing was a little off. Perhaps it was better, she lamented, when the things we want most in life come never at all, rather than sooner or later. When they come sooner, we live with the knowledge of what we've lost; when they come later we're only reminded of what it's too late to have. But she saw no sense in regretting the could-have-beens of life. It only made your heart heavy, subtracted from the beauty and wonder of the here and now. Gwen took another deep breath and slowly exhaled, detaching herself from the past as she heard her name being called.

"Gwen…?" Samantha was staring at her, smiling a little, a perplexed crease in her brow. "Where were you?"

"I'm sorry, I was just—"

"Having a private thought and I rudely interrupted. I'm sorry," Samantha said in good humor.

Gwen gazed into Samantha's dark-brown eyes. They were honest eyes, yes, but they were bedroom eyes, too, as deep and dreamy as Margot's. "I was just thinking that you remind me of someone I used to know."

"Not your ex, I hope. You know, the one you said you would have divorced by now?"

Gwen laughed. "Heavens, no. You remind me of my very first girl-crush."

"Do you still know her?"

"She died very young…a long time ago."

"How long?"

"Oh…" Gwen paused to think. "Over forty-seven years ago."

"Hmm…maybe I'm her, reincarnated. Maybe I've come back to you."

The thought startled Gwen. "Nice of you to take so long." She searched Samantha's face. "You came back too late."

"Late?" Samantha looked at her watch and smiled. "I was thinking I'm right on time."

Gwen parted her lips but was unable to think of a suitable retort. The mood became serious, and she thought it best to change the subject. "Feel free to touch or hold a vase."

"You read my mind," Sam said, as though sensing Gwen's need to lighten the mood. "I'd like to hold one…very carefully…just for the tactile experience."

"Knock yourself out, Sam." Gwen reached in front of her and opened a curio door. "Pick a favorite."

Without hesitation, she pointed to the red poppies.

Gwen lifted it from the shelf. "You have very fine taste."

"Shh! Don't tell me what it's worth. I'll get nervous and drop it."

"That's what insurance is for." Gwen chuckled, and her mood did lighten.

With two hands Samantha carefully accepted the proffered vase, but just as she did their bare arms touched. The feel of Samantha's skin brushing hers sent chills through her body. Call it chemistry, call it magnetism, but an undeniable electrical current sizzled between them. She knew Sam felt it too because they both froze for a moment before Samantha took the vase. Gwen watched as Samantha carefully rotated it in her hands, clearly admiring the full design, and then turned it over. "Eighteen ninety-six…" Samantha said.

Gwen looked on in surprise. "So you've learned to count in Rookwood years!"

"I have!" Samantha spoke like a proud student. "Liz taught me. I hope I'm impressing you in some small way."

Gwen tried to hide her smile. "In a big way, Sam."

"Well, I have to say you were right when you said I would fall in love."

"Was I?"

"Yes, you were." They were staring at each other now, not at the vase, and Gwen had the feeling they weren't talking about pottery anymore. If not for Isabel calling them for dessert, it seemed neither one would have managed to break their stare.

"Aunt Gwen?" Isabel called. "Are you two still in here?" She stood with her hands on her hips, Liz coming up alongside her.

"Uh-oh," Liz said to Gwen. "Sam's hooked. You're turning her into a pottery addict. Now she'll start buying up Rookwood and Weller pottery, and this time next year she'll be attending Collectors Anonymous meetings with the rest of us."

Gwen laughed.

"Go away." Samantha seemed to be only half joking. "Can't you see I'm in the middle of an intense sensory experience?"

Isabel and Liz had obviously become instant friends, and Gwen was glad to see them getting on so well. Business associates and social contacts, Isabel had plenty, but no intimate relationships. If Gwen couldn't interest her in seeking out a romantic relationship, then a close friendship would do for now.

"Come on, you two," Isabel said. "Dessert is served on the front porch. Liz and Sam brought us custard cream puffs, and Rosa has made a fruit salad. It's spiked with tequila, although she denies it. And she's making latte if you're interested."

"Rosa's making latte? She must be in a good mood. Sam? Latte?"

"Sure."

"Tell Rosa to make it four."

"All right," Isabel said, "but don't be too long. Liz wants to see the property."

"By all means, go on without us."

When the two young women retreated she returned her attention to Samantha, clenching the arm of her glasses between her teeth. She bit on it thoughtfully. "Okay, Sam, back to pottery. Are you up for a quick test before dessert?"

Samantha's brown eyes narrowed challengingly. "Test me."

Gwen smiled as she pondered her for a moment. "All right, then."

She slipped her glasses back on. "There's one last showcase over here," she said, leading the way. "You won't find any floral designs, just figurals and scenic pieces—vases, tiles, plaques, and such—all by different potters. Let's see if you can identify Rookwood from the rest."

Gwen adjusted a dimmer that brightened both the track lighting above and the lights within the case. The curio was enormous, but she saw Sam zero in on the Rookwood bookend she'd come for.

"Oh, wow—that's mine. I mean, yours, ours."

"Yes, it is…waiting for its mate for many years now." Gwen opened the double doors of the cabinet in which it was displayed.

Samantha surveyed the six or so shelves. All the pieces were beautiful, but some had that same haunting, ethereal style about them, with flying bats and owls against nocturnal landscapes. Another vase depicted a foggy swamp in the light of a blue moon. She took her time, keeping Gwen in suspense. "Should I start?" she asked.

"Go ahead."

Samantha was quiet for a while as she gazed at all the pieces of pottery, and then she began pointing. "Rookwood."

"Correct."

She pointed to another. "Rookwood."

"Yes."

"Rookwood…Rookwood…Rookwood," she called them, stopping at a life-like snapping turtle with a circle of holes in its back. "That doesn't look like Rookwood, but I love it."

"You should. It's Weller."

"Why the holes?"

"It's a flower frog?"

Sam trailed a finger along the snapper's spiked, dragon-like tail. "A snapping-turtle flower frog? I know florists use them to make arrangements, but the ones my mother had were flat disks with holes that sat in the bottom of vases, not ornamental like this."

"Well, during the thirties and forties all sorts of ceramic animal sculptures were made to hold water and display tiny buds and flowers too small for vases. Vintage flower frogs are very collectible right now. Besides putting flowers in the holes, people use them as pen holders, others to display vintage marble collections, and some keep them in the bathroom to hold eyeliner pencils, tweezers, and so forth."

"And what's that?" Samantha pointed to a blue-and-white cameo plate. "It's looks out of place with the other pottery."

"It is. It's English. Wedgwood. You might enjoy knowing that Charles Darwin married one of the Wedgwood daughters, Emma Wedgwood. She was his first cousin. Unfortunately, three of their ten children didn't survive. Others were intellectually disabled. In fact, Darwin's personal observations contributed to his essays against inbreeding."

"Geez…what a crash course this has been," Samantha said. "So, did I pass?"

"You more than passed." Gwen was amazed at Samantha's ability to identify and distinguish Rookwood from the others. "You *are* astute. And you have a great eye for detail."

"It's what made me such a good forensic investigator before I left the field to write full-time."

"Seriously? You were a detective?"

"No, a civilian. I worked for a crime lab."

"That certainly explains your sharp eye and fine investigative work, Detective Crowley."

Samantha did a double take, her mouth opening in surprise at the mention of her fictional sleuth. "How do you know about Detective Crowley?"

"I do my homework," she said quite nonchalantly.

"You've read my work?"

She edged her glasses down her nose. "Do you think I would entertain an author without first familiarizing myself with her work?"

Samantha shook her head, as if not quite knowing what to say.

"I will confess that Isabel told me about your books the other night. She passed along your first one she had in her library."

"Since our phone conversation two days ago you managed to read my first book?"

"I'm a professor. I read. It's what I do. Besides, I couldn't put it down. It's a hauntingly compelling story—atmospheric, mystical, your characters quite engaging. I stayed up half the night, unable to put it down. Tell me, though," she said, reaching in and taking the rook bookend from its shelf. "Detective Crowley is a ghost, is she not?"

Samantha looked at her incredulously. "How can you know that? Do you know how many readers are just now beginning to figure out that she's not real?"

"I didn't say she wasn't *real*…I said she was a *ghost*."

"Yes, well, what I meant is that she's *ethereal*, as opposed to *corporeal*." Samantha tilted her head and stared at Gwen. "I can't believe it was that obvious to you," she said, disappointment in her voice.

"Perhaps my recognition of the supernatural is as instinctive as your recognition of flowers. Now we can *both* be impressed." Gwen handed her the single rook bookend that was to be hers. "Let's take this outside so we can let them sit together."

She left Samantha standing there as she casually went about shutting off all the lights. As the room gradually darkened, the rook's body deepened from blue to black, the remaining curio lights reflecting in the rook's eye and giving it that strange glint of intelligence.

"But still," Samantha pressed, as Gwen circled the gallery, "I'm surprised you read my character so well…that you saw right through her. It makes me question my writing skills."

"Oh, don't ever question your skills, Sam. I love your storytelling. You're a superb craftsman. Suffice it to say," she said, circling back through the darkened room and coming face-to-face with Samantha in the shadows, "that I know a ghost when I meet one."

Chapter Ten

Isabel and Liz didn't wait for Gwen and Sam to join them. Liz wanted to see everything. After exploring the furniture inside the house, she had enthusiastically accepted Isabel's offer to see the grounds. They passed Rosa's stone cottage and, beyond a stand of pines, a second cottage under renovation. The cats' red barn was near the back of the house, its dozen residents meandering in and out. A few were friendly, but most kept their distance from Liz.

"My God, I've never seen this many at once," she said, marveling at the swirling colors of moving felines. "It's so wonderful that you've done this for them."

Isabel shrugged. "Some people think I'm the proverbial crazy-cat-lady in training," she said in a self-effacing tone. "But I don't care. It makes me happy to help something outside of myself. It's important to me that I go to sleep at night knowing that because I exist, something or someone suffered a little less today."

"I'm sure you sleep soundly." Liz watched with admiration as Isabel spoke, desire creeping in as well. Aside from the fact that Isabel's attire bordered on preppy—in a pinch, her white shirt and navy skirt might have doubled as a Catholic school uniform—there was something sleek and undeniably sexy about her. A natural sensuality. Her posture was perfect, and she walked with the aloof, languid stride of a cat.

"Animal welfare organizations are doing great things, and volunteers make such a difference," Isabel went on, "but even with the push toward a zero-euthanasia rate, over thirty percent of dogs and forty percent of cats that enter shelters don't make it out alive. That's over two million dogs and cats killed every single year. Just because they can't find homes."

"How heartbreaking."

"Well, it's a vast improvement over the numbers ten years ago, but finding good homes for puppies and kittens is harder than you'd think, and placing adult and senior animals is very difficult." She shrugged and gestured at the cats. "I'm in a position to help…and so I do."

"I think you're absolutely wonderful." Liz beamed. "And you might have just convinced me to adopt in the very near future." She softened her smile and put a hand to her chest. "I still have trouble talking about it, but my cat, Mars, and my Scottie, Skyler, both passed away a year ago. Skyler came to the shop and most everywhere with me, and I just haven't been ready to replace them. Maybe soon…"

They continued around, back to the front of the property, then strolled across the sprawling lawn and down to the water, to a path that would take them in a circle around the two-acre pond. The stone path was beautifully landscaped with ornamental grasses and blooms of blue and yellow flowers, and here and there white Adirondack chairs were tucked into the vegetation. The heady fragrance of wisteria, lilacs, and honeysuckle saturated the summer breeze, and Liz imagined herself whiling away a summer afternoon out here with a good book and a glass of iced tea.

Three cats followed them, one calico, one black, and an orange tabby. They paused when she and Isabel stopped to watch two Canada geese come in for a landing on the pond. The birds glided down, using their feet to brake against the water, and honked at Isabel in greeting. "Hey, guys," Isabel said, bending to reach for a plastic canister hidden behind a chair. She took out a handful of corn pellets and threw it to them.

Aside from recent time spent with Sam, Liz couldn't remember enjoying the company of a woman so much. She liked all types of women, especially Latinas, and Isabel had to be the prettiest one she'd ever seen. So bright and knowledgeable, too. Isabel was a walking Wikipedia when it came to subjects of interest, and Liz felt they could talk for days on end without ever running out of things to say. And if they did run out, Liz would be content to just stare in silent admiration.

Despite her diminutive stature, Isabel appeared strong and possessed a subtle but distinct androgyny that Liz found incredibly appealing. Isabel, she decided, was definitely gay. She just didn't know it yet. Liz studied her from head to toe as they walked—her small breasts, her smooth and feminine legs, her thin but nicely toned arms and shoulders—until the orange cat wove itself through Liz's legs and tripped her.

Without hesitation, Isabel reached and grabbed hold of Liz's hand to keep her from stumbling forward. Her hand was warm, a little rough from all the outdoor activities she obviously so enjoyed, but Liz liked the feel of a woman with working hands. "Thanks. Good reflexes." Liz laughed. "Better than mine."

Isabel held on until Liz had steadied herself, and Liz thought that if the circumstances were different, if she were on a date with Isabel, she would have reached for her other hand and pulled her in close for a kiss. The thought of doing this, of holding and kissing Isabel, sent a wave of arousal through her. But just as Isabel let go and they started walking again, something invisible distracted her, and she stopped.

Isabel soon turned and looked back at her. "Is something wrong?"

"No…it's just…I don't know." Liz held out her arms to the breeze and turned in a slow circle. "I feel something. Right here. It's so strange…like a heavy, almost palpable energy." A gust of warm wind blew toward them from across the pond, rippling the water and making a mess of Isabel's hair. Liz smiled at her, watching as every strand of hair—straight, dark, and shiny—fell back into perfect place.

Isabel wrapped her hair around her ear and tilted her head questioningly. "What kind of energy?"

Whatever it was vanished as fast as it had come. Liz shook her head and shrugged it off. "Probably just symptoms of my urban existence. I spend way too much time surrounded by buildings instead of trees," she said, combing her own hair back with her fingers because, unlike Isabel's, hers didn't fall back into place. "Do you get down to the city much?"

Isabel nodded. "Every two weeks or so…sometimes for auctions or the theater…a few times a year for the opera…but usually on business and for charity events."

"That's it? Never just to hang out?"

"No," Isabel answered, as if it would never occur to her to add mindless fun to her list of respectable things to do.

"I'm surprised you're fond of art deco," Liz said.

"Why, because the art form was a celebration of industrialization and urban living?"

"Exactly."

Isabel arched an eyebrow and retorted. "By the same token, you shouldn't like art nouveau because it was a Victorian celebration of *nature*."

"Oh, but I do love nature."

"You don't look like you love nature."

"Oh no?" Liz asked. Here she was again, being misinterpreted by yet another woman. She put her hands on her hips. "Please enlighten me. What *do* I look like?"

"You look like a Lladró statue—one of those chic deco ladies posed with an Afghan or greyhound."

Liz laughed. "I like those Lladró ladies. And if you ever stop by my shop, you might enjoy seeing me dressed up as a flapper."

"Maybe I will."

"I wish you would. Just let me know you're coming, because some days I'm open by appointment only, depending on how busy I am with clients." Liz smiled at her. "And about Lladró flappers and their dogs, do you know *why* those particular large-breed dogs were so popularly posed with women during the Roaring Twenties?"

Isabel held her head high. "Yes, I do. Because flappers represented the new and improved independent woman who had exchanged her Victorian lapdog for something bigger, sleeker, and bolder—a reflection of her changing self-concept, independence, and elevated social status."

"That's right, Ms. Wikipedia. It was the first time in history that a woman was free to go about her business without a male escort. She could drink and smoke in public, attend parties, enjoy jazz clubs with her single female friends…even enjoy casual sex for the first time in history."

The mention of *sex* seemed to shut Isabel down. She stopped talking, walked ahead to pick a cluster of flowers from a honeysuckle vine, and proceeded to nibble off the end of one and suck the nectar.

Liz was feeling a connection with Isabel—a connection that was mutual, she was sure—and she didn't want to say or do anything to scare Isabel away. "Oh, wow, honeysuckle? Give me one. I haven't tasted honeysuckle since I was a kid." Isabel handed her one and they stood side by side, pinching off the end of the flowers and sucking out the single drop of nectar. "Mmm…that's so sweet."

Isabel pulled off another clump of the delicate white flowers and shared it with her. "I suppose you're too busy living life in the city to stop and smell the flowers, huh?"

"*Taste* the flowers, you mean."

Isabel watched, smiling as Liz savored the honeysuckle as though it were a culinary delicacy, until Blue came rushing down the path with a racquetball in her mouth. "Personally," Liz said to the dog, "I like flappers, but as for their dogs? I much prefer rugged, short-legged Scotties."

"They prefer you, too," Isabel said as Liz picked up the ball Blue dropped at her feet and threw it. But Liz's aim was bad, and the ball landed in the water. Blue rushed to the edge of the pond, squealing frantically until Isabel grabbed a stick and fished it out for her.

"You throw like a city girl, too." Isabel evidently had a sense of humor.

"Now that's presumptuous. Did I say I was *from* the city? No, just that I currently *live* there."

Isabel shook water from her hand and wiped it on her skirt. "You mean you didn't live in the city until you married Samantha's brother?"

Liz's brow shot up in surprise. "Sam's brother? Where on earth did you get the idea I was married to Sam's brother?"

"My aunt said you were Samantha's sister-in-law."

"My *sister* is married to her brother, not *me*. I'm a lesbian."

As soon as Liz said the word *lesbian*, Isabel stiffened and quickly averted her gaze, as if afraid Liz's bright-green eyes might have the power to illuminate the subconscious desires kept secret in the hidden depths of her own. Isabel turned and walked, ignoring Liz's announcement and dropping the subject completely.

"I didn't mean to offend you."

"It doesn't offend me. I grew up around a lot of gay people. Aunt Gwen is gay."

Liz was about to say that Sam had already told her, but then thought better of disclosing the information Sam had shared. Instead, she kept quiet and smiled to herself as she followed Isabel, until that odd sensation stopped her again. It was as if one of the animals had brushed up against her leg, but the cats had fallen behind to watch the geese, and Blue was well ahead of her. "There it is again," Liz called to Isabel. "What *is* that? God…it's so strong…like a presence."

"You must be like my aunt. She feels things, too."

"Really? What kind of things?"

"I don't know." Isabel gave a casual shrug. "Spirits, I suppose."

"Spirits? You mean like ghosts?"

"Isn't that what you meant?"

"Not exactly, but now that you mention it, yes…there's a definite energy here. What is it?"

"Don't ask me. Ask them."

"Them who?"

"My aunt and Rosa. I don't feel things the way they do."

"You don't believe in spirits?"

"Not particularly. I think it's what you suggested before—the spirit of nature. The outdoors can be like that. Sometimes in midsummer, during the height of the growing season when everything is lush, you can sit out here in the early morning and actually hear things growing."

Liz smiled. "So, then you *do* feel things."

"Yes, but I'm more of an empiricist."

"A preference for the scientific method, huh? You observe, your aunt intuits?"

"Something like that." Isabel's voice was soft. "And you?"

"Ideally? I like to intuit my observations and observe my intuitions."

"Sounds complicated."

"Sometimes complications enrich our experiences, no?"

Isabel smiled. "I thought that was the function of literature."

"If you prefer to live vicariously, I suppose it is." Liz laughed, pondering her enigmatic companion as they came full circle and headed back to the house. She followed Isabel, smelling honeysuckle, tasting its sweet nectar lingering on her lips, and imagining how much sweeter Isabel's lips would taste.

❖

The sun in the west was blinding, but the air was now cool, and the trio of ceiling fans along the porch conducted both a breeze and a symphony of chimes.

Jacket flung over her shoulder, Samantha picked up the canvas bag she'd left on the porch and followed Gwen along the green-planked porch. "I like your chimes, especially the buoy bell." She gave it a soft push, and the black triangular bell sounded a deep, haunting *gong* that reminded her of being on the shore of a harbor. "You've quite a collection."

"Yes, but then…I'm a collector," Gwen said, laughing at herself as she made her way around the glass top of a white wicker table and gestured for Samantha to sit. "Some people would find them maddening, I know, but to me there is nothing more beautiful than the wind making music."

Samantha took sunglasses from her blazer pocket and sat across from Gwen. Liz and Isabel had apparently finished dessert and left behind empty cups and two discarded plates. "I once had an Aeolian harp," she said. "My ex has it now."

"A *wind* harp? Oh, my! Wherever did you find one? Years ago I read an article on Aeolian harps in a gardening magazine but never had the good fortune of happening upon one."

"I found mine in a shop in Connecticut. They're flat, about this long." Samantha demonstrated with her hands. "Just wide enough to sit on the sill of an open window."

"Well, if you give me the name of the shop, I'll definitely make a point of getting there."

Rosa interrupted just then, humming a tune, friendly as ever, as if their exchange in the kitchen had never taken place. Removing the empty plates and cups Isabel and Liz had left behind, she replaced them with a fresh tray of chocolate-covered strawberries, cream puffs, and two cups of latte. "Cinnamon?" she asked Samantha as she sprinkled some on top of Gwen's latte. She wondered if Rosa had a rapid-cycling mood disorder.

"May I ask a personal question?" she said when Rosa was gone.

Gwen smiled. "I may not answer…but go on and ask."

Samantha surveyed the landscape through sunglasses. "You didn't come to afford all this teaching philosophy, did you?"

Gwen laughed. "The Laraways have been in the paper business for generations."

"Paper?"

"Yes, you know, that white stuff they print your novels on? Writers might take trees for granted, but without them we would have no books, no recorded history. We'd all live in a world of hearsay, I suppose, just standing around…"

"Looking for shade."

"Good point."

"And for the record," Samantha said, "I *don't* take trees for granted. I often think of them when I'm printing out draft after draft, ream after ream of paper."

"I'm glad to hear it." Gwen took her cup, leaned back, and crossed her legs.

Samantha could have sat for hours, questioning her on a multitude of subjects, papermaking included, but she didn't want to overstay her welcome. "Well, your property is beautiful. I love the pond. I was admiring the view from the kitchen earlier. In fact, I spotted another dog down there."

"Oh?" Gwen replied in a voice caught somewhere between surprise and nonchalance.

"Yes. It might have been a German shepherd. I thought maybe it was another one of yours and asked Rosa if—"

As if on cue, Rosa interrupted a second time to place another tray beside Gwen. On it lay Gwen's sunglasses, a copy of Samantha's book, and a Montblanc fountain pen.

"*Gracias*," said Gwen.

"*De nada*," Rosa answered, glancing at Samantha as she hummed another upbeat tune and walked away.

"So…" Gwen put on her sunglasses and turned her attention to Samantha again. "Tell me the story of what led you here today," she asked, and listened with seeming fascination as Samantha recounted the role of fate in the recent turn of events in her life—the hurricane, the crow who saved her life and gave her the idea for the Detective Crowley mystery series, and eventually the purchase of the bookend that led her to Liz and to Gwen today.

"Synchronicity…a fascinating phenomenon," Gwen said.

Samantha's intellectual passions rose. "Funny you should mention it. After the hurricane, I started reading up on the notion of synchronicity. One essay in particular, written by Carl Jung, left a deep impression on me."

"It's wonderful. One of my favorites, and interesting that you enjoyed it," Gwen said, reaching for a cream puff at precisely the same time as Samantha so that their knuckles collided.

"Synchronicity," Samantha said.

"No. I think that was a collision," Gwen said, and they both laughed.

Samantha popped a cream puff into her mouth and sipped her latte while Gwen filled two bowls of fruit and whipped cream.

And just when she felt they were beginning to relate on a more personal level, here came Rosa again, carrying the rook bookend and changing the course of their conversation.

"Oh, look, Sam. Here comes our bride!" Gwen said as Rosa placed it on the table.

"Just so you know, mine's a bride, too."

"Of course she is. We wouldn't have it any other way, now would we?" Gwen smiled at her. "I just hope yours doesn't have cold feet about getting married."

"Nope. No cold feet. Just crow's feet." Samantha removed her rook from its bubble wrap and set it beside its mate.

"Flawless," Gwen commented as she inspected it. "It's so nice to see them together. A testament to arranged marriages, wouldn't you say?"

"And love at first sight," Samantha added without daring to look at her. She pushed her chair back and bent forward to study the birds at eye level. "When did the pottery close?"

"It produced pottery for over eighty years but never quite recovered from the Depression. It changed hands a few times, and at one point production ceased, but recently it came under new ownership and is actually back in business in Cincinnati. And in addition to the work of new artists, they're using original molds to issue revival pieces. Rookwood made architectural tiles as well, and some old estates in that area still have Rookwood mantelpieces and floors."

"So tell me this," Samantha said after examining the bookends again. "If we'd been alive in 1925…the year these rooks were made… where would we have bought them?"

"We?" Gwen seemed amused. "You mean if *we* had been on a shopping spree together in New York?"

"Yes…you know, in a past life."

Gwen raised an eyebrow. "Goodness, Sam, how many past lives have you lived?"

"I have no idea, but I'm sure we knew each other before today." Samantha laughed at herself then. "I know, you think it's a ridiculous idea."

"Not necessarily," Gwen said with a contemplative smile. "There is an undeniable familiarity that I, for one, cannot explain." Her gaze turned to the bookends, and she was quiet for a moment. "So. Let's see…if we were shopping together in New York City in the year 1925, we would have bought them in Tiffany's or B. Altman. Both were Rookwood dealers. All major cities had dealers—Chicago, Boston, Philadelphia, San Francisco, New Orleans, and, of course, Cincinnati."

"Hmm…Tiffany's, 1925…" Samantha trailed a finger down the back of each rook.

They both sat back then, cups in hand, admiring the bookends and listening to the sound of chimes until Samantha spoke again. "Name your price. I'll write you a check."

"What did I quote you on the phone?"

"You didn't. You said it all depended."

"On what?"

Samantha blushed. "On how much you liked me."

"Did I say that?"

Samantha had a feeling Gwen knew exactly what she'd said. She was being coy, teasing her, as she tended to do. Samantha couldn't hold back a grin. "Yes. That's what you said."

Gwen nodded. "Well, if that's what I said—and I do trust that what you say I said is, in fact, what I said—then I have no choice but to gift it to you."

"Absolutely not. I couldn't possibly let you—"

Gwen held up a hand. "If you insist on arguing I just might decide to keep my rook and outbid you on yours."

"But I—"

"Let's consider it your gold star for achieving an A in Pottery 101."

Samantha watched Gwen's face as she spoke, wishing she could see those sky-blue eyes, but then she decided that Gwen looked awfully sexy wearing sunglasses. "You're too generous, Gwen. I don't know what to say."

"Say no more." She handed Samantha her book and the Montblanc pen. "Autograph my copy, and we'll call it even."

"All right, but I'll have to throw in copies of the rest of my books."

"Deal."

A strong breeze stirred the chimes again, blowing a napkin off the table and running its unseen fingers through Gwen's waves of thick, golden hair. Samantha took the book and pen from her and thought for a moment before she wrote:

For Gwen—
I leave here affected, charmed, changed somehow,
by the woman who "knows a ghost when she sees one."
Fondly and with gratitude,
Sam Weller

Chapter Eleven

I can't believe she gave you the bookend," Liz was saying as they coasted down the tree-lined driveway and turned left toward the main road. An orange sun hung low behind the apple orchard and the great expanse of pastoral land in the distance.

"You gave me the Old Crow decanter, didn't you?"

"That's different, Sam. You're my relative, my out-law. Besides, that one bookend is worth several hundred dollars."

Samantha looked over at her. "You think she likes me?"

"Likes you? In case you didn't notice, she *adores* you."

Samantha's heart pounded. "How can you tell?"

"By the way she looks at you. Wasn't it obvious?"

"I'm not sure."

"That's because you were too busy adoring *her*. You're smitten."

"I am. Thoroughly and completely. She's unlike any woman I've ever known. I can't remember having had such an immediate connection with someone." Samantha hesitated. "If I ask her out on a date, do you think she'd say yes?"

"I don't think so, Sam."

"What? Why not? You just said she adores me."

"Yes, but I don't think she's the type of woman to have a fling with someone your age."

"I'm not looking for a fling. I'm ready for some sort of permanence."

"Permanence?" Liz attempted a smile, but it turned into a big yawn. "I don't think Dr. Laraway's your girl. A woman of her age and stature isn't about to start playing house and making babies with you."

"Babies! What are you talking about? Who said anything about babies?"

Liz shrugged. “I don’t know. Now that we can all get married, isn’t that what we’re supposed to do? Get married, make babies, and overpopulate the world like our straight counterparts?”

“It’s an option for those so inclined, but kids aren’t for me. I certainly don’t want someone to have babies for me…and I’m definitely too old to have them myself.”

Her brow shot up. “No shit, Sam. You’re in menopause?”

“Been there, done that. Two years ago. It’s great. No more tampons competing for space with my wallet and phone and all the other crap in my bag.”

“Wow, do you feel any different?”

“Hormonally?”

“Yeah. Hormonally, sexually.”

“I feel fine. No more progesterone, little estrogen, lots of testosterone…but somehow I think that’s always been my ratio.”

Liz was in the middle of another yawn when she laughed. “How’s your sex drive?”

“Considering one’s sex drive is testosterone-dependent? I’d say my drive is…in drive.”

“Whew. That’s good to know for future reference because I’d hate to reach a point where I no longer wanted to have sex. I can’t even imagine that.”

“God forbid.” Samantha glanced over at her and rolled her eyes. “Getting back to Gwen…now that we’ve established that she’s in her fifties, not in her nineties, why don’t you think she’d go out to dinner with me?”

“I’d say Gwen’s about sixty.”

“I was thinking mid-fifties.”

“More like sixty.”

“Even if you’re right, that would be, what, a twelve-, thirteen-year age difference?”

Liz reclined her seat a notch and settled back. “As long as you’re okay with that.”

“Age differences have always been common in the gay community. And you know what? They are in the straight world, too. I mean, how many middle-aged men are with women twenty years their junior?”

“You’re right. I just think Gwen would rather be with someone her own age. And considering you said someone *my* age is too young for you, I’m surprised you don’t have a problem with someone older.”

"All I know," Samantha admitted, "is that I left her twenty minutes ago, and I can't wait to see her again. She's beautiful and sexy and very youthful."

"She is, Sam. She's all those things. She's gorgeous. Considering I have next to no scruples, I'd sleep with her in a heartbeat if I didn't know her…and if I didn't have the hots for her niece."

"Uh-oh…here we go!"

"Yeah, well, don't get too excited, because I don't think it's gonna 'go' anytime soon."

"You actually came out to Isabel?"

"I did. Only because she thought I was married to your brother. She quietly freaked out when I told her I was a lesbian. But then before we left, she casually invited me along to an auction at Sotheby's Saturday evening."

"This Saturday? I told Gwen I'd love to take Bertha up to meet her crows, and she suggested Saturday."

"Ah, I see. So you're gonna use your crow to get into her pants." Liz snickered. "How clever."

Samantha frowned and shook her head. "I thought I'd talk you into coming along again, but I guess not."

"You're on your own. I'm meeting Isabel for dinner in the city before the auction, so plan on having Gwen all to yourself."

"Great. Maybe that creepy Rosa will disappear for the night."

"Aww, I love Rosa! Why do you say she's creepy?"

"I don't know. I caught her making the sign of the cross behind my back when I got lost and ended up in the kitchen. I mean, what's up with that?"

"She's probably just super religious, and something about you reminded her of the devil himself."

"Oh, geez, thanks!"

Liz laughed. "Give Rosa a break. She has a very heavy accent, and she's probably just self-conscious about her English. That's all."

"If you say so." Samantha decided to let it go. She preferred to spend her time thinking about being with Gwen. "Meanwhile," she said to Liz, "I can't believe you've already got yourself a date with Isabel."

"It's not a date-date. And don't worry. I'm keeping my hands to myself. If there's a chance of anything happening with Isabel, the last thing I want to do is scare her away. I get the feeling she's petrified of her own sexuality."

"Do you really think she might be gay?"

"Oh yeah…she's one of us. She just doesn't know it yet."

Samantha chuckled. "When I first saw her come in I thought she could be, but I wasn't sure. I don't have good gaydar."

"Isabel has that subtle androgynous thing going on—she and her hot little Latina self."

"Yeah, I know." Samantha laughed. "I saw you do a double take when she first walked in. And I caught you checking out her legs when you bent down to pet Loosey Goosey."

"Nice dog." Liz sighed and put her seat back another notch. "Great legs…"

"You're so bad." Samantha couldn't help but admire Liz's prowess, her easy confidence. She was so comfortable in her own skin. "Just be careful with Isabel," Samantha warned her. "She's my future wife's niece."

Liz laughed, but her laughter turned into another yawn. "Don't worry, Sam-I-am. Women are my area of expertise. I'll handle Isabel with kid gloves."

"And don't go hurting her. I know you like to love them and leave them, but—"

"Isabel is *not* the kind of woman someone leaves."

"Whoa! Are you saying Isabel is *relationship* material? Would that word *ever* come out of your mouth?"

"I don't know what I'm saying, Sam." She ran her fingers through her hair. "I can't even think about it. I'll make myself crazy," she said and yawned yet again.

Samantha yawned, too. "Stop yawning…you're making me yawn, and I have to drive us home."

"I'm sorry. All that fresh air knocked me out. Anyway, don't worry about me and Isabel. If anything ever happens it will be because Isabel initiated it. You have my word. I will be on my best behavior."

Samantha drove on in silence for a long while, her mind a restless tangle of emotions until she started talking again. "I don't care that Gwen is older. Sure, it would be nice if she were my age, but what if we were the same age and there was no chemistry between us? What good is being the same age in that case? I mean, how many people are perfectly matched on dating sites according to age, education, and common interests, and when they meet there's zero chemistry, no sexual attraction whatsoever? It happens all the time. Commonalities, including age, might be a good formula for friendships, but no one can predict or control the animal magnetism that attracts two strangers. It's either there or it's not. And it's definitely there with Gwen."

Samantha waited for a reaction, and when it didn't come she glanced over. Liz's eyes were closed, her mouth wide open, her head bobbing from side to side against the headrest. She'd fallen asleep. Samantha turned up the music and spent the remainder of the drive plotting a course of action to properly court and ultimately charm her way into Dr. Laraway's life.

Liz didn't wake up until they were on the Triboro Bridge to Manhattan. The lights, horns, cars, people—all of it harshly contrasted to the peacefulness of the country. "Gosh, Sam," she said when she came to. "I didn't mean to crash on you." She straightened up in her seat.

"Must have been all that caffeine in your latte," Samantha said sarcastically.

"Why are you taking me home? You could have dropped me off at the station where you picked me up."

"I was afraid you'd fall back asleep and wake up in some train yard in the middle of the night. I've been called to gruesome scenes in train yards."

"Well, in that case, thanks for maybe saving my life." Liz stretched and pulled herself together. "Hey, you're not mad at me, are you?"

"For falling asleep?"

"No, for letting the air out of your balloon. I'm sure Gwen will pump you up when you see her again. And if it makes you feel any better, I think you and Gwen would make a handsome and very compatible couple. You just need to be aware of some very real issues. You know what they say, *Know thyself*." Then she looked over at Samantha. "Who said that anyway? Is it in the Bible or was it Shakespeare?"

"Socrates."

"Oh."

❖

The nap had revived Liz, and when she got into her East Side apartment she stepped out of her shoes, peered mischievously at the phone, and on impulse decided to call Sam. She didn't want to try Sam's cell number because she didn't want her to answer. Instead she dialed her home number. After the greeting of a human voice and the raspy gibberish of a crow, she waited for the beep and began speaking in a low, breathy voice:

"Hello, my darling Samantha…it's me, Dr. Laraway…I want your body…I want all of you…right now…right here…on the table in my gallery…surrounded by all this dazzling pottery." She might have continued if she hadn't burst out laughing. "Had you fooled for a minute, eh? Ha! It's me, your out-law, just calling to wish you sweet dreams. Seriously, though, I just wanted to say that I know you left quite an impression on Gwen, and I have a feeling you're as heavy on her mind as she is on yours tonight. I mean that, Sam, seriously," she said, starting to laugh again. "Call me if you need to talk…unless you'd rather write Ann Landers for advice on falling in love with an older woman. In any case, let's get together and exchange date-night stories after Saturday. Love you…"

Still laughing to herself, Liz unbuttoned her blouse and let it slide off her shoulders. She walked around the bedroom, listening to her own messages, until the sound of Isabel's voice made her stop.

"Hi, it's Isabel. I tried your cell but it went to voice mail. Just wanted to make sure you got in safely. Would you give me just one ring so I'll know you arrived home? Okay then…see you Saturday."

What a sweet gesture, Liz thought. One of the disadvantages to living alone was that no one ever knew if you were safe or not. On some subconscious level, she often wondered what would happen if she never returned home, or better yet, if after getting home she tripped and hit her head. How long would it take for family, friends, or clients to notice she hadn't returned their calls? A few days? A week? Not if Isabel could help it. If Liz didn't ring her within the next half hour, Isabel would be the caring type to report her missing.

There was something attentive and nurturing about the young Ms. Laraway, not to mention the fact that she was intelligent, interesting, and so damn sexy. And what made her even sexier was that she was so unassuming. Liz found Isabel's grace and naïveté both puzzling and delightful. Compared to all the other women she'd seduced and bedded, Isabel was as much a breath of fresh air as a day spent in the country.

In her bra and skirt, Liz wandered over to her dresser. "Yes, Isabel," she said, smiling as she took off one earring, then the other, and dropped them on an antique jewelry tray. "I'm home…safe and sound…and trying to figure you out."

When she had taken off her skirt and slipped into a silk robe, Liz sat on the edge of the bed and fumbled through her purse for Isabel's card. She dialed, let the phone ring once, then hung up and smiled to herself. An auction and dinner, just the two of them. Ah...so she *had* hooked the fish. She was so good at this game, so adept at the sport of catch-and-release. But something told her that if she ever managed to reel this one in, she might not want to let her go.

CHAPTER TWELVE

Finding an Aeolian harp for Gwen had taken the better part of the day. Samantha had tried calling the seaside shop where she'd bought one years ago, but the store had gone out of business, so she ended up searching online for just the right wind harp. Express delivery would ensure its arrival by Saturday morning, just in time for her visit with Gwen.

Presentation, she had learned from her mother's flower business, was as important as the present, so later that day she scouted local card shops for just the right wrapping paper. She settled on a purple paper with a silver and gold stellar motif and chose three spools of ribbon to match.

Gwen had invited Samantha for dinner, but on Saturday morning she called to say that storms were expected by evening. "Why not come early," Gwen suggested, "so Bertha can enjoy the grounds and hopefully mingle with the other crows before it rains."

Samantha couldn't tell her she was waiting for a gift to arrive. "I have a few things I have to do, but I'll try to get there by three," she promised.

"And come comfortable. I'm in jeans," Gwen said, adding that the evening temperatures were expected to dip into the fifties.

Samantha's delivery came at twelve o'clock. The harp was perfect, just as she'd hoped, and she took her time wrapping it. Bertha watched intently as Samantha curled the ribbons with a pair of scissors, and when Samantha turned away she took the opportunity to grab and attempt to run off with them, except that they were attached to the box and she didn't get too far.

"You think you're slick, huh?" She cut off an extra length of silver ribbon and let Bertha play while she got ready. At Gwen's recommendation she slipped into jeans and a white short-sleeved shirt and grabbed a hoodie to take with her. It was after one by the time she gathered up Gwen's present and copies of her books, and put Bertha in a carrier in the back of the car.

The crow vocalized incessantly during the ride, her voice competing with the music. "*Kaa, kaa, kaa!*" she said, which translated to "Are we there yet, are we there yet?"

"We're going to see Gwen," Samantha repeated over and over, hoping the name would sink in, and with any luck, Bertha might bond with Gwen and help Samantha win her heart.

They made good time and were only a few miles from Stockbridge when the sun began to slip in and out of the clouds. Judging from the way they began to darken, she figured the expected storms wouldn't wait until evening. It was half past two when Samantha's SUV rolled along the gravel drive and came to a stop behind a white Mercedes. The moment she cut the engine Bertha fell silent.

"Wow…look at all *this*!" Samantha excitedly whispered to Bertha as she got out. She opened the carrier door and pushed her hand against the crow's breast. "Come see," she coaxed her. Wide-eyed and garbling, Bertha stepped onto her wrist. "Look at this pretty place. Go on… it's okay…go fly," Samantha encouraged her, but Bertha clung tight, climbing up to her shoulder and flapping her way up to Samantha's head.

"If you poop in my hair I'll kill you," she said, reaching up and taking hold of the crow with both hands. "I need to look good today, so go find a nice bird's-eye view of something." With that, she gently threw Bertha into the air and watched as she flew to the porch and landed on the railing. Immediately the crow began to survey the grounds, the sky, and the porch with its shiny, twirling chimes, until the raucous sound of cawing crows came from the locust trees on the side of the house. Bertha looked with astonishment as if to say, "Wow, they sound just like me!"

Bertha hadn't seen or heard one of her own kind since the hurricane had blown her out of her nest. "Nice to hear your native tongue spoken, huh? Do those crows sound like your mama?"

Samantha looked at her with affection and satisfaction, sorry that she'd left her at home the other day but so grateful for the opportunity to bring her here today. Samantha smoothed her hair and plucked a few tiny feathers from her shirt. Then she picked up a gift bag filled with her books, tucked the rectangular gift box under her arm, and walked briskly toward the house, trailers of silver, blue, and gold ribbons blowing up behind her in the breeze like the tail of a kite.

"Hello?" she called out, anticipating Gwen's face at the door. The front door was open, but no one was around. Isabel had most likely left to meet Liz in the city by now, and the idea of having Gwen to herself for the evening gave her a quiet thrill. Since leaving the other day she'd thought of little else.

"Gwen?" she called again as she reached the porch and was just starting to climb the steps when, out of the corner of her eye, she noticed the black Scottie sitting way out in the grass between the house and the pond. Blue sat with her back to Samantha, pretending not to see her, but Samantha knew the Scottie was too shrewd to be unaware of her arrival. If Liz had been with her, no doubt the dog would be all happy and bounding up the slope right now.

"Hi, Blue, good to see you, too," she called. "Looks like the sky won't be *blue* for long." Samantha chuckled to herself, but Blue didn't seem at all amused. She glanced at Samantha over her shoulder as if to say, "Yeah, I get it…my name is Blue and the sky is blue…that's too funny…you're a real riot. Why didn't you bring that pretty redhead I liked so much?" And then she turned back to stare at whatever held her attention.

Clouds quickly darkened overhead, hastening the coming of twilight, as the warm breeze swept through the grass and rippled the water surface below. Samantha loved summer storms, loved how everything seemed greener and more alive right before the sky opened up. She drew in a deep breath of fresh air, following Blue's line of vision, and in a beam of sunlight shining down between the storm clouds she caught sight of another dog down by the pond—the same one she'd seen from Gwen's kitchen window. The brown in its coat shone like gold in the sun's spotlight, and Blue seemed fixated on the animal.

Gwen was nowhere in sight, and since no one had been interested in answering her questions about the dog—let alone acknowledging the animal, for God's sake—Samantha set the harp and books on the bottom step and wandered off to introduce herself.

Samantha strolled through the grass and dandelions, careful not to crush the colorful splashes of wildflowers blooming on flimsy stems, until she reached the Scottie, who sat staring at the shepherd. About a hundred feet away, the strange dog stopped when it saw Samantha and stood at attention, its back to the water. Unlike the ill-mannered Scottie, it seemed to welcome her approach.

"Hey, Blue," Samantha said and crouched beside her. "Is that your doggie-friend down there?" And when Blue refused to acknowledge her, Samantha began singing the old ballad "Blue Moon." Slowly she reached to pet the Scottie's back as she softly sang, but then she saw Blue's mustache quivering and thought better of it. She'd read somewhere that dogs have many more facial muscles than humans and use them to communicate complex messages. Right now, the message was simple: *I'm not in the mood for doggie-talk...so quit patronizing me and stop that annoying singing.*

"Okay, be that way. See if I care." Samantha stood and walked past her, whistling the rest of the song as she moseyed toward the German shepherd. She continued down toward the pond, through the gently sloping grass, until she was within thirty feet of the dog, then bent down again. "Hey, boy."

Motionless, the dog only stared.

"*Girl,* maybe?"

A tail began to wag.

"Ah...so you're a *girl*? And what a *good girl*...so pretty, too."

Seeming excited now, the dog opened its mouth in something of a smile as Samantha rose and moved cautiously forward, stopping again when she was within ten feet.

"Who's my good girl? Come on...it's okay, come here," Samantha cooed, and patted her thigh.

Back and forth the shepherd began to pace, so lithe and swift and light on her feet that the grass and violets barely stirred beneath her paws.

Samantha spotted something orange in the grass. "Hey, what's this?" she whispered, picking up a squeaky-ball. She squeezed it, watched the dog's head tilt from side to side, and tossed it into the air a few times. "Look what I've got. Can you catch a ball?" She tossed it into the air again, then rolled it to the dog and watched as it came to a stop by her paws. The dog looked down at it and then at Samantha, apparently not quite sure what to do with it. She looked at the ball again and made a motion to pick it up, but then seemed to change her mind and stared up at Samantha, her forehead crinkling.

She was beautiful, although maybe not purebred. One ear was slightly tipped, but her black and tan markings were symmetrical, and in her eyes shone the distinct and imposing intelligence of a shepherd. Something else showed in her eyes, too: the sadness of a lost dog, a desperate longing, an anxious desire to find someone. It touched Samantha so deeply as to be unsettling. Samantha smiled to herself. She was probably reading into things, projecting her own desire for the beautiful woman she'd come to visit. Or maybe the humidity was getting to her. The breeze had stopped and the air felt heavy. Samantha almost wished she'd worn shorts. She needed something cold to drink.

"Are you lost, pretty girl, or are you just visiting?" she said to the dog. "Do you know Gwen?"

At the mention of Gwen's name, her tail broke into a full wag, and she cocked her head in seeming anticipation.

"Hmm…so you *do* know Gwen. I had a feeling…"

Thunder rumbled in the distance, and the dog began to pace, trotting several yards to Samantha's left, then turning and trotting to her right. Back and forth she raced, as though held back by an imaginary line, an invisible fence.

"You're not allowed to come here? All right then, I'll come to you." As she spoke she heard a dog panting, felt its hot breath on her back, and realized the Scottie had snuck up behind her. Samantha turned around and looked at her. "Where did you come from, and why are you panting so hard? Your shepherd friend here isn't panting at all. See? She's nice and cool. I guess you're absorbing heat because your fur is black. Maybe that's why you're such a hot-tempered Scot," Samantha said, wiping beads of sweat from her own brow.

Thunder rumbled again, dark storm clouds racing in overhead to obliterate the one beam of sunlight shining on the dog. The shepherd whose fur had gleamed in that beam of light now darkened in the hazy shadows of the impending storm.

Samantha wasn't allowed to have dogs in the house she rented, but she'd be buying her own house soon, if she could stop writing long enough to find one. If this dog turned out to be a stray, and if Bertha didn't mind, maybe she'd adopt her, take her home tonight. Of course, the shepherd didn't look like a stray. She appeared healthy, well fed, and perfectly fit.

Deciding the dog was harmless enough, Samantha closed the distance between them. She walked forward, bent at the waist, her hand held out. The dog's tail kept wagging with happy anticipation, and when Samantha got within arm's reach she crouched again, face-to-face with the shepherd. She reached out, moving toward the dog's throat, about to rub her chin, when all at once, Blue barked, Gwen yelled, and the shepherd's eyes widened.

"Sam, no—stop!" Gwen's frantic voice sounded from the porch. "Don't touch her!"

Mistaking the dog's joy at the sight of Gwen for fear, and startled by both Gwen and Blue's harsh reprimands, Samantha lost her balance and fell back onto the seat of her pants. Stunned for the moment and embarrassed that she'd toppled over, she jumped up and gave an inane wave. "It's okay," she called up to Gwen. "I was just—"

"Leave her be, Sam—*please!*"

The dog was oblivious to Samantha's presence now. Gwen held her attention. Samantha stared up at the white house, at Gwen leaning against the white porch railing, the crow perched on her arm. They seemed so far away. Thunder sounded again as Samantha brushed off the seat of her pants and walked back up the slope. Blue punched the back of her leg with her big rubbery nose, as if to herd and hurry her along without an ounce of respect. The indignity made Samantha feel as though she were a sheep being herded and told what to do.

Gwen watched her come up, stroking Bertha's back with her free hand and looking down at Samantha with what appeared to be both worry and apology. "I'm sorry, Sam…I didn't mean to raise my voice to you. I just…didn't want you to get hurt," she said.

Gwen let Bertha jump back onto the railing and took a seat in a wicker rocking chair. An empty one was waiting for Samantha, and on the table in between the chairs sat a pitcher of sweet tea, lemon and spearmint sprigs floating among the ice cubes.

Feeling a bit foolish and, she had to admit, a little insulted by being scolded like a child, she scooped up the gift and the bag of books and climbed the steps to the covered porch. Bertha had jumped down and was stomping around in a shallow pan of water Gwen had put out for her.

"How was your trip?" Gwen asked as she filled two glasses with tea. But when she looked up and saw the colorfully wrapped gift, her eyes flew open, and she set the pitcher down. She looked wonderful in her tight white jeans and blue T-shirt that matched her eyes. "For me?" she asked.

Samantha set the books by her chair and handed her the wrapped box. "For you," she said, and cleared her throat.

"Oh, Sam, it's wrapped so beautifully. Too beautiful to open!"

"How else will you get to the beauty inside?" She sat down beside

Gwen. So that was that. They weren't going to address the visiting dog. Samantha was decidedly put off by the secrecy. "I was only trying to pet her, Gwen. I've been around dogs my whole life. I didn't mean any harm."

"I know. Have some tea, Sam. You look thirsty."

She was, and she took a long drink. "That's the dog I saw the other day."

"Uh-huh. She's very elusive."

"Not with me she's not."

"So I see," Gwen said, the gift in her lap, her attention shifting to the loud cawing of crows and then to Bertha, who'd hopped to the other end of the porch to look for them. "I'm so very happy and honored to make Bertha's acquaintance. What a beautiful crow she is, and so affectionate—just like her fictional character. And these books…and this gift…" She shifted the box on her lap. "May I?"

"By all means," Samantha said, marveling over Gwen's composure. She had an amazing tranquility, a serenity, but Samantha was beginning to wonder if it wasn't a rehearsed tranquility, a practiced serenity—all of it part of a professorial persona long in the making. And in the process, she seemed to have developed quite a knack for changing subjects and controlling conversations. But when Gwen opened the harp, the thrill in her voice and genuine delight in her eyes made Samantha soften and forget her analysis of the poised Dr. Laraway.

"A wind harp?" Gwen beamed.

Samantha gestured at all the hanging chimes along the porch. "Now your orchestra is complete."

"Oh, Sam…I don't know what to say. I didn't expect this…but thank you so very much." Her smile was broad as she reached across and stroked Samantha's arm, squeezed her hand. "Will it play for us, do you think?"

"That's up to Aeolus, keeper of the four winds," Samantha said, as a flash of lightning lit a sky that was turning from day to night in a matter of minutes. The breeze stopped again, and an eerie stillness enveloped them. Even the chimes fell silent. "You may need to ask one of them to blow and play your harp…and they like to be addressed by name."

Gwen smiled. "I know they do. I learned that from Detective Crowley in your book. She sends Bertha off daily to deliver a message to each of the four winds."

Samantha smiled even though she didn't want to. "That's in the second book."

"I couldn't wait for a hard copy, so I started the second one on my Kindle last night." She paused and thought for a moment. "Boreus is the north wind…Zephyr the west wind and…" She stopped, seeming unable to recollect the other two.

"Notos is the south wind, Eurus the west wind, in Greek mythology, at least. They have Latin names, too, but I can't recall—"

Before Samantha could finish her sentence, a strong gust of wind blew in with a fury, combing the chimes, striking deep and haunting gongs on the buoy bell, and sweeping up the loose wrapping paper from the porch floor. Gwen tried to grab it but missed and began to laugh. "I don't know which of the four winds this is, but it must have heard us call its name."

Samantha jumped up to snatch the paper and ribbons, but they blew up over her head and set sail off the porch. She chased the paper down the steps and out into the grass, the first heavy plunks of raindrops hitting her head.

"It's okay, Sam. Let it go," Gwen said, laughing at Samantha's failed attempts to catch up with the colorful mess.

But Samantha caught up and stepped on the paper. As she bent to pick it up she couldn't help but look down at the pond. And there it was, the dog, still standing there, still staring up at the house. The sight of the lost, lonesome animal upset her.

"I'm sorry, Gwen," she said, when she was back under the cover of the porch, "but this storm is going to be something fierce, and that poor dog's still down there with no shelter." She looked at Gwen, bothered by her indifference. "Don't you feel bad for her?"

Gwen shifted uneasily in her seat but didn't answer.

"Why does everyone around here ignore the poor dog?" Samantha frowned and let out a frustrated breath. "I know you know her…because she knows you."

Gwen looked at her incredulously. "Why do you say that?"

"Because when I said your name she got excited." Samantha shook her head and walked to the end of the porch that overlooked the water. "Can we at least bring her in out of the rain until the storm passes?"

"No." Gwen placed the harp on the seat beside her and joined Samantha at the railing. Blue followed her, keeping a sharp eye on

Samantha. “I wish we could,” she said and softly rested her hand on the small of Samantha’s back. “but we can’t.”

“Why not? Does she have an owner? I was thinking that if she’s a stray, maybe I could take her home with—”

“*What?*” Gwen seemed stunned. “Take her *home*?”

“Yes, well…if she doesn’t belong to anyone, I’d be willing to take her.”

Gwen looked at her as though she were speaking another language. Her hand fell away from Samantha’s back, and she closed her eyes. “You can’t take her home, Sam.”

“Why not? Whose dog is she?” Samantha refused to let Gwen dismiss her questions.

Gwen brought a hand to her mouth, covering it as if trying to keep herself from saying what Samantha was pushing her to say. Her arm dropped to her side then, and she gave a sigh of resignation. “She’s mine, Sam. If you must know the truth, she’s my dog.”

“Yours?” Sam turned to her, totally confused.

Lightning flashed, a clap of thunder startling her as wind ripped through the trees. Branches bent and swayed, loosened leaves whirling in the air like confetti. The dog by the pond seemed to grow nervous, pacing that imaginary line, vying for Gwen’s attention. And then the sky opened and the downpour came, her fur changing from brown to misty gray as a curtain of rain obscured her outline.

“I don’t understand. If she’s yours, what’s she doing down there in the rain?”

“Waiting…” Gwen said, her voice tinged with anguish. “She’s waiting for me.”

“Then let me help. What can I do? I’ll carry her up if she’s sick or something.”

“Sick?” Gwen shook her head. “Oh, Sam…I’m afraid it’s much, much worse than that.”

“Worse? What could be worse than—”

“She drowned.”

“Drowned?” Samantha felt her face pale. “You mean she…she *almost* drowned?”

“She’s dead, Sam. She’s been dead for seven years.”

Chapter Thirteen

The world seemed to fall silent as Samantha stood staring at the dog from the porch. She was only vaguely aware of the windswept rain lashing her face, of Gwen urging her to come in the house. And then Gwen had gone away, although for how long she couldn't say. Now she was back, touching Samantha's arm, saying something, but the words seemed far away. Her own body felt distant, as if she were merely an eavesdropper on her own conversation.

"Sam…come with me. Come in from the rain."

She finally managed to speak. "I just can't…I feel so…so *confused*."

Gwen touched her shoulder, tugged on her sleeve. "Look at me."

Even the sensation of Gwen's touch was dream-like, her emotions fragmented. Slowly the noise of the world returned to her ears, the cacophony of wind and rain and chimes making it hard to organize her thoughts, let alone her legs.

The dog was still out there staring up at the house, its storm-darkened image pulsating with each flash of lightning, as though caught in a strobe light.

"How can she not be actually there?" Samantha asked. "She seems so *real*."

"She *is*, Sam…a real *ghost*."

"A ghost?" She wiped rain from her forehead with the back of her hand. "A ghost," she repeated, as if saying the word aloud would help her come to terms with what her eyes beheld. To think she had talked to the dog, tried to initiate a game of catch, almost touched her—or maybe she had touched her. She couldn't be sure. Looking at her now, she seemed so lonely, so sad. "I can't *process* this," she whispered to Gwen.

"Come," Gwen said, taking hold of her hand. "We can process inside."

Another bolt of lightning seared the sky, and the dog, as if still subject to earthly sensations, cringed at the crack of thunder. Pinning her ears, tail tucked between her legs, she hung her head low and turned toward the water. Tears welled in Samantha's eyes.

At the pond's edge the shepherd stopped and looked back at them, squinting against the downpour, until another thunderous *boom* shook the ground and sent her slinking like a coyote into the water. No, not into the water. Across the water. Her paws broke the surface as she padded along, but it appeared she was wading through nothing more than a puddle.

Samantha's mouth hung open as she watched. "How deep is it out there?"

"Six, maybe eight feet in the middle."

"My God," Samantha said, wiping another spray of rain from her eyes, "she's walking on water."

Body paling against the stormy landscape, the dog began circling, scratching at the water with her paws, scratching the way a dog fluffs its blanket before bedding down. She curled herself into a ball then, wrapped her tail around her face. And as if she'd never been more than a watercolor painting, the rain washed her away, brown, black, and tan hues fading until nothing was left but the hazy outline of a white spirit.

Gwen started to speak, but her voice caught in her throat. She didn't ask Samantha to come inside again. Instead, she took her firmly by the hand and led her to the front door.

"Wait!" Samantha said, coming to her senses in a panic. "Where's Bertha? I've got to get her—"

"Everyone's inside, safe and sound. Now come," Gwen said, and led her through the house to the living room.

A fire was laid but not yet lit on the hearth. Bertha was standing on a beach towel that had been spread out for her, pecking at something that resembled a granola bar, and Blue was politely inspecting the crow, who stood almost as tall as the short-legged dog. The Aeolian harp was out of its box and resting on the coffee table. Gwen moved a few throw pillows out of the way and then gently pushed down on Samantha's shoulders until she sat, zombie-like. Beneath the green shades of brass lamps, lightbulbs flickered in rhythm with the storm.

"Don't be alarmed if we lose power for a few minutes. It happens here during storms," Gwen said. She stood over Samantha, her fingers combing Samantha's damp hair with tender concern. "How about a dry shirt and a hair dryer?"

"I'm fine, really. Just damp." Samantha patted her shirt. "I'm already air-drying."

"You don't look so good, Sam. You look like—"

"Like I just saw a ghost?" Samantha snorted.

Gwen's expression was apologetic. "I was about to say you look like you need a drink."

"I think I look like I need a drink, too." She gazed up into Gwen's beautiful blue eyes, close enough to wrap her arms around her waist, and she would have had they been on different terms.

Gwen shook her head at Samantha. "Name your poison."

"Bourbon, if you have it."

"Bourbon it is. Let me make us drinks, and then I'll light a fire and we can talk."

"Where's Loosey Goosey?" Samantha asked, looking around and noting the pit bull's absence.

"At a festival with Rosa. They left early this morning. Rosa's gentleman friend, Eugene, is in a *bateria*, a samba band. She went to hear him play. I imagine it's over and they're keeping dry under a tent, or maybe at Eugene's by now," Gwen said, a little too cheerfully, as though pretending they were enjoying a perfectly normal afternoon and she hadn't just dragged Samantha away from an apparition.

Samantha called Bertha to her, but the crow took off after Gwen, the curious Scottie following with her nose to the bird's butt. "Bertha? Come back here," she called.

"It's okay, Sam. Let her explore."

"I don't want her pooping all over your house."

"Relax…I'll take care of it," she said, and then Gwen, the crow, and the Scottie left the room in single file.

Samantha sat alone, listening to the thunder, the rain pelting the glass windows. It seemed she and her bird both were slowly losing their hearts to Gwen, and Samantha wondered if she might be losing her mind as well. She'd just seen a ghost, for God's sake…a real ghost like the ones she researched and wrote about in her paranormal mysteries. Granted, this wasn't her first supernatural encounter—hadn't most people had at least one?—but the other encounters were nothing compared with what she'd just witnessed.

Twice since her mother passed, she'd caught a whiff of the fleeting but distinct scent of her perfume, and once while sleeping at an old inn, she'd felt something tug the covers at the foot of her bed. And of course, over the years, she had participated in many spooky exchanges with friends over strange phenomena that defied explanation: the unexplained bang or creak, hearing one's name called when all alone, even the toppling over of a picture frame or other object connected to someone deceased, or the sensation of being touched. Samantha could recall a few times that she'd been somewhere—standing at the sink washing dishes, say—and felt something brush her leg, tap her shoulder. Yet all these subjective sensations and testimonies shared among friends were arguable, easily rationalized. But to actually *see* a spirit, to be an eyewitness to an apparition—what could be more conclusive? The fact that she had seen a ghost with her own eyes, interacted with something as visible as a living, breathing, flesh-and-blood dog was indisputable.

A crash of thunder shook the house as Gwen returned with drinks and tapas on a tray. Just as she set the tray on the coffee table, the electricity went out, and they looked at each other in the dim light of the stormy afternoon.

"There they go," Gwen said. She looked around to make sure Bertha wasn't underfoot and then removed the screen from the hearth and drew a long wooden match from a box on the mantel. "I think a fire will warm you up and give us more light."

Samantha picked up her rocks glass and downed half her drink in one gulp. "What is…what was your dog's name?" she asked, almost choking on the bourbon and wiping her mouth on her arm as she watched Gwen light the fire.

"Alley. I found her as a stray in the Bronx when she was very young and very pregnant, and had her fourteen years. She was the dog love of my life. You know how it is, Sam…we love all our animals, just as we love all the people in our lives, but there's always that special one, the one that steals your heart and takes a big piece of it when they go."

"Can I, uh…ask what happened to her?"

"She went through the ice," Gwen said, her voice constricting. "She was old…it took us too long to get to her."

"But she…she looked so young out there."

"Because what you see is spirit. And spirit, as you saw for yourself, remains forever young."

Samantha recalled a Bible scripture her mother used to quote. "Behold," she said in an absent whisper, "I make everything new again."

"Ah! The book of Revelations," Gwen said, her back to Samantha as the logs caught and the fire began to blaze. "Something of a theologian, are you?"

"No," Samantha said. "My mother taught Sunday school. Just before she passed she was embarrassed by how bad she looked…and she quoted that scripture, promising that the next time we saw her…in heaven…she would be young and beautiful again."

"Well, now you know it's true." She placed the screen back in front of the fire, then coaxed Bertha from the floor onto her arm and stood facing Samantha.

Flames danced like spirits on the hearth behind Gwen, turning her blond hair into a halo of light and silhouetting her face so that, all in all, she appeared ethereal. It suddenly occurred to Samantha that Gwen herself might be a ghost, as dead as her dog. The prospect made her almost woozy, but when Gwen brought Bertha to her face, making silly sounds and letting the bird nibble at her lips, she seemed reasonably carnal again.

"What an exquisite creature," Gwen said, guiding the crow over to Samantha's arm. Bertha cawed her contentment, pecked gently at Samantha's chin, and then flew back to the floor to stare at the crackling fire, first with one eye and then the other.

"She's not going to want to go home," Samantha said.

"I may not let either of you go home in this weather." Gwen took her drink in her hand and sat sideways on the sofa, facing Samantha, one leg tucked underneath her. "I would love to have spent more time with the crows I raised, one in particular, but the other unlocked and opened the aviary door and both escaped, although they continued to live on the property."

"How did a crow manage to open a door?"

Gwen raised a brow. "Why, with a *crowbar*, of course."

Samantha grinned in spite of herself. "Very funny."

Gwen stroked Samantha's cheek with the back of her fingers. "At least I can make you smile."

"At least…" Samantha said, her smile slowly evaporating as she sighed and shook her head. "Seeing her changes everything, Gwen. Seeing a ghost changes *everything.*"

"I know, Sam. I know it does. The implications are astonishing, life-affirming. Or I should say, *afterlife*-affirming."

"She's always there?"

"No. Once or twice a month I'll see her waiting out there for me, always confined to the pond area, at least when she's visible. But these past few days…I don't know why…she's been there constantly."

"Incredible." Samantha said more to herself than to Gwen. "It's a real case of obsession." A loud crack of thunder sent Bertha scurrying and flying up to the towel Gwen had draped across the arm of the sofa nearest Samantha.

Gwen's brow knitted. "Obsession?"

"Yes. It's said to happen when spiritual entities can't move away from people they were devoted to in life. They may not understand they're dead and remain stuck in the location where they died, sometimes for years, trying to communicate and influence their loved one at every turn. Sometimes to the benefit, sometimes to the detriment of the living." Samantha petted the smooth, glossy feathers of Bertha's back. "Maybe Alley can't move on, either because she's too attached to you…or because she doesn't know anyone on the other side that can distract her from you and help her transition."

Gwen listened intently, seeming to weigh every word of what Sam was saying. "That's been my guess," she said. "There's no one she would have known and loved during her life that has passed over, no familiar spirit to meet and guide her to the light." She stopped speaking for a moment. "Rosa believes this property is a portal…just like the one your fictional sleuth uses to travel between realms. And since my secret is out, Sam, I will confess that I've seen others down by the pond."

"Animals or people?"

"Both. Many years ago, I saw a young and very stately looking woman who literally vanished in the blink of an eye. Months after that, I saw an older man on a horse as clear as day. I was standing on the porch, and he and the horse were facing the water. I was barefoot, and when he didn't respond to my voice, I ran into the house to get my shoes. When I came back out he was gone. It had been raining for days and the land around the water was soggy. I went down to investigate, expected to see prints, but found none, no sign that a horse or anyone had been on that path.

"A few weeks later I spoke with the owners of the property behind us. They did and still do have horses, but my description didn't fit anyone they knew. So as most people would do, I convinced myself that the horse had trotted off into the woods instead of taking the path, even though I knew a horse would have difficulty getting through those dense woods. It just didn't make any sense."

Gwen sipped her martini and stared into her glass before meeting Samantha's eyes again. "Rosa sees spirits all the time, harmless comings and goings of cloudy, transparent figures, but that was it for me...until Alley appeared. Of course, the experience of seeing her was much different for me than it was for you today. She was my dog, Sam. I loved her dearly and had to bear the heartbreak of her tragic death. I couldn't explain away seeing her, couldn't convince myself that she was a neighbor's dog, because I recognized her and knew she was dead. But beyond the grief of losing her and the initial shock of seeing her ghost, her presence served as a comforting confirmation of immortality. It's one of the reasons I stopped teaching."

"You stopped teaching because of seeing her ghost?"

"Well, the *implications* of seeing her ghost. As you say, Sam...it changes everything."

Gwen put a spoonful of olive tapenade on a cracker and held it to Samantha's mouth. "Open up," she said, and Samantha took the cracker in her mouth. "Actually, I still give lectures at various universities, but after seeing her I felt as though the question motivating my academic pursuits had been answered, and I decided to take a break and devote more time to the family business."

They were sitting side by side, curled up like lovers in front of the fire, close enough to kiss, and Samantha might have made an advance had she not felt emotionally disabled at the moment, still struggling to fathom what she'd just experienced.

Gwen sipped her cocktail. "The other day," she said, "I told you that you reminded me of someone I once knew. She wasn't my lover...I was only a teenager with a hopeless crush at the time. And even though that adolescent love was never consummated, Margot was a significant part of my life. She triggered a pubescent explosion of sexual awareness that made me realize why I'd never had any interest in boys."

The rain and thunder grew louder, the downpour of rain overtaking the tinkling of chimes so that only the resonating gongs of the buoy bell were audible. Gwen rested a hand on Samantha's knee as she spoke. "Her sudden and untimely death was significant for me as well, because I'd never lost anyone I cared about, not even the family dog or cat up until that point, and I just couldn't wrap my head around the mystery of mortality...couldn't grasp the concept of how someone so alive could stop being alive. I mean, is there any greater horror for the sentient than the prospect of insentience? Sitting here as we are, Sam, living, breathing sentient beings…can you imagine the day when you will no longer have a conscious thought, an opinion, a feeling, because you will no longer *be*?"

Samantha tried to force a laugh. "I try not to give it much thought."

"Well, I gave it too much thought, perhaps. It became my personal grail quest and turned into a career for me," she said. "During my first year in college I took courses in metaphysics and theology, and that same year my paternal grandfather died. He was a larger-than-life man—generous, intelligent, opinionated, very humorous—an energetic entrepreneur who, along with his own father, started the family business. And when I saw him at the wake, all I could think was… where is he? Where is everything that made him who he was? Where is the passion, the lifetime of accumulated experience and knowledge… the jokes he loved to tell? Where has it all gone? It seemed everything had evaporated, just like that. His body was there, but he wasn't." Gwen gave a faint smile and shook her head. "And I wondered then, as we all do, if personality is purely an organic illusion—an electrochemical magic show like scientists would have us believe—or if personality is spirit, and that his spirit had simply stepped out of its body the way a hermit crab discards its shell to find a more suitable home."

Gwen smiled, patted Samantha's thigh, then put her glass down and got up to add another log to the fire. Bertha was perched on a towel draped over the arm of the sofa now, falling asleep, and Samantha kept a light hand on her back to keep her from hopping down.

Lightning struck again, a flash of bright white flooding the house, then returning the room to the cozy yellow glow of the fire. "I don't know about you, Sam," Gwen said as she stoked the fire, "but I was raised a Christian in the Protestant church and naturally taught to believe in heaven and hell and the eternal life of the soul—*human* soul—but these things we accept through faith and without any proof. I guess it was my search for proof that led me toward theology and metaphysics, all for the purpose of trying to answer the one question we all ask."

"Is there life after death?"

"Exactly," Gwen said, "that eternal quest for spiritual confirmation. During that time I entered a very existential period of my life. My personal journey led me away from the family business and toward academia. And then we had more deaths in the family. We lost our dogs and cat, more grandparents, and several years later, we lost Maria, my brother's wife…Isabel's mother. I was thirty-six, an assistant professor on a tenure track by then. Isabel was just four years old."

"What happened to her?" Samantha asked.

"A private plane crash over the Atlantic, a few miles off Martha's Vineyard. It started out as a romantic getaway. She had left Isabel with me for the weekend to meet my brother, William, who was flying in from Boston." Gwen put the poker down and walked back to Samantha. "People think money is everything, and it does buy many comforts, but it can't buy love, and it can't bring back the dead." Gwen shrugged. "Anyway, Maria's untimely death only deepened my metaphysical quest, and I immersed myself in academia. It's hard to explain all that I felt."

The rain seemed to be slowing, but the wind was wild, racing along the porch, rattling the rafters. Samantha could hear its fury shuffling the wicker furniture on the porch.

"You don't have to explain," Samantha said. "I understand completely. I went through a similar struggle when my mother died, except *my* sense of existentialism probably borders more on the macabre than yours."

Gwen sat down again, drawing both legs under herself and leaning close to Samantha on a pillow. "Tell me," she said, giving her full attention. The logs crackled, flames falling and rising in rhythm with the moans of the wind. The lights flickered and came back on, the glow from the green lampshades softly highlighting Gwen's beautiful features.

"Well, my mother wanted to have her ashes scattered in her gardens. It was a late September day...and as I watched the breeze carry her through the autumn blooms she loved so much, I wondered the same things you did. My mother was an encyclopedia of flora—if it grew on God's green earth, she could name it. Like you, I wondered where all of it had gone—her knowledge, her interests, her love of nature's beauty. I remember wondering that day if the brain is perhaps comparable to a computer's hard drive, crashing at the time of death... and hoping that whoever created her had bothered to back up her files on some celestial flash drive so that her mind could transfer over and continue in a parallel universe."

"You needn't wonder anymore. Alley is obviously on that flash drive. Of course, the consequences of being a person versus a dog may alter the state or quality of that afterlife...but as you have seen for yourself, death has not obliterated her. She *is* existing in the afterlife."

"And if one soul survives death, we all do."

"We must," Gwen said.

Samantha nodded thoughtfully. "I have to say that, in as much as your metaphysical quest led to the study of philosophy, I think mine unconsciously led to writing paranormal mysteries."

"And let me say that Detective Crowley is not only an outstanding investigator but a brilliant and engaging philosopher."

Samantha laughed. "You think so?"

"Physically compelling, too," she said with a knowing wink. "She reminds me of you."

As Gwen's eyes played upon her face, Samantha felt a magnetism she'd never experienced before, the force of its pull far too strong to be one-sided. She didn't feel as emotionally numb as she had a half hour ago. Her head was clearing, and she was once again aware of this sexual attraction. "Speaking of psychic investigators," she said, keeping herself in check, "did you ever consult one about Alley's appearance?"

"Heavens, no! For what purpose? So my colleagues could hear about the eccentric Professor Laraway who, half out of her mind, can be seen walking her pet ghost at night, a dogless leash in one hand, a pooper-scooper in the other?" She waved a hand in the air.

Samantha laughed. "I suppose you're right."

"You know, Sam, as we age and face the losses that time and experience bring—death of loved ones, broken dreams, unrequited love, to name a few—we come to learn that grief is a very private affair. We may attempt to express it to others, and others will attempt to understand and offer comfort…but in the end we're left alone with our grief…left alone to find resolution." She stopped and stared at her. "Seeing ghosts falls into that category of private affairs, wouldn't you agree?"

"I do," Samantha conceded.

"For years I wanted to believe in an afterlife," Gwen explained. "Under the guise of a scholar I solicited accounts of ghostly sightings, near-death experiences…all from fairly credible sources. And while I wanted to believe and even thought I *did* believe, I always had doubt. You know the old adage, *to see is to believe*." She paused. "You yourself write about ghosts, Sam, about life after death, but before today…did you truly believe in ghosts?"

"If you had asked me yesterday, I would have said yes. I mean, I don't think I could write believable paranormal mysteries if I didn't believe in a spiritual realm. But now, having seen a ghost with my own eyes, I realize that before today I *wanted* to believe more than I *did* believe." She swallowed from her glass and stared at Gwen, the corners of her mouth creasing in a self-deprecating smile. "Do most people who see her remain as calm as I did?"

Gwen rolled her eyes and shook her head. "Most people don't see much of anything. And I must say you made Rosa very nervous when you spotted Alley from the kitchen window. I myself didn't sleep that night. I thought about you, wondering what enabled you to see her. And then today, when I saw her out there interacting with you, responding to you...my God...I panicked. I'm so sorry."

"I'm sorry, too. I wanted to be at my best today," she confessed. "But instead, you saw me fall on my ass and then nearly faint at the sight of a ghost—you know, a ghost just like the ones I write about with such authority," she said, mocking herself.

Thunder shook the house again, and while the rain seemed to be slowing, the wind was worsening. In one more swallow she finished her drink and held her glass up as if in a toast. "Here's to making better impressions."

Gwen bit her bottom lip, clearly holding back a smile as she stretched her arm along the back of the sofa. "You made your impression several days ago...over the phone and again in person. You couldn't make a bad impression if you tried." Softly, she cupped Samantha's face with her hand. "You are an exceptional woman, and the fact that you saw her ghost—that you were *able* to see her—only endears you to me more." She let her hand slide from Samantha's cheek, softly pinched her chin. "Your color is coming back."

"Only because you're making me blush."

Gwen smiled, a rush of admiration in her eyes. Or was it desire? Samantha couldn't be sure. She wanted to close the distance between them, wanted to kiss her, but she didn't dare. Gwen wasn't seducing her. She knew that. Gwen's gesture was one of tenderness, affection. She was caring for Samantha right now, helping her through a bout of *post-ghost trauma*. If Samantha kissed her, if she crossed that line tonight, she feared it would all be over. She regarded Gwen for a moment and then asked, "Why me? What allows one person and not another to see a ghost?"

Gwen shrugged. "A combination of factors, I would think—emotional availability, perceptual style, sensory integration, extrasensory perception, and so forth. I can count the people who have seen her ghost, although I shouldn't say people, because Blue sits and watches her for hours at a time. Goose, on the other hand, doesn't seem to notice her at all. She also appears differently to people. I see her as you do, in color…Rosa sees her as a white spirit…and then there's Isabel, who wouldn't recognize a ghost if she bumped into it."

Samantha laughed. "I hope she made it to the city okay in this weather."

"Believe me, nothing could have stopped Isabel. For all the worrying she does about others, she's a bit of a daredevil, a very physical and confident young woman. She'd ride a horse through a hurricane if she wanted something on the other side of the storm. And by horse, I mean that ridiculous Mustang she drives! Tonight it was Liz on the other side of that storm. I don't think I've ever seen her so excited over a friendship."

"Liz really enjoyed her company. But she was concerned that her being gay might have put Isabel off."

Gwen looked shocked. "Liz is gay?"

"I thought you knew."

"How would I know? Liz doesn't look gay."

"Neither do you. And what about me?" Samantha smiled. "Am I that obvious?"

"That's hard to say. You're more androgynous, but you told me you were gay before I met you. I don't think someone straight would necessarily think you are, but—" She threw her hands up in the air. "Oh, hell, Sam, I don't know what we're supposed to look like anymore."

"Well, Liz is very open about her sexuality. She was concerned, though, because when she told her, Isabel quickly changed the subject."

"And still Isabel met her for dinner? Hmm…this is getting *very* interesting."

"If you're worried about Liz stepping out of line, don't be. I'm sure Liz would never—"

She laughed. "Are you kidding? I'd pay Liz to step out of line with my niece. I like Liz a lot. I liked her the moment I met her. It's Isabel, not Liz, I'm worried about. My niece has never shown a romantic interest in anyone. I don't mean to speak against her. God knows any man or woman would be lucky to have her. But for some reason she's sexually…*clueless*, for lack of a better word. I don't think it's at all healthy for a twenty-eight-year-old to be so repressed."

As far as Samantha was concerned it wasn't good for anyone, and she only hoped she wouldn't have to repress her own feelings for Gwen indefinitely.

Seeming distracted, lost in thought now, Gwen got up and began to pace, one arm tucked under the other, a thumbnail working itself between her teeth. "So, Isabel is aware that Liz is gay…and she drove down to the city to meet her for dinner. Hmm…this is good news, Sam. It means Isabel has a crush. You know, the going joke between her father and me has always been that Isabel hit puberty, but puberty never hit Isabel." She looked at Samantha and nodded her satisfaction, a twinkle in her eyes.

"I'm just glad you're okay with Liz being with her."

"Okay? I'm ecstatic! I've always had suspicions about Isabel, but I figured she needed to work herself out." She stopped moving and looked at Samantha. "How are you feeling? I know the day's events are a lot to digest," she said, her face softening. "Are you up for dinner yet?"

"I think so."

"Good, because Rosa prepared paella for us."

"I love paella. But I have to warn you, so does Bertha."

"Well then, it's paella for three. Blue already ate the plate of chicken and rice Rosa left for her. I just have to warm dinner and set the table."

"I'll set it," Samantha offered.

"Why don't I do it while you set up my new harp and convince the wind to play for us?"

As soon as Gwen disappeared, the room seemed suddenly large and spooky. Bertha, who had been fast asleep, opened one eye at the sound of a sputtering log toppling over in the fireplace. Embers popped and crackled, and an eerie feeling filled Samantha. She turned to look at the row of windows behind her, half expecting to see the face of the ghost-dog staring in through the sheer white curtains. There was nothing but the darkness and the pounding wind. It battered the chimes, banged on the windows, shook the doors, as though searching for a way in.

Samantha inspected the harp, then walked around the sofa and opened the middle window several inches. As soon as she did, the hungry wind grabbed the curtains, and when she set the harp on the sill, it wasted no time making music. Like some invisible composer, it claimed its instrument and strummed the strings.

"Oh, Sam," Gwen whispered as she tiptoed back into the living room. "Is that it?"

"Yes." Samantha untangled herself from the curtains that blew up around her and smiled.

Softly, quietly, Gwen came up from behind and put a hand around her waist. “The sound…it’s ethereal. And with the chimes and bell it all sounds like an opera.”

Samantha gave her a sidelong glance and nodded, pleased with Gwen’s reaction. “Sort of Wagnerian, like the *Ring*, isn’t it?”

“Yes…almost primordial.”

Ghostly fingers played at the harp strings. And the more the wind gusted, the louder its haunting music grew. But then, beyond the rustling of trees, came another low and melodious voice. Samantha turned her ear to catch it. “Listen,” she said, struggling to separate it from the other sounds. “Do you hear that?”

“I do…” Gwen whispered. “It’s the wind howling.”

“It’s not the wind. Listen.” Samantha swallowed. “It’s her, isn’t it?”

“How could it be? She never makes a sound.” Gwen let go of her waist, reached for her hand, and slipped her fingers in between Samantha’s. “She hasn’t had a voice since she died.”

Samantha squeezed her hand tight. And there it came again, distinct this time, the mournful and summoning howl of a lone canine. The curtains blew wildly, billowing up again and enveloping Gwen and Samantha as they settled. Speechless, motionless, they stood hand in hand like two sheet-ghosts.

And the wind played on, as though remembering, reciting the sound of the first wind that ever blew.

Chapter Fourteen

In a cozy back corner of a Moroccan restaurant, Isabel waited at a table for two. With heavy rain in the forecast, Liz had suggested they meet here. It was just around the corner from Sotheby's, which meant making it to the auction without getting soaked. Her phone beeped, and she reached in her bag to read a text from Liz: *stuck in traffic, see you in five minutes.*

Isabel touched the yellow rose in the table vase, gently rubbing a soft petal between her fingers, then smoothed her hand over the tablecloth, checked her watch, and sipped the basil-jalapeño martini she'd ordered. She had performed this ritual three times in ten minutes—smoothing, checking, sipping—until finally she opened her auction catalog and tried to concentrate. But she just couldn't. She was too restless. No, restless wasn't the word. She was a wreck. And when she looked past the raindrops on the glass windows and saw Liz standing on the sidewalk, closing and shaking an umbrella, she felt almost sick to her stomach.

Isabel didn't know how to act, how to *be*. Sure, she'd invited Liz to the auction, but then Liz had asked her to dinner. Had she accepted an actual date without knowing it? It wasn't like her to say yes on impulse, but something about Liz had made her do just that, and now the knot in her stomach had her thinking she'd made a mistake, gotten herself in too deep.

The last and only person she'd been physical with was Wayne Howard on the night of her high school prom. She'd known him half her life, and he'd been obsessed with her about that long. He was athletic, handsome, and well-groomed, and any girl in school would have traded places with her in a heartbeat. She wanted to want him, wished she could be attracted, but nothing beyond his friendship had ever appealed to her. Even with clothes on she didn't like the feel of his body against hers, didn't care for the smell of his skin, and only tolerated kissing him. In fact, she never did understand why he had a reputation for being a great kisser because, after high school, Isabel decided she'd be happy if she never kissed anyone ever again. But these couple of days, sitting in corporate board meetings, Isabel had daydreamed about Liz, wondered what it would be like to kiss her. At times she became so lost in thought her secretary had expressed concern and asked if she was feeling all right.

Like her aunt Gwen, Liz seemed so comfortable with herself, with her sexuality. She probably had many girlfriends, kissed tons of women. In her daydreams Isabel was one of those women. But tonight was real life, and her own inexperience embarrassed her. She prayed Liz wouldn't try to kiss her because she wouldn't know how to properly kiss her back. The thought that it might even happen sent a wave of panic rolling through her. She had no business having come tonight. But short of escaping through the restaurant's bathroom window and running to the parking garage, it was too late to cancel. She took a swallow of her drink, straightened her black suit jacket, and smoothed the front of her white silk blouse.

The maître d' must have known Liz, because as soon as she walked in, he kissed her on both cheeks, took her umbrella, and helped her slip out of a black trench coat. Isabel watched the two chatting, exchanging words in hushed whispers until they laughed aloud. Liz's laughter was infectious. Her energy, her radiance, seemed to fill the room.

Heart pounding, Isabel drew in a deep breath and waited. A moment later the maître d' pointed, directing Liz's roving eyes to her. Smiling in recognition, Liz raised her hand and wiggled her fingers in greeting. Awkwardly, aware of her hands trembling, Isabel wiggled her fingers back.

Liz looked as wonderful as she had the other day, but tonight her short auburn hair seemed darker, thicker, wavier, and she exuded a presence that turned heads and stirred in Isabel an unfamiliar and overwhelming excitement that rapidly extinguished what little appetite she had left.

In a black sleeveless dress and flashing an ear-to-ear smile, Liz approached the table holding a purse and a small shopping bag. "Hi, you," she said in a low voice when she reached the table. She paused, her sparkling green eyes taking in Isabel's whole face, as though Isabel were a tall glass of water and Liz couldn't stop drinking until she'd swallowed every drop.

Isabel shyly greeted her. "Hi..."

"Sorry I'm late. Marco said you already had a drink, so I ordered myself a martini." Squeezing around to Isabel's side of the table, Liz set the gift bag in front of her, then leaned down and kissed her cheek. "It's nice to see you again," she softly whispered in her ear.

Isabel inhaled Liz's heady fragrance, felt Liz's damp hair brush her face. "Me, too. I mean...it's good to see *you*." She kept her hands in her lap so Liz wouldn't see them shaking.

Liz smiled down at her and then moved to the other side of the table. "I don't know what's going on out there tonight, but the traffic is awful. I finally had to get out and walk the last block."

"What are you wearing?" Isabel asked, and when Liz looked down at her dress Isabel corrected herself. "I meant your perfume... you smell good."

"Oh. Thanks. It's Burberry London."

"A perfect choice for this London weather we're having," Isabel said.

Liz laughed as she settled into her chair. "Yeah, I guess it *is* apropos of this rain—what a night, huh?" She paused as the waitress placed a martini in front her and handed them menus. "At least you got here before the rain. Did you take the train?"

"I drove. I'm parked in a garage around the corner."

"I thought of calling back after we spoke to tell you to bring a change of clothes in case the storm didn't let up. Except by the time I heard a weather update, I figured you were halfway here."

Isabel peeked at Liz's long, slender hands and polished nails. She could still feel the sensation of Liz's kiss on her face and absently raised her fingers to the spot where those lips had touched her cheek. And then she put her hands on the shopping bag. "Is this for me?"

"Uh-huh. Something I saw in a window yesterday and couldn't resist." Liz gestured to the bag. "Open it."

Isabel reached in, digging through the colorful tissue paper, and pulled out a hard, dog-shaped object with a velvety coating. "A Scottie *nodder*?"

"Yep. It looks new, but it's a vintage piece from Germany, molded from papier-mâché and flocked like the original nodders—not like those heavy resin ones they make nowadays."

Isabel sat it on the table, tapping the Scottie's nose so that the head bobbed, first from side to side, and then up and down. She loved it instantly. And she appreciated Liz's unexpected thoughtfulness. "I have a Scottie collection, but this might end up being my very favorite. It's so…"

"*Kitschy*, don't you think?"

Isabel smiled. "It is. It's wonderful."

"So now when you're in the car, stuck in traffic or hitting potholes and bouncing over speed bumps, you can amuse yourself by asking it yes or no questions."

Isabel laughed, her awkwardness slowly dissipating. "It will ride home on my dashboard tonight. Thank you…thank you for thinking of me," she said, and carefully stuffed the nodder back into the bag.

Liz watched her. "It would be hard not to think of you. I had such a wonderful time the other day."

"So did I." Isabel tucked her hair behind her ear, then lowered her head. "You look very pretty tonight."

"Who, me?" Liz grabbed her damp hair. "God, I'm a mess! My hair and the rain do *not* get along. And then my hair and all the rest of me got blown around in that wind when I ran the last block."

"Then the wind and rain serve you well." Isabel tried to smile, but her lips were so tight the corners of her mouth trembled.

"Well, thank you." Liz's smile came easy. "And might I say that you, too, look very pretty." She lifted her martini glass and waited for Isabel to do the same. "So, here's to the mutual admiration of two new and pretty friends."

The word *friends* made Isabel feel more at ease, took the pressure off, and she was able to toast without shaking and spilling her drink. Fortunately, she'd already finished half of it. "*Salud*," she said.

"*Salud*." Liz drank but then furrowed her brow. "What's that you're drinking?"

"A basil-jalapeño martini."

"Gin? Vodka?"

"Jalapeño-infused tequila."

"Wow. Is it hot?"

Isabel shrugged. "Not much heat, no. Taste it if you like." She pushed the stem of the glass toward Liz.

Liz drank and waited a moment. "Mmm…savory. I taste the fresh basil," she started to say, but then her eyes bulged and she began to fan her mouth with her hand. "Isabel! Are you kidding? Not much heat?" She reached for her water goblet. "I'm on fire."

"Here. Eat some bread." Isabel handed her the basket that the server had just set on the table. "Bread works better than water." She folded one arm and brought the other hand to her mouth, pinching her lips between her fingers to keep from laughing as she watched Liz frantically tear off a piece of bread and chew.

"Go ahead and laugh," Liz said after she swallowed, chasing the bread with more water. "But just you wait until I discover *your* weakness."

Isabel let go and giggled. "I'm sorry. I didn't mean for that to happen. It just doesn't taste that hot to me."

Liz shook open her cloth napkin and patted her lips before laying it across her lap. "You like a little fire, huh? I feel like I'm sitting here having dinner with Frida Kahlo."

Isabel looked at her quizzically. "The artist? Why do you say that?"

"Because she was known to enjoy large quantities of tequila and jalapeño peppers."

"Really? I know she had a reputation for drinking tequila, but I didn't know about the jalapeños."

Liz frowned. "All right. I made up the part about the jalapeño peppers. But being half Mexican and living in Mexico, I'm sure she ate a lot of them."

This remark made Isabel giggle again, and Liz grinned. "You've seen the movie *Frida* with Salma Hayek and Ashley Judd, haven't you?"

Isabel shook her head. "I don't think so."

"Well, you may not know, but Frida was bisexual, and there's a scene in the movie where the men are at a club having a tequila-drinking contest. They bet that whoever can hold the most tequila gets to tango with a beautiful young lady who's there. So in walks Frida to join the challenge, outdrinks all the men, and not only gets to tango with the young woman, but passionately kisses her on the dance floor. It's a great scene if you ever get to watch the movie."

Isabel didn't know how to respond, so she just nodded and opened her menu, making a mental note to put the movie in her Netflix queue as soon as she got home. Isabel loved to dance and secretly felt curious about watching two women tango.

After they ordered, Liz pulled an olive off a toothpick with her teeth and stared at Isabel as she slowly chewed. "Speaking of Latina women," she said, her eyes playing on Isabel's face, "where did you get that gorgeous bronze skin…and those golden eyes? You look nothing like Gwen."

Isabel shrugged. "My mother was Brazilian."

"Ah, that explains a lot. Have you ever been there?"

"Brazil? Several times. Mostly with my father."

"Hmm…so you speak Portuguese?"

"I'm more fluent in Spanish, but yes, I can manage Portuguese. And what about you? How did you end up with red hair and not a single freckle?" She looked at Liz's porcelain skin and those large green eyes that seemed to shine their light into Isabel's soul and touch something no one had ever reached before.

"My father's Irish, my mother's Italian."

Isabel pushed her hair back from her face "And where did you learn Spanish?"

Liz laughed. "Who told you I speak Spanish?"

"Rosa. She was impressed. She really likes you."

"I like her, too." Liz sipped from her glass and shrugged. "Well, let's see…I took Spanish in high school and enjoyed it. And then in college I became interested in Spanish Revival interior design and got to spend a semester in Spain. After that I dated a few Latina women here and there and…I don't know, I just picked it up little by little. Not that I speak much—just enough to identify furniture, order food, and ask directions." She looked at Isabel sideways and twisted her lips. "So you're half Brazilian, huh? Does that mean you can dance the samba?"

"I love samba dancing. There are many different samba styles, though." She paused and smiled, feeling shy. "*Sabes cómo samba?*"

"Ha! Yeah. I can samba—*gringo* style," Liz said with self-deprecating wit. "Maybe one day you'll teach me how to dance a real samba."

For a moment Isabel felt like the more experienced one, which boosted her confidence. It was strange how being in Liz's company was both unnerving and comforting. She hesitated and then said, "If you don't have plans two weeks from today, I'd like to invite you and Sam to my aunt's surprise sixtieth birthday party. We'll have a DJ, but Rosa's boyfriend's samba band will be playing as well."

Liz's face lit up. "A surprise party? Where?"

Isabel's stomach was empty, and her drink was going right to her head. "On the property," she said, and reached to butter a piece of bread. "I know we all just met…but my aunt is very fond of you and Sam. I'm sure she'd love to see you both there."

"Then I'm going to say yes right now for both of us. I'm sure Sam wouldn't want to miss it. How do you plan to pull off a surprise?"

"We've asked her best friend and colleague at the university to invite her down for a guest lecture that Friday. Knowing my aunt, she'll want to see some exhibit at some museum. Carol will have her spend the night and keep her in the city until at least two on Saturday. We're asking guests to arrive by three."

"We'll be there."

They stopped talking long enough to look at menus, and after they'd ordered, Liz gestured at the auction catalog by Isabel's side. "So tell me what you have your sights set on tonight."

"I'd really like two things. One is a rare first edition of *Huckleberry Finn*, printed with a wrong date of 1894. When it came off the press and the error was realized, the publisher had the title page cut out and another glued in its place to reflect the correct publication date of 1885."

"And what might that mistake be worth today?"

"It depends on trending prices, but I'm hoping it'll stay under two thousand. Also, there's an 1897 first edition of *Mother Goose in Prose*, illustrated by Maxfield Parrish."

Liz's face lit up. "I saw that listed when I looked online. I can't say I'm familiar with Parrish's children's books. I didn't even know he illustrated them. But I *adore* his sensuous women, especially the androgynous nudes. I have two hanging in my bedroom. I love those saturated colors and that idealized neoclassic style…and I'm really excited about seeing the illustrations in the book you're after." Liz tapped the auction catalog. "And did you see the Icart print? I see they're offering an original signed print of *Martini*."

"I know it well," Isabel said. "It's the one of the woman on a barstool with her dogs."

"Yep. A Scottie's on the floor, and sitting on the barstool next to her are two terriers. Jack Russells, maybe. I have a small print of it hanging in my kitchen."

"Are you bidding?" Isabel asked.

"On that original? No. I don't think I can afford to. I'm just happy for the opportunity to see it up close."

"I like Icart, too. I have an original print of his *Illusion*."

"Uh-huh. That's the one with cigarette smoke rising up and turning into a nude woman," Liz said excitedly. "Why didn't I notice it the other day? That's not like me. Where was it hanging?"

"On the wall behind the bar."

"I didn't see a bar."

"The bar's in the ballroom."

Liz's brow shot up. "You have a *ballroom*?"

"Well, sort of. It's an empty room we keep for dancing. There's nothing in it but the bar and sound equipment. I guess I skipped it on your tour because you were interested in seeing furniture, and we have none in there."

"Well, you'll have to show me at the party." Liz thought for a moment, then reached for the catalog and opened to the listings. "You know what else I can't wait to see? These two sketchings by Romaine Brooks." She tapped the page. "Do you know anything about her?"

"Only that she specialized in portraiture—very dark portraiture."

"Yes. She was known for her subdued palette of grays. And when she wasn't painting commissioned portraits, she painted portraits of androgynous, cross-dressing women—sometimes *extremely* masculine women—including her own famous self-portrait, and her even more famous portrait of Una Troubridge, the English aristocrat."

"Una Troubridge I'm more familiar with," Isabel said. "She was the renowned literary translator who introduced the French writer Colette to English readers."

"That's right." Liz nodded. "Una Troubridge was also the long-time lover of Radclyffe Hall, the author of *The Well of Loneliness*."

Liz paused, as if waiting for her reaction, but Isabel maintained a poker face. Isabel knew the book; her aunt had a collector's copy in the family's library. Banned for obscenity when first published in 1928, it became an international best seller, the single most ground-breaking novel ever written about women loving women. Isabel had eyed it many times but couldn't say why she'd never read it.

"Una was married to a man when she met Radclyffe Hall at a party in Paris in 1915," Liz said. "She fell in love and left her husband that same year. In fact, it's suspected that Una inspired one of the characters in Hall's book. They became inseparable, adopted very masculine styles of dressing, and made no secret of their sexual relationship. Eventually they bought a home together in London. They even raised champion dachshunds and griffons."

"Dogs?" Isabel asked.

Liz laughed and nodded. "Yeah, hot dogs and those little monkey-faced ones. They had French bulldogs, too. I suspect the dogs kept Una company while Radclyffe was out having affairs with other women." Isabel finished her drink and gestured to the server for another round. "But getting back to Romaine Brooks, she was another one who never pretended to disguise her sexuality. At one point Brooks married a gay man, a close friend. He needed her as a 'skirt' to cover up his homosexuality. But Romaine wasn't into skirts. She preferred suits. After they were married he decided she looked too much like a dyke and demanded that she wear dresses and behave in a more feminine manner when out together in public."

Isabel listened with the enthusiasm of a child being told a tale. "What did Brooks do?"

"She divorced his ass!"

Isabel laughed out loud.

"And that was that!" Liz laughed with her. "Anyway, Romaine Brooks became good friends with Radclyffe Hall. During the nineteen twenties Hall introduced Brooks to her lover, Una, and Brooks painted Una's now-famous portrait. It's the one of her wearing a tailored suit and monocle and posing with her two prized dachshunds—gifts from Radclyffe Hall."

Isabel listened, quietly captivated by Liz's ability to impart history with such soap-opera flare. Yet her mind wandered. She knew next to nothing about the personal histories and social lives of the authors and artists whose work she was so well acquainted with. Probably because she was emotionally inept. That's what was wrong with her. How could she love books and art, yet pay such little attention to the real-life dramas, the intimate relationships and love lives that inspired those works? Why did she pay so little attention to her own desire for intimacy? *Because I'm socially stunted and emotionally challenged,* she thought. *That's why.*

"Isabel?" Liz looked at her sideways. "Hey…did I lose you?"

Isabel snapped to attention. "No. No, not at all."

"I'm sorry. I'm talking too much, aren't I? Sometimes, when I'm really enthused, my brain derails and goes off in different directions."

"No, really, I…I find everything you talk about interesting."

"Well, all I really started out to say about Romaine Brooks is that she moved to New York City in the nineteen thirties, and people assumed she had stopped painting. But she lived another forty years. After her death, photographs of numerous oil and charcoal sketches were discovered, but the original artwork remains largely unaccounted for. Now, little by little, those sketches are popping up here and there. Like these two." Liz pointed to a page in the auction catalog and handed it back to Isabel.

Talking about books and artwork put Isabel on familiar ground, and, as always, discussing subjects and people other than herself made her feel less self-conscious, less put on the spot. As she lost herself in conversation her appetite returned, and she realized she was hungrier than she thought she had been.

Isabel was quiet for a moment and then said, "I'm sorry to use my phone at a dinner table, but…would you mind if I did for just a minute? It's important business."

"Of course. Go right ahead."

Isabel kept her phone in her lap as she busily typed away, and a minute later she smiled and put her phone down. "Thanks."

They talked nonstop over dinner, and by the time either of them thought to glance at a watch, they had little more than an hour to preview items up for bid. Isabel motioned for the check, but Liz had apparently arranged to pay the bill when she first arrived.

"Liz," Isabel said, disappointed, "I wanted to take *you* to dinner."

"Are you crazy? It's the least I could do after your hospitality the other day. Come on. Let's go. You can take me out for coffee later."

With no time to spare, they left the restaurant and made a dash for Sotheby's. Arm in arm, they shared Liz's umbrella, laughing and splashing their way through the pouring rain in nearly identical trench coats.

Chapter Fifteen

The rain had slowed to a drizzle by the time the auction ended. Isabel was high bidder on the items she set out to acquire, and Liz couldn't help but marvel over her. In the restaurant, Isabel had been adorably self-conscious, as endearingly awkward as a teenager, but at the auction Liz had seen a different side: a confident and calculating businesswoman one wouldn't want to cross in a business deal. Watching her in action was enlightening, and being at an auction house such as Sotheby's was, as always, like being in a museum as they perused items up for bid. Especially Icart's *Martini.* It was wonderful to see it in person. There were several floor bidders, and Liz participated in early bidding, but at fifteen hundred dollars she had to resist the impulse to continue. In the end, she watched the other bidders lose as well when the print sold to an absentee high bidder for twenty-eight hundred dollars.

Seemingly satisfied with herself, Isabel held Liz's gift bag in one hand and dug the other deep into the pocket of her London Fog as they waited in the parking garage for an attendant to bring the car. When it finally came down the ramp, Liz looked in wide-eyed shock at the silver horse on the grill of a shiny black convertible.

"Isabel! You drive a *Mustang*?"

"Mm-hm. A sixth generation."

"Wow. My dad has two vintage Mustangs."

"Really?" Isabel's eyes grew as wide around as Liz's. "He collects cars?"

"We're all collectors. It runs in the family—except for my sister, who only collects designer clothes," she said, too fixated on the approaching Mustang to elaborate.

If sex appeal and sensuality could be attributed to cars, this one dripped it. It was the sort of sports car Liz imagined herself driving, but her van proved more practical these days for transporting antiques. It was the only practical thing in her life.

"You are full of surprises, Isabel," she said as the attendant pulled up and got out. Isabel handed him a tip and stood by the open driver's side door as Liz moved slowly around the car. She trailed her fingers over the sleek exterior as she circled and began singing the song "Hey Pretty," by Poe.

The attendant smiled at Liz and winked at Isabel as he walked away.

"I know that song," Isabel said to her.

"It should be your theme song while driving this car." Liz ran her hand over the hood and came full circle, until only the open car door separated the two of them.

"If you can sing and drive at the same time, you're welcome to drive it to wherever we're having coffee. And then I'll take you home."

Liz looked at her, excited. "Seriously? You'd let me drive your Mustang?"

"Sure." Isabel backed away from the door and gestured for Liz to get in.

"I haven't driven a stick shift in years."

"It's an automatic with paddle shifters."

"Fancy. And in that case I will not refuse, but…hey, pretty," she said, looking playfully into Isabel's eyes, "if you're going to take me home, why don't I just drive us there now, and we'll have coffee at my place."

Suddenly Isabel quickly averted her eyes and stared down at her shoes, and Liz sensed her quiet panic. "Isabel, I don't bite. And I'm only a few blocks from here. One hour and I'll send you on your way…although I'd still rather you stay and not have to travel home." She smiled tenderly at her nervous companion. "I make really good cappuccino…and I baked some brownies to die for this morning."

Isabel seemed to consider the invitation. "Do you put walnuts in your brownies?"

"Excessive amounts."

The corners of her mouth turned up, and she shrugged. "Then okay, I guess," she said, her voice hesitant and barely above a whisper.

Thank God for walnuts. "Great. Then let's get this party started." Liz flashed a sly grin as she slid into the plush driver's seat. Isabel made her way around to the passenger side, and as soon as she got into the car she took the Scottie nodder from its bag and placed it in the center of the dash.

Dancing in place and humming the song again, Liz buckled her seat belt and smoothed her hands all over the car's interior. "What a fucking sexy car!" she said, then immediately put her hand to her mouth. "Sorry…I curse when I get really excited." And when she saw Isabel looking at her with amusement, she rubbed Isabel's chin between her thumb and finger. *You're as fucking sexy as your car*, Liz wanted to say, *and when I'm done driving it I'd love nothing more than to drive you—all night long.*

Instead, she let go of Isabel's chin and spoke to the Scottie on the dash. "You're going to have so much more fun living in Isabel's Mustang than you did in that boring store window, don't you think?" She tapped its velvety nose, and the dog's head nodded in agreement. "See?" she said to Isabel. "He agrees."

Isabel laughed, which made Liz want to take hold of her chin again and kiss her on the lips. Taking a deep breath, she put the car in drive, pulled out onto 72nd Street, and then made a quick right onto York Avenue. "How's the Mustang's safety record these days?"

"Good, although I'm not exactly sure how it rates. I tend to choose cars based on performance, not safety."

Like I choose my women, Liz thought. "Oh, Isabel, this car is *so* turning me on! I'd like to open it up on the highway with the top down one of these days," she said as they drove around the slick city streets of the Upper East Side. "And you really are full of surprises—operas and auctions and *Mustangs*! Who would have thought you'd be driving around in a muscle car—a street machine, as my dad calls them."

"What Mustangs does he have?"

"Not just Mustangs. He actually owns an auto body shop and for years has done restorative work on vintage cars. He was also an amateur race-car driver, although I shouldn't say amateur because he used to rally race, and that can be harder than being a circuit driver. Anyway, he's made a small fortune restoring and selling classic cars, but he keeps several in his own collection. I'm not sure what all he has right now, but I know he still has an '81 Camaro, which I used to drive in high school…a '72, or maybe it's a '73 Dodge Charger…a '57 Ranchero…and the two Mustangs, a '67 convertible and a `68 Shelby—"

"No! A Super Snake?" Isabel got so excited that she uncharacteristically hollered the words. "Is it white with blue stripes?"

Liz glanced over at her and laughed. "My, my, my…the young lady certainly knows her Mustangs. I'm impressed, Isabel. My father would be, too," she said, happy she'd found a way to break through Isabel's reserve.

"Some Super Snakes have sold for hundreds of thousands."

"My dad has argued that over the years. Whenever my mother complained about him spending so much time and money on vintage cars, he'd tell her that the return on his investments would be their retirement money. My mom buys a lot, too, mostly Depression and Vaseline glass, which she sells on Etsy and eBay. She loves going to estate sales and antique flea markets, so on Sundays after church my dad drives her around in one classic car or another. He likes turning heads and talking cars with people while she shops."

"God, I'd *love* to race a classic Shelby."

"Race?" Liz raised her eyebrows. "Really?"

"Well, maybe not race another car, but I'd love to experience driving at a hundred and twenty miles an hour. What could be more exhilarating?"

Having sex with Isabel would run a close race in the exhilaration department. Liz gave her a playful glance. "So you like to go fast, huh? Do you ever get pulled over driving this?"

"All the time."

"Ha! I bet you do. Any speeding tickets?"

"Only one," Isabel confessed. "Most troopers expect to pull over a young guy with an attitude, and when they find a woman in a business suit, they don't know what to do, except let me go with a warning."

"Well, just so you know, I wouldn't let you go," Liz teased. And as she began circling her building, looking for a parking space, the wheels began turning—the ones in her head. She was planning a trip to Maine next week to do some furniture hunting and see her parents. Their home was in Paris, but they also had a seasonal lakefront cabin a few towns over in North Waterford. If she could figure out a way to get Isabel to make the trip with her, maybe she could talk her father into planning a surprise for Isabel. He knew all the people at the speedway in New Hampshire. It was only an hour's drive, and…yes, her wheels were turning. She smiled over at Isabel, gripping the steering wheel in secret excitement as she broke out in a few more bars of Poe's song.

Isabel didn't sing along, but she appeared captivated by Liz's animated and high-spirited personality, her ability to let loose and have fun. Parking wasn't fun, though, and after circling three times, Liz pulled up in front of her building and honked at the doorman.

Ben, a stout and jovial man, squinted at the car but didn't recognize Liz until Isabel rolled down the passenger window and he bent down to see Liz in the driver's seat. "Ms. Bowes, is that you?"

Ben was used to Liz coming and going with women. One time he'd shook his head in amazement and asked how she managed to get more female visitors than all the single men in the building put together. "It's because I'm way prettier than all the men in this building," she'd told him. Ben had laughed and wholeheartedly agreed with her.

"Hey, Ben," she said, "I need a solid. Can you guard this car with your life for about an hour—move it if you have to?"

"No problem," he said with a broad smile. "Leave the keys."

Liz got out first and looked at him as he stepped off the curb to admire the front of the Mustang. "Isn't it gorgeous?" she said.

"What, the car or the young lady in the passenger seat?"

"Both." Smiling, Liz waited for Isabel to get out, then handed her the keys and let her lock the car. "I trust Ben," Liz assured her.

"If you trust him, I trust him," Isabel said, passing him the keys.

"Take your time, ladies. If anything comes up, I'll ring you upstairs."

"Thanks, hon," Liz said. She slipped him a folded bill and then grabbed Isabel's hand and led her into the building.

When they got off the elevator and into the apartment, Liz set her bag on a hall table and turned on the lights. She watched Isabel take in the spacious living room's bold but inviting color palette: lime green, black, and white. A tweed area rug with all three colors covered a good portion of the dark-stained floors, and against the left wall was a curved deco-styled sofa upholstered in a tapestry of overlapping green leaves on a black background. Sheer black curtains covered a sliding door to the terrace, and in front of them stood an artificial birch tree, its interwoven lights accenting a luxurious zebra-print chaise lounge. Floor lamps and an oversized glass cocktail table completed the grouping, all of it facing a mounted television and an exquisite art-nouveau bookcase that took up half the wall. All in all, the opposing styles and bold colors merged in a strikingly exotic arrangement that lent a botanical liveliness to the room.

"Wow…this is striking," Isabel said. "And I want to look at everything. But first I need to use the bathroom, if I may."

"Of course. First things first." Liz smiled as she hung their raincoats on an oak coatrack and then led her down the hall to a doorway just past the bedroom. "I'm going to start coffee, so when you come out, give yourself a tour."

Afraid of terrifying Isabel by taking her into the bedroom, Liz grabbed the opportunity to sneak in while her guest was in the bathroom. She turned on the Tiffany-style lamps on the mission nightstands, their red and white and amber glass illuminating a romantic fusion of 1920s Spanish revival and American Craftsman furniture. A dark-oak Stickley bed rested against creamy walls, a delicate red-and-white floral quilt balancing the heavy wood and adding a feminine feel to the room. On her way out, she passed the dresser and switched on an electric hurricane lamp, its glow highlighting the large Maxfield Parish prints of scantily clad women hanging on either side of the dresser's large mirror.

Liz dashed into the kitchen and had the espresso maker going by the time Isabel emerged. She saw her disappear into the bedroom for a moment and then watched her come out and wander down the hallway, pausing to study the Icart and Erte prints of even more sultry women before slowly making her way toward the living room and kitchen.

Isabel wandered through the living room and over to the nouveau bookcase, stopping to run her hand along the wood and examine the book titles and treasures contained within. When Liz looked up again, Isabel was leaning against the kitchen archway, tucking a strand of dark silky hair behind her ear, then folding her arms. "You certainly are an instinctive connoisseur," she said over the noise of Liz frothing milk. "I love the way you integrate styles."

"Why, thank you. The thing I love about revival styles is being able to create a feeling of being transported when you walk into a room."

"Well, you have a wonderful visual feel for blending eras," Isabel said. "A flair for juxtaposition, I guess you'd call it."

Liz turned off the machine and twisted her lips thoughtfully. "Hmm…an instinctive connoisseur with a flair for juxtaposition. I like the sound of that." She filled two cups halfway with espresso and began adding steamed milk. "Maybe I should use it as a slogan on my business cards." She smiled at Isabel. "Cinnamon?"

"Please." Isabel moved around Liz, looking at the mix of new and vintage dinnerware behind glass cabinet doors.

"My decorating philosophy," Liz explained, as she took out a tray and gathered plates and napkins, "is based on a firm belief in the attraction of opposites. I think it can be applied to anything from furniture to relationships. I love blending two distinctly different pieces, pieces that would appear to clash, like Victorian and modern, say, and see how each complements and accentuates the unique aspects of the other."

"You said you design interiors?"

"Sure. It's what I do," Liz said, setting their cappuccino and dessert on the tray. "I worked for two firms after graduate school, but since I like to incorporate antiques, hard-to-find and sometimes one-of-a-kind pieces, it made more financial sense to deal in furniture. For me, there's a greater profit in being a dealer who designs than a designer who buys from dealers. Not to mention lower costs for clients."

"So you're for hire?"

I'm for anything you want me to be. "What did you have in mind?"

"The empty guest cottage. The kitchen was just updated, but I have no idea what to do with the rest of it."

"Are you kidding? I'd love to get my hands on that cottage. I'm thinking contemporary farmhouse meets seaside cottage."

"Western Massachusetts is a little far from the sea."

"You'll think it's right outside your door when I'm done with it."

Isabel bit her lip for a second. "I think I'd like that. And I'd like to do business with you."

"I'm not doing business with you, Isabel. But if you're up for picking out paints and colors and shopping and decorating, we'll do it together. It would be an exciting weekend project. A pleasure project."

"I don't know how good I am at decorating, but I'm up for it." Isabel moved past the cabinet, and when she spotted the print of the lady sitting at a bar with a Scottie at her feet and two terriers on a stool, she tapped on the frame. "Ah, here's your *Martini* print! I was wondering why I didn't see it anywhere."

"Yep, that's it. Small, but I love it. Seeing that original tonight was incredible, wasn't it?" She picked up the tray and gestured for Isabel to follow. "Come on. Let's get comfortable inside."

Isabel looked around the living room as she sipped her cappuccino and bit into a brownie, complimenting Liz on all of it. She seemed far more relaxed than she'd been at dinner, but even now she sat stiffly on the edge of the sofa.

Liz smiled at her and patted the throw pillows. "Isabel, slide back and get comfortable before you fall off the edge."

"I'm fine, really," she said, one corner of her mouth turning up in a self-effacing smirk. "Some people like living on the edge…I prefer to sit on it."

"Ha!" Underneath her reserved exterior, Isabel Laraway had a good sense of humor. "Judging from the car you drive, I'd say you also like to ride on the edge, too."

"Sitting, riding—I figure as long as I'm seated, not too much can go wrong," Isabel said before biting into her brownie again.

"Enough walnuts for you?"

Her mouth full, Isabel nodded and patted her lips with a napkin, and Liz realized that just the fact of being here, alone with Liz in her apartment, represented a huge step for Isabel. As long as they were talking about subjects in general—books, art, cars, cats—Isabel maintained good eye contact, but when addressing anything of a personal nature she shyly looked away, as she did now when she asked Liz, "Do you live here alone?"

Liz stared at her beautiful profile. Isabel was the epitome of demure—modest, unassuming, so unaware of her sex appeal. Liz smiled to herself. "Yes, I live alone. Did you think I lived with a woman?"

Isabel shrugged and sipped her cappuccino. "I didn't know."

"Well, I don't. I've never been that serious about anyone. And I don't have a girlfriend," Liz said. "I mean, I have girlfriends from time to time, but not *a* girlfriend. How about you?" She gently pried. "Anyone special in your life? Any boyfriends?"

Isabel shook her head. "I'm too busy for that sort of thing."

"All work, no play?"

"Something like that."

"Don't you ever want to make time?"

Isabel looked perplexed. "Time for what?"

"Time for romance. Time for spending time. That's what happens when you fall for someone, right? You want to make time to spend time."

"I don't fall for people that way."

"I see."

Isabel really was clueless, and Liz found her naïveté absolutely fascinating. "Well, Ms. Laraway, I'm honored that you made time to spend time with me. I can't tell you how wonderful it is to have so much in common with a new friend." Liz slipped out of her shoes and got comfortable on the sofa. She held her cup in both hands, turning sideways so that she faced Isabel, and approached the subject carefully.

"Speaking of spending time…and considering that wonderful cottage waiting to be filled with furniture…I have a proposition."

A hint of worry washed over Isabel's face. "A proposition?"

"Yeah. Do you have plans next weekend?"

Isabel looked at her. "Not particularly."

Liz suppressed a smile. How funny it was that the demure Ms. Laraway, who had no time for spending time, seemed to have an awful lot of it on her hands. "Well, I'm making a trip to do some treasure hunting. If you'd like to come along, we might find some great things for the cottage."

"Where are you going?"

"Paris."

"Paris, France?"

"I'm not at liberty to disclose that information. All I will say is that you can bring the dogs if you like, and the three of you will have your own private bedroom."

"I guess that rules out France."

Liz grinned. "You never know with me. But I guarantee we'll have fun and get lots of ideas for decorating. Departure time is Friday, early morning before traffic starts. I'll have you home Monday night. That's all I can tell you right now, except that you need to pack appropriately because Paris gets really cold at night, even in summer."

Isabel's countenance was a combination of intrigue and worry. When she opened her mouth to answer and nothing came out, Liz held up a hand. She was making a quick study of Isabel's body language, learning when to push forward and pull back, and right now she knew enough to pull back. "No pressure. Don't give me an answer now. Discuss it with the dogs," she said with a crooked smile. "Let me know tomorrow."

Isabel nodded as she brought her cup to her mouth, and after she drank she got up and walked across to the nouveau bookcase, pointing to a framed photograph of a younger Liz on the dock of a lake with two Scotties. "Were these yours?" she asked in a soft voice.

"That was taken close to ten years ago." Liz answered with a wistful smile. "The smaller one was my little Scottie-girl, Skyler. Jock belonged to my parents. God, I miss those babies so much. And you know, Isabel, I'm still amazed that you have a Scottie. Occasionally I spot one in Central Park and can never resist asking to pet it, but other than that I don't see many around."

"Have you ever been to Hyde Park in the Hudson Valley?" Isabel asked.

"President Roosevelt's house? Of course. I think it's so cool that both Fala the Scottie and the family's German shepherd are buried there alongside Franklin and Eleanor."

Liz thought it best not to ask any more personal questions tonight. She gave Isabel control of the conversation as they talked about cats and dogs, and city versus country living. Liz answered questions about the vintage furniture in her apartment, her antique shop and interior-design business, and they were both shocked when Ben rang Liz to say he'd be going off duty soon. What felt like minutes had been almost two hours, and it was eleven o'clock by the time Liz walked Isabel down to her car and gave her a friendly hug.

"I hate knowing you have a long trip," Liz said after Isabel started the car and rolled down her window. "And I won't go to sleep until I know you're home, so promise you'll call the minute you pull in the driveway—before you even get in the house."

"I promise."

"And no speeding!"

"No speeding." Isabel grinned. "I'm very careful at night and always keep a close eye out for wildlife."

Liz watched and waved as Isabel drove away and then thanked Ben again and went back into the building. Who would have thought hugging someone in a damp raincoat could be so physically arousing? God, how she had wanted to hang on to that hug, to hold her close and discover Isabel's lips with her own.

❖

Heading back uptown, Isabel picked up the FDR to the Triboro Bridge, then took the Cross Bronx Expressway to the Hutchinson River Parkway and headed north. When she was well out of the city, she set her cruise control at 65 mph and turned on the radio.

She felt strangely energized. The sensation was inexplicable, but somehow she knew her life had changed tonight. An unfamiliar, delirious sort of heart-pounding happiness filled her. Had she just been on an actual date? She'd spent the last ten years politely declining dates with countless young businessmen, and now she'd finally gone on one. With a woman. With Liz Bowes, the vivacious, redheaded, green-eyed beauty who probably had more women than she knew what to do with.

Of course, neither of them had verbally confirmed that they were on an actual date, but it had certainly felt like one. And while the thought of a weekend away with Liz scared her no end, she couldn't wait to spend more time with her.

That's what happens when you fall for someone, Isabel. You want to make time to spend time.

She replayed Liz's words over and over in her head. Possibly for the first time in her life she understood the meaning of wanting to spend time. And she wanted to spend more of it with Liz. Did that mean she was falling for her? She looked to the Scottie on the dash, as if for an answer, and just as she did, the Mustang hit a bump and set the Scottie's head in motion.

Yes, yes…yes, it does, it nodded.

Suddenly Isabel panicked. Who was she kidding? She was so out of Liz's league. What would Liz want with someone so uptight and inexperienced, someone who didn't even know the first thing about touching and pleasing anyone? Tonight Liz hadn't expected anything from her. But next time Liz would probably try to kiss her, and the next time she'd probably want to—

How humiliating would it be to admit to Liz that in all her twenty-eight years she'd never been sexually intimate with anyone? She could never bring herself to do it. Just thinking about it made this wonderful delirium turn into the same dread she'd felt while waiting for Liz in the restaurant. In the morning she would call Liz, tell her she'd checked her calendar and, unfortunately, did have standing plans for the weekend.

And then what? A close platonic friendship might develop over time. Isabel might even become Liz's best friend and confidante, listening to her discuss her many girlfriends and steamy love affairs while she herself kept her own feelings of unbearable desire and jealousy a lifelong secret. How pathetic would that be? She hated letting fear and embarrassment make decisions for her, but it was probably best. Isabel turned up the volume on Sirius radio, letting the percussive beat of electronica and dance music pound the negative thoughts out of her head.

These past few days, fantasies of kissing Liz had left her aroused in ways she'd never thought possible, left her wanting to relieve the ache that worked its way between her legs. And she almost had, except that, having done so, she'd never be able to look Liz in the eye again. And then tonight? Liz's soft lips on her cheek sent crazy chills up her spine, and as nervous as she was, their parting hug made something inside her want to melt into Liz's arms.

Isabel had never given much thought to whether she might be gay. All she knew was that she wasn't sexually attracted to men. And now? The realization overwhelmed her. Could she actually be falling for a woman—a woman she enjoyed so much but barely knew? She blasted the music and stepped on the gas, keeping her eyes on the road and avoiding eye contact with the Scottie. But in her peripheral vision it kept nodding its unequivocal answer:

Yes, yes, yes, Isabel, yes…yep, uh-huh, yeah…oh yeah!

Chapter Sixteen

Last night's storm had left behind a picture-perfect Sunday morning. The air was cool, the sky a beautiful blue, the light breeze just enough to stir the chimes. The only thing missing was Sam. Gwen wished she had stayed for breakfast. Bertha, on the other hand, had invited herself for breakfast, lunch, and dinner. Indefinitely. She had refused to leave with Samantha.

Captivated by crows on the property, and focused on a particular bird who had taken an intense interest in her, Bertha had acted like a defiant teenager when it came time to leave. She'd hopped around in the grass, just out of Sam's reach, letting her get close, then darting away.

"Don't you want to come home with Sam-Sam?"

Nope, she'd cawed, and after several unsuccessful attempts at nabbing her, Samantha gave up and agreed to let her stay for a few days. But when Bertha had heard the motor of Samantha's car, she'd panicked like a child watching a parent leave. It seemed Bertha wanted to stay, but she didn't want Samantha to go.

Flying out and landing in the driveway where Gwen stood waving good-bye, Bertha ran along the gravel, chasing the black Range Rover on foot until Gwen caught up and offered her arm as a perch. All those black feathers couldn't hide the expression of worry on Bertha's face. Gwen softly kissed the crow's cheek, and when the SUV disappeared from sight, she allowed Gwen to walk her back to the house.

Raucous voices of unseen crows came from the trees, but in the grass a silent and solitary crow kept a watchful eye on Bertha. Perched on the edge of the porch table now, Bertha nibbled on toast, scrambled eggs, and an assortment of fruit. Gwen rubbed the bird's neck and smiled affectionately, momentarily distracted from Rosa's sulkiness.

It irritated her that Rosa pretended not to speak good English in Sam's presence, and with Samantha gone she was back to babbling in English. Granted, her accent was heavy, her grammar not always correct, but she spoke with fluency.

"Why don't you like Ms. Weller?" she flatly asked.

"Did I say I don't like her?"

"You certainly act like you don't, so let's clear up any misunderstandings right now."

Rosa folded her arms, her bottom lip protruding in something of a pout.

Gwen waited. "Well…?"

Rosa huffed and puffed and finally answered. "I don't like the way that dog shows itself to her."

Gwen's brow furrowed. "Why do you say 'that dog' like she's some kind of intruder? It's Alley. You knew and loved her when she was alive."

"*Sí*, when she was alive. She doesn't belong here anymore."

"I know that. We all know that. And I would help her move on if I could, but I can't. I don't know how."

As much as it had comforted her to see Alley in the beginning—to lay eyes on proof of life after death—Gwen sometimes couldn't bear to see her stuck between worlds, so forlorn, sorrowful. More and more, Alley seemed depleted of the energy needed to cross that proverbial Rainbow Bridge, and Gwen feared her soul might be growing stagnant. "You know it breaks my heart to see her trapped where she died, but yesterday with Samantha she was so," Gwen shrugged and shook her head, "so animated, happy…more connected to this world than I've ever seen her."

"Tell me this," Rosa said. "When I see her in the corner of my eye and then look right at her, what happens?"

Gwen regarded her tentatively. "She disappears. Isn't that what you always say?"

"*Sí!* And you can look right at her all day long, but what happens when you walk down there to get closer?"

"She…she disappears."

"*Sí!* So why she let Señora Weller get so close?"

"I don't have an answer, Rosa. All I know is that Alley likes Samantha. And I love that Samantha has the emotional and spiritual capacity to experience a ghost. It says a lot about her character."

Rosa's mouth tightened. "That…that *espíritu*," she said with a wave of her hand, "has no interest in that woman. She's using her to get to you."

"Oh, come on now. *Dramatica, dramatica*…always such drama, Rosa." Gwen brought a hand to her face and rubbed her forehead to fend off the headache her housekeeper was giving her.

Rosa narrowed her dark eyes. "I know you have feelings for that woman. And that *fantasma* knows it, too."

"Nonsense." A piece of scrambled egg fell from Bertha's beak onto Gwen's leg. She picked it off her thigh and threw it over the railing to Bertha's gentleman caller standing in the grass. He gobbled it, obviously happy for the offering, and Gwen threw him a piece of toast to go with it.

"You think I'm *loco*?" Rosa shook her head. "In life, that dog never left your side. She knew everything you felt, all your moods. Isn't that what you always say, that she could almost read your mind?"

"And what of it?"

"She can still read you. She senses what you feel…and she'll find your weakness. That weakness will be her way to you."

"You're not making any sense."

"Just remember what I tell you." Rosa pursed her lips and looked away. "*Ten cuidado!*"

"Be careful? Of what should I be careful?"

"Bringing that woman here."

"Sam?" A flush of anger rose in Gwen's cheeks. "I will tell you right now, Rosa. I don't know when I've enjoyed someone's company more, and I will *not* have her made to feel unwelcome in this house. Are we clear?"

Gwen heard the screen door open and looked up to see Loosey and Blue coming out, followed by Isabel in shorts and a T-shirt and holding a coffee cup.

Rosa turned around to see Isabel walking the length of the porch, then quickly turned back and leaned forward on her elbows. "I'm warning you, that *espíritu* is up to no good."

"Good morning, darling," Gwen called out cheerfully as Isabel approached, and then she raised a reprimanding eyebrow at Rosa and lowered her voice. "Enough of this ridiculous talk."

Isabel's face lit up when she caught sight of the crow. "Oh my God, is that Bertha the celebrity crow?"

"In the flesh." Gwen flashed a smile.

Loosey and Blue lifted their noses to smell Bertha, but when the crow turned and stabbed their noses with her formidable beak, they both decided the scrambled eggs were of greater interest.

Isabel sat down next to Gwen and looked between her and Rosa as if sensing the tension. "Is everything okay?"

"Everything's fine," Gwen said with another forced and perfectly peaceful smile.

"You're so beautiful, Bertha," Isabel cooed. Gently she stroked the bird's neck. And then she asked, "Where's Sam? I saw her car when I pulled in late last—" She blushed.

Gwen knew it had suddenly struck Isabel that she and Samantha had spent the night together. "I insisted Sam stay in the guest room because of the weather…and because she had a little too much to drink after seeing a ghost."

Isabel looked at her. "Alley?"

"Uh-huh."

"Why am I the only one who never sees anything?" she said, seeming almost disappointed. "Even Liz described feeling a presence when we walked around the pond the other day."

"Did she now? Hmm…how interesting." Gwen nodded. She liked the idea of Liz being emotionally uninhibited enough to perceive the extrasensory. She'd actually gotten that vibe from her when they first met. And the thought that Liz might be getting another kind of vibe from Isabel pleased her most of all. "Well, suffice it to say Sam experienced a lot more than a presence." She stopped to drink the last of her coffee.

Rosa smiled at Isabel. "So? How was your night out, *chica*?"

"We had a great time," Isabel said, and then she blushed again, as though worried her feelings for Liz might be transparent.

And they were. Gwen could tell she'd enjoyed herself. "I'm so glad the two of you hit it off. Any plans to see her again?"

"She's going to help me decorate."

"Oh? What will you be decorating?"

"Well…" Isabel chewed on a fingernail for a second and then stared into her coffee cup. "I was thinking the other day that, um…that maybe I should move out."

"Out?" Gwen raised her brow in surprise. "You mean off the estate?"

"No…more like into the empty cottage…you know, to give you more privacy in the house."

"I see. And it would give you more privacy as well…and you and Rosa would get to be neighbors." Gwen winked at Rosa and stifled a laugh. "I think it's a fabulous idea."

Isabel seemed surprised. "You do?"

"Absolutely. And it's very nice of Liz to offer her services, considering she's an interior designer."

"I proposed hiring her, but she refused. She wants to do it with me."

"How generous of her. I'm sure she'll make it beautiful."

"That's what I was thinking." Isabel hesitated. "She's going away this weekend to shop for furniture and, um," she squirmed in her chair, tucked her hair behind both ears, "she wanted me to go with her, thinking we'd get some decorating ideas for the—"

"Go!" Gwen said before Isabel could even finish her sentence.

"I don't think I can. Lori at the shelter needs help trapping some feral—"

"Isabel," Gwen said, "the shelter will be there when you get back. Go have fun."

"But I'd have to take Monday off, and I have an important morning meeting scheduled."

"Your father will handle it."

"I'll feed the cats for you," Rosa offered.

"And I'll watch the dogs," Gwen said.

"Liz told me I could take them."

"The dogs? How sweet of her to invite them along. And you know Blue, who couldn't care less about people, is crazy about her."

Isabel put her head down and nodded. "I'll think about it."

"There's nothing to think about, Isabel. Tell her you'll go."

"But—"

"Isabel?" Gwen arched an eyebrow and used her sternest tone. "It's settled. Call Liz today and accept her invitation."

Isabel chewed her fingernail again and then put her hands in her lap and didn't say anything more.

Gwen was not easily aggravated, but between Isabel and Rosa—the virginal niece and the histrionic clairvoyant—she'd had just about enough. Last night had been a special evening with a remarkable woman, and all Gwen wanted was to sit alone and process these unexpected feelings Sam stirred in her. The moment she had laid eyes on Sam—or was it as early as their first phone conversation?—she'd known instinctively that she could fall in love, fall as hard as the smitten crow who was courting Bertha.

He flew up onto the low branch of a nearby tulip tree and called to her. Bertha hopped to the porch railing and paced back and forth until caution gave way to curiosity and she mustered the courage to fly out and join her admirer on the same branch.

While Rosa and Isabel sat watching the two crows, Gwen disappeared into the house. "Excuse me," she said. "I need more coffee." And after pouring another cup she took the opportunity to sneak through the house to the back porch. The soft chirping of songbirds came through the screens. She plumped a pillow and settled into a yellow wicker chair with her coffee to quietly ponder both the mystery writer and the mystery of love.

❖

Liz was relaxing in bed with coffee and *The New York Times* when the bell rang. She shuffled through the dark living room and felt the wall for the intercom. "Yes?" she said, and when the caller spoke she immediately recognized Sam's voice.

"I need to talk," Samantha said.

"What are you doing down there?"

"The pressing question is how do I get up there?"

"What's the password?" Liz asked.

"Bacon and egg on a roll."

"How would you like your coffee, miss?"

"Milk, two sugars. Why do I feel like I'm at a drive-thru?"

"Thanks for your order. Please drive around to the sixth floor." Liz buzzed her in, gathered plates and napkins on a tray, and by the time Samantha got off the elevator and to the door, she had Sam's coffee waiting on the night table opposite hers.

Samantha walked in with a broad smile. "Top of the morning to you," she said, handing Liz the breakfast bag and walking past her.

"I would have made breakfast for us if you had called, but thank you. I was getting hungry."

As Samantha wandered into the dark living room, Liz grabbed her by the hand and pulled her down the hallway to the bedroom with its unmade bed. Samantha paused in the doorway. "We're having coffee in bed?"

"We always have coffee in bed on Sunday morning."

"We do?"

"Yes." Liz gathered up sections of the newspaper on the bed and dropped them onto the floor.

"Your coffee is on the night table," she said, placing a tray in the middle of the bed and climbing back in. "Why are you in the city today, and why so early? I figured you would have been with Gwen until late last night."

"I slept there."

Liz stared. "You slept with her?"

"I said I slept *there*, not with her. She wouldn't let me drive home because of the storm…and because of other unforeseen circumstances, which I'll tell you about in a moment. Of course, I would have slept with her, but all she offered me was a toothbrush, a T-shirt, and the guest room." Samantha pointed to the wall. "I love these." She stopped to examine the Maxfield Parrish women on her way around to the other side of the bed. "Anyway," she said, stepping up to the first print, "we were up early having coffee on the porch, and she wanted me to stay for breakfast, but I have to deliver a manuscript tomorrow and need to sit and read through the entire thing today."

"Where's Bertha?"

"With Gwen."

"You left your crow there? I'm shocked."

"Not as shocked as Bertha was to discover she's a crow and not a person." Samantha talked with her back to Liz as she moved from one print to the other. "Bertha had a bad attitude this morning…suspicion mixed with resentment. She finally figured out she's adopted and that I've been hiding the truth of her identity. And worse yet, there's a boy-crow hot on her trail. Can you believe that?" She turned and faced Liz. "I feel like the mother of a teenage daughter who wants to start dating. I want to meet his parents."

Liz laughed. "Well, the good news is that you have another excuse to go back there. Very clever, Sam."

Samantha grinned. "That, too." She stood at the foot of the bed and looked around the room. "It's really beautiful in here. Very romantic. I can understand why you like to eat in bed."

"It's not like I serve dinner in here, silly." She fluffed the pillows and shams on Sam's side and patted the bed. "Come on, climb in. Don't be afraid."

Samantha looked at her askance as she kicked off her shoes. "All right, but don't try anything funny, because I'm saving myself for Dr. Laraway."

"Don't worry. You're completely safe. I'm saving myself for the young Ms. Laraway."

Samantha drank from her cup. "Good coffee. Thanks," she said as she got in bed. "So how was the book auction?"

"It wasn't just books. It was *ephemera*."

"Ephemera? As in *ephemeral*?"

"Precisely. Things that deteriorate over time: books, prints, posters, postcards, magazines, letters. Things made of paper don't survive the test of time as well as other antiques, which means fewer of them exist, and that can make them very valuable."

"I get it. Between you, Gwen, and Isabel, I'm on my way to becoming an honorary antiquarian." Sam took two sandwiches from the bag on the tray and handed one to Liz. "Did you have a good evening with the heiress apparent?"

"Oh God, Sam! Did you have to say that?" Liz let her head fall back against the shams and stared at the ceiling. "Shit, she is an heiress, isn't she?"

"I believe that's the proper title for a young woman who stands to inherit the family fortune."

"Stop!" Liz said, groaning and running her fingers through her hair. "I can't even think about it." She looked over at Sam. "Are we pathetic? Look at us, both under the spell of the Laraway women."

Samantha set her cup on the tray, stretched out alongside Liz, and propped herself on her elbow. "You really like her, huh?"

"Like her? I'm crazy for her."

"You think she might have tendencies?"

"Tendencies? Isabel's a sexy little dyke disguised in heels and a skirt suit. She just doesn't know it yet. Or maybe she does and it scares her."

"So nothing happened?"

"Nothing."

"Aww…the serial seductress didn't score, huh?"

"That's not exactly true. Getting her up here for coffee was a score."

"I'm surprised you didn't at least kiss her."

"Isabel is pure and unspoiled, and I'm trying to keep my thoughts that way."

"Gwen thinks Isabel has a crush on you."

"*Whaaat?*" Liz sat up, nearly spilling her coffee. "Did she really say 'crush'? Did she actually use that word?"

"She did." Samantha bit into her bacon sandwich. "Gwen had no idea you were gay, and when I told her you were, she seemed thrilled that Isabel had taken a liking to you."

"You're kidding me—Gwen was *thrilled*?"

"She was. She more or less said that Isabel's never cared for men. So go for it."

"Nope. I woke up thinking about Isabel," Liz said as they ate, "and I've decided I will not make any sexual advances. Romantic overtures, maybe, but nothing physical. If she makes a first move I will gladly take the lead, but I promise to restrain myself."

"Why restrain?"

"Because I really, *really* like her, Sam, and I'd be terribly upset with myself if I scared her off and lost her as a friend. I'm fine with letting her set the pace as long as I know she wants me." Liz smiled. "Isabel is so worth waiting for."

"No doubt she's worth the wait…but this behavior is sort of out of character for you, isn't it?"

"Very out of character," she said, squinting at Samantha's lips as she talked.

"What's wrong? Do I have food stuck?" Samantha picked up a napkin to wipe her mouth.

Liz stopped her and pushed the napkin away. "No, no food, but…" She reached with a fingertip and lightly rubbed the side of Samantha's upper lip. "I'm seeing the hint of a mustache there, Sam. You need to let me wax that for you."

"Hey." Samantha pulled away. "Leave my mustache alone." She smiled and pretended to smooth it out. "It's taken me over forty years to grow it."

"I seriously hope you're joking," Liz said, but then her cell phone rang, and she reached for it on the night table. When she saw the number she jumped out of bed. "Oh my God, it's Isabel." She put a finger to her lips and left the room.

In a few minutes she was back, jumping up and down, grinning like a maniac. "Isabel said yes. She said yes! She's coming with me next weekend."

"What? Where?"

Liz danced around the room, then crawled back in bed on her

knees, sat back on her heels, and bounced excitedly. "Last night she asked if I would decorate the empty cottage with her, and since I was planning to drive up to Maine for a furniture hunt, I suggested she come along. I didn't expect her to say yes." She grinned again. "This is so great. I get Isabel and the dogs for three whole days!"

"You're staying with your parents?"

"We'll stop for dinner, but we'll stay at the cabin. I want to take her kayaking and show her I'm not the city girl she thinks I am. And best of all, I'm hoping my dad can pull some strings and take Isabel to the speedway. Did you know she loves muscle cars and drives a Mustang?"

"Gwen mentioned it last night, but I didn't see it this morning. I guess it was garaged. I never would have pegged her for driving a Mustang."

"Me neither. And her dream is to race a car. I want to make that happen."

"Making that dream come true should earn you a few brownie points."

"My walnut brownies already earned me brownie points."

"You have brownies?"

"Yeah. You want some?"

"Sure. Not right now, though. Tell me about Craig. You think he can set something up for Isabel?"

"You know my dad. If it has anything to do with cars, he'll arrange it."

"Hmm…" Samantha smiled. "So this is next weekend, huh? That leaves Gwen home alone. I might take advantage of the situation." But then Samantha's smile turned to a frown. "Any chance of taking Rosa with you?"

Liz rolled her eyes. "Geez, Sam, what is it with you and Rosa?"

"Ask Rosa. She hates me. Why, I don't know."

"Maybe she's just being protective and questioning your romantic interest in Gwen."

"Well, last night was not exactly conducive to romance." She paused and studied Liz. "I need to tell you something. And I don't want you to think I'm crazy."

"What happened? Tell me."

Samantha took a deep breath, puffed her cheeks, and blurted out, "I saw a ghost there yesterday. As clear as day. The ghost of Gwen's dog."

Samantha waited for Liz to burst out laughing, but she didn't. Instead her jaw dropped open. She put her sandwich down, wiped her hands on a napkin, and rearranged herself so that she now sat cross-legged, staring at Samantha. "By the pond, right? Tell me you saw it by the pond."

"Yes, by the pond. That's where the dog drowned. I saw it from the kitchen window the day we went there, but Rosa blew me off when I asked about it, so I figured it was just a neighbor's dog that had wandered onto the property. And then yesterday when I arrived, Blue was sitting in the grass watching the same dog. I swear it looked like a real dog, and it was happy to see me…so I walked down there and got close. Almost close enough to touch. I think maybe I did touch it before Gwen screamed and made me leave it alone."

Liz just listened intently and kept nodding.

"Gwen sees her, too," Samantha said. "She says her spirit seems confined to the area where she died."

"I *knew* it. I just knew I felt something there. While Isabel and I were walking I distinctly felt something brush up against my leg, and after that I felt—I don't know, it's hard to explain—a heavy presence, a pressure around me like something was standing there. I told Isabel, but I don't think she believed me."

"Gwen implied that her niece is sort of repressed when it comes to opening up and allowing herself to experience the more spiritual side of life." Samantha closed her eyes and shook her head and breathed a sigh of relief. "I'm so glad you believe me."

"Oh, I believe you, Sam. I do." Liz drank her coffee and thought for a moment. "A ghost-dog. Wow…this is so incredible."

Samantha rambled on, recounting every detail of her stormy night with Gwen. So lost was she in sharing the life-altering experience of seeing a ghost that she seemed not to notice Liz getting up and coming back with a waxing strip for her upper lip.

Another pot of coffee and an hour later they were still talking, lost in conversation about their shared new world: a wondrous world, rich and heady, filled with spirits and rising passions.

CHAPTER SEVENTEEN

Samantha pulled up to the Red Lion Inn in Stockbridge and took in the New England charm of an inn dating back to the Revolutionary Era. With over one hundred rooms, it took up half of Main Street. As a child, she'd seen Norman Rockwell's famous winter painting of this scene on Christmas cards, and while researching ghost stories in recent years she had noted it referenced in books on American historical and haunted inns. Samantha called Gwen from the car. It was the perfect place to have lunch with her.

"It's me," she said when Gwen answered. "I got into town early."

"Where are you?"

"At the Red Lion Inn, about to snoop around for ghosts and take you to lunch."

"As it so happens, I was sitting here thinking I should take you to lunch and show you a little bit of the Berkshires."

"Too late. I beat you to it. I've been reading about this place for a long time, and since Detective Crowley always begins a new case by meeting her clients in one dark tavern or another, I thought it would give me ideas for the next book."

"Where will you be, in the courtyard?"

"Why spend a perfectly beautiful and sunny day outdoors, when we can enjoy the ambience of a dark and haunted tavern?"

"I can't think of one good reason." Gwen laughed. "Give me fifteen minutes."

"See you then." Samantha couldn't wait to be with her again. It was all she'd thought about. That and Bertha…and the ghost-dog.

They hadn't seen each other for three days, not since Sunday morning, although Gwen had called every day with updates on Bertha's adventures with a gentleman caller who had captured her attention.

Without the crow, her house had seemed terribly empty these past few nights. She missed the bird something fierce, and although she'd never admit it to anyone, news of Bertha's newfound boyfriend stabbed her with a deep pang of jealousy. The thought that Bertha might not want to come home broke Samantha's heart, but if her bird's affection for another crow was anything approaching her own affection for Gwen, it was only fair to let Bertha choose. That crow had changed her life—saved her life—and she'd have to find a way to love her enough to let her go.

Samantha got out of the car and followed the brick walkway that led between two stone lions and up to a porch that ran the length of the enormous white inn. Over a dozen rocking chairs were lined up, all occupied by chatting guests relaxing with colorful drinks. Pushing her sunglasses to the top of her head, she entered a lobby that looked like a large living room, and when the hearth came into view she imagined how cozy the inn must be with a fire roaring on a snowy winter's night.

She wandered casually down the hallway, peeking into antique-filled rooms that offered additional seating with more privacy. In a sunny alcove at the end of the hall, an ornately carved Victorian rocking horse came into view. It stood as high as a real pony, and beside it two guests played chess on an antique game table. Beyond that lay a gift shop and not much else. Samantha turned and walked back in the other direction until she found the main dining room. Another fireplace, lace and fine linens covering the tables, and a collection of countless teapots decorating the shelving along the crown molding gave the room the formal feel of another century. But she wasn't looking for this one. On the website, she'd seen other dining areas at the inn: the underground Lion's Den, housed in the cellar, the outdoor Courtyard, and the Widow Bingham's Tavern that should have been here on the main floor.

Samantha must have looked lost because an enthusiastic staff member stopped to offer assistance, the young woman's perky ponytail swinging and slapping Samantha in the face as she cheerfully turned to lead Samantha through a doorway that took her into the tavern's bar. Samantha smiled and thanked her, taking a minute to marvel over the dark wainscoting and squeaky wide-planked floors marked with centuries of wear. Adorning the walls were the original gas lamps, now electrified and illuminating red-checkered tablecloths and bentwood chairs. All in all, it seemed a likely spot for resident ghosts to gather, and a rustically refined and romantic setting for dining with Gwen.

A soft murmur of conversation came from a handful of people

having lunch. The six stools at the short bar were empty, and Samantha got up on one. Through a glass door on her left she saw the Courtyard with its umbrella-covered tables, outdoor bar, and bustling crowd of diners. Beyond that she spotted two other barn-like structures, and judging from the vintage photographs hanging on the tavern's walls, she presumed those buildings were renovated stables that once accommodated the carriage horses of weary travelers.

A distinguished gray-haired bartender in a black vest and bowtie emerged from a doorway, turning up the cuffs of his white shirt as he came to greet her. "Avoiding the heat or the crowd?" he asked, sliding a cocktail menu toward her.

"A little of both," Samantha said, looking down at a list of this week's Prohibition Era drinks. She trailed her finger down the curious cocktails until she stopped at a Bee's Knees. "Hmm…lavender-infused honey with lemon and gin? I have to try this…but how does it relate to Prohibition?"

"Well, during Prohibition," he said, pouring ingredients into a stainless-steel shaker, "speakeasies needed to mask the smell of bathtub gin in case the cops made a raid, so they'd add honey and lemon and sometimes herbs, like lavender." A few shakes and he poured the purple-colored elixir into a frosted martini glass and smiled. "If you don't like it I'll make you something else."

Samantha lifted it to her lips. It was cold, almost icy, and she smelled the lavender before she tasted it. "Very nice," she said, letting her taste buds fully appreciate the sweet honey and lemon zest. "In fact, this is so good, I'm going to trouble you to make another one for my lunch date, who'll be here any minute."

While he complied and she had the bartender all to herself, Samantha took the opportunity to engage him in conversation about rumored hauntings at the inn. "Any ghosts around from the Prohibition Era?"

"Where do you think we get our recipes?"

Samantha laughed and quickly got him talking about the inn's ghosts. He shared hearsay concerning hauntings and reports of paranormal activity—especially room 301, an apparent hot spot for spirits—until movement outside the glass door caught her eye, and she turned to see a tall, slim blonde in dark sunglasses walking up to the door through the Courtyard. She wore white cropped pants and a loose floral top, a large and most likely designer bag hanging from her shoulder. The sight of her was arresting. That this woman was here to meet her filled Samantha with pride and nervous anticipation.

Gwen removed her sunglasses as she came through the door, seeming to give her eyes a moment to adjust to the dim light as she scanned the room and spotted Samantha at the bar.

Samantha slid off her stool at Gwen's approach, feeling the dizzying effects of both the woman and the libation she'd started drinking on an empty stomach. "Hi," she said, opening her arms.

"You know, Sam," Gwen whispered, hugging and keeping Samantha in her embrace long enough to speak against her ear, "if it's a ghost you want to see, you didn't have to come here."

"I know."

Gwen let go and smiled at the lavender-colored cocktails on the bar. "Bee's Knees? What a nice surprise."

"You've had one before?"

"I have. They're delicious."

Samantha frowned. "I was hoping to turn you on to a new experience in Prohibition Era drinks."

"Well, I've never had one with you, so it will be a new experience. Shall we sit?"

Once they'd taken their drinks and moved to a table, Samantha sighed with satisfaction. She couldn't think of anyone she'd rather be with or any place she'd rather be, except maybe in bed, making love with Dr. Laraway.

"I hope I didn't forget my glasses," Gwen said. She set her bag on her lap, and as she dug through it, Samantha stole a moment to secretly admire her face.

Samantha was sure Gwen had been to a salon since she'd last seen her. Her blond hair had more highlights than it had last week and seemed a few inches shorter than Samantha remembered. What had fallen around her shoulders now barely touched them, and the shorter length gave her hair more waves.

Samantha squinted, closing her eyes just enough so that her vision blurred, erasing the years from Gwen's face and allowing her a glimpse of what Gwen had looked like as a young woman in her thirties. And then she slowly opened them again, letting her eyes time-travel back to the precious present.

She smiled to herself, decidedly enamored of the seasoned woman sitting across from her. She'd always been attracted to older women, although she herself was now as old as the older women she'd admired in her youth. There was something about character lines, signatures of life's experiences…those visible accumulations of the many surprises that raise the brow, deep thoughts that furrow it…disappointments and sorrows that turn down the corners of the mouth, and the endless delights that turn them up again and crease the cheeks with laughter over life's amusements and absurdities. And while many women would do anything to erase those character lines, Samantha found that they added an alluring depth to a woman of a certain age. On Gwen, those gentle lines lent a sensual maturity, a rich complexity and unapologetic confidence to her still-beautiful face.

Gwen pulled out her eyeglasses, hung her bag on the chair, and turned back as Samantha continued to smile at her. "What?" she said, her blue eyes catching the light of the old electrified gas lamps that hung on the wainscoting above their table.

"Nothing." Samantha still smiled. "I was just thinking that you cut your hair."

"I did. Do you like it?"

"I do. And your pink nail polish. You weren't wearing any last time I saw you."

"You don't miss a thing, do you, Detective Crowley?"

"Not on you, I don't."

Gwen held her gaze, the corners of her mouth twitching. "I'm beginning to think you have a crush on me, Ms. Weller."

"You have no idea, Professor."

"Oh, I think I do."

"Is that an admission of a reciprocal crush?"

Gwen only answered with a tentative, flirtatious smile and raised her glass. "Here's to sunny days spent in haunted taverns with a mystery writer who has herself become an intriguing mystery."

Their glasses touched, but before Samantha could take the conversation to a more personal level, Gwen steered it away, as she was adept at doing. "And speaking of mysteries," she said, "I started your third book yesterday."

"Really," Samantha said, content to let Gwen take the lead for a while. Just knowing her feelings were reciprocated was enough to sustain her for now. "How far along are you?" she asked as the waitress brought menus and filled their water glasses.

"Not too far. The ailing Mr. Minerva, having discovered that Mrs. Minerva has secretly kept a mistress throughout their marriage, has just expired and in an act of vindictiveness is attending his own funeral in hopes of taking possession of Ms. Edwards, the town's affluent Realtor and his widow's long-time lover."

"Just your average paranormal soap opera, isn't it?" Samantha laughed. "However, the late Mr. Minerva isn't taking possession of Ms. Edwards. He's attempting an auric attachment."

"Right, I read that, an auric attachment. I actually looked it up but couldn't find anything on the subject. I take it to be a form of possession, no?"

"Not exactly. Possession would be the act of a spiritual entity entering the body of someone. In the case of auric attachments, the intrusive spirit remains outside the body, sort of piggybacking the aura of a vulnerable person and feeding off its energy." Samantha opened her menu. "You'll understand it as you read on."

"Did you make that up?"

"Auric attachments? No," Samantha said, her eyes immediately drawn to the day's special—fresh crab cakes. "I stumbled upon the phenomenon while researching something else." She looked over the top of her menu. "As far-fetched as it sounds, many paranormal researchers believe that certain medical conditions, such as Epstein-Barr syndrome and other energy-zapping afflictions, are often misdiagnosed cases of auric attachments."

"Is that so?" Gwen put on her glasses and opened her own menu. "And how do they propose to establish a correlation, let alone a causal relationship?"

"Well, what's interesting is that in one study, over five hundred patients were interviewed about their recent histories. Within two weeks prior to the onset of symptoms, it turns out that more than seventy percent had been in a funeral parlor, a cemetery, or a hospital—all likely places to encounter newly deceased souls who haven't yet transitioned. And some of those souls, perhaps not yet knowing they're dead, or not wanting to accept that they're dead, look to attach and feed off the electromagnetic field of a susceptible person."

"Now there's a scary thought. Talk about being in the wrong place at the wrong time. So…in the case of Mr. Minerva's ghost," Gwen said, "by attaching itself to the aura of his wife's mistress, he's hoping for what, vicarious conjugal visits, a theoretical ménage à trois?"

Samantha laughed. "Something like that, yes, unless Candice Crowley can detach him from Ms. Edwards's aura and send him on his way."

"Hmm." Gwen was silent for a moment. "You know, there's a new-age center here in the Berkshires that offers aura photography every so often. I went the summer before last and dragged Isabel along."

"Really? I've always wanted to do that. How does it work?"

"I believe two photos are taken simultaneously and then superimposed—one of you and the other of your electromagnetic field. When we sat in front of the camera, we had to place our hands on electronic pads," Gwen explained. "It's a complicated process, I'm sure, but vibrations from the electrical charges are sent to the camera and translated into colors. I read somewhere that Tesla actually invented the aura camera at the turn of the last century, part of his research in robotics."

"Tesla? Now that's interesting. I wonder if he took pictures of pigeon auras."

"Pigeons?" Gwen raised her brow. "All living things have auras… but why would he photograph a pigeon's?"

"Tesla loved them. During the years he spent living in New York hotels he was known to take in injured pigeons he found in Central Park." Samantha grinned at Gwen's quizzical expression. "I only know this because my grandfather, a retired engineer, was a homing-pigeon hobbyist and fascinated by magnetoreception, nature's GPS. When I was little and we still lived in Texas, he'd bring along a couple of birds on every family road trip. When we got to where we were going, sometimes a hundred miles or more from home, we'd release them. As they flew away he'd proudly say, 'Those birds will be home before us.' And they always were."

"Amazing. I wonder what gives some birds that biological compass."

"Magnetite. Possibly in the cells of the inner ear…and extra brain cells that store information on the earth's magnetic field like a GPS stores maps." Samantha closed her menu. "I'm having the crab cakes."

"I'm going with the lobster roll," Gwen said. "Should we share a salad?"

"Sure. You choose," Samantha said as the waitress approached. She liked the idea of sharing anything with Gwen.

After they ordered, Samantha leaned back and folded her arms. "So tell me about your aura. What did it look like?"

"Well, mine was mostly green and orange, and above my head were five distinct balls of glowing light, a half circle of orbs, which I was told were spirits." She paused to sip her lavender cocktail. "I was expecting the interpreter to say they were guardian angels, you know, spirits of people or animals I'd loved and lost and who were now watching over me. But he said they were 'universal spirits'...spirits who knew me but whom I did not know personally."

"Higher-level beings...unseen forces connecting you to them." Samantha considered this information. "Maybe that connection is what gives some of us a consciousness of something greater than ourselves... while others don't feel that connection and never give it a thought."

"That's exactly what I took it to mean. Some people never think beyond what they're having for dinner, what movie they want to see, what plans they have for the weekend, while others always wonder where they fit into the larger scheme of things."

Samantha finished her cocktail. "And what about the colors of your aura? Do they have a meaning?"

"Green was a sign of harmony and balance, I believe, a oneness with nature. The orange represented independence, playfulness, creativity...a sense of adventure. I'll show you the photograph when we get back to the house. If I can find it."

"Definitely. I'd love to see it. And next time you hear of it being offered, please let me know," she said as their salad came. "And what was Isabel's aura like?"

"A lot of yellow, but mostly bright red."

"Red being what, anger?"

"Actually, no. They say kids and animals often have bright-red auras. It indicates a strong physical nature, an almost childlike awe and appreciation of the physical world. And that's Isabel," Gwen said as she took a fork and pushed half the salad onto Samantha's plate. "If she can't pet it, play with it, drive it, dance to it, climb or swim through it, it doesn't exist. I told you that's why I think she can't see Alley. She's spiritually blocked."

Samantha speared a piece of arugula and feta cheese. "Why do you think?"

"Part of it might just be her practical nature, but I'm sure a lot of it has to do with losing her mother so suddenly and at such a young age. I think that acute physical absence taught her to cling to things that are substantial, solid, reliable. Things she can wrap her arms and her head around. But I'm hoping something will happen to open her up, and I have a hunch Liz will prove to be a catalyst."

"Liz is making a trip to see her parents and do some antiquing this weekend. I think she might have asked Isabel to join her," Samantha said, not sure how much she should say about Liz's surprise plans for Isabel.

"I know," Gwen said. "Liz called me yesterday."

"She did?"

"Mm-hm. We had a nice conversation. She didn't have to call. I mean, Isabel is twenty-eight years old. She certainly doesn't need my consent. But I appreciate Liz asking if I was comfortable with her father arranging for…" Gwen frowned as she ate and shook her head in mock resignation. "…for Isabel to race a stock car!"

"Don't worry. Craig won't let Isabel do anything he doesn't think she can handle. If worse comes to worst, he won't let her drive at all, and she'll get the thrill of going 140 miles per hour strapped in the passenger seat with a helmet on."

"I certainly feel better knowing that. Do you know them, her parents?"

"Craig and Gina? Sure. They're wonderful people. I drove up there with my brother, Jason, when he and Lisa were first engaged. We spent a night at the house and a couple of nights at their lakeside cabin. I suppose that's where Liz and Isabel will be staying."

"In the cabin?" Gwen gave a thoughtful nod, making room on the table as the rest of their food came.

"And before the wedding I spent a weekend with her parents at Jason and Lisa's weekend place in the Hamptons. In fact, until a couple of weeks ago, I knew them better than I knew Liz."

"Well, I'm glad you and Liz are making up for lost time. And I'm beyond thrilled that she and Isabel have connected. I just love Liz," Gwen said.

Over lunch Samantha told Gwen about all the reading she was doing on American art pottery and about the Weller vase with foxes she'd won on eBay the other night when the house had felt so empty without Bertha and she couldn't sleep.

After they'd finished eating and were waiting for coffee and a slice of key lime pie to share, Gwen said, "I know you can't wait to see Bertha. I know she misses you."

"I hope so, because I miss her, too. Something awful. You wouldn't think the presence and personality of one little animal could fill so much space and leave such a void in its absence."

"Oh, but they do. Every time I say your name, whether she's sitting on the porch or in the tree with her smitten friend, she stops what she's doing to look at the driveway and listen."

"She knows the sound of my car. These past few nights I've been wishing she could transition into spirit form like she does in my stories and pay me spectral visits."

"I do love how you have her character flying through portals so small she can only fit through them in spirit form." She gave Samantha a sideways look and arched one eyebrow. "I detect a creative and clever fusion of Norse mythology and quantum physics."

Samantha shook her head in wonderment. "How is it you have such immediate insights into my literary secrets?"

Gwen laughed. "It's been years since I've read Norse mythology, but the earthbound Detective Crowley sending her crow up into the ether to locate and communicate with spirits reminds me of the god Odin. In human form, if I remember correctly, he saw out of only one eye and relied on his raven to see and tell him things."

"Two ravens. Hugin and Munin, which translate to something along the lines of *thought* and *memory*. Odin also had two wolves to hunt and keep him nourished, but he sent out the ravens every morning to fly around the globe and report back with news on everything happening in the world."

"Now we have the internet for that."

"True." Samantha laughed. "I suppose Odin's ravens are obsolete."

"But Detective Crowley's crow isn't. Odin's ravens might have circled the world, but Bertha travels between dimensions to locate the dearly departed and help solve cases. And the microscopic portals she accesses resemble wormholes—those hypothetical shortcuts through the universe that connect parallel dimensions and might provide access to the past and future, if only we were small enough to fit through them." Gwen gave a thoughtful smile. "I'm assuming you have a good understanding of physics to write what you write."

"A very basic understanding." Samantha grinned. "I'm not as smart as I sound."

Gwen laughed. "You're certainly smart enough."

"Well, as you know, my background is in biology and forensic science, not physics. When I get ideas, I try to learn enough that my novels make theoretical sense." Samantha paused as the server brought coffee. "I know we exist in *space-time*, three dimensions of space, one dimension of time, all of it governed by gravity, electromagnetism, and the two nuclear forces."

"That's the basis of classical physics that made way for the industrial revolution and astrophysics." Gwen poured cream and stirred her coffee. "Its focus, though, is on the macrocosm, on harnessing those forces. But the quantum mechanics that makes today's technology possible, including all those electronic devices we can't seem to live without, focuses on a microcosm invisible to the naked eye. And what goes on in that subatomic world is shocking. So shocking that some physicists suspect the universe may be part of an intelligent design... that the *big bang* might not have been an accident...that we could be living in a simulation, right alongside other dimensions hidden from our senses because," she tapped the side of her head, "our minds are trapped inside this organic computer programed to function in only a three-dimensional world."

"You're talking about string theory." Their dessert arrived and Samantha slid the plate between them. "All matter is composed of vibrating strings of energy, like strands of pearls, in a ten-dimensional universe that can be worked out mathematically but not yet proven."

"Well, the math doesn't work without at least ten dimensions. There may be many more, depending on which version of superstring theory appeals to you."

Samantha gazed at Gwen, delighted by the quiet excitement of their conversation. "And what, may I ask, makes a philosopher so interested in quantum physics?"

"All philosophers are fascinated by it. And if that 'theory of everything' they're working on ever succeeds in reconciling Einstein's general theory of relativity with quantum mechanics, it may prove to be the holy grail of not only science but of philosophy and theology."

"Hmm." Samantha stuck out her bottom lip as she pondered this possibility. "I guess I can see how the two fields share a similar quest."

"Absolutely. Philosophers ask *why* we are here, why *any* of this is here, and physicists ask *how* it is here." Gwen cut into the key lime pie with a fork and held it out to Samantha's mouth. "Open up," she said.

Samantha took it, still feeling a little awkward, still mildly intimidated by Dr. Laraway but pleased by the intimate gesture. "Mmm, that's really good."

Gwen watched with the hint of a smile as Samantha savored the tangy bite and swallowed. "You've read about particle accelerators."

"Atom smashers."

Gwen laughed. "Yes. There's the famous Large Hadron Collider, for one, and thousands of others in nuclear-research laboratories around the world. And while applications in everything from nuclear medicine and robotics to quantum computers are astounding, the philosophical implications are truly uncanny." She paused to sample the key lime pie. "Mmm. That *is* good," she said. "But here's what fascinates me. You can pair two particles of light, two photons, so that they become unified, intrinsically linked. Then you can separate them again—keep one here and send the other three hundred miles into space. You'd think the two would be separated forever. But they aren't. They continue to read each other, correlate, communicate. Anything you do to one affects the other. No one knows how."

"Entanglement."

"That's right. Quantum entanglement. Spooky action at a distance, as Einstein called it. And since we're all made of particles, entanglement could explain why we stay emotionally connected to certain people even when separated by great distances. Or why, when we're thinking of someone in particular, the phone suddenly rings."

"That is spooky." Samantha picked up a fork and helped herself to another bite of pie. "Do you think entanglement could explain love at first sight?"

"Hmm…" A glint of amused acknowledgment danced in Gwen's eyes, as though she knew where this was leading, but she kept her tone academic. "Well, let's see. If you use entanglement to explain it, then love at first sight would really have to be love at *second* sight, wouldn't it? Two strangers who catch each other's eye at a party and feel an instant attraction would have to have been previously paired, intimately linked…perhaps in one of those past lives you've mentioned."

Samantha tried not to grin, but she couldn't help it. "In other words, what would seem a first meeting would really be a reunion, a moment of recognition between separated soul mates…or twin flames, as they're sometimes called."

"Exactly." Gwen rested her elbows on the table, coffee cup cradled in both hands, and peered at Samantha over the rim as if to gauge her reaction. "The other night, when you gave that analogy about your mother's soul being backed up on a cosmic flash drive…well, it got me to thinking about an article I wrote not long after Alley started appearing."

"On entanglement?"

"That and other concepts, like nonlocality and superposition, which means that once things are linked together in a quantum system they're able to exist in multiple states at the same time. I started wondering whether the force of a soul entering an earthly body at the speed of light causes it to somehow divide. Maybe one half enters us and the other remains in the other dimensions, feeling, experiencing, recording the events of its corporeal life."

"So what happens to the mortal self here on earth is happening to the eternal self somewhere else." Samantha considered this. "I'd love to read your article."

"When we get back to the house I'll give you a copy of the journal in which it appeared. I think you'll recognize a lot of your own thoughts and ideas."

"Do you think you and Alley are entangled?"

"On a fundamental level I think we're all entangled. And if there's a God, then we're entangled with our creator, no? How else is it possible to pray and be heard?"

"Wow, that takes wireless communication to a whole new level… or would that be wireless *communion*?"

"Ha. That's funny, Sam. Wireless communion it is. But bottom line, as much as classical physics deals with certainties and predictabilities in the universe, quantum physics deals with probabilities and possibilities. And the possibilities are absolutely mind-blowing."

"My mind *is* blown." Samantha licked whipped cream off her lip and smiled. "Thank you for agreeing to have lunch with me. I enjoy your company…and our conversations. They're as rich as this key lime pie," Samantha said and finished the last bite.

"Ditto." Gwen smiled just a little and hesitated before she spoke again. "Do you have plans for the Fourth of July?"

"It's this weekend already, isn't it? I totally lose track of days when I'm writing."

"If you're free, I have two tickets to a Saturday-night performance at Jacob's Pillow."

"What's that?"

"One of the oldest internationally acclaimed dance festivals in the country. It's just a few miles from here. If you'd like to join me, we can have dinner on the grounds, under the tent. I'll make reservations."

"I'd like that."

"And you know the guest room is always there for you, Sam, so think about spending the night. We can stay up late, watching the stars and pondering the probabilities and possibilities of the universe."

Samantha saw her opportunity and dared to take it. "And when we're finished with that…can we discuss the probability and possibility of us?"

Gwen was about to finish her coffee when she put her cup back down and sighed. "Sam, I'm going to be honest," she said, a wistfulness washing over her face. "One evening just last week, I was relaxing with music and a magazine when the phone rang—an out-of-the-blue call from some mystery writer looking to marry off her bookend—and I haven't been the same since." She reached across the table, smiling affectionately as she covered Samantha's hand with her own. "I felt an instant chemistry over the phone, as crazy as that might sound, and when I laid eyes on you, the physical attraction was immediate. But I'm content with my life and not looking to complicate it."

"Is that what I am, a complication?"

"A surprisingly wonderful and deeply tempting complication that's had me walking around in a deliciously delirious fog these past few days."

"I've been walking around in the same fog. That must have been you I bumped into." Samantha took Gwen's hand and ran a thumb back and forth across her palm.

"I love reading your books, Sam. And I love being with you. You make me laugh and wonder and look up words I don't know." She slid her hand up to Samantha's wrist and squeezed it. "If I were ten years younger, or you ten years older, I could fall madly in love with you. But an age difference of over twelve years is a big issue. For me it is. I do, however, look forward to what promises to be a very dear and lasting friendship."

Samantha didn't hear most of what Gwen said. Her brain didn't pay attention to the part about issues, age differences, or friendship. All that registered was, *I could fall madly in love with you.* That's all she needed to hear. She'd met her soul mate, her twin flame. They were entangled. Samantha was sure of it. Now she just needed to figure out a way to turn a probability into a predictability, a possibility into a certainty.

CHAPTER EIGHTEEN

Isabel was sitting on the porch steps with her duffel bag and the two dogs when Liz arrived at seven on Friday morning. In long shorts, sneakers, and a hoodie, she looked like a kid waiting for the bus to take her to summer camp. Liz still couldn't believe Isabel had agreed to come. It stirred in her the excitement of a hunter who'd captured its prey, but instead of eating this one she'd be keeping her as a pet.

Liz rolled down the window of the van, lowered her sunglasses, and looked at Isabel over them. "Good morning, darlin'. You ready to rock and roll?" she asked with a big grin.

It seemed Isabel would have preferred to rock and roll herself right back into the house, but she stood her ground. "Ready," she said.

The dogs watched expectantly, their faces lighting with recognition as Liz got out, stuffing something into the pocket of her skinny jeans, and crouched to give them an exuberant greeting. "Hi, babies!" she called out. Blue rushed off the porch, clearly overjoyed to see her again. Loosey Goosey followed in close pursuit, her rump wiggling in rhythm with the stump of her docked tail. "I have a comforter for them to lie on," she said as Isabel carried her duffel bag down the steps. "You can arrange things any way you want." And then she stood and looked at Isabel. "Is Gwen asleep?"

"I think so. Why, would you like me to make coffee?"

"No. I had a venti vanilla latte from Starbucks over two hours ago. I really need to pee." She smiled crookedly. "Would you be able to get me a pen and paper and let me into the cottage?"

"Of course!" Isabel's eyes wandered down to the bulge near the crotch of Liz's pants.

Liz caught the concern on her face. She looked down at herself and laughed. "Don't worry, Isabel. I'm not packing." She pulled it out and held it up. "See? It's a tape measure. I need to take some measurements in there."

"Sure." Isabel nodded. I'll get the key."

When Liz came back out, Isabel led her quietly past Rosa's cottage and unlocked the door of the vacant one. It was empty except for a sawhorse and power tools scattered on a floor that had been taken down to the substrate. The dogs pushed past them to sniff and explore the large room.

Morning sun poured in from a skylight, drawing Liz's eyes to the unfinished wood on the cathedral ceiling. "New pine planks?"

"Some had to come down because of a leak in the old roof, so we replaced them all."

"Nice." They stood side by side, their soft voices echoing in the hollow space. "What are you going to do to them?" Liz asked.

"Whatever you think."

"Really?"

"You have free rein."

"Oh, goody!" She stared up at them. "Let's have them whitewashed." She looked at the rustic stone fireplace on the far-right wall. "Wood-burning?"

"Yes."

"Those stones are beautiful. What's the square footage in here, around four hundred?"

"About that. And then there's the bathroom and bedroom." Isabel pointed to closed double doors to the left of the kitchen.

"Maybe we could get rid of those solid doors and put in a sliding barn-wood door with some nice rustic hardware."

Isabel's eyes lit up. "That's a great idea. I love those doors."

Liz ran to the bathroom and, when she came out, stopped in the kitchen to inspect the new granite counter and bar. "Four stools here," she said, making mental notes to herself, then smoothed her hand across the white stone with specks and blotches of black and gray. "Beautiful," she said. "What about the floor?"

"Rosa's boyfriend, Eugene, has a flooring business. He was here last week. We were thinking oak with a walnut stain."

"With this gray stone fireplace and beautiful granite?" Liz frowned and shook her head. "Call and tell him to hold off. I'm picturing a driftwood-gray finish like we discussed, something wide-planked with a nice matte aesthetic. Eugene can install it. If you want to meet me in the city I can take you to see—"

"It's not necessary. I love everything you're describing."

"Do you have a budget?" Liz asked.

"No."

Silly question, Liz thought. "Well then, if you'll trust my taste I can order flooring pre-finished from an ecofriendly company I use. They make nice hardwoods with a quality birch core, all manufactured from sustainably sourced wood, which I would think is important to you."

"Absolutely. Do it."

Turning in a circle to look at everything, Liz clasped her hands and held them to her chest. "I'm so excited about decorating. It's a great space with great energy. And it's going to be beautiful!" She stopping turning when she caught Isabel staring at her. She detected something she hadn't seen in those golden-brown eyes before. A glint of admiration, a hint of curiosity, a speck of desire, if she wasn't mistaken.

Caught staring, Isabel quickly looked away and tucked a strand of dark hair behind her ear, something Liz noticed Isabel doing whenever she felt suddenly shy. It made her want to gently back Isabel up against the wall and kiss her right there. Instead, she got busy taking measurements, calling them out for Isabel to jot down.

Ten minutes later they were on the road, taking Route 102 a few miles to the Massachusetts Turnpike, and it wasn't until they reached the toll booth that Liz finally asked, "So? Have you figured out where Paris is?"

"Well, when you invited the dogs, I knew we weren't going to France." Isabel glanced at her with a smirk. "So, I looked up towns named Paris in the United States. Did you know there are twenty-three?"

Liz laughed. "I did not know that."

The only ones close enough to reach in an afternoon are in Connecticut and New York, but since you said summer nights get really cold, I figured we'd be heading farther north. That would put us in Oxford County, Maine. So my answer is Maine. Final answer."

"Ha! Maine it is." Liz laughed at herself for thinking she could keep their destination a surprise. "I should have known I couldn't fool you, but don't think you're too slick, Ms. Laraway. I still might have a surprise in store for you."

An hour later they stopped at a rest area and ate breakfast in the car. Isabel had already fed the dogs, but they enjoyed a few bites along with some treats Liz had bought for them. And then they were on their way again, listening to music and talking about New England as they drove through Massachusetts and New Hampshire.

"I've always wanted to go to Salem," Liz said.

"You need to book well in advance if you want to go near Halloween."

"You've been there?"

"Yeah, but I'd go again," Isabel said, as if offering to accompany her.

"How about the Cape? Have you ever been to Provincetown?"

"Many times. Growing up, I spent the month of July there almost every summer. Gwen and Jean, my aunt's ex, always rented a house on the bay…until they separated."

"That must have been like going through a divorce."

"It was. Jean was family."

It was so strange that Isabel had grown up with two lesbians, exposed to gay men and women and the LGBT community. She knew all about Commercial Street and its restaurants, all about the comedy and drag shows. She talked about Gwen always attending book signings at Womancraft, about being on the beach at Herring Cove with their dog, Alley, about spending time along Whale's Wharf while Gwen and Jean went to tea dances at the Boat Slip.

Yet Isabel seemed so sheltered, so out of touch, as though she didn't know where she belonged in all of it. She was a paradox, unless Liz's gaydar had developed a serious glitch. Who knew, maybe Isabel really was straight. Maybe she just had a low sex drive, little desire for romance, and preferred to focus on the family business and her many other interests. "Do you keep in touch with Jean?"

"I used to spend a weekend with her every so often, but considering she left my aunt for one of her graduate students, it was awkward. Especially after they moved in together."

"I can understand that." Liz looked over at her. "What's Gwen doing this weekend?"

"She has tickets for a performance at Jacob's Pillow. I'm sure Sam's going with her."

"What makes you so sure?"

Isabel shrugged. "It sounded like they had a date. I can tell my aunt likes Sam."

"Did you ask her?"

"No. I would never do that."

Isabel had such rigid boundaries. "So what makes you think she's crushing on Sam?"

"She's just been acting strange…different."

"How so?"

"I don't know." Isabel shrugged again. "She's been reading Sam's books a lot. The other day she went clothes shopping with a friend. And then she went for a manicure and pedicure, something she hasn't done in a long time. She's been walking a lot, too. She often takes Blue for a stroll down the road before dinner, but this past week she's been doing a mile or more, and Blue has been coming back exhausted."

Liz acted nonchalant, but inside she was screaming with excitement. Maybe Sam was about to get lucky after all. New clothes? An increased interest in one's own appearance? Yep, definitely a telltale sign of a budding romance.

The long trip seemed to go faster than it usually did. After they'd crossed the bridge into Maine and reached Portland, Liz pulled into the first gas station she saw, but her back tire missed the entrance and jumped the curb with a bang that startled everyone in the van. "Whoa! Sorry, girls."

Isabel flinched, then looked over at Liz and in a very calm voice said, "Would you like for me to retrieve your muffler while you're pumping gas, or would you rather leave it here and pick it up on the way home?"

"Ha! You're very funny, you know that?" Laughing, she popped open the gas tank and got out. "I'll be right back."

Smiling, Liz leaned against the van as she pumped gas. They were here. Another forty-five miles inland and they'd be in South Paris. Maybe their next trip would be to Salem in the fall, or perhaps Provincetown for Women's Week, if Liz got her way. Amazing. For the first time in her life she found herself making plans with a woman—*wanting* to make plans—and imagining a ton of things she'd like to do with Isabel.

❖

Craig Bowes stood outside watering flowers, a big black Lab lying beside him in the grass when they pulled in. He was handsome, in his early fifties, the male version of Liz. In tight jeans and a form-fitting shirt with the sleeves rolled up, he looked trim and muscular—the kind of guy who stays in shape working for a living. His thick, wavy hair was rusty red, like his daughter's, and it was easy to imagine that in his youth, he'd lived for adventure, especially if it came in the form of pretty women and fast cars. He dropped the hose and walked toward them.

"Hi, Dad!"

"Hey, sweetheart!" he called, the black dog rushing ahead of him.

"Zoe!" Liz grabbed the dog's snout and planted a kiss smack on her lips. "How's my sister from another mister, huh? I've missed you so much!"

"And I get sloppy seconds, huh?" Craig said. "You're supposed to kiss your father before you kiss the dog!" He gave her a kiss and a big squeeze, then turned to Isabel. "Is this the young lady who likes muscle cars?" He shook her hand and kissed her cheek just as his wife's voice called out.

"Are they here already?" In denim shorts and a black tank top, Liz's mother, tanned, with dark hair in a ponytail, came out of the restored farmhouse. Blue eyes aside, her coloring was such that people would have thought she was Isabel's mother, not Liz's. "Where's that Scottie?" she said as soon as she'd kissed Liz and given both of Isabel's hands an affectionate squeeze.

"Dad, do you think Zoe will be all right if I let the dogs out?" Liz asked.

"You know she doesn't have a mean bone in her body. If they don't like her I'll lock her up."

But the dogs were happy to get out. Nose-to-nose, nose-to-butt, they made their introductions, and then Zoe's attention shifted back to Liz and Isabel.

When Gina saw Blue, she put her hands together and pressed them to her lips. "Oh my God, Craig. Look at the Scottie! I've heard all about you, Blue. You, too, Loosey Goosey!"

Blue was pleasant and wagged her tail, which made Liz wonder why Samantha turned the dog off so much.

"Aww...she's beautiful," Craig said as Isabel ducked into the van and came out with two bottles. She handed them to Gina. "From a winery in the Berkshires."

"White wine? You must have read my mind, Isabel. We're having fish, and I was sure I had a bottle of white in the house. I must have seen it at the cabin, though, and I didn't have time to run to the liquor store.

"Honey?" she said to Liz's dad. "Would you take these so I can help Isabel with the dogs?" Gina handed over the wine and grabbed their leashes, talking baby talk while letting them relieve themselves, then led them in the house.

The decor in the old farmhouse had a contemporary flair but kept in style with the architecture. "I love your home," Isabel said, glancing around at low-beam ceilings and a cast-iron stove. Craig had built a lighted showcase for Gina's collection of vintage glass. It covered almost an entire wall, and Isabel was immediately drawn to it.

"Why, thank you. It helps having an interior designer in the family." Gina took her daughter's face in one hand and squeezed it before going in the kitchen and coming back with fresh-squeezed lemonade for Craig and Isabel. "Have a look around while Liz helps me for a minute," she said to Isabel and took Liz by the hand.

When they were in the kitchen and out of earshot, Gina whispered to her. "She's very pretty. I like her. She's like us."

"Like us?"

"You know, she likes Scotties and she's also a collector."

Liz smiled. "Yeah. I'd like to collect *her*."

"I assumed you were dating."

"Not yet. I'd like to take it in that direction, but we're friends for now," Liz said and went on to give her mother the short version of how she and Sam had just recently met Isabel and Gwen.

Her mother opened the oven and put the haddock in to broil. "You've known her less than two weeks and brought her to meet your parents? That's a first." She searched her face with a knowing smile. "I think you've already fallen for her. Something's different about you, Liz. You seem…settled, more centered."

That meant she was generally uncentered and unsettled. This was the part where a conversation with her mother could easily turn into a quiet argument. Settled and centered implied that Liz didn't seem her usual all-over-the-place self, that her attention was focused. Liz let it go, because Isabel did make her feel settled. She hadn't been to a bar in over a week, hadn't felt the usual itch to go out dancing or meet new women over drinks after work. She hadn't even answered texts from the friends with benefits she occasionally bedded, like Skyler or Taylor. Somehow, she preferred Isabel's company, even if it didn't involve sex.

Liz looked at the six ears of corn on the counter. "Want me to husk these?"

"No. I've learned a better way to cook corn. It's amazing. Leave the husk. Just cut an inch off the bottoms. Four minutes in the microwave and the husk and silk will slip right off."

"Yeah?" Liz took a knife and did as her mother said.

"And let's get all the dogs fed before we sit down to…will you listen to them talking in there? I can tell your father likes her because he hasn't shut up. I hope he doesn't spoil your surprise."

They stopped to eavesdrop for a minute, and Liz peeked through the kitchen doorway to watch Isabel and Craig talking about vintage muscle cars. Liz had never seen Isabel so animated. But just as Liz ducked back into the kitchen she heard a noise, and her father shouted, "Gina, quick! We got a spill!"

Gina rolled her eyes. "That's code for *Zoe's tail knocked over a glass.*" She grabbed a roll of paper towels and rushed inside.

There was Zoe, sandwiched between Isabel's legs and the coffee table.

"I'm so sorry," Isabel said, reaching over the dog's back to pick up the glass, a magazine, and a small vase of wildflowers so Craig could sop up the mess.

"Don't you dare apologize for this dog," he said, pretending to be angry. "We've lost count of the glasses and beer bottles that tail has knocked over."

"She can't help it," Liz said. She took the empty glass into the kitchen and came back with a fresh one for Isabel and a sponge for her mother.

Gina and Craig wiped and dried the table while Zoe watched, wagging her tail like it had all been a big joke, until Craig straddled the dog and grabbed her tail. "You see this tail, Isabel? Guess how long?"

"Geez. I don't know." She laughed. "Over a foot, I'd say."

"Eighteen inches." He wagged it in his hand. "As thick and strong as a bat." He let go of it and pointed a finger in her face. "One more time, and chop-chop," he warned the dog. "I'm gonna make a nice soup with this tail."

Liz laughed. "Faux oxtail soup?"

"Oh, stop." Gina waved a hand at her husband. "He's always threatening to cook her tail. He doesn't even have it in him to get mad at that dopey dog."

When they were ready to sit, Craig opened the bottles of white wine Gina had chilled and set them on the farm table that could comfortably seat ten people. Isabel admired the barn-wood candelabra with Edison bulbs hanging down and complimented the cook once they'd started eating.

"So," Gina said, "Liz tells us your family is in the paper business?"

"Yes. Laraway Paper."

"Laraway..." She stopped eating, making a sudden connection. "Laraway! Oh my God, that's the copier paper I buy at the office supply store. We've got it right here in the house. No wonder your name sounded familiar when Liz told me."

"Wow. It's sort of like having a celebrity here, huh?" Craig smiled at Isabel. "I don't know how much you know about Maine, but the state has a logging history that goes back over two hundred years," he said. "It's one of the most forested states in the country right now."

Isabel nodded. "You've got about twelve million acres of softwoods up north and most of your hardwoods down here in the southern parts of the state. Over ninety percent is privately owned."

"You know more than I do. I guess you would." Craig was clearly impressed. "During the seventeen and eighteen hundreds most of those forests in central and southern Maine were cleared for farms, but eventually farming took a dip."

"And when farming declined your forests grew back," Isabel said. "Maine actually has more forests now than it did a hundred years ago. The state probably harvests over fifty thousand acres a year, but they no longer harvest trees faster than they can grow. No clear-cutting, like they used to do."

"That's what sustainability is all about, right?" Gina asked.

"It is," Isabel said. "The pulp and paper companies, along with those that make other cellulose-based products, comprise one of the largest industrial sectors in the world. And as you might imagine, the industry has the greatest impact on global forests." She put her fork down and drank her wine. "Fortunately, silviculture is quite advanced these days. In fact, the Laraways have pioneered some very important environmental technologies."

"Silviculture...that's like what, forestry?" Craig asked.

"More or less. It's basically the practice of achieving the most sustainable timber production while *protecting* water and wildlife," Isabel stressed. "Today we can grow more timber per acre than ever before in history, and at the same time do more than ever to improve the quality of habitats for fish and wildlife. Of course, wherever there's money to be made, you're going to find greedy and unscrupulous businessmen who'll exploit any resource to make a dollar. We're very careful about buying from private land owners."

Gina sat with an elbow on the table, her chin in her hand, obviously captivated by everything Isabel had to say. "How many reams of paper can you get from a tree?" she asked.

Isabel smiled. "It all depends. A forty-foot tree about six inches thick might produce sixteen reams on average."

"Yeah?" Craig said, as captivated as his wife. "From what kind of trees, pines?"

"Used to be pines, all softwoods, but with so many advances in pulp-processing technologies we can use just about any kind of wood these days."

"This is so fascinating," Gina said as she took the second bottle of wine and reached to fill everyone's glasses.

Liz put her hand over the top of hers. "None for me, Mom. I have to drive, and I want to get to the cabin before dark. I'm exhausted."

Craig winked at Liz and she nodded. "Speaking of driving," he said, "what plans do you ladies have for tomorrow?"

"I have a list. Three barn sales, two estate sales, and the two usual antique flea markets. I'm looking for clients, for the shop, and for the cottage I'm helping Isabel decorate. Whatever we don't get to tomorrow, we'll hit on Sunday."

"Gee, that's too bad. I was hoping Isabel might want to drive a stock car on the track."

Isabel, who had her glass to her lips, almost choked on her wine. She coughed and cleared her throat, staring between Craig and Liz like an expectant, wide-eyed kid.

"Aww…Dad, that's so nice of you, but we have our hearts set on shopping." She turned to Isabel. "Don't we?"

Isabel looked between them, decorum seeming to suppress her urge to blurt out her true desire.

Gina gave her daughter and husband a glance of reproach as she hand-fed the remaining piece of fish to the three dogs. "Enough, both of you. Stop teasing her."

Liz looked at Isabel across the table and grinned. "My dad knows the owners of a speedway not far from here. He's arranged for you to drive a stock car tomorrow," she announced, then coyly added, "if you want to."

Isabel couldn't even speak but nodded vigorously.

"Good. Then it's all set," said Craig with a smile as mischievous as Liz's. "How about I pick Isabel up at the cabin, say about eleven. That'll give you two time to wake up, relax, and have breakfast."

"We stocked the fridge for you yesterday," Gina said. "You've got bacon and eggs, bread, butter, milk, and a pound of coffee. There's plenty to drink, and whatever else you need you'll find in the pantry."

"We'll get over to the speedway by noon or so," Craig went on. "You'll need instruction first, so figure on being there for a few hours."

"Mom, why don't you drive to the cabin with Dad in the morning. You and I can take the van and do a run-through of half the places on my list, and the rest Isabel and I will hit on Sunday. That way we can get over to the speedway to watch Isabel."

"Sounds like a plan," Gina said. "And before it gets dark, why don't you take Isabel out back and pick some blueberries for pancakes this weekend? They're a week early this year for some reason. Have you ever had wild Maine blueberries, Isabel?"

"I don't think so."

"They're tiny, but sweet as sugar."

And they were. Liz pushed the first one she picked between Isabel's lips, and they ate a bunch more as they moved through the half-acre blueberry patch with the dogs. "Thank you for having your father do this for me," Isabel said. "I can't believe it. I'm so excited I don't know what to say."

"Excited? Oh, my God." Liz laughed. "Do you know what it was like holding it in on the ride up here? It took everything in me not to tell you."

They began losing light as they each filled a small basket of berries, and by the time they left and arrived in the tiny village of North Waterford it was dark. Liz turned on to a back road and headed west for another two miles. "The nice thing about Kezar Ponds," she said, "is that they're shaped sort of like an open hand, your fingers being land, with the water of the great pond running between them." She slowed down and turned into the long, narrow driveway of the cabin, the headlights shining on a painted sign nailed to a tree. It was white with a green frog and read: HAVE YOU BEEN INVITED? The floodlights clicked on, and a small log cabin came into view.

"Do the dogs like the water?"

"Blue could spend hours wading through lily pads looking for fish and frogs, but Loosey loves to swim."

"Then let's keep them leashed until morning, because the water is right behind the house, and it's really dark back there."

Isabel took care of the dogs while Liz got their bags out and unlocked a door that led into a small open kitchen. She flipped the light switches and then walked around the counter to turn on the lamps in the living room.

"My grandfather built this cabin in the fifties," Liz said. "It's not much, and it's only seasonal. No heat, except for this woodstove."

Liz followed Isabel's eyes as she took in the shabby-chic décor that gave the room a wonderfully cozy and bohemian feel. The vibrant colors of a braided rug added color to the dark split-log walls, and a paisley couch with red, yellow, and blue pillows was big enough for several people to sink into.

"It's perfect. And charming. Like something out of a storybook," Isabel mused.

Liz opened the sliding doors on the back wall. "Come see the porch," she said, and patted her thigh for the dogs to follow. They looked at Isabel for reassurance, then at each other as if to say, *this is so much fun, isn't it?* Finally, they followed Liz out to the screened porch, their noses lifting to the rich scents drifting in off the water. A table with benches sat at one end, two papasan chairs and lamps for reading at the other.

Liz turned on a yellow porch light and unlatched the wood-framed screen door that faced the water. Pushing the dogs away, Isabel stepped outside with her. The moon played on the water's rippled surface, its light just enough to outline two lounge chairs at the end of the dock and two kayaks resting on the sand of a small beach. Trees grew tall on either side of the cabin, casting a wall of darkness.

"It's wonderful," Isabel whispered. "I could spend the whole summer—" A haunting call similar to the melodic howl of a wolf sounded.

"Loons," Liz said. She looked at Isabel in the dark and smiled.

"I've never heard them in real life."

"That's the *wail*. They use it to call back and forth to their mates. The males also yodel and hoot. And if you hear something that sounds like a crazy woman laughing, that's the tremolo. It means they're advertising and defending their territory."

A tremolo took Isabel by surprise just then. "Oh, wow…" She stared at Liz and laughed softly. "If you hadn't just told me, I would have thought a witch was cackling and run back into the house."

They stood in silence for a few more minutes, the vocalizations and the chilly air raising the hair on their arms until Liz started to shiver. She felt the heat coming off Isabel's body and wanted to wrap hers around her, but she didn't. She sighed, a happy sigh, thrilled just to have this woman standing beside her. She folded her arms and listened to the soul-stirring wails and tremolos echoing in the darkness. And as they stood shoulder to shoulder, it occurred to Liz that somewhere along the way between Massachusetts and Maine, she had fallen in love with Isabel.

Chapter Nineteen

The last person Gwen wanted to be bothered by today was her brother. It was two o'clock, and she expected Sam soon. Dinner reservations weren't until six, but Sam wanted time with Bertha.

Gwen had already showered, dried her hair, and fixed her face, but decided not to dress. In shorts and a tank top, she'd grabbed her clippers and wandered out to the gardens behind the house to check on the vegetables, cut flowers for a vase, and pick mint for the sweet tea she'd just brewed. She let her thoughts wander while she worked, entertaining fine and private fantasies of Samantha Weller, until the sound of tires on gravel interrupted her daydreams.

She peeked around, expecting Sam to have arrived, but here came Bill's silver BMW, pulling up alongside Eugene's red pickup that had been parked there all night. Rosa had met him in church two years ago, and ever since, the two had spent the weekends committing ungodly acts.

No doubt Gwen's brother was passing by on business and wouldn't stay long, but today his visit seemed an intolerable intrusion. Clippers in one hand, mint and flowers in the other, she started around to the front of the house, coming to a halt when she saw him get out, leave the car door open, and dart for Rosa's cottage. Gwen ducked behind a fig tree and watched as Rosa opened the door before he even knocked and quickly pulled him inside.

Her birthday. They were probably making secret plans for her sixtieth birthday next weekend—most likely a dinner party at a restaurant with family and a few close friends. And, of course, Gwen would do her best to feign surprise and thank them all for attending.

What she really wanted for her birthday was a time machine, a magical clock to turn back the years—turn back *her* years, not Sam's.

Gwen sighed. No sense wishing for the impossible, and really, aside from the fact that she had secretly fallen for a woman twelve years her junior, she couldn't complain. She was healthy, a breast-cancer survivor, and thanks to good genes and moderate exercise, she had a body that many younger women would envy—except for the scar beneath her breast, which was really no worse than scars women had from breast enhancements. All in all, and despite that fact that over time the body had a way of reorganizing, redistributing itself, she was in good shape for almost sixty, good enough that she could still dance for days and whup Isabel's butt on the tennis court. On a good day at least. Gwen could still hear her father's optimistic voice: *Aging may not be the most delightful of experiences, but always remember, Gwenie, that every day above ground is a good one.*

She hurried along the side of the house, creeping past the empty cottage, sneaking past Rosa's, then ran up the porch steps and into the house. When she heard his car door slam, she pretended to be just coming out with a pitcher of mint-filled tea. "Bill!" She set the pitcher next to a tray of glasses on the table. "I wasn't expecting you."

"Hey, Gwen." He came up the steps in a navy-blue suit and white shirt with no tie, a briefcase in his hand. He was a tall, burly man with Gwen's blue eyes and blond hair.

Three years younger than his sister, he was often mistaken for the older sibling, decades of boating and water sports having given him a permanent tan and the weathered good looks of a sea captain. It was funny how sun damage, battle scars, a wooden leg or missing hand like Captain Hook's could strangely enhance a man's rugged sex appeal. But not a woman's. The manmade rules of human aesthetics favored only the gender that made them.

"Sweet tea?" Gwen needed to stop thinking of her birthday and getting older before she depressed herself.

"That'd be great." He took off and hung his jacket on the back of his chair before he sat. "I'm just getting back from that meeting with Kyle Richards in Boston yesterday." He retrieved a folder from his briefcase as he updated her in his usual meticulous and verbose manner, but Gwen wasn't paying attention. "You'll need to read through all this and sign the last three pages," he said and handed her the folder. "I would have sent them home with Isabel, but I understand she's away."

"She is." Gwen opened the folder, took one look, and closed it. "Bill, I can't do this today. I'm pressed for time. I have a dinner date and tickets for the Pillow."

"A date? With the writer?"

"Ah, so Isabel told you. Funny how the little snitch never mentions a word about her personal life but likes to advertise mine."

"She only mentioned that a popular mystery writer had come to the house for a piece of Rookwood, and that the two of you had become fast friends, and," he stopped and looked around the porch, "and that the writer's pet crow was staying here with you."

"Well, then, she's told you everything there is to tell."

He drank from his glass, gagging as he swallowed and coughing up a mint leaf. He picked it off his tongue. "For Christ's sake, Gwen. Why do you put plants in your tea?"

Gwen frowned and didn't bother to answer. She patted the folder. "I'll read through all this tomorrow and send it back with Isabel on Tuesday."

He nodded. "She never mentioned where she was going. The secretaries said she'd be away and that I should run her Monday morning meeting." He looked at Gwen sideways. "What's Isabel up to? It's not like her to go off alone like that."

"She's not alone. And I'd advise you to prepare yourself for a possible romance brewing."

Bill's eyes bulged. "What?" He leaned back in his chair, his expression a mixture of joy and shocked disbelief. "You're kidding me. Who is it?"

"A worthy suitor, in my estimation. I don't have time to go into detail right now, but it's someone I approve of, and so should you...*if* and when the time comes."

Bill gave a husky laugh. "At this point I think we'd approve of just about anyone who is stable and loves her, wouldn't we?"

"Can I have that in writing?"

"Why?" He looked at her askance. "Who is this fellow, anyway?"

"The fellow's a lady, the sister in-law of the writer. Her name is Liz Bowes. She's an interior designer and antique dealer with a business in Manhattan. She's bright, charming, and miraculously—I stress *miraculously*—she's managed to pull Isabel out of her shell."

Bill didn't look so happy anymore. "Oh, come on. Isabel isn't gay!" He waved a hand, dismissing the thought. "You don't know what you're talking about."

"Oh, I think I do, Bill."

"Nonsense. She's just...you know, slow to mature."

"Slow to mature? She's twenty-eight." Bill was in denial. The more Gwen pushed him on the subject, the more agitated he became. She kept her naturally authoritative voice gentle but firm. "Bill…how often do you tell me about young and eligible businessmen approaching Isabel after meetings, trying to strike up a conversation and ask her out?"

"All the time. All the young men like Isabel."

"But she doesn't like them. Isn't it you who always says that those men are all but invisible to her?"

Bill bent forward, his arms braced against the table like a bulldog. He balled one hand in a fist, the fingers of the other drumming to a beat only he could hear. "I just want her to have a happy, normal life."

Gwen flushed. "What's *not* normal is the fact that your twenty-eight-year-old daughter has never had a romantic relationship, not a single date her whole adult life! *That's* not normal. And it's not because young men don't ask her out. It's because she declines." Gwen paused, pacing her words, keeping her tone even. "And since when does my brother speak of being gay as not being *normal*?"

"Jesus, Gwen. That's not want I meant." He raked a hand through his hair, tried to drink his tea again, but the pointy stem of a mint sprig poked him in the nose, causing both his nostrils and temper to flare. He reached in the glass, pulled out the whole clump, and tossed it over the porch railing like he was throwing a baseball. "You gotta stop with these damn weeds before you choke someone."

"It's only mint, Bill. Calm down. You look like you're about to have a stroke."

"Do I? Would you like me to? Because I feel like I just might." He wiped his hand on a napkin and then folded it and dabbed the sweat beginning to bead on his forehead.

Gwen rolled her eyes, an exaggerated roll that probably made her look as silly as she had when they had bickered as children. Something about her expression made him catch himself, and he finally acquiesced. He leaned back and took a deep breath, his cheeks puffing as he exhaled through tight lips. "All I meant by *normal* is that I…I just want her to have an *easy* life, you know? I want her to be accepted."

"Accepted?" Gwen raised her brow. "We're white Anglo-Saxon Protestants, Bill. We grew up in a high-status social group of other stuffy, nosy, and dreadfully boring white Anglo-Saxon Protestants. And what did you do? Straight out of college you went on a business trip to Brazil with our father and fell in love with a brown-skinned, Spanish-speaking Latina woman. The first time she flew here to visit, you took her to the yacht club, oblivious to the disapproving stares. And do you remember what you said when Mom told you people were whispering behind your back?"

Bill frowned. "I told her I didn't give a rat's ass."

Gwen gave a soft chuckle that made his face soften. "That's exactly what you said. And you married her. You were so in love, so proud to be her husband, so proud when she gave you Isabel. And if I'm not mistaken, your second marriage five years ago was to a biracial woman," she said, referring to her brother's current wife, Sheila, who was a shade darker than Isabel's mother. "So don't tell me that social acceptance has ever been high on your list of importance." She looked at him with stern tenderness. "You've always followed your heart, Bill. It's one of the things I admire about you. It's why you were the first person I came out to. You supported me and convinced Mom and Dad to do the same."

"Yeah, but..." He looked out into the lawn where two black crows were chasing a terrified cat. "I was hoping for a grandchild, you know. We need an heir."

"Well, thanks to modern science and the gradual social evolution of our species, gay people are marrying and having children. So don't give up on an heir yet."

Bill ran a hand over his face, scratched the back of his head, then finally held up his hands. They fell to his thighs with a slap. "All right...so when do I get to meet this woman who's interested my daughter the way no man has?"

The frantic *caw* of a crow sounded just then, and before Bill knew what was happening, Bertha swooped down and landed on the railing beside them. "Geez!" He put a hand to his chest and looked at the noisy bird.

Gwen laughed. "This is Bertha...the writer's crow."

"She almost gave me a heart attack. She looks more like a raven. She's huge, bigger than the ones you raised that time," he said, marveling over the excited crow.

Bertha looked at Bill, then turned to Gwen and shouted her caws as if trying to communicate some important news the way she did in Sam's stories. "Bertha, honey! What is it?"

Bertha didn't have time to play charades. She turned around, looked back as if to say *follow me*, then swooped and took off at top speed toward the driveway.

"Wow," said Bill. "Look at her go."

They watched her fly until she rounded the bend of white birch trees and disappeared from sight. Bill's cell phone rang just then, and he reached into his jacket pocket. "It's probably Sheila expecting me home by now. I should have called from the car." Home was in the Hudson Valley, just a few miles over the New York line.

Curious to know where Bertha was going, Gwen left Bill to talk and went down the steps. She heard Bertha in the distance, then silence, and then the sound of gravel. A moment later Sam appeared in her black Range Rover, her window down and Bertha perched on the door. Gwen watched, amazed, as Sam pulled up alongside the silver BMW.

"I guess she still loves me." Sam smiled. "She was standing on your mailbox and flew out to meet me as I turned in from the road."

"She tried to tell me you were coming."

Bertha made garbled happy sounds as she tugged on Samantha's earrings, pecked at her shirt collar, her lips, tapped her teeth with her beak as Sam laughed and turned her head away. She got out with the crow perched on her wrist and hugged Gwen with her free arm.

Gwen inhaled her intoxicating scent. God, Sam looked so good in tight white jeans, a black shirt, and pointy gray booties. Still aroused from her garden fantasies, Gwen had a vision of taking her by the hand and leading her up to the bedroom. "You look nice," she said and was just complimenting her outfit when Bill approached from behind.

"You must be the writer," he said.

"Bill, this is Samantha Weller."

"A pleasure meeting you—and your crow." He extended a hand, and the two exchanged pleasantries until he glanced at his watch. "I better run. Sheila made dinner reservations."

Gwen winked at Sam. "I'll be right with you. There's tea on the porch. And if you want Bertha in the house with you tonight, take her in now. You won't see her later, otherwise. I haven't wanted to worry you about her whereabouts, but the last two nights she refused to come in." Gwen pointed to the other crow in the tree. "We tried to talk what's-his-name into coming inside for the night with her, but when he wouldn't, Bertha insisted on sleeping out here with him."

"It's okay if she wants to be with him," Samantha said. "I know she's falling for that rogue crow…and it's killing me, but," Samantha kissed Bertha on her cheek, "whatever makes her happy."

Samantha got her bag from the car while Gwen walked Bill around to his. Bertha was clearly thrilled to have her back. She hopped off Samantha's arm and flew to the porch railing, coaxing the other bird in her native tongue until he flew from the tree and came to land next to her. Gwen and Bill turned to watch as Bertha cawed at Samantha, as if to say, *look what I found, Sam—a crow like me!* Samantha had seen Bertha's gentleman caller at a distance the other day, but he'd been too wary to get this close.

Gwen turned back to the open arms of her brother and gave him a hug. "I love you, you know," she said.

"Yeah, me, too." He let go of her and got in his car. "She's pretty, by the way."

"Who?"

"The writer." He started the engine. "She reminds me of someone, but I can't think of who right now. She's a little younger than you, no?"

"Yes, but not as young as *your* wife."

He chuckled as he shut the car door and rolled down the window. "Good for you, big sister. It's about time someone turned your crank."

"No one's turning anyone's crank, Bill. We're just friends."

"Yeah, yeah, sure. I saw the way you looked at each other." He put the car in reverse and shot her a teasing grin as he backed up. "You better take Janis Joplin's advice and get it while you can, honey!" And before she could respond he rolled up the window.

Gwen shook her head as he drove away, then went to the porch to find Sam sitting and Bertha standing on the table facing her. Bertha's eyes were closed in ecstasy, her head drooping as Sam kissed and rubbed her lips back and forth against the soft feathers.

"Hold still," Gwen whispered and picked up her phone. "I want to get a picture." Sam froze for the camera, her lips on the crow's head, her hand resting along its back, and Gwen was instantly reminded of a painting. She took the picture, smiled at it, and turned her phone so Sam could see the screen. "Woman with a crow. Have you ever seen Picasso's painting by the same name?"

"Really?" Bertha nibbled at Sam's chin, and she resumed her petting and kissing. "Picasso painted a crow? Would that be a cubistic crow?"

"It was done shortly before he invented cubism," Gwen said, thinking she ought to have a framed print made for Sam, something large that she might hang on a wall over the desk where she wrote. "It was toward the end of his blue period. I believe the model was the daughter of the owner of a café that Picasso frequented, and she often sat there, having her morning coffee with her crow."

Gwen searched the internet as she spoke, bringing up an image of *Woman with a Crow*, and handed the phone to Sam.

"Oh, wow, this is wonderful! How did I not know about this painting?"

"I don't know why it didn't occur to me to mention it earlier. It just dawned on me when I saw you sitting here…looking like her."

Sam studied the woman for a long while. "I love how her long fingers on the crow's back are symmetrical with the wing. It's as if they're somehow biologically connected…related by nature, you know? It's so strange that she's beautiful, yet crow-like, and the crow almost human-like. They have the same profile."

Gwen had never examined the painting from that perspective. The oneness of woman and crow was astonishing, really, and watching the rich exchange of emotion between a crow and the woman here with her today was astonishingly beautiful.

Chapter Twenty

With half the van full from a successful furniture hunt, Liz and her mother reached the speedway just in time to see a blue-and-white Sprint Cup style car zooming around the track. Craig was sitting in front of the bleachers beside a younger man.

"Hey, guys," Gina called.

"Oh my God, Dad. Is that Isabel?"

"Yep. She's riding shotgun with Robert."

Rob was Craig's close friend and a professional driver. Liz had known him all her life. "How fast are they going?" she yelled from where she stood.

"Around a hundred and thirty. Maybe more. She'll drive next, with Rob coaching her through the two-way open-mic radio. You know the drill. You've driven with me," he said as Liz and Gina made their way down to them.

"Hey, gorgeous!" said the guy next to Craig.

Liz smiled, surprised to see him. "Hi, Brian."

"I was talking to your mother." He winked at Gina.

"Hey, slow your roll, cowboy," Craig warned him.

"Oh, so it's like that, huh?" Liz played along with Brian. He was in his thirties and had worked for Craig since graduating from high school. He'd also spent most of his twenties in love with Liz, until one day she had to set him straight. Unlike other assholes who would have insisted she just needed to be with the right guy, Brian respected that she was attracted only to women and had moved on.

He hugged her. "Eh, I guess you're sort of gorgeous, too, even if you do look like this one over here," he said, pointing a thumb at Craig.

"Uh-huh," said Craig. "And maybe I should tell them that you've been hitting on Isabel all morning." He looked at Gina and Liz. "Rob and I had to threaten to lock him in the trunk of a stock car if he didn't behave."

"Oh, really?" Liz still had Brian in an embrace when her father said this, and she slid a hand around to the back of his head, grabbed a handful of his long, blond hair, and pulled back just hard enough to make him squeal. "Keep your paws off my friend and be a gentleman. You hear me?"

"Okay, okay. Ouch!" He laughed, but when she let go, he quickly rubbed his scalp. "I didn't know she was taken."

"Well, now you do." She squeezed his cheeks in one hand. "So go find your own girl to marry before you lose those good looks of yours."

Liz settled next to her mother and watched as the race car rocketed flag to flag two more times. When it stopped, she ran down onto the track.

Isabel got out wearing a helmet and a zippered jumpsuit, and Liz shrieked with delight. "Oh my God, you are so fucking adorable."

"Hey, I heard that. Watch that mouth of yours." Gina scolded her from where she sat.

Liz laughed with delight as Isabel removed her helmet, her straight and shiny dark hair spilling out and falling into perfect place. "You really are fucking adorable," she repeated in a hushed voice only Isabel could hear.

Isabel grinned. "My jumpsuit's a little big, though."

"She's a beauty, isn't she?" Brian said, coming up from behind. And when Liz reached for his hair again he ducked out of arm's reach. "Hey. I'm talking about the car, I swear. We did the detailing."

Craig walked around the blue-and-white car, stroking it as if he were petting a live animal. "Yep, she's a beauty, all right. I was explaining to Isabel that this is a spec car," he said, "not your average stock car. Aside from slight variations in the body shape and engine, it's built to NASCAR specifications." He turned to Isabel with a big smile. "How was it?"

"Breathtaking! I mean, literally, we went so fast it almost took my breath away." She looked at everyone and then at Robert as he got out of the car. "That was so awesome, Rob!"

"Then let's get you in the driver's seat and get ready for more awesome," he said, coming around and taking off his helmet to kiss Liz hello. His short, stylish hair had turned completely white since she'd seen him last, and it made his blue eyes seem even bluer.

Isabel tugged Liz's arm. "Could you get my cell phone out of my jacket over there and record me?"

"I'm way ahead of you, sweetheart. I have my mom's video camera ready."

"I'll use the camera," Gina said. "You take Isabel's phone."

Rob waited until the filming crew was ready, then buckled Isabel in the driver's seat and checked her radio. "All right," he said as he put his own helmet back on and got into the passenger seat. "You ready to unleash six hundred horsepower on the track?"

Obviously overjoyed, Isabel gripped the steering wheel. "Ready!"

"Go get 'em, kiddo," Liz shouted as they all returned to the bleachers.

The shy, conservative, self-conscious Isabel was gone, and the new and improved Isabel was on fire, her adrenaline-fueled passion for racing stripping her reserve. And somewhere in all of it, Liz was convinced that one day she'd strip Isabel's latent passion for women as well.

Liz and her mother began filming as one of Rob's crew members gave the thumbs-up and the green flag flew. Isabel hit the pedal to the metal, and the V8 roared down the track.

Eight laps around the oval Magic Mile, and Isabel topped out at almost 120 mph. And while Isabel unleashed horsepower, Liz learned what it took to unleash Isabel. Most women she'd known needed only a drink to loosen them up; Isabel needed a ride in a race car.

When it was all over, Isabel was presented with a detailed lap-time sheet and printout of her top speed, and Craig thanked his good buddy for giving them this private time on the track.

"Next time," Rob said, "you'll share the track with other cars and get to experience some side-by-side racing."

Yeah, next time, Liz thought. Hopefully there would be many next times.

On the way back to the cabin, Gina rode with Liz so Isabel could ride with Craig in his vintage Dodge Charger. Liz drove behind him, following the car to a popular roadside clambake. Craig fought to pick up the tab, but Isabel absolutely insisted on treating them all to dinner. On a picnic table overlooking a lake, they feasted on clams, chowder, Maine lobster, and corn, and talked about cars, mostly. Liz was amazed at how much Isabel had learned about car mechanics in one afternoon: acceleration and braking, driving lines, track geography. And she asked Craig all about rally racing.

"It's one thing to be a circuit driver who's been around the same track a thousand times," he said, "and quite another to be a rally racer covering five to two hundred miles of unfamiliar terrain—old logging and forest roads, closed public roads, mountain passes—any surface in any kind of weather. And rally cars, mind you, have to be street-legal. Nothing like you drove today. Lots of Fords, Chevys, Mitsubishis, and Subarus, like the WRX I always use. And then there's your co-driver, who uses a route book and some computerized equipment to guide the driver by describing conditions and obstacles ahead—intersections, trees, cliffs, and so on. Can't win without a co-driver, and you might likely kill yourself without one. Rally racing is a team effort."

"I'd love to do that," Isabel said with conviction.

Liz and her mother looked at each other. They had been starving and were happy to eat while Isabel and Craig talked, but Gina had had enough. "Okay, you two, if I hear the word *car* one more time today, I'm going to shoot myself."

Liz laughed. "Isabel has discovered a new passion, so you know I'm going to hear it all night long."

"Listen, I don't know what you ladies have planned," Gina said as they finished eating, "but your father and I are going home to take care of Zoe, and then to watch fireworks at nine o'clock. You want to join us?"

"We have to get back to the dogs, too," Liz said. "We've left them for six hours, so I think we'll just hang out on the water and let them play."

Isabel couldn't thank Craig and Gina enough for her day at the track, and when they parted, Gina hugged and kissed her. "I have a hunch we'll be seeing more of you."

"I hope so," Isabel said.

On the way back to the cabin Liz made a quick stop at the liquor store for tequila and mixer, and another one at the general store for avocados and limes.

After the dogs were fed, Isabel took them out back to play ball and explore the sandy shore while Liz made margaritas and guacamole with chips, and carried everything out to a table between the two lounge chairs on the dock. And at Isabel's request, Liz went back for the bottle of tequila, shot glasses, a salt shaker, and two wedges of lime.

"Do you want a sweatshirt?" Liz called out to her.

"No, I'm okay," Isabel called backed back.

They had changed into shorts and T-shirts, but it was getting cool, and Liz threw on a hoodie.

Isabel had spread a beach towel on the dock and given the dogs rawhide bones. She watched Liz fill the shot glasses and get ready to suck a lime wedge. "You're doing it all wrong," Isabel said, an amused expression on her face.

"Am I?"

"Lick, slam, suck."

"Mmm..." Liz waggled her eyebrows. "I like it when you talk dirty."

"I'm not talking—" Isabel hesitated, seeming to grow self-conscious for the first time all day. "It's just the proper way to drink tequila, that's all. Make a fist," she said, and poured salt in the web of Liz's thumb. "Lick the salt, slam the shot, suck the lime."

Liz watched Isabel demonstrate and then copied her. "Mmm...so that's the order of things, huh? Works well."

"Most gringos suck the lime first."

"Ha! Well, this gringo is happy to follow your lead."

Isabel tasted her drink and looked at her. "You do make a perfect margarita, though. And your guacamole is outstanding."

"Why, thank you." Liz relaxed in her lounge chair as Isabel took her glass and walked to the edge of the dock. Across the water, beyond the line of evergreens and between the tall silver trunks of beech trees, the summer sun leaked its fiery palette of pink, rose, and golden yellow into the pre-dusk sky. Liz had witnessed a thousand sunsets from this very spot, but now it was the sight of Isabel against those brilliant streaks of color that captured her attention.

Isabel put her free hand on her hip and stared out at the landscape. Evidently the adrenaline rush from racing had her still too pumped to sit still. "Driving today was so incredible," she said, her back to Liz.

Isabel's *body* was incredible. Liz let her eyes graze over it, taking in the soft outline of muscles in her bare arms, the light golden-brown skin of those lean and shapely legs. As the tequila kicked in, Liz started feeling frisky. She wanted to come up from behind, run her hands over Isabel's tight little ass, wrap her hands around her waist. *Lick, suck...* she'd drink Isabel like a shot of tequila. She imagined taking her into the shower...then into the bedroom. Maybe she'd gently tie Isabel's wrists to the headboard, just tight enough to secure them and make her squirm with anticipation. She pictured herself between Isabel's legs, pushing them wide apart, and not letting her close them until Isabel came in her—

"I love your parents," Isabel said.

"Huh?" Liz said, although the word came out sounding more like a moan. Her shorts felt suddenly tight, and she pulled at the crotch, reached for her drink, trying to shake off her arousal.

"Your parents." Isabel turned around. "They're so wonderful." The tequila seemed to be relaxing her, and she stretched out in a lounge chair beside Liz. "Your mom's beautiful, and your dad's very handsome. You look just like him."

"If that's a third-person compliment, I'll take it."

"If you want a direct compliment," she said shyly, and without looking over at Liz, "you're as pretty as he is handsome."

Pretty enough to kiss? Liz wanted to ask. But she didn't. The last thing she needed was Isabel thinking Liz had brought her here to seduce her. Isabel would feel trapped. She'd probably want to go home, and the rest of the weekend would be uncomfortable for both of them. Liz would behave and do what she'd never done before, which was to get to know a woman before she slept with her. And really, she wanted to know what made Isabel tick, wanted to know all about her—past, present, plans for the future. "What about your parents? I understand you work with your father…and that you lost your mother long ago."

Isabel poured them another shot of tequila. "I did. I was four when she died in a plane crash."

"Four is very young. Do you remember her?"

"I'm not sure. I know that sounds terrible, but I really don't know. I have pictures, scenes in my head…but I don't know how many are actual memories. My mother was a photographer. She took hundreds of photographs of all of us, herself included. So sometimes I wonder if my mind has created false memories from constantly looking at photo albums throughout my childhood. I do remember her perfume, though." She looked over at Liz. "Did you know that human infants recognize their mothers by their smell? It's how most animals forge immediate ties with their mothers…maybe with the exception of birds, who have a pretty poor olfactory sense."

"That's so interesting," Liz said, zippering her hoodie and stuffing her hands into the pockets. "So how would you describe your mother's scent?"

"Like sunshine and orange blossoms and spice. I'd have to ask my father the name of the fragrance she wore. He kept that last bottle for a long time. Sometimes, when I was little, I'd walk into his room at night and catch him spraying it on his wrist and holding it to his nose. He'd just say he missed her and would let me smell, too. I'm not sure what he did with that bottle, but knowing my father, he still has it."

"He never remarried?"

"He *is* married. He didn't date again until I finished high school, or at least not that I knew of. Years later my aunt told me that he was adamant about not bringing women to the house for fear that I'd think he was betraying my mother or putting another woman before me. So, I had my father and I had Gwen. And Jean, Gwen's girlfriend, too. Gwen's really been a mother to me." Isabel stopped to pour them both another shot and sat back again. "And then when I was first in college he met Shelia, the art director of the advertising agency that handled the Laraway account. They married while I was in the MBA program at NYU, and now they live in the Hudson Valley near our corporate office. Sheila's a very nice person, very sincere. She makes my father happy, and she's always treated me well."

Liz was so glad that Isabel, perhaps under the influence of tequila, was opening up about her personal life. "Well, I'm sure that through it all, your mother has been with you in spirit."

"I don't think so," Isabel said as they watched two black-and-white loons quietly swimming and diving for fish, too far from shore to see their red eyes.

"No?" Liz asked.

"No. I know people like to talk themselves into believing their departed loved ones are with them in spirit, protecting and watching over them like angels. It's a nice sentiment, I suppose, but I've never once felt my mother's presence. One day she was here with me, the next day she was gone. I've never felt anything but her absence."

Liz's heart broke for the little girl who had lost her mother, and she wished Isabel would come to her and sit between her legs so she could just wrap her arms around her.

Isabel turned and faced her then, but Liz could hardly see her in the fading light. The dogs had finished their bones and treats, and Loosey was fast asleep on the beach towel, but Blue was still awake, sitting near the edge of the dock, staring at the water and the distant loons.

"What do you imagine Blue thinks about?" Liz asked.

"Hard to say. She stares off into space a lot, sometimes for hours. I'm never sure if she's caught up in philosophical meditations or meditative stupors."

Liz laughed and checked her watch. It was nine o'clock, and the temperature was quickly dropping as fast as the light was fading, a thick, swirling fog forming over the water and obliterating their view of the loons.

"Holy smoke!" Isabel said. "When did that fog roll in? It wasn't there a minute ago."

"That's what happens when the temperature drops so fast and the water is warmer than the air. I told you it gets cold up here at night. Believe it or not, campers, hikers, and even elderly people who wander off can suffer from hypothermia in Maine, even in summer."

"Wow…it's really spooky. I love the gloaming, here especially."

"The gloaming?"

Isabel nodded. "Twilight." And then she sat and pointed at the bats flying low over the water, flitting in and out of the fog, searching for a mosquito dinner.

Some people would have thought the sight before them looked like a scene from a horror movie, and it did, but Isabel was enchanted. And so was Liz. But she was freezing, too. "Time to go inside, Isabel. I'm cold. I don't know how you can sit out here without a hoodie."

"I'm starting to feel it now."

They carried everything back inside, grabbed a flashlight, and took the dogs for a quick walk around the front of the cabin. On the way back in, Liz checked the outdoor thermometer. Fifty-two degrees.

Liz took a shower first, and while Isabel was in there, Liz got out extra blankets and left one on a chair in Isabel's room. The dogs had already jumped up on the bed, both of them as excited as little kids to be staying in a cabin in the woods. But when Isabel came out of the bathroom in a nightshirt, she quickly apologized and tried to call them off the bed.

Liz stopped her. "Where do they sleep at home?"

"With me," said Isabel.

"Then leave them be. They're my guests, and I won't have them sleeping on the hard floor." She turned back to the dogs. "Isn't that right, you sweet little babies?" They looked at each other and then at Liz, their eyes twinkling in wholehearted agreement as they rolled onto their backs for the belly rubs Liz proceeded to give them.

"Would you like some hot tea or something else to eat?" Liz asked.

"No, nothing for me. But thank you."

Liz said good night, made herself a cup of herbal tea, and took it into her bedroom. But even a hot shower and hot tea couldn't warm her up. It had been a long day after a long drive yesterday, and all the tequila they'd had should have knocked her out, but she was too cold to fall asleep. She lay awake, rubbing her feet on the sheets to warm them until she couldn't stand it anymore and called out, "Are you all asleep in there?"

"We were," came Isabel's answer.

Liz laughed to herself. "Good. I'm glad you're all warm and toasty, because I'm freezing my ass off in here."

After a moment of silence came the sound of Isabel giggling.

"I'm glad my hypothermia amuses you," Liz called back.

Another moment of silence, another giggle, and Isabel said, "You can sleep in here with us…if you're that cold."

"Yeah?" Liz didn't wait for an answer. She jumped out of bed, carefully padding across the dark kitchen and straight into Isabel's room. The dogs took up the foot of the bed, but Liz didn't mind curling into a ball, careful not to kick them as she pressed her feet up against what must have been Loosey's warm back. "Oh, bless you, Goose," she murmured. With no heat in the cabin, it was definitely a three-dog night, but two dogs, plus the heat emanating from the hot-blooded Brazilian next to her, was even better. Liz faced Isabel, happily melting into the comfort of what felt like a warm cocoon. "*Gracias, señorita*. I think I can fall asleep now."

"*De nada*," came a tiny voice. "And it's me who should be thanking you. I don't know how to ever repay you for today."

"You don't have to. Seeing you so happy is payment enough." Isabel's face wasn't far from her own, but Liz couldn't make out her features in the dark. "I mean, if you really feel the need to repay me, you can always take me to the beach this summer in your Mustang convertible…or buy me a drink…or maybe just give me a lap dance, and we'll call it even. Whatever you deem appropriate."

And when an awkward silence filled the room, Liz sucked her teeth and rolled her eyes in the dark. "I'm just kidding. Good night, Isabel. Go to sleep," she said, and rolled over.

Isabel turned over, too, and as she did her foot touched Liz's foot, and there came another giggle. "Are you wearing socks?"

"I am." Liz giggled back. "We gringos aren't as warm-blooded as you Latinas…but my feet are actually getting hot right now." Liz used her foot to push off one sock and then the other, and kicked them out from under the covers.

"How haunting. I just love hearing the loons," Isabel whispered.

"I might have to buy a little waterfront cabin up here, something on the New Hampshire-Maine border near the speedway, so I can race cars all day and listen to the loons all night."

"As long as you invite me to decorate."

"Of course."

They were quiet then, the echoes of loons filling the silence. Moonlight playing on the water cast rippling shadows on the walls, and it wasn't long before their eyes closed and the haunting wails and tremolos lulled them into a deep sleep.

Chapter Twenty-One

Gwen stopped to put on a denim jacket over her sleeveless black dress as they exited the theater. She almost wished she'd worn slacks, and shoes instead of these flimsy silver sandals. It was much cooler than it had been two hours ago when they'd dined outdoors under a white tent on the sprawling lawn. She and Sam had enjoyed the view of the woods and the big post-frame theaters that harmonized well with the rustic ambience of a barn-studio and several old houses dotting the well-landscaped property. Now a National Historic Landmark, Jacob's Pillow had started as a farm in the seventeen hundreds and later served as a stop on the Underground Railroad for slaves escaping to Canada. In the nineteen thirties a famous choreographer had purchased the property with the dream of establishing an all-male dance company that would change the public's not-so-masculine view of men in dance.

"Look." Samantha pointed to a bonfire blazing in celebration of the Fourth of July. Most of the Pillow's patrons seemed to be heading home, but many were making their way over to the fire.

Gwen watched Sam staring at the blazing flames. Something about the curious glint in her brown eyes, the way she cocked her head in wonder reminded Gwen of how Bertha looked when fixated on an object of interest. She smiled to herself. "Would you like to get something to drink and sit by the fire for a while?"

"Let's do that," Samantha said excitedly.

"I could really go for a cup of hot coffee."

"Coffee sounds great."

Gwen hooked her arm around Sam's and led her through the crowd, along a wide gravel pathway. It forked in one direction toward the parking lots and in the other to an outdoor café and bar.

"This is such a great venue," Samantha commented as they carried their cups back to the fire and grabbed the last of the low chairs placed in a circle laid out around it. "And the performance was outstanding, especially that last dance. Such incredible kinetic power. It was like a fusion of heavy metal and classical music."

They stared at the bonfire as they talked, leaning against one another's shoulder in a friendly sort of snuggle, and Gwen was glad for the fire's heat and the warmth of the coffee cup in her hands. "That's classical modernism, with its often raw and brilliant elements of jazz and rock."

Samantha glanced around at people sitting in pairs, their backs to the starry darkness, the fire casting an orange glow on all the faces. "Thank you for bringing me."

"I'm so glad you enjoyed it." Among the mostly straight couples Gwen picked out several gay pairs. Pride week at the Pillow was in August, the last performance followed by a dance, and Gwen would be sure to get them tickets for that. "To be honest, I kept from telling you this particular performance was set to classical music because I thought you'd pretend to have made prior plans."

"And miss a date with you? I'd have suffered through almost anything." Sam smiled over at her. "And don't make assumptions, because I actually do enjoy classical music."

"Do you really?"

"Well…in small doses, I'll confess, but I do have an appreciation."

Gwen laughed. "Since we're confessing, I must tell you that I have a thing for the romantic eras and…uh…a love for waltzes."

"Waltzes!" Sam shot her a look of surprise. "Then you happen to be in luck."

This time it was Gwen's turn to be surprised. "You're kidding me."

"I kid you not. Years ago my ex signed us up for a ballroom-dancing course through some LGBT group in the city. It's not something I would have done on my own, but I ended up liking it more than she did."

"And you learned to waltz. Hmm…" Every time she tried to dismiss her deepening feelings, tried to find reasons not to let herself fall for this incredible but younger woman, something else emerged—another thing in common—to strengthen the force of the pull that was increasingly testing her resistance.

"I'm not ready for *Dancing with the Stars*," Sam teased her, "but with a quick refresher course I could certainly manage the box and progressive step…if it's a slow waltz, you know, at the walking pace. I wasn't too good at a fast waltz or making turns without bumping into other couples."

Done with her coffee, Gwen set her cup down and pulled her jacket tighter around herself. "What if you had the dance floor all to yourself, with no couples to bump into?"

"Do you know a place?"

"The perfect place. But we'll have to go back to the house."

"Now?"

"Whenever you're ready."

Samantha finished her coffee, got up, and extended a hand. "I'm ready."

They strolled back along the softly lit pathway to Gwen's white Mercedes in the parking lot and took the back roads to Route 8. Fifteen minutes later they were turning into the tree-lined driveway. The headlights lit their way until the porch lights of the grand white house came into view. Rosa was gone for the day, a soft light burning in the bedroom window of her cottage, and with Isabel and the dogs away, Gwen enjoyed a welcome sense of privacy she hadn't felt in quite a while.

Sam followed her as they walked to the house, but as Gwen climbed the porch steps she felt Sam fall behind and turned to find her searching the darkness. "Looking for ghosts?" she asked.

"Mmm." Sam nodded. "Do you think she's around tonight?"

"You won't see her anywhere but the pond. If she's not there she's somewhere out in the ether." Gwen thought of Rosa's warning. "But it's too dark down there, and I think it's best you stay away from her."

"Why?" Sam frowned like a teenager arguing a curfew. "This is all so extraordinary, proof of life after death, as you say. It's changed the way I think about death, the same way it's changed yours, and—" Sam threw her hands up. "This is what I write about, what *you've* written about. We've been given a chance to witness an observable threshold between life and death, a dimension beyond comprehension—we've actually interacted with a ghost!"

"*You've* interacted with a ghost. That's the point, Sam. I've been seeing her for the longest time, waiting for me in that one spot, her face without emotion. But until the day I saw her engaging you, I'd never seen her move, never seen her expression change. That's why it came as such a shock to me." Gwen put a key in the door lock. "I don't know what it is about you or what it means, but I think it's best if you don't pay her any more attention." Sam didn't respond, but Gwen heard her frustrated huff of resignation as she opened the door and let them in.

A black cat greeted them in the foyer, and Sam stopped to pet it while Gwen turned on some lights. "I'll show you where we'll dance," Gwen said, and led them into the dining room to a set of double doors that disappeared into the wall when she slid them apart. She flipped two light switches and the room came to life, the faceted crystals of the chandelier sprinkling the floor with enchanting patterns of light. "Will this give you enough room without bumping into anyone?"

"I'll say."

"Isabel calls it my ballroom."

Samantha's mouth opened as she took in the empty space. Left to right it measured a good thirty feet, and at least twenty across to a wall of tall, white-paned windows that looked out onto a slate patio surrounded by shrubs and blooming flowers. A few white cast-iron bistro tables and chairs gave the patio the feel of an English garden from an earlier time.

"Yep, I think Isabel's right. *Ballroom* would be the proper term," Sam said. "It appears to meet all the criteria."

Gwen placed a hand on the small of Sam's back and pointed to the left. "The bar's over there. Why don't you make us drinks while I put on my dancing shoes."

"Sure." Sam smiled. "What can I make you?"

"A gin martini, shaken and very dirty. You'll find olives and a bottle of brine juice in the refrigerator behind the bar. Make it taste like the ocean for me."

"The ocean?" Sam gave her a sideways glance. "As you wish, Professor. I feel like you keep testing me, giving me assignments."

"So far you're earning straight As."

"Well, in that case, Dr. Laraway," Sam rubbed her hands together and began unbuttoning her shirt cuffs, "let's see if I can simulate the ocean for some extra credit."

"You do that. You'll find plenty of sodas and mixers for whatever you want. And if you're hungry," she said on the way out, "Rosa should have left a small platter of cheese and fruit in there."

Gwen went upstairs to freshen up and slip into black pointy-toed flats that dressed up her black dress as it were, then gave herself another spritz of perfume on the way out. Sam was busy at work when she returned, with several open bottles and a shaker on the bar. Gwen went to the sound equipment on the other side of the room. "You're familiar with *Sleeping Beauty*, of course."

"Of course," Sam called back to her. "I have a thing for Disney villainesses."

"Not princesses?"

"Nah. Princesses are too sweet and simple. I prefer a more edgy, complex woman. Besides, the villainesses are far sexier."

"I'll have to keep that in mind." Gwen laughed. "Do you remember the theme song?"

"To *Sleeping Beauty*? Hmm...I can't remember the title offhand, but..." Sam put the top on the martini shaker and paused before she started shaking: "Da-duh-da...da-da da-da...duh...da-da...da-da..."

"That's it. 'Once Upon a Dream.'" Gwen sang along with Sam's humming.

"Yes. 'Once Upon a Dream'!" Sam called out as she vigorously shook the shaker.

"It's my favorite from Tchaikovsky's *Sleeping Beauty* ballet—'The Garland Waltz,' or 'Grande valse villageoise.' When Disney first produced the movie in 1959, lyrics were written for it, and it became 'Once Upon a Dream.' And then for the movie *Maleficent*, the more recent remake of *Sleeping Beauty*, Lana Del Rey covered the song."

"So we're dancing to Disney?"

"Well, I adore this version, and it's really downtempo, a good starting point until we get used to dancing together." Gwen put the song on repeat and walked over to take a stool at the bar, the hauntingly sultry voice of Lana Del Rey filling the room.

Sam had rolled up the sleeves of her black shirt, and it was unbuttoned just enough that when she leaned down to put the brine back in the refrigerator, her cleavage and the outline of a black bra gave Gwen an intense rush of quiet desire. "Most people don't realize the waltz is an incredibly romantic dance," Gwen said, trying to distract herself from the sweet ache Sam was giving her. "They confuse it with the minuet, which is also in triple time, but a far more prudent and stately frolic without the tight body contact of a waltz."

Sam filled two martini glasses and placed one in front of Gwen. "I really like this song. It'll make for a slow-motion waltz, which is just what I need to get back into practice."

"Don't worry. We'll get you back into practice." Gwen regarded her with a suggestive smirk as she lifted the toothpick from her glass and pulled an olive off with her teeth. She chewed it slowly, then raised the glass to her lips. It was wonderful having Sam here all to herself, and for a moment she imagined they lived here together, just the two of them, Sam working by day in one of the guest rooms turned into a study, or in the gallery with its mood-setting lights illuminating the library table where she'd write, in view of the pottery she was coming to love. Perhaps in the early mornings she'd write on the porch, or on the patio overlooking the gardens, her avian muse beside her. And soon enough there would be the welcome disturbance of several more crows if Bertha started a family.

"How is it?" Samantha stood behind the bar, her dark eyes expectant, and Gwen was suddenly struck by her sex appeal. Her hair had grown a little since they'd first met, and the evening breeze had tousled and swept it forward. It was a particularly nice look, Gwen decided, the look one's hair has after lovemaking, and she had an urge to run her hands through it, mess it up some more.

"Well?" Sam waved a hand in front of her face. "Have I transported you to the ocean?"

"Ah, yes. It's perfect, Sam. One sip and I was somewhere sailing on a schooner, the salty air in my face." She touched a fingertip to the foam in her glass. "I don't think I've ever seen anyone shake a martini so vigorously as to produce sea foam."

"No flotsam and jetsam, I hope." Sam smiled as she came out from behind the bar with another martini glass in her hand and touched it to Gwen's.

"Are you having one, too?"

"I am. My sweet tooth prefers sweet drinks, but I decided to try a tastes-like-the-ocean martini just to experience what *you* like."

"I like *you*," she said and watched Sam take a sip. But when Sam's mouth puckered, she laughed. "Not good?"

"It's pretty awful."

This made her laugh again. "Sam, don't be silly. Let me make you—"

"No, no." Sam held up a hand to her. "I'm determined to enjoy this." She took another sip without puckering this time. "Geez, that's strong. Another five minutes and I'll be too drunk to know what it tastes like." She set her glass on the bar. "Now…about that dance, Professor."

Gwen parted her lips in a flirtatious smile. Another sip of her drink and she got off the stool and offered her hand. "Madam…?" she asked, and led Sam to the middle of the room.

Beneath the crystal chandelier, Sam took Gwen's hand in hers and placed the other flat against her shoulder blade while Gwen raised her free hand to cup Sam's shoulder. Perfectly postured, heads held high, Gwen pressed the right side of her torso against the left side of Sam's. "Do you want to be my lead or follow?"

"I'll be your lead, although you might have to lead me leading you for a minute."

"My pleasure."

"Let's try the basic box step."

"Okay…visualize the box," Gwen said as they began moving to the music. "On the downbeat your left foot comes forward into the left corner…right foot slides forward into the right corner…and now the left foot comes over to close with your right foot. Step, slide, close… nice. Now the right foot steps back to the right corner, left foot back to the left corner…and close. *One*-two-three, *one*-two-three…now let's rotate the box by making a quarter turn."

"Counterclockwise."

"Always counterclockwise."

The quarter turn was tricky, and they had to begin again a few times, but despite what seemed a waning confidence, Sam quickly remembered the waltz, and within minutes they were moving as smoothly as if they'd danced together a hundred times. For half an hour they danced, alternating between the box and progressive step, until they slowed to a stop.

"You're better than I expected," said Gwen. "Next time we'll dance to a faster Viennese waltz…maybe work in a combination of hesitations, turns, and whisks."

"What I'd like right now," Sam said, keeping Gwen in their breast-to-breast embrace, "is to work in a combination of kisses."

Gwen's chest swelled as she gazed, breathless, into Sam's wanting eyes and then at the mouth slowly reaching for her own. She placed her fingertips against Sam's lips. "Please don't, Sam…because I don't have the willpower to resist you."

Sam gently closed her hand around Gwen's fingers and pushed them away from her lips. "You should have stopped at *please don't*," Sam said, and kissed her anyway, a soft, lingering kiss that left Gwen speechless, and before she could find her voice Sam kissed her again, deeper this time.

"Sam, I…"

"Shh…" Sam whispered against her lips, and when she kissed her a third time, Gwen surrendered, her mouth melting into Sam's, the low moan that escaped Sam's throat sending a rush of desire that settled between her thighs.

"I want you…so much," said Sam, her words coming in a husky whisper. She rested her forehead against Gwen's and caught her breath.

"I want you, too, but I—" She hugged Sam to hide her expression, her vulnerability, the conflicting emotions that engulfed her. Happiness, fear, desire. She couldn't remember when she'd felt such a strong sexual attraction. She felt more alive than she had in years; from head to toe her skin yearned to feel the full length of Sam's naked body against hers. The thought intensified that sweet ache. But if they crossed the boundary line of friendship tonight, there would be no going back.

As Gwen stood facing the windows, embracing Sam and giving in to the idea of taking her upstairs, she caught sight of a small, wavering patch of fog on the patio. With a shudder, she gasped.

"What's wrong?" asked Sam, pulling back in alarm and staring at her.

"She's here."

"Who?" Sam let go and turned around.

Gwen watched in shock as the white patch solidified into the monochromatic shape of a dog. It stood watching them, a spectral voyeur, its white eyes intent on Gwen—a vision that broke her heart and made her feel faint for a moment. "My God, she's like the negative of a photograph."

"What do you mean?" Sam said, letting go of Gwen and moving closer to the window.

"Tell me what you see."

"I see her, a brown dog…but she's very…very thin."

"Thin?"

"Yeah. I mean I can almost see through her." At the right end of the windows was a glass-paned garden door, and Sam made a move for it.

"No! Don't go to her." She grabbed Sam's hand and held her back. "Something's happened to her. Something's wrong," she whispered, more to herself than to Sam. "What's allowed her to leave the pond?"

Gwen remembered Rosa's words: *Be Careful.* Ten cuidado. *That* espíritu *is up to no good*. The warning sent chills up her spine.

❖

In the middle of the night, Samantha awoke in the guest room that was becoming her home away from home. A persistent whining, a far-off whimpering had roused her from a deep sleep, unless she'd only dreamed it. It was hard to tell. Wherever the noise came from, it was gone now, and the house was still. The faint blue light of a nightstand clock lit the room, and Samantha turned her head on the pillow to read its luminous hands. Three thirty.

She should have been in Gwen's bed, not alone in this one. She'd finally broken through Gwen's emotional barriers, danced and kissed her way into her heart. She was on the verge of a beautiful seduction, and no doubt they would have made love tonight had the canine apparition not appeared to foil her plans, sober lust, and quickly change the mood. Damn dog.

Samantha folded her hands behind her head, her eyes fixated on the ceiling. Strange how Alley had appeared to her in living color and to Gwen as a photographic negative. A negative…a photograph. An idea came to her. If the dog was still on the patio, maybe she could snap a few pictures. It would be interesting to see if the ghost could be recorded, or if, like a vampire, its image would defy capture. Only one way to find out.

She threw back the covers, pulled on a pair of shorts, and grabbed her cell phone. Quietly opening the bedroom door, she peeked across to Gwen's room. It was directly in front of hers, on the opposite side of the staircase. She wished she was in there with her, reveling in the afterglow of lovemaking and enjoying the intimate pillow talk that might have gone on until the sun came up. But the ghost-dog had jolted Gwen to her senses, and she'd seemed distant after that, preoccupied, more worried than amorous. When she bid Samantha good night, she did it with a tender kiss to the cheek and a hug into which she'd mumbled a halfhearted apology for having crossed a line she hadn't meant to cross. The woman she'd danced with had disappeared, and as much as Samantha wanted to slip into that room to find that woman again, she knew sex was off the menu. At least for tonight. Which left time for a sleepless mystery writer to conduct some well-overdue paranormal research.

She tiptoed to the staircase, her feet sinking into the yellow floral carpeting as she held on to the wide banister and followed the path of woven flowers down the winding stairs. But when she reached the bottom, a floorboard creaked, which brought the questioning meow of the black cat. It rushed to Samantha, slinking in and out of her legs, mewling its nocturnal boredom. The only way to silence it fast was to scoop it up, and she carried the cat with her, using the flashlight on her phone to find her way into the dining room. She paused, listening for any noise, afraid the creaks and mews had roused Gwen from sleep, but when no sounds came she put the cat down and parted the doors to the ballroom. Better to keep the lights off, she thought, and crossed the room to the windows. The patio was dark, and the glare of the phone's light on the glass made it hard to see anything until she was right up on the glass pressing her phone against it.

And there it was, no longer brown, but as Gwen had described it—a photographic negative—now curled asleep on the outdoor mat with its back to her. As if sensing her presence, and faster than Samantha could track her movement, the dog repositioned itself so that now it was standing, facing her, the white pupils of its black eyes locked on her.

Samantha startled when those eyes met hers. She dropped her phone, and the light went out. Her heart pounded as she fumbled to turn it back on, although it wasn't fear she felt. She'd never felt fear, only awe and dizzying wonderment. It was a ghost, after all, and what harm could the dead really do? Besides, it was the spiritual remains of a friendly, albeit sad dog, a beloved family pet that had met its tragic demise on the property. It was lonesome, isolated, trapped in the three-dimensional world of the living. Why her appearance left Gwen upset, she didn't know.

Samantha moved over to the glass door, inspecting it for signs of an alarm. The last thing she needed was to set off a fury of bells and whistles that would send Gwen rushing down in a panic. She hadn't noticed her setting an alarm before bed, so it was safe to assume that here in the country, Loosey Goosey, the resident pit bull, was the security system. Samantha turned the lock on the knob, gently slid the bolt lock back, and eased the door open just enough to squeeze through without letting the cat slip out.

Two owls hooted back and forth, one right by the house, the other answering from the distance, and she imagined Bertha asleep out here, part of the wildlife now, cozied up in a tree with that rogue bird who had stolen her heart. Samantha experienced that hopeless, heartsick feeling of a parent whose child who had run off to join a gang. And in the midst of the hoots and hollers of owls, she listened to what sounded like the soft hum of a high-voltage transformer coming from the apparition. Against the black of night the apparition glowed and shimmered as though lit from within. Pure spirit, pure energy, Samantha thought, as she dared to edge closer.

Another step tripped the floodlights. The patio lit up, and the dog became brown again, as lifelike as any living dog, except that she was slightly transparent, enough that Samantha could almost see the legs of a bistro chair through her body. How absolutely incredible! She'd worked with dead people for eighteen years—well, mostly with their DNA—and had never once seen a spirit. Too bad she couldn't have seen and interacted with them the way she did this dog; they might have helped solve the mysteries of their deaths as she did in her stories.

The ghost-dog wagged its tail, bowed its head shyly, as if not sure it was going to be petted or reprimanded. Without Gwen around to scold Samantha, she didn't hesitate. Kneeling on the slate, inches from the dog's face, she reached to pet it.

Her hand sank into the dog's head, a strange electrical current tickling her hand and flowing up her arm, not strong enough to give a shock, but somehow energizing. It left her with the same invigorating feeling people often experienced right before a thunderstorm, when static electricity and negative ions saturate the air. Her hand trembled with adrenaline as she turned on the camera. She'd come out to take a picture of the dog, but this occasion was too momentous to not include herself. With her left arm lightly draped over the dog's back, she held out the phone, looked at the dog, and smiled. But just as she snapped the picture, the lights in the ballroom came on, and Gwen's horrified face appeared in the window.

Caught in the act. Samantha jumped up and stood at attention as Gwen opened the door and stared in disbelief. "What on earth? Are you out here taking selfies?"

Samantha gave a crooked smile. "Just one."

"All alone? It's the middle of the night, Sam."

Alone? It occurred to Samantha that Gwen could no longer see her dog's ghost. And when she glanced down she herself could barely see it. The spirit was fading, evaporating around her feet. She stepped to the side and gave a sheepish shrug.

Gwen's tone was stern. "You're not out here looking for Alley, are you?"

"No. Of course not. A bird outside the window woke me up," she said, lying as she went along. "I thought it was Bertha calling me…and I came out to see, and…" The owls began to hoot again, just in time to give credence to her story. "Turned out it was just these noisy owls, and not Bertha, so…"

"So, you took a selfie?" Gwen had that look of a professor who suspected a student of cheating on an exam. "Bertha's a crow. They sleep at night. You know that." She took a deep breath and shook her head at Samantha. "You gave me a scare, Sam. I almost came down with a gun."

"You have a gun?"

"Yes. We're not in New York City. People here keep guns."

"I'm sorry I scared you."

"I was worried you might be wandering down to the pond… looking for things neither of us understand too well."

She was finding it hard to look Gwen in the eye without telling the truth. "Sorry I woke you…I'm going back to bed."

Gwen looked at her oddly. "Are you okay, Sam?"

"I'm fine."

"Can I get you something to drink?"

"No."

"Well, all right then…"

Samantha was glad to get back to her room. As soon as she closed the door she climbed back into bed, excited to check her photo. There was no dog, though. In the picture, she was kneeling with her arm held out, looking sideways at something that wasn't there, a stupid smile on her face. She looked insane. Gwen must have thought she'd gone nuts, but better for her to think that than to think Samantha had deliberately gone against her wishes and snuck outside to engage the ghost of her dead dog.

Something bothered her, though, as she lay there trying to fall asleep. Something about the room had changed. The atmosphere was different, heavier. It suddenly struck her that something had followed her inside, and she wasn't alone anymore.

Chapter Twenty-Two

Liz and Isabel had hoped to make better time coming back, but Monday's rush-hour traffic slowed them down as they crossed into Massachusetts. Liz was exhausted. They'd had a good workout this morning, kayaking and then swimming with the dogs, and yesterday had been nonstop. After a blueberry-pancake breakfast Sunday morning, they'd taken the dogs on a short hike to a nearby waterfall and then spent the rest of the day rushing from sale to sale until the van couldn't hold much more. There was room for books, though, and Liz made a point of taking Isabel to a few little-known shops tucked away along the back roads that would have heaps of musty old books sure to contain a few treasures.

And Isabel had found those treasures, a whole box full, her biggest find a complete set of oversized reference books entitled *Character Sketches of Romance Fiction and the Drama.* Replete with illustrations of wood engravings, etchings, and brilliant photogravures, the collection was a reader's guide to plot and character summaries of the world's most beloved stories. Isabel kept one out for the ride home and for two hours kept Liz entertained with stories ranging from *Don Quixote* to *Puss-n-Boots*. When Isabel grew tired of reading, she went over the book's anatomy, commenting on the leather and cloth cover boards, the gilt-tooled motifs and silk-moiré end sheets. She said her thirty-dollar purchase would easily bring three hundred if she were inclined to sell, which she wasn't, and she didn't mind that the books' spines were moderately rubbed because, as Isabel put it, the internals were exquisite.

Liz was sure Isabel's "internals" were just as exquisite, but she was beginning to doubt she'd ever find out. She'd finally met a woman she could actually be with for days without wanting to run away, but something told her this love might be, in the end, unrequited—karma's way of kicking her in the ass for the many hearts she'd broken.

"This may sound like a stupid question," Liz said, "but why did you get that old dictionary? I mean, with the internet, does anyone even buy *new* dictionaries anymore?"

"They're just fun to read, souvenirs of the past…reminders of change, progress, the passage of time." She shrugged. "I love looking up words that don't appear."

Liz looked at her oddly. "Words that *don't* appear?"

"Yes." Isabel paused. "Take the word *teenager*, for instance. It didn't appear in a dictionary until after World War Two. And you won't find *automobile*, *telephone*, or *camera* in dictionaries from the early 1800s."

"Ah, because they didn't exist back then. Hmm…I never thought about that."

"It must be fascinating to be a lexicographer—someone who compiles dictionaries."

"I can't think of a more exciting job."

Isabel made a face at her. "I like old encyclopedias for the same reason. It's interesting to look up people, theories, inventions that have changed the world and the way we think, and not find them there because they hadn't yet been born, or developed, or invented." Isabel looked over at her with the cutest apologetic smile. "I know. You think I'm eccentric."

Liz laughed. "Engrossing, yes. Quirky, maybe. Eccentric? You're too young to be eccentric. Check back with me in a few decades, and I'll let you know."

Isabel gave a soft snort of laughter as she unscrewed the top of a water bottle and took a drink. She had let her reserve down over the weekend, and Liz loved seeing her this animated and talkative.

"Do you think we can stop at the next rest area?" Isabel asked.

"I was just about to suggest that. I need coffee, and I know these dogs need to stretch their legs." She glanced at Blue and Loosey, who were sandwiched together right behind the front seats. "Aww…you babies are such good travelers," Liz said to them. "I'm sorry the ride back isn't as comfortable as the one going up."

"If you're tired, I'll drive the rest of the way," Isabel offered.

"Yeah? Well, if you handled a race car, you can handle the van… if you don't mind."

"I love driving. I could drive all day long."

Liz smiled over at her. "I think I learned that about you this weekend."

Gwen and Rosa had finished eating and were having coffee on the porch when the phone rang. Rosa ran back in to answer it, and when she came back out she looked at Gwen's bare feet. "That was Isabel. You better go get your sneakers. They'll be here soon and need help unloading."

"Really? How did she sound?"

"So excited. She go on and on about a video of her racing a car." With a mimicking gesture, Rosa flapped her fingers like a talking puppet. "*Boca del motor!*"

Motormouth. That was a good sign. It meant Isabel was having a great time. Isabel tended to grow introspective and self-conscious when she stayed quiet for too long. Gwen nodded her satisfaction. She'd done well to force her to go away.

It was dusk when the van pulled up, and Rosa and Gwen were ready to help. The dogs bounded out like kids returning from a great adventure, so much to tell but no words for all they'd seen and done. Liz was the first to kiss both Rosa and Gwen and hand them a basket of wild Maine blueberries, two jars of jam, and a bottle of blueberry wine. Rosa took the gifts, and Gwen gave Liz a tight squeeze. Her warmth and energy were infectious. Isabel would be crazy to pass this woman up. "Thank you so much for taking her," she whispered to Liz.

And then Isabel kissed her hello. "So?" Gwen asked. "You had a good time?"

"The best. I want to be a race-car driver!"

Gwen just shook her head. She'd sent Isabel off in hopes the weekend would lead to romance, not a career change.

"Wait until you watch the video," Liz said. "Isabel was amazing, a real natural on the circuit…and she just happens to look adorable in a helmet and jumpsuit." And when Isabel blushed, Liz changed the subject and looked up at the porch. "Is Bertha still here?"

"Mm-hm. She's somewhere in the trees, probably in bed for the night." Gwen gave a helpless shrug and shook her head. "I can't get her to come into the house at night anymore." She turned her attention to Isabel to make a subtle point. "It appears Bertha has decided to grow up, fall in love, and make a life with her new companion."

"Oh boy…" Liz said. "I haven't talked to Sam. She must be heartbroken."

"I think she's more upset than she lets on. And 'oh boy' is right," Gwen said. "Rosa and I have determined that Bertha's either a lesbian… or Bertha's *Bert*."

Liz's jaw dropped, and she covered her mouth. "Oh no! Bertha's a boy? How can you tell?"

"Well, for starters, we witnessed Bertha mounting the other bird," Gwen said with a poker face. "And then we stuck around for the copulation, just to be sure."

"Oh, no. How did Sam take it?"

"She doesn't know. I'm waiting for her to adjust to the idea of Bertha wanting to live here before breaking the news."

"Poor Sam," Isabel said, before politely interrupting the conversation. "Listen, I think we should pull the van around to the barn and unload before it gets too dark." The cottage wouldn't be ready for furniture for a few more weeks, and the barn would provide dry storage and give them space to clean and work on the pieces they'd bought.

"Yeah. Let's do that. And then I really need to hit the road."

"You're not hitting any road," Gwen said. "Sam's room is ready for you, and dinner's on the stove."

Isabel looked at Liz. "Please stay," she said. "I know you're tired, and I'd rather you didn't drive home."

Rosa got the dogs into the house so Liz could back the van around to the barn. Isabel directed her in, shooing away the outdoor cats that ran out of the open barn to greet her.

"My goodness!" Gwen said when Liz opened the back doors of the van. The space was packed, piled to the ceiling.

"Everything up front is for the cottage. The rest is going back with me to the city."

They began by sliding out a huge stack of barn-wood panels that Liz would use as a wall covering in the bedroom. She'd find the perfect color paint for the other three walls, something cooler than taupe, warmer than gray, that would complement the weathered wood and pop the white of the rustic birch headboard they'd found. If any panels were left, they'd build a pot hanger for the kitchen wall.

Isabel pulled out a lobster trap and held it up for Rosa to see. "You think Eugene will help us turn this into an end table?"

"You know he'll help you do anything, *chica*."

Smiling, Isabel carried it into the barn, careful not to trip over the dozen cats inspecting the items, then took a moment to pet and talk to each one of them. "Did they eat yet?"

"Everyone's been fed," Gwen said as she lifted out the first of two heavy stoneware pieces and squealed with delight. "Burley Winter," she said, immediately recognizing the pottery. "These must be a hundred years old." Both were half brown and half white. One was a five-gallon whiskey jug that would look nice on the floor with dried flowers or pussy willows; the other was a two-gallon butter crock that would serve as a utensil holder in the kitchen.

Rosa picked up a large bulbous lamp with two hands, its round glass globe encased in a metal cage. "What's this?"

"It's an onion lamp," Liz answered. "An old reproduction of the lanterns used for nighttime working on fishing schooners. We thought it would look great hanging over a small table in the dining area."

"You know, Liz, I really like your sense of style," Gwen said, and then she winked at Rosa. "When this cottage is done, I might want to move into it and let the girls have the house."

Isabel shot a nervous look at her and then glanced away, as if embarrassed by the fact that Gwen always saw clear through to her emotions.

"You know I would never refuse that house, and I wouldn't change a thing in it," Liz joked as they lifted out the remaining items: the headboard and weathered barn window, the glass panes of which Liz would replace with mirrors; a narrow hall table Isabel would refinish; a hand-carved, life-size loon; two vintage fruit crates for magazines or books; a huge galvanized basket to hold fruit; and an old milk can that would make a perfect stand for a pot of flowers outside the cottage door.

The only thing left was the largest and heaviest of their finds—a vintage cupboard almost as wide as the van and six feet high. The original white paint was worn along the edges and crackled all over, so that the dark wood beneath showed through. Untouched, it would make a perfect pantry or maybe even a bookcase. The cupboard was lying on its back, and Liz and Isabel slid it out almost all the way, letting the far corners rest on the bumper until Gwen and Rosa came around.

"It's very heavy, so let's each take an end and carry it flat until we get it into the barn," Isabel suggested.

"Okay," said Liz, "on the count of three. One, two—"

The four of them lifted, but after a few steps Rosa started losing her grip. "*Espera, espera!*" she yelled, and they all stopped.

"All right, all right, we're waiting." Gwen rolled her eyes. "Hurry up, before I lose my end."

Rosa struggled for a moment, then let her end slip to the ground. *"Ay, Dios mío!"* She leaned forward and held her abdomen.

"Are you okay?" Liz asked with sudden concern. "Did you hurt your stomach?"

"No, no, is not my stomach." Rosa huffed and puffed, mumbling in broken English as her hand moved down to her groin. "Is my lady parts. I think they just fell out."

Gwen made a face at Rosa, struggling to hold on to her end and trying not to laugh. "Did you drop your uterus?"

"*Dios mío!* I drop something for sure. Is in my underpants."

Isabel's eyes widened. "*What?*"

"I no wanna look because…whatever drop out, I can't put it back."

One glance between Gwen and Liz, and they both tightened their lips to keep from laughing. Still holding the heavy load, which was feeling heavier by the second, Liz raised one foot behind her and pretended to inspect the bottom of her shoe. "I think it was an ovary you lost, and it's not in your underpants anymore. I just stepped on it."

Gwen played along. "I hope you don't need it anymore, Rosa, because it's flat as a pancake."

That was all the four of them needed to start heaving with laughter, and the harder they laughed the weaker their arms got, so that one by one they lost their grip and let the cupboard slide to the ground.

Gwen gestured at Liz and tried to speak, but she was laughing so hard the words came out in squeaks. "Don't fret, Rosa. I'm sure Liz, our resident antiquarian and designer, will repurpose and turn it into something beautiful for the cottage." And with that they broke into another fit of laughter and laughed until they couldn't breathe, Isabel included.

"Oh my goodness…let's give this another try," Gwen said when they'd regained both their composure and the strength to lift the cupboard again. Liz and Gwen picked up one end, and Isabel moved Rosa out of the way and took the other end by herself.

"*Dios mío!*" Rosa complained as she watched them carry it. "Why you get something so heavy, *chica*?"

"Never mind that," Isabel said, and when Rosa looked away Isabel mouthed the words *drama queen*. "Just keep the cats out of the way for us so we don't trip. *Por favor*."

It was almost dark by the time they were done, and Gwen walked back into the barn to shut off the lights and turn on a nightlight. "I'll lock the cats up," she said to Isabel. "You two go wash your hands and have dinner."

While Liz and Isabel brought the van back around to the house, Gwen and Rosa shut the barn doors, keeping the cats safe from wandering coyotes and the early morning crows who mercilessly chased them for pure enjoyment.

On the way back to the house Gwen looked up at the rising moon and stars and thought of Sam. She always thought of Sam. No matter what she was doing, that woman had become permanent background music, and she regretted that their passion had cooled the other night. It was not just seeing Alley, but seeing her on the patio, that had filled her with terror. For as long as Alley's ghost had appeared, it had always been by the pond, and she'd never been afraid; after all, who wouldn't want to see the spirit of a beloved pet, a confirmation of their continued existence? Yet something about her unexpected appearance outside the windows of the ballroom struck fear in her, and for the first time ever she worried that the vision might be a bad omen.

"It's a nice night," she said to Rosa and looked around. "It's supposed to be cool again."

"*Sí,*" Rosa said. She began humming and spread her arms as she walked, as if feeling for something palpable in the air. When she reached the porch, she stopped and looked back at Gwen. "It's gone," she said.

"What is?"

"The *fantasma*. The *espíritu.*"

Gwen looked at her, perplexed. "Alley?"

"*Sí.*"

"Gone where?"

Rosa shrugged. "I dunno…maybe to the other side…but she's not here."

It was strange how Gwen could see the ghost of her dog clear as day but never actually *felt* her presence, and how Rosa always felt her presence but never saw more than a white mist. And then there was Sam, who could see and feel and *communicate* with the ghost, for God's sake. There was something about Sam, but Gwen hadn't quite figured it out yet.

Had Alley, after several years of being earthbound, of being unresolved, *unfinished*, finally found a way to cross the invisible chasm between life and death? Whatever had happened, Rosa would insist that

Sam had played a part, and for this very reason she'd kept from telling her about the ghost coming up to the windows the other night.

Tears welled in her eyes as she started walking again. Was it possible that her dearly departed dog truly had departed? That she would not see her again until she herself crossed that chasm? She felt ashamed of herself just then, ashamed to think her beloved companion had come to the window, maybe only to say good-bye—*so long, farewell until we meet again*—and that she had recoiled from the sight of the dog she'd loved with all her heart.

Gwen climbed the porch steps and paused to wipe her tears. She ran a finger under each eye, careful not to smudge her eyeliner. Then she pulled herself together, put on a perfectly enthusiastic smile, and went inside to make drinks and hear all about the girls' trip to Maine.

Chapter Twenty-Three

In the dream it was winter, the morning cold and gray, a heavy snow falling quietly. It wasn't too deep yet: just enough to cover the feet of the black crows noisily gathered in the middle of the frozen pond. Something was going on out there. The birds seemed to be circling an undulating mound of snow on the ice, but the mist and whirling flakes distorted her vision, making it hard to get a good view of what was attracting the crows' attention.

Samantha couldn't see herself, but she knew this was her home and that she had lived here for a long time. So long, that she had grown old here. Her hips ached on cold, wet days like this, and the discomfort would soon drive her inside, but for the moment she wanted to sit with her memories, very fond memories, of being young in this glorious place. She stared out, remembering a woman and a girl who ice-skated every winter on this pond, holding hands as they raced and glided, until one would slip and they both laughed. She remembered bounding toward them with the effortless vibrancy of youth, trying to stop before she reached them and plowing into them instead, slipping and sliding and sometimes flipping over. This made the woman and girl laugh more. Oh, how she loved their laughter...how she loved the woman and the girl. Oh, how she loved these memories of days that were no more.

Now in the winter of her own life, she was content to trade those wild romps for quiet comforts. And the best of comforts was lying beside the woman by the fire at night, just the two of them. The woman would hold a book in one hand, while the other hand came to rest on her, to gently massage her sore hips, rub her ears, softly scratch her head. This woman was her world. Being next to her was heaven. From time to time she would turn her head from the flames of the crackling and mesmerizing fire to gaze up at the woman and think how much she loved her.

Her nose twitched just then, catching the scent of burning wood wafting from the chimney, and she knew that both the woman and a warm fire were waiting for her inside. Breakfast would be waiting, too. She rose to head back, but just as she did the crows spotted her and stopped cawing. In the silence, she heard the snow falling and then the mewling of a cat. The girl's cat. An alarm went off in her, adrenaline numbing the ache in her hips. She stepped out onto the ice. Moving cautiously, purposefully, Samantha looked back only once to see the trail of paw prints she left behind, and in the crazy way that dreamers dream, she knew instinctively that those paw prints belonged to her.

Farther out she went, hesitantly padding her way, until she could see the white cat clearly. Half of a cat, really. It was submerged to its waist in water, too weak to pull itself out of the hole, but its sharp claws clung to the ice. It struggled to keep them securely anchored, lest its upper body follow the bottom half into the smothering, icy darkness. When it saw and recognized the dog approaching, hopeless mews strengthened into desperate cries for help. She whined and whimpered at the cat and then crouched, lowering herself to her belly and crawling forward. Inch by inch she edged her way to the break in the ice. And when her paws reached the hole, she pushed her face forward. The cat looked at her as if staring into the face of a miracle and, in a flash, used the dog's long snout as a ladder. Retracting the claws of one paw from the ice, it reached with an arm, anchoring those same claws into the dog's paw. And then in a flash, the claws of its other paw let go of the ice and hooked onto the dog's snout. In one more swift movement, it clawed and climbed its way over the dog's back and was gone, saved.

She felt the piercing needle-like pain of cat claws, but it was nothing compared to her fear as she tried to push herself up and heard the ice groan. Her legs splayed, she tried to push up again, but her paws kept slipping, and when tried instead to turn herself around to crawl back, the ice cracked beneath her belly.

She opened her mouth to scream for Gwen but had no voice. Help me, help me, help me!

The vibrations of the cracking ice grew louder until they woke Samantha up, and she turned her head on the couch to see her cell phone bouncing around the coffee table. She grabbed it, looked at the screen in a daze, and answered when she saw Liz's name.

"Hey there," she said, her voice raspy, the words coming in heavy breaths.

"Did I interrupt? Are you having sex with someone?"

"No."

"Are you having sex with yourself?"

Samantha laughed. "No." Liz's decadent humor was a welcome distraction from the awful dread of drowning that still filled her chest. She sat up and scratched her head.

"Am I catching you at a bad time?"

"Perfect timing, actually. I was having a horrible dream. You woke me up right before I died, so thanks for that."

"You were *dying*?"

"Yeah, but it wasn't me…I mean, it *was* me, but in the dream I wasn't a person. I had the body of Gwen's—oh, never mind." Samantha rubbed her face again and ran fingers through her hair. "Just a crazy dream. I think my brain was streaming psychic residue from thinking so much about that ghost-dog."

"Alley was her name, right?"

"Yeah." Samantha got up and took the phone into the kitchen to put on a pot of coffee.

"Why are you sleeping so late, anyway? It's almost noon."

"I've been up writing since six. I crashed on the couch an hour ago and must have passed out."

"Starting a new book so soon?"

"Two books. I'm working on the next in the series and also trying something different…something for a woman's audience. I got this idea for a story and want to see if I can work it out on paper."

"Another paranormal mystery?"

"Sort of…"

"What's it about?"

"Ah, it wouldn't be a mystery if I told you. All I will say is that it involves a romance."

"Ooh! Am I one of your characters?"

Samantha laughed. "Absolutely. You'd make a really good character in a novel."

"Is Isabel in it, too?"

"If you want her to be."

"Of course I do. Just do me a favor and make sure my character has sex with Isabel's character, because it's not going down in real life."

"Uh-oh." Samantha turned the faucet on and filled the coffeepot.

"How'd you make out this weekend…or should I ask, *did* you make out this weekend?"

"No. We definitely did *not* make out. We had a great time, though. Isabel and my parents hit it off, and she was ecstatic over racing a car. She was so adorable and did so well. I'm sure she'll make you watch the video."

After a long pause, Samantha could hear Liz blowing out a breath of frustration.

"What's wrong?"

"I don't know, Sam…I'm falling big-time for this one, but…I'm beginning to think she's not gay. Maybe she just isn't terribly interested in the whole dating scene and chooses to be celibate."

Samantha scooped coffee into the filter. "What makes you think that?"

"I can't explain it. I mean, she's smart, interesting, surprisingly funny, and—God, Sam, we're *so* good together—but there's something…something almost *adolescent* about being with her. I feel like she's twelve and I'm thirteen, and we're besties having sleepovers."

"Liz, come on, just kiss her already and see what happens." Samantha pulled out a kitchen chair and sat while the coffee came down. "If a kiss turned the frog into a prince, maybe your kiss will turn the girl into a woman."

"Nice fairy tale, Sam, but I don't think so." She blew out another breath. "If she would only give me a signal, one sign, just a hint that she wanted to be kissed, believe me, I'd take over from there. But she hasn't, and I'm scared of doing anything that will freak her out and send her into a panic. I'm telling you, she's emotionally delicate, and I can't bear the thought of losing her friendship if—hold on a second," she said. Sam heard muffled shouts, horns blowing, and then Liz yelling, "Yeah, fuck you, too, dickwad!"

Samantha chuckled. "Ah, home sweet home. You must be approaching the city line."

"I'm in the city now, can't you tell? I'm at the bridge. It's been so peaceful driving through New England these past few days. I didn't hear a single horn. Now I'm back in New York, and everyone's in a fucking rush to reach a destination that's apparently more important than anyone else's. Assholes!"

"Why don't you just turn around before the bridge and come here? I'll make lunch."

"I can't. I have to get to the shop and empty the van. Jake from the coffeehouse next door offered to help me unload if I got there before one. Anyway…I take it you were no more successful than me at making out this weekend."

"What makes you say that?"

"Well, we got in late yesterday, and Gwen insisted I stay the night in 'your room,' as she put it. So, if you spent Saturday night in *your* room, that's means you didn't spend it in *her* room."

"That would be an accurate statement. But we did make out…and we danced the waltz."

"You kissed? Really? And you *waltzed*?"

"One of my many hidden talents." Samantha snickered. "And to be honest, I'm sure it would have gone a lot further if the ghost hadn't shocked Gwen with its unexpected appearance so close to the house."

"O-M-G. The ghost-dog…I've been thinking about that. What happened?"

"What happened is sure to distract you from driving. Call me when you're home and settled tonight, and we'll talk."

"Okay. Also, just to let you know, I'm heading back up on Friday so I can help Isabel supervise the party planners early Saturday morning. She said for you to come up and hang out with Bert if you want."

"Who?"

There was silence and then muffled laughter on the other end. "Bertha. I said *Bertha*. Your crow. Remember her?"

"Mm…I'd love that, but I have two book signings Friday. One in the afternoon at Strand and the other at Barnes and Noble."

"Strand? Funny, but Isabel was talking about Strand being her favorite bookstore."

"Of course it is, because in addition to new and used books, she can surround herself with signed, leather-bound copies of *Ulysses* and Twain and all the other literary icons in the rare-book room upstairs. And that's where my signing is."

"Damn, I'd really, really like to go, and I know Isabel would, but…"

"Don't worry. I'll have others." Samantha got up and poured herself coffee. "I'll spend Saturday night, though. I'm sure neither of us will be in any condition to drive home after the party."

"Goody. We can share the bed in your room, because it doesn't look like I'll be in Isabel's bed, or you in Gwen's." She laughed, although she didn't sound at all amused. "And the other three guest rooms will be occupied. Isabel's father and his wife are coming, along with a few cousins and a lot of Gwen's colleagues and friends."

"And they're all staying at the house?"

"I think most are staying at the Red Lion Inn."

"Well, then, it's a date—me and you."

"Does Gwen know about your book signing?" Liz asked.

"Nope." Samantha spooned sugar into her cup and went to the fridge for cream. "I figured I'd lay low these next few days because I didn't know what Isabel's plans were, and I didn't want to interfere with the party plot. How are they getting Gwen out of the house?"

"Gwen's best friend and colleague, Carol, came up with a plan weeks ago. The philosophy department has been trying to get Gwen to come down for a guest lecture, so Carol pushed her to agree to this Friday morning under the guise they'll turn her visit into a birthday celebration. Gwen's driving down Thursday to stay with Carol and her husband. After the lecture Friday, they'll have lunch and shop and whatever, and then Saturday morning Carol's taking her to the Met. Apparently there's a Picasso exhibit Gwen wants to see. Gwen thinks the family is taking her out for dinner, so she'll want to head home early, but Carol will keep her in the city until at least one o'clock. Guests were asked to arrive no later than three, and hopefully Gwen won't arrive until four."

"Sounds like a plan." Samantha carried her cup back into the living room and flopped onto the couch. "Tell Isabel I'll head up Saturday morning. I can spend some time with Bertha and help out."

"Nothing to help out with. Isabel has a full staff. Anyway, let me go, and I'll call you this evening. I *really* want to hear more about that kiss. And about that ghost…God, it's all so bizarre, isn't it?"

It was beyond bizarre, and Samantha's ghostly encounters were fueling wonderful ideas for a new book. Her publisher might not want it, but if she could knock it out in a month, she was sure her agent could sell it.

❖

Samantha spent the rest of the day and Wednesday catching up with chores and returning calls from her brother, father, and several friends who had left messages days ago. Of course, not having to constantly clean up after a sloppy crow gave her a little extra time. It was the only thing she *didn't* miss about having a large free-range bird in the house.

On Thursday she set out to find a birthday gift for Gwen—something with meaning, something that symbolized their first dance together…their first kiss. She wasn't sure what she was looking for, but she'd know it when she saw it. A jeweler in town sold artisan jewelry, and she went there first, but nothing really caught her eye, so she got back into her car and drove to Tiffany's in Westchester.

Samantha went from showcase to showcase, quickly browsing the collections. And then she saw it, a simple and beautiful rose-gold pendant, two large interlocking circles held together in a gold knot. A perfect symbol of two bodies embraced and waltzing…loving.

"Paloma's melody," a soft voice said, and at the same time Samantha heard the saleswoman, she read the words in the showcase: Melody Collection by Paloma Picasso. *Melody*…it was perfect!

"Where does the Picasso come in?" she asked.

"Paloma is Picasso's daughter. She's one of Tiffany's longtime designers," the woman said, as if this should be common knowledge.

"May I see it?"

In jeans and a T-shirt, her wallet in her back pocket, Samantha didn't look like a Tiffany's regular. The woman hesitated for a moment. "I have it in silver."

"I want to see the rose gold," Samantha said, pointing to the pendant that first caught her attention. When the woman placed it on the counter, Samantha smiled to herself. This was it, exactly what she'd had in mind. "How much?"

"Twenty-four."

Samantha stared at her. "Twenty-four?"

"Hundred."

Samantha raised her brow and nodded thoughtfully. "Twenty-four hundred…"

The woman smiled and reached into the showcase for the silver one. "The silver is four hundred and seventy-five."

Samantha glanced between the two. The truth was that the money was coming in and not much was going out these days. She was too busy writing to spend it. And Gwen had, after all, been generous, very good to her. She'd put her up on more than one occasion, and Bertha had taken up residency under Gwen's supervision. Besides, a gift like this was an investment, wasn't it? An investment in the future of a relationship. "I'll take it," she said.

"The silver?"

"The gold."

An hour later Samantha was back home, walking in the front door and happily swinging the pretty blue bag that held the pretty blue Tiffany's box. Mission accomplished.

She spent Thursday evening and most of Friday writing, giving herself only an hour to shower and slip into a sleeveless black shirt and black suit. Mystery fans seemed to like her best in that color. And then she drove to the station and caught the train. She'd thought of driving in, but with Friday traffic she'd never make it.

A meet-and-greet and signing at Strand took longer than expected, and without much time to spare she rushed out to hail a cab to get to Barnes and Noble uptown.

"Eighty-sixth and Lexington," she said to the driver. "As fast as you can."

"*Ay ay ay!*" the driver said. "All the way uptown in Friday traffic? I try my best, *mami*, but this isn't a helicopter, you know."

The voice and accent rang a bell, and just as Samantha leaned forward to squint at the driver's photo-license, she heard the crack of gum. "Mayra Ramos…we meet again."

Ms. Ramos gave a cocky smile in the rearview mirror. "I remember you…a few weeks ago, right? What'chu up to, *mami*?"

Samantha watched a pink bubble forming in the mirror and laughed. "Still blowing bubbles, huh?"

"If I don't chew, I'll smoke. I need something in my mouth," she said, and the next thing Samantha saw was an eye winking at her over a pink bubble that hid her mouth and nose.

"I just hope you can see over those bubbles. If I'd known I'd run into you, I would have bought you a lollipop."

Ms. Ramos sucked the air out of her bubble, her tongue jutting out like a bird in a cuckoo clock. Samantha made sure her seat belt was secured, and when she looked up again, Ms. Ramos was still staring at her. "I think maybe I've seen you in the Village…you go to women's bars?"

Takes one to know one, Samantha thought. "Not really. My friend does, though."

"What's your friend's name?"

"I don't think you'd know her."

"I know everybody."

Samantha laughed. "Liz."

Ms. Ramos's eyes narrowed in the mirror. "She have red hair?"

"She does."

"Yeah. I know Liz. We play pool sometimes." She cracked her gum. "She likes the ladies…and the ladies *love* her."

Mayra Ramos talked all the way, but at least talking kept her from blowing vision-obstructing bubbles. She got Samantha to the bookstore with five minutes to spare and was rewarded with a generous tip and a promise to say hi to Liz.

A brief meet-and-greet, a half hour of questions and answers, and she settled down at a table to sign books and move the line as fast as possible.

Pen in hand, Samantha opened the first book placed in front of her and looked up at a young woman. "I'm making this out to…?"

"Christina," said the woman. "I'm so happy to meet you, Ms. Weller. I have everything you've written."

"I'm happy to meet you, too, Christina. Thanks for coming today and for reading my books."

Just as the young woman turned to go, another book was handed to her. Samantha glanced up to greet the next fan, and there stood Gwen. Her eyes were as blue as the lapis jacket she wore, the white shell beneath it accentuating the matching stones of a heavy gold and lapis necklace. The enticing glint in her eyes made Samantha's pulse quicken and her heart pound.

"Where on earth did you come from?"

Gwen didn't answer. She looked her up and down with a tantalizing smile and spoke in a hushed tone. "You look very mysterious dressed all in black."

Still stunned to see her, Samantha looked down at her suit and tugged on the lapels of her jacket. "My mystery-writer's costume," she said with a grin.

"And where is the mystery writer going when she's done here?"

"Anywhere you want me to."

"Good." Gwen tapped the cover of her book. "You can make that out to Gwen."

Samantha opened the cover to see Gwen had written inside: *Staying at the Waldorf. Meet me at Peacock Alley.*

For Gwen, Samantha responded with her pen. *Looking forward to picking up where we left off on the dance floor.* She shut the book and handed it back to her.

Gwen peeked inside and closed it. With a teasing smile and a slow wink, she turned and left, walking past Samantha and leaving a trace of perfume that Samantha couldn't wait to chase.

CHAPTER TWENTY-FOUR

The Waldorf," Samantha said and shut the yellow taxi door. Traffic was heavy but at least she was on the East Side and just needed to get to Midtown. She texted Gwen that she was on her way. All she could think about was the invitation in Gwen's eyes, the intention in her smile. Despite the knot in her stomach, Samantha couldn't get there fast enough.

The taxi dropped her at the entrance on Park and 49th Street, and she walked through the revolving doors and up the short staircase. She'd been to the Waldorf twice, both times to meet her agent for drinks at the Bull and Bear, but never to Peacock Alley. Looking up at the grand crystal chandelier, she crossed the immense floor mosaic, passed the freestanding Waldorf clock with its bronze reliefs, and marveled over the classic styling of New York's art deco masterpiece—the black pillars and lighter woods, the gilded ceilings of the corridors—until she reached Peacock Alley and made her way to the bar and lounge. It took her only a moment to spot Gwen sitting at a cocktail table in a plush armchair, her back to Samantha. Food and two champagne glasses, giant strawberries perched on the rims, were waiting.

Sneaking up from behind, she leaned close enough to smell the perfume she'd chased. The intoxicating fragrance was as challenging and complex as the woman wearing it. "May I have this dance?" she whispered in her ear.

Gwen looked up with a welcoming smile, her eyes following Samantha appraisingly as she set her briefcase beside a chair and unbuttoned her suit jacket. "It is a dance, isn't it?"

"What's that, romance?"

"Mm-hm. Romance, courtship. It's just another kind of dance. And at our respective ages, we can assume we've both danced this dance many times. Partners change, but the dance is the same…and the dance always ends."

"You'd make a great motivational speaker, you know that? I'm getting depressed already." She made a face and shook her head. "For the record, Dr. Laraway, I've *never* danced this dance. Not to *this* music." She draped her jacket over the back of a chair and sat opposite Gwen. "And I don't anticipate the music ending anytime soon…so stop trying to talk yourself out of me."

Gwen stroked her chin but didn't respond, because that's exactly what she'd been doing from the start—talking herself out of Samantha. However, she'd obviously failed to make a strong argument for herself, or she wouldn't have canceled plans with Carol to check into a hotel.

Samantha looked at the food. "What's all this?"

"I took the liberty of ordering a few small plates, although I should have asked if you like seafood. It's all the Peacock serves."

"I do. It looks wonderful."

Gwen gestured with a sweep of her hand. "We have a shrimp and lobster cocktail…pan-seared diver scallops…and my favorite, peekytoe crab and caviar with lemon, chives, and a scrumptious cucumber mayo. I didn't know if you'd eaten or not. If you prefer dinner we'll move to a table."

"This is more than enough," Samantha said, sinking into the comfort of the plush chair and looking around.

Gwen reached for the glasses and handed one to her.

"What is it?" She was thirsty and drank before Gwen could answer.

"A strawberry contessa. Gin, champagne, strawberry syrup, and muddled berries. And hopefully sweet enough for your sweet tooth."

"Delicious. Tastes like punch. But the glasses are so small. I might have to have another. And another after that." Samantha grinned.

Gwen laughed and motioned to the server for a double round.

Samantha helped herself to a scallop, spread some caviar on a toast point, and looked around. "I've been to the Bull and Bear, but never here."

"Then it's good you're here to see it," Gwen said as she ate. "The Waldorf is closing soon for renovations. Many of the rooms are being turned into condos."

Samantha's phone beeped, but she ignored it. She had a feeling it was Liz and Isabel trying to track down Gwen. In a little while she'd sneak a text or call them from the ladies' room. "So, Dr. Laraway…how did you know I'd be at the bookstore?"

Gwen told her about coming in to give a lecture, about spending last night and this afternoon with her friend Carol. "I always make a point of stopping in Barnes and Noble when I'm in the city, and my stop there this afternoon proved quite fortuitous. I saw your book and a flyer with your picture and decided to change my plans. I wanted to arrive in time to hear you speak, but by the time I checked in here, showered, and changed, the traffic was horrendous." She looked disappointed. "Why didn't you tell me you'd be there? You know that Isabel and I both would have come in. And where was Liz? Did she know about it?"

Caught off guard, Samantha didn't know how to respond. "You just missed her. She stopped in with a friend, but they had theater tickets and couldn't stay long," Samantha lied. One good thing about being a writer was the ability to make up stories on the spot. "I wanted to call you, but when I spoke to Liz the other day, she mentioned you had a birthday coming up this week. I figured you had plans and didn't want to interfere."

"You're anything but an interference."

And why didn't you tell me it was your birthday?" she said, putting the onus on Gwen.

"I was trying not to think of it. It's tomorrow, and I know my brother has something planned. Most likely dinner at a restaurant with the family and some company people," Gwen said without much enthusiasm. "I'd love nothing more than to invite you and Liz, but I'm not supposed to know about it."

"That's okay. We'll just have to take you out for another celebration, maybe early next week?" Samantha suggested.

"I'd like that."

Their plates empty, Samantha sat back with her third drink. She was tipsy now and eager to change the subject before she slipped and said something to raise Gwen's suspicions. "Tell me why you changed plans with your friend to come here."

Gwen propped her elbow on the arm of her chair, her chin coming to rest in her hand, and stared at Samantha. "I can't explain it, Sam, but I…I have an instinct for you. After that first conversation on the phone, before I even laid eyes on you, I had an instinct for you."

"Is that the same as feeling me in your bones? Because I feel you in my bones…this deep-down primal magnetism that pulls me to you in a way I've never been drawn to anyone."

Gwen looked away for a moment as if to catch her breath. "I don't know how good I'll be at this, Sam. I, um…I haven't had much casual sex."

Samantha raised her brow in mock surprise. "You mean you've *had* casual sex?"

Gwen chuckled. "A few times, in my youth…and once a few years ago, but it was rather disastrous."

"Do tell," Samantha said, finishing the shrimp and lobster cocktail. "I'm all ears."

Gwen hesitated. "If I weren't on my second drink, and if I hadn't had that martini before you arrived, I would *never* in a million years be telling you this, but…well, a couple of years ago friends talked me into a blind date with a colleague of theirs who was here on sabbatical from California. She was younger, probably your age, and I was mildly attracted. Not crazy about her, but attracted enough to see her again. I knew she was returning to California, so that took the pressure off. On our second date, things took an intimate turn, and I decided to just not think about it and go with the flow. I hadn't been with anyone since Jean, and having sex with someone new seemed a good way of…oh, I don't know…overwriting the old files, I suppose. Anyway, in the heat of passion she excused herself, and a few minutes later came back wearing this…*monstrous* prosthetic."

"A strap-on?" Samantha laughed.

"Sam, I swear it was as long as my arm. I've never seen anything so big in all my life. And I knew that if I let that go in one end it would have come out the other."

Samantha had just started to drink and almost spat out her strawberry contessa. Gwen quickly handed her a napkin, and Samantha held it to her lips, trying to swallow without choking. "How did that turn out for you?" she said when she could speak again.

"It *didn't* turn out! When I politely declined in quiet horror, she complained that she wanted to 'feel herself inside me,' as if it were a real penis, nerve endings and all. To this day I can't figure out what she meant. If a woman wants to *feel* herself inside another woman, then wouldn't she use her fingers?" Gwen waved a hand in the air. "I guess things have changed," she continued. "I was born during the women's movement. Penises were so out of style back then. Feminists didn't need men to fulfill their lives, and lesbians certainly didn't need penises for sexual fulfillment. But now?" She shrugged. "Now all the young lesbians seem to want a penis…or at least the experience of having one. I don't know, Sam, maybe I'm just old school, but are there any lesbians left who enjoy having a woman's body and enjoy loving another woman's body without the drama of carting around an extra appendage in a gym bag?"

"Well, having had this conversation, I'm glad I left mine at home," Samantha said in a deadpan manner. "Not to worry you, and not to boast, but mine's a little too large for a gym bag. I carry it discreetly in an old saxophone case. But never into the city. I'm always afraid I'll leave it behind in a taxi."

Samantha couldn't keep a straight face any longer, and neither could Gwen. They both covered their mouths, shaking with laughter until they laughed out loud and caught the attention of people sitting at the bar.

Gwen reached for a napkin and dabbed the corners of her eyes. "So that's my casual-sex story. I'm glad I could amuse you," she said, still laughing. "Do you have one to share?"

"I've had several short-term relationships, but no casual sex, so I'm afraid I don't have any anecdotes to offer."

Gwen nodded, her smile slowly dissipating. Her expression grew serious, and she looked away. "I haven't been with anyone since my surgery," she said out of the blue.

The self-assured professor, usually the epitome of confidence, seemed suddenly unsure of herself. Samantha softened in understanding and waited for Gwen to look at her before she spoke again. "I love every inch of you, sight unseen. Haven't you figured that out by now?" She smiled gently. "And, you know, I'm pushing fifty. Lately, a number of imperfections have been springing up here and there. If you'd like to see them, I'd be more than happy to give you a private, guided tour."

Gwen stared at her for a long while before answering, and then one corner of her mouth turned up. "I think I'd like that."

"Then either you check out of this dump and come home with me…or take me to your room." She stopped to finish her third tiny drink. "Of course, if you're overwhelmed by the physical intimacy associated with either option, we can keep in style with the new generation of lesbian hipsters and sext instead."

"Sexting. Yes. I've read about that. How exactly does it work?"

"Well, you would go to your room right now, and I would stay here and send you text messages, telling you how much I desire you, describing the things I'd like to do to you. And then you'd sext me back, telling me how excited I was making you and about the things you imagine doing to me…and so on and so on."

"Huh!" Gwen nodded. "I suppose that could be fun. I'm getting excited just listening to you tell me about it. But if it's all the same to you, Ms. Weller, I think I'd prefer to leave the *T* out of sext." She drained her glass, as if she needed those last few drops to fight her inhibitions, and reached for her bag. "Let's go upstairs."

Samantha was on top of the world, possibly happier than she'd ever been. Here she was, sitting in the Waldorf with the woman of her dreams, and that woman had just invited her to continue their evening in private. With the rush of the day over and the strawberry contessas kicking in, without Rosa or the ghost-dog to foil a second seduction, she finally had Gwen right where she wanted her—all to herself. Tonight she was going for the gold.

❖

The elegant decor of the room was softly faded but still rich with the history and magic of the Waldorf. Gwen shut off the overhead light as she came out of the bathroom in a black negligee, something she'd picked up while shopping with Carol after her trip to the bookstore earlier today. Nothing extravagant, nothing too revealing, just something simple, slip-like, that ended above the knee: tasteful and age-appropriate, she liked to think.

The drapes were open, and Sam was facing the window that looked out at the Chrysler Building from the twenty-third floor, frantically typing on her cell phone and too busy to notice Gwen coming out.

Gwen smiled to herself and watched her for a moment. She'd come to adore everything about this woman: the way she thought, the things she thought about, the way she spoke and wrote about them. And she loved her curiously androgynous look—the tailored shirts and slacks, always accessorized with feminine touches, like the hint of makeup and the low-heeled pumps she wore.

So much for cultivating a friendship, for confining the sexual attraction to those private fantasies she frequently entertained. The fantasies weren't enough anymore. Ever since they'd danced and kissed the other night, the urge to consummate this attraction had been unbearable. Against that urge she had fought, finding reasons why this love affair should never be. Yet here she was, throwing caution to the wind, throwing everything to the wind—self-discipline, better judgment, all of it. But how long would it be before Sam threw her to the wind? She asked herself this question over and over again. If her same-age partner had left her for a younger woman—a graduate student, to boot—how long before this younger woman left her for an even younger one? *Get it while you can,* her brother had joked, and at some point today she'd come to agree with his philosophy.

Checking into a hotel had been a good decision. Away from home, away from reason, away from Alley's interference, she felt her fears suddenly far away, leaving only this aching desire to take their place. All that mattered was being with Sam in this moment, allowing herself the pleasure of knowing her intimately and without consequence. She came up behind her then, slipping her hands around Sam's waist and pressing them against her stomach. "Sexting your other girlfriend, are you?" she whispered.

"Ah, you caught me," Sam said without looking at her. She covered Gwen's hands with one of her own, quickly hitting the send button on the phone she held in the other. Then she powered it off, set it on the sill, and turned around in Gwen's arms. Her lips parted in surprise at the black negligee. "Mmm…what's this?" she said, smoothing her hands over the soft, silky fabric.

"Just something I picked up in a hurry."

"Well! As long as you're not in a hurry now…" Her hands glided down over Gwen's hips, up to her torso. One slid between her breasts, up to the thin line of lace along her neck, and then both stroked her bare arms. "You have great shoulders," Sam said.

"Tennis," Gwen murmured.

"Hmm…so that explains why the ball's in your court." Sam smiled, pushed down a strap, kissed and bit one shoulder blade.

Gwen laughed softly, but the sound turned into a soft moan as Sam's lips explored her neck, her jaw, her throat. She tilted her head back, luxuriating in the exquisite pleasure of being touched. It had been so long. And never ever had it felt this good.

As Sam's lips found hers, Gwen opened her mouth and kissed her deeply, and when Sam's hands reached around to her buttocks, gently spreading and pulling up on them, she gasped at the sudden pressure between her legs. The sound of her pleasure seemed to drive Sam wild, and she pulled Gwen close, backed her up against the bed, and reached down to pull up her negligee.

Gwen put a hand between them and pushed against Sam's chest. "And what's *your* hurry?" she teased her. "I want that private tour you promised." Slowly she trailed her fingers down Sam's sleeveless shirt, opening each button as she went.

Gwen held Sam's gaze as she undressed her, taking in the fine details of her face, the moist and supple lips now swollen from kissing, her thick and shapely eyebrows. And the bright brown eyes that usually regarded her with inquisitiveness and sincerity were now dark, glassy, dilated with desire.

"Gwen, I want you so—"

"Shh." She smiled and took her time, making Sam wait, enjoying this feeling of sexual power over her right now. When she reached the last button she pushed the shirt off her shoulders, and as it fell to the floor she reached around to Sam's back to unclasp the black bra that contrasted against her fair skin. She had wanted to do this the other night while watching Sam bending over behind the bar. Oh, how she'd imagined sliding her hands inside to cup and play with her breasts as she did now. Gwen held Sam's gaze as she explored her, moving her hands down over her abdomen, over the surprisingly hard muscles beneath her soft skin. "You have a beautiful body, Sam. I think you lied about those imperfections."

"As long as you keep these lights low, I'll pretend to have lied," Sam whispered, her muscles tightening even more as Gwen unzipped her pants.

Gwen slipped a hand down inside and watched Sam's eyes close, her mouth open. She felt the pounding of Sam's heart, listened as her breathing became ragged. And Gwen, too, had to catch her breath. She hadn't expected to find Sam this aroused, and cupping the center of that arousal in her hand sent her own soaring to another level.

"You see what you do to me?" Sam said, her words hoarse in between heavy breaths. "This is how I've been since I met you. It used to feel good…then it became an ache, which still felt good," she said with a forced laugh that seemed to catch in her throat. "And now it just hurts. I hurt for you all the time," she said.

"I might have an antidote."

"You *are* the antidote." Sam started to shimmy her way out of her pants, urging Gwen along. When her legs were free, she reached again to gently tug the bottom of Gwen's negligee and, in one smooth movement, pulled it up and over her head.

Gwen watched as Sam's eyes roamed her body, the space between them, then drew Gwen to her. Kisses that were slow and tender became wild and desperate. The room had been pleasantly cool with the air conditioner on, but now it felt as though it had been turned off. Heat rose between their naked bodies, their stomachs slick with perspiration as they held on to each other, kissing, slipping and sliding against one another's skin, blindly reaching in a frenzy to pull back the white covers. They fell together in the sheets then, and in an instant Sam was on top of her.

"I want to take that ache away," Gwen whispered.

"Oh, you will...after you watch me take yours away."

Gwen joyfully submitted, arched her body, desperate to be taken, needing to be taken. She opened herself completely, giving her body and soul to this woman who so skillfully ravished her.

A long while later, they lay facing one another in the quiet of the room. Lost in thought, Gwen stared at her in admiration as she traced Sam's eyebrows with a fingertip, trailed it down her nose and across her lips.

"What are you thinking...?" Sam asked.

"How comfortable I am with you...how sexy you make me feel... how wonderfully delirious I am right now." She cupped and stroked Sam's cheek. "And you? What's going on in that beautiful mind of yours?"

Sam's dark eyes were half closed. "I'm thinking I could do that all over again." She grabbed hold of Gwen's thigh, pulling and draping her leg across her own body. "I love the way you taste. Fruity..."

"Sam!" she said, and knew that even in the low light Sam could see her blush.

"Well, you do." Sam smiled crookedly, rolling forward so that half her body covered Gwen's now. She buried her face in her neck. "You taste like...like peaches and plums...apricots and honey and—"

"Stop!" Gwen said, but she had started to laugh.

"I didn't realize you were so modest."

"I am."

"Then I feel privileged to have penetrated that modest exterior."

"Oh, you penetrated it, all right." Gwen looked at her adoringly, then lifted her head off the pillow and pulled Sam's mouth to hers. "You've completely drained and dehydrated me," she said after a long kiss. "I need to use the bathroom...and I need something to drink, but I don't know if I have the strength to stand yet, let alone walk."

"You've left me weak, too, so I don't think I can carry you. I might be able to drag you, but to prevent injury you might try getting there on your own."

Gwen laughed as she got up. "Why don't you see what drinks that minibar has to offer us."

"You want a drink-drink?"

"God, no. I'm still working off the martini and contessas," she said, and made her way to the bathroom while Sam went to the minibar.

"Perrier, soda, juice…?" Sam called to her.

"Perrier. And, please, make yourself a drink if you like."

Sam was back in bed drinking a Snapple when Gwen returned. She opened the bottle of Perrier and handed it to Gwen. "Hydrate."

Gwen took a long drink, then stretched out alongside Sam. She propped herself up on an elbow and ran her hand up and down Sam's body.

Sam watched her with a lazy smile. "You make me happy."

"I could spend the rest of my life making you happy. Although perhaps not the rest of *your* life," she added as an afterthought.

Sam frowned. "Why do you say things like that?"

She looked away, and as she did caught sight of the time. "Can that clock be right? It's past midnight. Goodness, Sam, we've been making love for over three hours."

"Is that a complaint or an observation?"

"Hardly a complaint." Gwen leaned forward and kissed the side of her mouth. "But I should inform you that somewhere in the throes of passion, I turned sixty."

"Happy birthday, sweetheart. I'm upset that you'll have to wait for a present, but it's your fault for not telling me you were having a birthday."

"You *are* my birthday present…my gift to myself, as it were." She smiled. "And I must say I thoroughly enjoyed unwrapping it." She paused for a moment, overcome by a fleeting sadness that seemed to come out of nowhere.

Sam stroked her cheek with the back of her fingers. "Talk to me."

"Well, for one, when you're my age I'll be seventy-three. And when you're eighty, I'll be…well, I probably won't…but if I am, there won't be much left of me to make you happy."

"You know what? I shouldn't be here with you right now. In fact, you should never have met me. I should have died five years ago when my car was crushed beyond recognition by that tree."

"Do you ever think you *weren't* supposed to die, that something or someone invisible made you notice that bird and got you up and out of that car because it wasn't your time to go?"

"That appears to have been the case. My point, Professor, is that being younger doesn't guarantee longevity. Younger people die before older people all the time. I spent years working with dead people—their DNA, at least—and most of them weren't past their prime. There are people not yet born who will die before both of us." Sam inched closer to her. "Let me tell you a story."

"Ah...here comes the casual-sex story after all."

Sam laughed. "I told you, I don't have casual sex. This is a love story. About Agatha Christie and her second husband, who, as it so happens, was almost thirteen years her junior."

"Almost thirteen years, just like us, huh? What a coincidence."

"That's why the telling of it seems apropos."

"Hmm...so tell me this story that is sure to address and quiet my concerns."

"Well, after divorcing her first husband, Christie went on an archeological dig in the Middle East to research a novel. She was headed somewhere else, but because of transportation issues ended up in Bagdad, where she met Max Mallowan, a renowned archeologist, who agreed to be her tour guide as a favor to friends. He was twenty-six, she was thirty-nine. The chemistry was immediate. They became instant friends and fell madly in love. Max proposed more than once, and Agatha declined more than once because of the age difference. He persisted, eventually she gave in, and they were married that same year, days before her fortieth birthday. Their love affair lasted forty-five years, until her death at the age of eight-five. Max died two years later at the age of seventy-four. So despite the age difference, they died only two years apart." Sam grinned. "True story."

"A very charming and convincing one," Gwen said, "but it's not dying before you that frightens me...it's living long enough to see the day that you no longer find me attractive."

Sam didn't respond right away. She stared at her with sleepy eyes and ran her fingers through Gwen's disheveled hair.

"My hair must be an awful mess."

"A wild and wonderful mess. It looks great." Sam smiled and played with it some more. "You know, either of us could go to several dating sites and find plenty of women in our respective age groups... but there's no guarantee of any chemistry, sexually or otherwise."

Gwen gathered her in her arms and sighed, and she rested her head on Gwen's breast. "I hate to admit it to myself, Sam, but I've never experienced chemistry quite like this."

"It was there that first day we met. I couldn't say anything then, but I was struck with this strange sensation of déjà vu...like I'd known you before…like we weren't meeting for the first time but returning to each other from another place in time." Sam's hand moved in soft circles over Gwen's stomach. "That chemical attraction was strong. We mix well together. We even smell good together."

"Sam!" She gave her arm a playful slap.

"But it's true. We do."

Gwen sighed, squeezed her tight, and put her nose to Sam's hair. "Yes…our scents do mingle well," she said, and felt Sam smiling against her breast.

Sam buried her face in Gwen's skin and mumbled, "…love stokes its raging fire…as the heady fragrance of desire…fills the room like sweet perfume…"

"Mmm…are you poetizing?"

"I am."

"Did you just think that up?"

"I did. You're a source of spontaneous inspiration."

"It's wonderful. I told you once before, you should try your hand at poetry." Gwen kissed her head. "Maybe one day you'll write a poem for me."

"Maybe I will," Sam said, and cuddled close.

Chapter Twenty-Five

In that place between sleep and wakefulness, Samantha couldn't tell if the tingling in her legs was coming from a dream or waking her from one. Her eyes sprang open, and she was acutely aware of a heaviness below her knees, a deadening pressure pinning her ankles. Gwen was sound asleep, tangled in her arms, and Samantha's first thought was that the weight was coming from Gwen's legs stretched across her own. The moisture from their lovemaking seemed to have dried and sealed them together during the night, and she tried to lift her head as much as she could without waking Gwen. In the early dawn, the room was still dark, but something darker than the room itself lay at the foot of the bed. And unless her eyes were playing tricks, the round and indistinct shape seemed to be rhythmically heaving.

The sight of it, the physical pressure of its presence on her feet sent her into a quiet panic. She fought back a scream, yanking her legs from under it and jerking her feet until she kicked them out from the covers.

"Sam? What's wrong?" Gwen said, awoken by the commotion.

"Something's in bed with us!"

"What?" Gwen peeled herself off Samantha's body and quickly reached for the lamp.

Samantha jumped out of bed, shaking one foot and then the other until the feeling in them returned.

Gwen sat up, a hand held to her chest, and looked around the empty room. "You scared me to half to death. I thought there was an intruder."

"It *was* an intruder. I don't think it was alive, though."

"A ghost?"

Samantha nodded. The hair on her arms stood on end, and she crossed them, rubbing her shoulders until the sudden chill passed. "At the foot of the bed…something heavy was on my legs. It made my feet fall asleep." She might not have been so forthcoming with anyone else, but Gwen would believe her. After all, neither of them would ever again dismiss the reality of ghosts.

Gwen patted the bed. Samantha crawled back in and snuggled close but kept her eyes on the foot of the bed. "Do you think the Waldorf has ghosts?"

"Considering the hotel has been world renowned since the nineteen thirties, I'm sure a few expired guests and employees are wandering the hallways."

Samantha was quiet for a minute. "Do they allow pets?"

"The Waldorf has always pampered pets of the rich and famous." Gwen stroked Samantha's arm as she spoke, calming and lulling her back to sleep. "Is that what you think you saw…an animal?"

"Could have been…I'd prefer an animal to some long-dead bellboy on my legs."

"I'm sure you know this from your own research, but one of the most commonly reported ghostly encounters is the feeling of something at the foot of the bed, kneading or pulling the blankets."

"I know. I didn't feel movement, just my feet trapped. It reminded me of…" Samantha's words trailed off as she lost herself in a memory.

"Tell me," Gwen said.

"The last time I felt something like that was when I slept with a dog. Did I ever mention Arthur, my Weimaraner?"

"You did. Arthur the ghost runner, who followed the scent of flowers…"

"Yeah. He always had to sleep with part of his body touching mine. Arthur was a big boy, and sometimes I'd wake up to that same feeling of being pinned down. And there he'd be, his long legs draped across my ankles, his heavy paws and chin resting on my shin. That's what this felt like. God, that was so creepy."

"You don't think it was him."

"Of course not. Arthur crossed the Rainbow Bridge more than twenty years ago. And if his spirit were still around, I don't think he'd come looking for me at the Waldorf."

Gwen's soft laugh came as a murmur, and Samantha touched the hand that was stroking her. She rolled onto her back and gathered Gwen in her arms.

They were quiet then and must have fallen back to sleep, because the next time Samantha opened her eyes the room was bright and cheerful, the sun having chased away the night-loving spooks. Samantha heard the water running and then the shower cut off. She stretched and glanced at the clock. Almost nine. She would need to keep Gwen occupied until two o'clock.

"Good morning, darling," Gwen said as she came out of the bathroom in a robe and sat on the bed beside her. "I ordered coffee. We can have breakfast downstairs."

Samantha touched her face. "What are your plans for the day, birthday girl?"

"Well, I had intended to see a Picasso exhibit at the Met, but when I read that *Woman with a Crow* is there, I decided I should see it with you."

"What time is your surprise dinner tonight?"

"I should turn my phone on and call my brother. I think reservations are for seven. I'll be fine as long as I'm home by five."

That would keep guests waiting for over two hours. Isabel wanted her there at four, and with Carol out of the picture, the responsibility of ensuring a timely arrival was on Samantha. "How long is the exhibit running?"

"Through August."

"Could we save it for next week?"

"We could."

"Why don't we do that? I have to leave town this coming Wednesday for a few days. I have signings in DC on Thursday, Baltimore on Friday, Philly at noon on Saturday, and then I drive home. Pick a day after that and we'll go." She rubbed her hand up and down Gwen's arm. "I haven't been to the Met in years. It would be nice to take our time, have dinner out…turn it into a date."

Gwen raised an eyebrow. "Hmm…I like the idea of more dates with you."

"The other thing," Samantha said, fibbing as she went along, "is that I didn't exactly plan on bumping into you yesterday. A friend of mine had to leave her car in the shop, and I promised I'd give her a lift back before three this afternoon."

"That's fine," Gwen said. Someone knocked at the door just then. "Coffee's here."

"Do I have time for a quick shower?"

"Of course."

As soon as Gwen went to the door, Samantha got up, grabbed her phone, and made a beeline for the bathroom.

"There's a toothbrush for you in there, Sam, and—"

"Ah. So you were that confident you'd get me up to your hotel room and seduce me?"

"Reasonably confident, yes."

Samantha shook her head. "I'm such a cheap date. Shameless, too," she mumbled.

"And help yourself to whatever else I have in there."

"Thanks." Samantha closed the door and turned on her phone. Five missed calls from Liz and Isabel. She dialed Liz and turned on the shower to drown out her voice.

"Sam! Why is Gwen's phone off? Do you still have her?"

"I have her."

"*Did* you have her?"

"I did. And she had me. More than once."

"Damn. I'm jealous. No action here. Not that I expected any. Are you taking a shower with her?"

"No. I'm running the water so she can't hear me. I can't talk. We have to check out soon. I'll get her to come home with me and won't let her leave until two. That'll get her there by four. I'll call when she leaves. I won't make it for the surprise, obviously."

Samantha hung up and showered quickly, helped herself to toothpaste, deodorant, and powder, then wrapped herself in a towel. When she came out she spotted a coffee pot on a tray in the sitting area, *The New York Times* beside it. Gwen sat on a love seat reading the Arts and Leisure section, which she quickly discarded when she saw Samantha. "Mmm…come here to me," she said.

Samantha went and sat beside her, kissed her softly.

Gwen played with the strands of damp hair hanging down over Samantha's forehead. "I'd take you back to bed if we didn't have to leave."

"And I'd let you." Sam kissed her again, then turned to pour coffee, but it was there waiting for her.

"I think I know how you take your coffee by now."

"I think you know how I take more than just my coffee." Samantha cradled the cup in two hands and curled up next to her. "How are you getting home?"

"I have my car."

"Then I have an idea. Instead of breakfast here, why don't you drive me home, and I'll make us breakfast there. I'm always at your place, and I feel like you have no…no context for me."

Gwen pursed her lips and thought. "I'd love that, yes. Then I get to see where you write."

"You will. And it'll put you an hour closer to home."

Samantha had no choice but to put back on her suit, and Gwen sported a short-sleeve shirt and tight, stretchy white jeans that had Samantha walking behind her just to admire the view until they got into Gwen's white Mercedes.

Traffic wasn't too bad getting out of the city, and they made it into Westchester just before eleven. Gwen dropped her off in the train station's parking lot, then followed her a short distance to the tiny Tudor nestled at the end of a quiet, overgrown street.

Samantha was glad she'd shopped and cleaned the other day, glad she'd changed the sheets before she'd left for the city yesterday. With any luck she'd lure Gwen into them and keep her occupied until two o'clock.

She unlocked the door and held it for Gwen. "Welcome to Dark Shadows."

The Tudor's original stained-glass windows were beautiful but didn't allow sunlight to filter through. Not that there was ever much sun; the house itself faced northwest and was completely shaded by the canopies of enormous oak trees lining the block. When the autumn leaves fell there would be more light. The house was always brightest in winter.

"It's charming. The perfect abode for a writer of paranormal mysteries, if you ask me," Gwen said as she walked in and looked around. "I've always loved Tudors, both English and Spanish. The window art is magnificent."

"You know it's not mine. I guess it's sort of pathetic that I'm living in someone else's house, furnishings and all. Only the bed and what's in the study belong to me—and that." She pointed to a freestanding perch. "I figured I'd leave it in case Bertha decides to move back home."

Gwen gave a sympathetic look. "I'm sorry she's not here with you."

"Don't be. The Laraway estate offers more attractive living options. I'd have made the same choice."

"It's not the place. It's what she's found there—other crows."

"I can't compete. So it's just me for now, until I find the inspiration to house-hunt."

"In Westchester?"

"Who knows. Now that I'm retired from my first career and writing full-time, I'm not tied to a location. I can write from anywhere. I just don't know where *anywhere* is yet. I'd even thought of moving back to Texas to be closer to my father."

Gwen smiled, but her smile seemed forced. "Is that your plan?"

Samantha put her hands around Gwen's waist. "I actually love New England, and I've grown especially fond of a particular woman who lives there. So, no, it's not my plan." Samantha smiled. "What would you like for breakfast?"

"What's on the menu?"

"Anything you want. Bacon and eggs, pancakes, French toast… or my signature breakfast, a spinach and feta-cheese omelet with fresh farmers' bread."

"Mmm…your signature dish sounds delicious. I'll help you, although I'm not too good in the kitchen. I've never really had to cook. And I certainly didn't peg you for the culinary type."

"I love to cook. I just don't do it much because I have no one to cook for." She gave Gwen a quick kiss. "Any messages from your brother?"

"I still haven't checked. It would help if I turned on my phone."

Samantha let go of her. "Why don't you do that? I'll make coffee and start breakfast."

Gwen settled on the couch, and Samantha went into the dining room, turning on lights as she walked into the small kitchen. She got coffee going, poured orange juice, and took a glass out to Gwen.

"Ten voice mails, probably birthday messages…one missed call from Bill…and five missed calls from Isabel," she said.

Samantha turned on some chill music and set the volume low. "You better call Isabel. I'm just running upstairs to get out of these clothes. I'll have breakfast ready in twenty minutes."

Gwen was on the phone when she came back down in shorts and a tee, and by the time she was off the phone, breakfast was cooking and the table was set with brightly colored plates and several burning jar candles.

"Well, I was thoroughly chastised for having my phone off all night," Gwen said as she came in. "But I was right. Reservations are for seven." She looked at the table and around the room. "It's very cozy in here. I feel like we're in one of those dark and haunted taverns you like so much."

Samantha laughed. "Maybe that's why I picked this house. It's conducive to writing what I write about," she said, going back and forth to the kitchen to bring out coffee, their omelets, and the fresh bread she'd sliced and heated in the oven. "There's just something about the dark, you know? Just like there's something about a woman in black."

"I'll take the woman in black," Gwen said, and began eating once Samantha joined her at the table. "This is delectable. My compliments to the chef."

They relaxed after they ate, talking, lingering at the table over a third cup of coffee. Samantha kept careful track of the time. She needed to keep her for an hour and a half, no more, no less. "You said you wanted to see where I write."

"I would absolutely love to," Gwen said, and started to clear the table.

"Leave it, birthday girl. I'll take care of the dishes later." She got up and gestured for Gwen to follow.

Up the narrow staircase they went, turning right on the landing and into the room she'd made her study. Gwen stopped, her face lighting with amusement at the life-size skeleton donning a velvet top hat and bowtie. A large horseshoe-shaped desk faced out to the room, and the skeleton sat in a chair on the other side of the desk, as though Samantha were in the habit of regularly conversing with it. "I know that man!" Gwen said, pointing with surprised delight. "It's Professor Crowley, Detective Candice Crowley's great-great-uncle. I so enjoy him crawling out of bed—out of his grave, as it were—to walk the cemetery with Candice and speculate on unsolved cases. And it's nice that he thinks to collect worms for Bertha."

"Well, he appreciates having something to occupy his time and thoughts. It eases the monotony of eternity."

"It's an honor to meet you, Uncle Felix." Gwen curtsied to the skeleton. "Your conjectures are brilliant." And then she nonchalantly made her way around the desk, stopping to examine the assorted piles of papers there: printed chapters of a manuscript, research papers, copies of Gwen's published articles, and a book that looked brand-new. She tapped the cover with a fingernail as she passed it. "*Philosophy for Dummies*? Hmm...giving yourself a crash course, are you?"

Samantha felt a little embarrassed. "Well, you see, my new girlfriend's a philosopher. I'm trying my best to impress her."

"She's very impressed, in case you haven't noticed." Gwen sat in the high-back office chair, pulled the chain on a banker's lamp, and looked all around the room.

Samantha knew exactly what she was looking for. She walked to the barrister bookcases across from the desk and turned on a tiny spotlight overhead. It lit the Rookwood bookends.

Samantha held out a hand to them. "Mine and yours."

"There they are…the 'mine and yours' that brought me and you together." Gwen gave a knowing smile. "They look lovely…very happy…yet they still have that air of omniscience, don't you think?" Gwen leaned back in the chair, admiring them, and then her eyes moved to a huge plug-in jack-o'-lantern on the floor. "Does it always feel like Halloween in here?"

"Always. I find it inspirational," Samantha said, and watched as Gwen's blue eyes settled on a framed painting that hung beside the bookcases. In it, a large, whimsical crow wearing worn black boots walked through an autumn cornfield, its feathers cape-like.

Gwen studied the anthropomorphic bird, then looked at the empty wall on the other side of the bookcase. "I have something coming that will fill that space perfectly."

"You got me something? What is it?"

"I'm not telling." Her attention shifted to Samantha's laptop and printer and another scattering of papers. "What are you working on now?"

"Two books. The next in the series and something new…a paranormal romance. I don't expect it to appeal to my current audience, but my agent's shopping it."

"A romance? Between women?"

"I don't have it in me to write a heterosexual romance."

Gwen sat back, her arms draped on the arms of Samantha's office chair, and gave a calculating look. "Is it a mysterious romance?"

"Didn't you once tell me that love is its own mystery?"

"I did, yes."

Samantha smiled and held at her hand out to Gwen. "Come and see the one other piece of furniture I own," she said, and led her across to the bedroom.

Gwen paused in the doorway. "You certainly are a master of mood," she remarked. "And please don't take this as an insult, because it's not, but I feel like I went from Halloween through a portal to another place in time. This room has old-world charm and the ambience of a high-class brothel."

Sam laughed out loud and flopped down on the red down comforter. "It must be all the red. I have a thing for red. But if you say brothel, then we'll pretend it is." She patted the space next to her, and when Gwen came close enough, she grabbed and pulled her down onto the bed. "I will delight in servicing you…and you can leave the money on the dresser on your way out."

"How about I pay you in writing supplies? With a lover who owns a paper company, you need never buy another ream." She stared up at Samantha, searched her eyes. "The truth, though, is that I would pay for you. That's how much you make me want you."

It seemed like only yesterday that Gwen had rejected her advances on the basis of age. And then, just that fast, Gwen had seduced her, and here they were, lying together, kissing so passionately. It still felt like a dream, and Samantha had yet to thoroughly realize this wonderful and unexpected reality. An idea came to her suddenly, and she pulled away and smiled. "Stay right where you are," she said, leaving Gwen stretched across the bed.

"I don't trust that devilish grin," Gwen said, a hint of caution in her voice. "What are you up to?"

"Being it's your birthday, my services are free today," she said, and disappeared into the bathroom.

"I'm warning you right now, Sam, if you come out of there with a saxophone case, I'll be out of here and in my car before you can open it."

Samantha laughed and came back out with a flat, round jar. "Today's special is a birthday massage."

Gwen sat up and checked her watch. "Sam, I…I really should get going soon. Time has a way of running away from us. Last night, minutes turned into hours."

"Don't you worry. I'll have you out of here in an hour," Samantha promised, although she'd need to keep her a little longer than that. "And you'll leave here feeling great. So will my hands."

"How's that?"

"My hands spend most of the day held rigidly over a keyboard. Sometimes I think they might permanently stiffen like this," she said, holding up her hands and curling her fingers like monster claws. Massaging someone is good exercise for them. It'll loosen my fingers."

"Your fingers felt loose enough last night."

Samantha regarded her seductively. "Take your clothes off, sweetheart." She put the jar down and pulled off her own shirt.

"Since when does the masseuse take her clothes off?"

"That's the rule. If the masseuse and the masseuse-ee have had sex prior to a tantric massage, then the masseuse must be naked as well."

"Did you just make up that rule?"

"Maybe." She winked at Gwen. "But it's a good rule, designed to maximize my experience as well as yours."

Gwen stood up and shook her head. "I don't know what it is, but I think I'd let you talk me into just about anything."

"You say that like it's a bad thing."

Gwen looked at her with hesitation but didn't argue. She stripped down to her underwear while Samantha drew back the covers. And when Samantha turned back around, she hooked a finger in the waistband of Gwen's panties and let the elastic snap back. "These, too," she said, and kicked off her own shorts.

Reluctantly, Gwen did as she was told and stretched across the bed.

"If it's too cool in here I can turn up the thermostat."

"It's perfect."

"How about the music? Too loud?"

"It's fine. Are there speakers in here, or is the music coming from downstairs?"

"I have wireless speakers everywhere. If you must know, I'm music-dependent when it comes to writing. I write different scenes to certain songs that I keep playing on repeat—in the house and in the car." Samantha knelt on the bed and straddled her, and as soon as she felt Gwen's warm body touching her between her legs, she grew excited.

Samantha scooped out a glob of body butter, warming it in her hands before starting on Gwen's shoulders and neck. She spent time there, her caresses deep and slow, before shifting to her arms. From Gwen's wrists to her shoulders, she moved her hands up and down in long strokes.

"Mmm…I'll have to have a whole truckload of paper delivered for this," Gwen said as Samantha focused on her back, finding and kneading each muscle with the tips of her fingers and heels of her hands.

Discovering Gwen's body, learning points of pleasure by her soft murmurs, triggered a rush of desire that made Samantha wet.

Gwen writhed, rose a little, and pushed herself up between Samantha's legs. "Did you just spill some hot body butter on me?"

"Mm-hmm…it's not from the jar, though."

"You're far too good at this, Sam. How many women do you service in this brothel of yours?"

"I swear, I've been with only one other woman in this house." She glided her hands up and down Gwen's body, grazing the sides of her breasts with just the right amount of pressure, then bent forward, trailing her lips over Gwen's skin in a line of kisses from her lower back to her neck. "And she wasn't you, so she doesn't count."

The more she worked on Gwen's body, the softer and silkier her own hands became. She got off and kneeled beside her, alternating between firm and feather-like touches as she worked on Gwen's lower back, the outside of her thighs, and down to her legs. And then slowly she worked her way up again, this time massaging the inside of her thighs. When she sensed Gwen's arousal, a sudden change in her breathing, she stretched out alongside her.

"I didn't know I was feeling any tension until you took it all away," Gwen whispered.

"The point of a tantric massage is not to take away the tension, but to send it all to one place." Samantha whispered in her ear as she slipped her left hand between the back of Gwen's thighs, then expertly slid the other beneath her stomach and down to cup her tightly. "It's to send it all here so you can release it yourself…all at once."

"Did you make that up, too?" she asked, her breathing becoming heavy.

"What if I did?" Samantha whispered. "Would you object?"

"How could I possibly…"

"Then spread your legs for me, and I'll help you release that tension."

"God, Sam…" Gwen opened her legs, relinquishing control of her own body.

Samantha stayed on her knees, her breasts and stomach pressing against Gwen's back as she found her from behind, the slippery fingers of both hands meeting as she stroked and massaged her to a quick climax.

"Oh, Sam, I can't…I can't stop it, I—"

"Don't stop," she whispered, working both her hands and bringing Gwen to the edge of an orgasm. "Just let it come…"

And it did, Gwen's cries of pleasure putting Samantha on the verge of her own climax. She kept Gwen in her hands until her breathing slowed, then turned her over and settled between her legs to find her own rhythm.

But Gwen rolled her back over and climbed on top of her. "Oh, no…you've worked hard enough." She ran a hand between her thighs. "Let me take care of you."

"You don't have to reciprocate…I know you need to leave…"

"With you like this? It won't take me long," Gwen said. "I don't think you'll last a minute in my mouth."

And she didn't. She exploded almost the instant Gwen took her.

It was a few minutes before Samantha could think straight, another before she could see straight enough to look at the clock. Ten minutes to two. She needed to get them up and showered and send Gwen on her way. "It's almost two."

"See what I mean about time passing when we're together?"

"I'll run the shower and get you a towel."

"I'll shower when I get home," Gwen said in between deep kisses. "I don't want to wash you off me yet. I rather like what you said last night about the 'heady fragrance of desire,' and I do like the idea of keeping you close to me all the way home."

Samantha didn't know what to say. Gwen had no idea what she was headed home to—sixty or more people waiting to bombard her with hugs and kisses and birthday wishes. But she couldn't warn her, and she couldn't force her to take a shower. "Come on. How about a quick one with me?"

"Nothing's quick with you. Besides, this body butter feels wonderful. I should let it do its job before washing it off. My skin feels wonderful."

Gwen's mind was made up. Pushing the suggestion would only raise her suspicions. Samantha couldn't do anything except watch as Gwen picked up her clothes from the floor and carried them into the bathroom.

Samantha jumped up, grabbed her shirt, and pulled on her shorts. She'd try to act casual and, after she walked Gwen out to her car, would quickly do the dishes, shower, and dress, then get on the road, hopefully no more than thirty minutes behind her.

Chapter Twenty-Six

One side of the Laraway driveway, as far as Samantha could see, was lined with cars. Others were parked along the shoulder of the country road. She pulled up behind the last of them, and as soon as she got out she heard the muffled sound of voices, distant laughter, and the percussive thumping of music. It wasn't easy to walk up the gravel drive in one-inch heels, and as she concentrated on not slipping, there came a *whoosh*, and something sharp grabbed her shoulder.

"Bertha! You scared the daylights out of me." She reached over her shoulder to pet the crow's back. "Thanks for that rush. You have no idea how much I miss you scaring me. Every single day I miss it," she said, pressing her hand against the bird's breast. After Bertha stepped onto her hand, she brought the crow around to her face. "Even with all this noise you heard me coming, huh? It makes me feel good to know you miss me."

Bertha's eyes widened, and she looked at her strangely, first with one eye and then the other. In a flash, as if something had frightened her, she flew up to a branch over Samantha's head and began cawing.

"Aww…I know you're nervous." Samantha looked up, using a hand to shield her eyes from the sun shining through the trees. "Are all those people interrupting the peace and quiet of your new country estate?"

Spreading her wings, Bertha lowered her body on the branch, dipped her head, and squawked.

"Why are you yelling at *me*? I'm not the one who invited them all," Samantha said, but just then her phone rang, and she dug it out of her pocket and answered. She'd texted Liz fifteen minutes ago to say she was almost there but doubted Liz would hear or check her phone with everything going on. "I didn't think you'd see my message."

"I hear Bertha. Why is she screaming like that?"

"She has the jitters. Probably all those people and so much noise."

"She's been fine until now. Where are you?"

"Coming up from the road. I can't walk too fast in this gravel with dress shoes."

"Why'd you park all the way down there? Bring the car up. Isabel saved a space for you at the top of the driveway."

"Oh, good." Sam went back to the car. When she pulled into the driveway she stopped under the branch where Bertha was still perched and rolled down the window. "Come on and ride with Sam-Sam. Oh, come on, Bertha," she pleaded, but the crow wasn't budging. She dropped from the branch and flew up the driveway, staying low between the trees and gliding around the bend. Samantha followed her in the car.

Liz was waiting with a drink in each hand when she reached the top of the driveway.

"Beautiful dress," Samantha commented as she got out with her gift and looked Liz up and down.

"Thanks." Liz's glance darted to the little blue bag dangling from Samantha's fingers, and she gasped. "You went to Tiffany's? What'd you get her?"

"A gold necklace."

"Whoa! You must *really* like her."

Samantha smirked. "Eh…maybe just a little bit."

"And you." Liz waggled a reprimanding finger in her face. "You were asked to *occupy* Gwen today, not seduce her."

Samantha gave a crooked smile. "How would *you* know what I did?"

"Trust me, I know the look of a woman who's just had sex, okay? Besides, her hair looked like she'd just rolled out of bed, and when I hugged her…well…never mind." She handed Samantha a margarita. But just as Samantha took the glass from her, an odd expression came over Liz's face, and she looked around. "There it is, Sam…that strange feeling, that weird presence I felt the first time we came here."

"I bet it's the ghost-dog. She'll show herself to me soon enough. I'll let you know when she does," Samantha said, taking pride in the fact that she could see the ghost better and more often than anyone else. It somehow trusted her, she was convinced, and she was coming to think of it as her ethereal pet. Whether she had latent psychic abilities or the dog had simply decided to make herself visible, Samantha felt as though she'd been chosen, specially selected to serve as intermediary for the lonely, earth-bound spirit.

"What a party, huh?" Liz said.

"I'll say. It looks like a wedding reception." Samantha could see two huge white tents, the walls and ceilings covered in tiny white lights. In one was the DJ, a huge, portable dance floor, a band set up, and a long bar; in the other were round dinner tables set with white tablecloths and balloons floating up from colorful floral centerpieces. The lawn featured cocktail tables and chairs, most of which were occupied. It had been eighty-five degrees and humid when Samantha left her house, but the sun wasn't strong now, and the country air was dry and very pleasant. "How many people?"

"Isabel estimated seventy-five, give or take a few."

People who weren't at the cocktail tables were already dancing, others standing around holding drinks and talking in small groups. At a glance, Samantha could easily distinguish the business people from the academic types. "Was Gwen surprised?" Samantha asked.

"Surprised? Try horrified." She pursed her lips and shook her head disapprovingly, as if it were all Samantha's fault. "She obviously knew what was going on the moment she saw all the cars parked, but you know Gwen—always gracious and composed. She didn't miss a beat. She drove right up with a big smile and rolled down her window to wave at the crowd as they all cheered and yelled surprise. But her eyes were frantic, and as soon as she caught sight of Isabel and Rosa, she pointed to the back of the house, then opened the garage door from the car and pulled in. Rosa knew she'd been given a direct order to sneak her inside. The three of us ran in through the front and unlocked the back door. Gwen instructed Isabel to have the DJ announce that she would be with her guests momentarily, as soon as she was appropriately attired. She was happy to see me, though, and gave me a quick hug before running upstairs," Liz said with a knowing smirk. "And she left additional orders for you to report to her the moment you arrived." Liz pointed a finger at her again. "You're in big trouble."

"Uh-oh."

"Uh-huh. Come on, I'll walk you to the house."

Samantha tasted her margarita, and just as they started to walk, Isabel came through the crowd, Blue and Loosey Goosey trotting alongside her. She was dressed in a tight-fitting, silky white shirt tucked into low-rise black pants, and on her feet were patent-leather loafers with a crocodile print. "What a sharp-looking little dyke," Samantha whispered. "Does she really think the long hair throws people off?"

"I think it throws *her* off…and it's throwing me off, Sam. I'm ready to give up." She let out a heavy sigh, talking faster and lower as Isabel approached. "I slept in bed with her last night because Rosa and a woman they hired to help out were busy getting the guest rooms ready. Carol and her husband are spending the night, along with a couple of cousins who flew in for the party. It was another fun and cozy adolescent sleepover—me, Isabel, Loosey, and Blue."

When the dogs spotted Liz and Samantha they raced ahead of Isabel. But midway Blue stopped short and took a few cautious steps back, a low growl rumbling in her chest. She stared at Samantha for a moment, then ran off.

"Geez," Liz said. "At first that dog couldn't care less about you, and now she's scared to death."

"She's not scared. She just hates me…like Rosa hates me."

"Shh…" Liz nudged her as Isabel came up to them.

Isabel turned with a puzzled face to watch her Scottie disappear into the crowd and then shrugged.

Samantha put her gift bag down to greet the exuberant pit bull. "Hey, Goose!" she said, scratching the dog's back and patting her side. Then she straightened and smiled at Isabel.

The moment their eyes met, Isabel blushed, obviously aware that Samantha had spent the night with her aunt, but she put her arms around Samantha and hugged her anyhow. "Thank you for being here and for helping pull off the surprise. Fooling my aunt is *never* an easy task."

"Look at you two," Liz said, holding her hands out to both of them. "Your outfits almost match."

Isabel looked down at herself and laughed. "They do. And we also match the servers, in case you haven't noticed." She waved an arm at the wait staff walking around with hors d'oeuvres and then checked her watch. "Gwen needs to get out here, but she wanted you to go in and see her before she does," Isabel said to Samantha.

"I was just walking her there," said Liz.

Liz left her by the porch, and Samantha went into the house. She sipped her margarita and set it on a table in the foyer before heading upstairs and knocking on the bedroom door.

"Who is it?" Gwen called out.

Samantha hid the gift behind her back and put her lips to the crack in the door. "Your masseuse."

A moment later the door opened halfway, and there stood Gwen in a sleeveless, off-white dress and one matching high heel. The other shoe was in her hand, and she let it drop to the floor. Holding on to the doorknob for balance, she slid her foot in and pulled the heel on. Then she quickly yanked Samantha into the room, closed the door, and backed her up against it. "How could you let me leave without a shower?" Her tone was accusatory, but her eyes were dreamy, and she was smiling just a little. "I've never been so embarrassed! I had body butter in my hair. And I smelled like...like us," she said, sliding her hand seductively between Samantha's legs and squeezing the inside of one thigh.

"I'm so sorry." Samantha kept the gift behind her back, picturing the embarrassing scene and trying not to laugh. "I tried my best to get you in the shower. If I'd persisted, you'd have known something was up."

"And when I saw Liz...I was shocked, but so happy, because I knew that meant you were coming."

Samantha withdrew her arm from behind her back and held up the blue gift bag. "A peace offering," she said. "If you don't have time to open it, I'll put it in the pile outside."

"Don't you dare," Gwen said. She took the bag over to a table between two chairs opposite the four-poster bed and turned on a lamp.

"I know you didn't get to see Picasso at the Met today, but at least you'll get to have something made by his daughter."

Gwen just stared at her after she opened it. "Sam, I...I don't know what to say. This is...*very* special." She took the necklace out and draped it across her palm. "Paloma Picasso. I love her jewelry. I have a brooch from one of her older collections."

"This is from the Melody collection. The entwined circles reminded me of our first dance."

Gwen touched it again. "And I can't wait to dance with you tonight, although we won't be waltzing to that house music Isabel has going." She handed it to Samantha. "Would you put it on me?" she asked, turning around and lifting her hair.

Once Samantha fastened it, Gwen walked over to a cheval mirror and smoothed her fingertips over the gold piece. "It's beautiful, Sam... so is the symbolism. Thank you so very, very much...but really, you should *not* have done this."

"Yeah, I should have." Samantha came up from behind, putting her arms around Gwen's waist and kissing her cheek. "Happy birthday, sweetheart."

Gwen turned and hugged her, then pulled back and stared at her, her expression more serious than Samantha had ever seen it. "I'm falling in love with you, you know."

"I'm way ahead of you."

They stared at one another for a moment, neither saying anything, until Gwen leaned in, her lips stopping just before they touched Samantha's. "I want to kiss you so much," she said, "but we'll end up with lipstick all over our faces."

"I'll collect that kiss later. Unless I'm banished to the guest room again."

"Not a chance. You're sleeping with me tonight…and we might actually sleep. I'm exhausted, and I know you must be, too."

"I am. In a good way, though." Samantha reached with a finger to push a strand of blond hair from her face. It seemed Gwen had put some mousse in her hair and let it dry on its own, and the look was sexy, summery. "You look gorgeous. And you better get out there."

"I know. Time to make my *second* grand entrance." She took a deep breath and exhaled. "Come with me."

"No. I'm going out ahead of you." Samantha kissed her cheek, her lips sliding up to Gwen's ear. "Go greet your waiting guests and don't worry about me. I already know a few people here."

As Samantha went down the stairs with Gwen following her, she heard the hurried sound of heels racing across the tiled foyer. And here came Rosa in a bright-red dress and a flower in her coiffed hair. She was rushing toward the staircase, watching where her feet were going and not looking ahead until she reached the first step of the staircase and nearly bumped into Samantha.

"Oh!" Rosa looked between Samantha and Gwen. "*Señora Weller. Buenos!*" She greeted her in an overly friendly and exaggerated tone, all for Gwen's benefit, no doubt. "Welcome to the party. It's *so* good to see you again." And then she shot Gwen her pasted-on smile, as if to say, *Is this what you want—am I acting friendly enough?*

Samantha smiled. "It's good to see you, too, Rosa. What a lovely red dress. My favorite color." Samantha glanced back at Gwen with a wink, then bypassed Rosa.

"Well done, nicely rehearsed," Gwen said, complimenting Rosa's staged congeniality with an edge of sarcasm. "You're an absolute pleasure when pretending to be pleasant."

But Rosa wasn't listening. Gwen saw her make the sign of the cross, her other hand clinging to the banister as if to steady herself as she watched Samantha pick up her drink in the foyer and continue outside. Gwen reached the last step, but Rosa's rotund body was blocking further passage.

"Excuse me. Can I please get by?" And when she didn't respond, Gwen tapped her on the shoulder.

Rosa jumped. "*Dios mío!*" And when she turned to Gwen her dark skin was as pale as a ghost, if that were possible.

"Rosa? What's wrong? You look faint. Sit right here and let me get you water."

"No, no, no!" she said, shaking her hands at Gwen. "I'm fine. You go."

"I'm not going anywhere. You look like you're about to collapse."

"It's not me, it's..."

"It's what? Talk to me."

Rosa clasped her hands and clutched them to her chest. "You get mad when I talk. Just go. *Vamos!*"

"I'm not mad, Rosa. I'm worried. Tell me what's wrong before I call the paramedics."

The front screen door opened and Isabel walked in, all smiles. "Aunt Gwen? Are you coming? We're all waiting for you."

"I'm on my way, honey. Go on out. I'm right behind you." She waited for Isabel to leave and looked at Rosa's face. Her normal color had returned. "What was all that about?"

"The *espíritu*," she whispered. "It's back..."

"Alley?" Gwen looked at her incredulously. "Rosa, dear, I don't think so. You feel her, but I *see* her. And I haven't seen her in a week. Even you said her spirit might have left."

"*Sí*...it left with Señora Weller. Now they're back..."

"But I...I was just with Sam. And I did *not* see Alley."

"It's hiding behind her."

"What?" In the past twenty-four hours Gwen had seen all of Sam. She'd seen her from the front, from behind, and everywhere in between. "Please, Rosa, don't do this. I have a crowd of people waiting and a party to attend." Gwen pressed a palm to her forehead. "I cannot have this conversation now." Gwen stepped off the last stair and pushed past her. "Stop calling Alley 'it.' And *stop* calling Samantha *señora*!"

"See? You tell me to tell you things and say you won't get mad, and then I tell you and you get mad."

Gwen took Rosa's hands and squeezed them. "I can only imagine how hard you've been working for this party, and I thank you from the bottom of my heart. But you can relax now. Go have a good time with Eugene and Carlos, and enjoy the party. Let the waitstaff handle the rest, okay?" She kissed her on the cheek. "Are you sure you're okay?"

"I'm okay." She let go of Gwen's hands as Gwen walked away. "I just hope you and Señora Weller will be okay," she said under her breath.

Gwen stopped and looked back. "What was that?"

"*Nada*," Rosa said and followed her out.

Isabel was waiting on the lawn, and as soon as she saw Gwen at the door she signaled to the DJ. The music stopped, and his voice rang out through the speakers to ask for everyone's attention. "Let's give it up for the birthday girl!"

The people clapped and cheered as Gwen came down the porch steps. Samantha stood next to Liz, clapping and watching as Gwen began moving through the crowd, greeting guests with the grace of a socialite and the charmed reserve of a professor.

"I want to be her when I grow up," Liz said. "She's so classy. And she looks stunning…not to mention that healthy glow you've given her." Liz nudged her with an elbow. "You're glowing, too. I'm happy for both of you."

"Thanks." Samantha breathed a sigh of contentment. "Every relationship, every woman I've ever known…none of them compares to her. Do I dare call her mine? God, Liz…last thing I remember, I was off to the city by myself for a book signing…and then she showed up like something out of my wildest dreams, and…I can't believe we're together. Pinch me so I know I'm not dreaming," she said. And Liz did.

"Ow! That hurt." Samantha rubbed her arm as a server passed them with a tray. Samantha took an Asian meatball on a toothpick, dipped it in sauce, and popped it into her mouth. "I'm starving," she said, but when she turned to grab another, the young man had moved on.

Out of nowhere, Isabel came rushing over. "You must be hungry, Sam. Come on. There's a delectable appetizer buffet under the tent. It's been there for over an hour. Go make yourself a plate before they take it away."

"I was just about to suggest that," Liz said.

For all her naïveté, Isabel was very attuned and attentive, and Samantha had a strong feeling that she was far more observant and perceptive than she let on. She just didn't know how to express her sensitivity. "Thanks, Isabel. I think I will."

As the three of them walked toward the tent, the music picked up, and two young men dancing called out to Liz.

"My new best friends," Liz said to Samantha. "The Latino one is Carlos, Rosa's son. The white guy is Phillip, his 'roommate' from vet school."

"Roommate? How convenient. They look like a couple."

"Ya think?"

Isabel seemed shocked. "Oh, I don't think so. They've been best friends for almost four years. Phillip even comes for Thanksgiving. And during winter break they come to ski because Phillip's from Alabama, and it doesn't snow much—"

Liz raised her brow. "Isabel, trust me on this, okay? Carlos and Phillip are lovers."

Isabel's entire body tensed. Even Samantha noticed it.

"Relax," Liz said to her. "I didn't say they were *murderers.* I said they were *lovers*. That's a *nice* thing for people to be." She shook her head in defeat, then looked at Samantha and crossed her eyes as if to say, *now do you understand what I'm dealing with here?* "Go eat, Sam," she said, "and then meet us at the bar."

Samantha went to the buffet, filled a small plate, and looked out on the lawn for a place to sit. People were leaving the cocktail tables, making their way to the bar and dance floor, and Samantha was headed for an empty chair when a deep voice called out her name. A good head taller than most everyone there, Bill Laraway appeared, waving at her over the crowd, gesturing for her to join him. As Samantha skirted her way around the people and tables, she saw him tap the shoulder of a black woman beside him. He said something to her and pointed, and the woman quickly put her fork down and patted her mouth with a napkin. The woman was tall as well, slim and model-like, with her hair pulled back in a chignon.

"Samantha! Please, join us," he said. "I'd like to introduce you to my wife, Sheila, Isabel's stepmother. I'm not much of a reader, so you'll have to forgive me if your name wasn't familiar. But my wife's an avid reader, and apparently we have a few of your books hanging around our house."

Immediately, Sheila offered her hand. "It's a distinct pleasure to meet you, Samantha. I'm a fan of your work."

"Why, thank you, Shelia." Samantha put her plate down, noting the huge diamond on her ring finger and the diamond tennis bracelet on the wrist of the hand she shook.

"And I can't believe I met the real Bertha earlier."

"The party has her out of sorts," Samantha said. She scanned the property and zeroed in on Bertha and her crow-friend across the lawn, quietly staring at her from the white branch of a birch tree. "If there wasn't a commotion, she'd be on my shoulder, and you'd get to pet her," Samantha said, and walked around the back of Shelia's chair to shake hands with Bill.

He opened his arms and gave her a bear hug instead. "Thanks for holding on to my sister today…and for making her happy. Her attention isn't easily captured, you know, but you seem to have all of it," he said with twinkling eyes. "And by the way, that's a beautiful necklace you got her."

"Gorgeous," Sheila added.

"And how was the Waldorf?" he asked.

"Bill!" Sheila said and gave him a look like he should mind his own business.

"What? I'm just talking about the hotel." He looked at his wife innocently and then to Samantha said, "Your sister in-law and I were talking about the hotel's art deco architecture and interior, and hoping most of it will be preserved during renovations."

"Ah, my sister in-law…so you've met Liz," Samantha said.

"We have." His bottom lip protruded, and he squinted one eye and nodded as though he'd already made a careful assessment of his daughter's would-be suitor. "She's terrific. We had a wonderful conversation. She's very attractive too…and *very* charming."

"That she is," Samantha said.

"We're happy she and Isabel have connected. Isabel is finally coming into her own, albeit slowly, and I think Liz will help her."

Sheila pressed her lips into a subtle woman-to-woman smile meant only for Samantha, and Samantha read the polite disclosure in that smile. Bill might have been clueless all these years, but it appeared that Sheila had long suspected Isabel would one day come out of the closet. And then intuitively, she shifted the conversation back to a more comfortable social level. She asked about the new book while they ate and, being in the advertising business, talked enthusiastically about the graphic design of Samantha's book covers.

It appeared news traveled fast in the Laraway family, especially with Liz around to assist in the dissemination of that news. Both Bill and his wife now knew Samantha and Gwen were an item, that they'd spent the night together, and they couldn't have been happier. Neither could Samantha. She hadn't expected Bill to be this excited to see her, and Shelia's warmth made her instantly feel like membership in the Laraway family had just been approved.

CHAPTER TWENTY-SEVEN

Here you are." Gwen stood behind Samantha's chair, delighted to see the three of them getting on so well. She put her hands on Samantha's shoulders and smiled at her brother and sister in-law.

"We were having a nice chat," Sheila said.

"I see. Isabel has us all sitting together for dinner, so you can chat more later. Do you mind if I steal Sam for a dance?"

"Not at all. We're headed that way, too." Sheila began dancing in her chair as the DJ made a segue from house music to classic disco. And when Patti Brooks's "After Dark" started playing, she got up and looked at her husband seductively. "Come on, baby. Let's burn some calories together."

Bill looked at her with a stupid, crazy-in-love grin, and if Samantha hadn't known they were married, she'd have thought they were newly together. He got up and regarded his sister with concern.

"Have you eaten anything other than the olives in that martini?"

Gwen put a hand to her stomach. "I had a few hors d'oeuvres, but I can't handle much right now. I will at dinner." She took Samantha's hand then, and when they were out of earshot she said, "Come on. I want to show you off."

"I've been lying low, not sure what to say if anyone asks how I know you."

Gwen stopped short. "Sam, everyone here—colleagues, business associates, friends and neighbors—is here because they mean something to me. And anyone who means anything knows who and what I am. Most of them knew me while I was with Jean, and over the past few years many have made failed attempts to either set me up or talk me into online dating. Needless to say, they're all dying to meet you." She touched her necklace. "By the way…I've received many compliments."

The caterer caught Gwen's attention just then and pointed to plates covered with foil. "Isabel had me set aside plates for the dogs. Do you know what she wants me to do with them?"

The caterer was a fabulous chef who handled all the Laraway occasions. "Thanks, Irene. I'll ask her right away."

"Wait," Samantha said and looked around. It took only a moment to locate the Scottie above the crowd. She was sitting way up on the porch, her black body and pricked ears outlined against the white house. Her eyes were locked on Samantha. Loosey was stretched out next to her, presumably asleep. "Would it be all right if I took their food to them? Blue was frightened of me before…it'll be a peace offering."

Gwen looked at her oddly. "Sure, Sam. I'll wait for you by the bar."

Irene uncovered the plates, and Samantha balanced one in each in hand. Loosey rose when she heard Samantha's approach and excitedly stepped in place at the smell of food coming. "Hey, girls, I've got dinner."

As soon as Samantha put her foot on the first step, Blue stood and took a step backward. Another step had the Scottie backing up more, until her rump hit the front door and she showed her teeth. "Okay, okay, take it easy. It's food. You make it very hard for me to like you, you know." Samantha didn't dare take another step. She bent and slid one plate to Loosey, who dug right in. Samantha gave the other plate a good shove in Blue's direction. Halfway to the tent she glanced back to see them both eating. That Scottie wasn't making it easy for Samantha to win her over.

Gwen was in the middle of a crowd, laughing and talking as Samantha approached her. She reached out a hand to her and raised the other to one of the two bartenders. "What's your pleasure, darling?"

Samantha eyed the long line of top-shelf liquor. "Patrón and pineapple juice, if he has it?"

"I do," he said, and when she had her drink in hand, Gwen slipped her arm around her waist and began introductions. Samantha didn't expect to remember many names by the end of the night, but she tried to commit to memory at least those of Gwen's cousins and close friends. With the music so loud, it was hard to converse without yelling, but she did her best to make small talk and was thankful when Bette Midler's

"Do You Want to Dance" came on and Gwen whisked her away to the dance floor.

"You look radiant," Samantha said as they danced.

"I was just thinking the same of you."

"Do you think we've radiated one another?" Samantha grinned.

"That and then some."

Samantha pulled her close, and they instinctively found a steady rhythm, a perfect fit.

Just before the song ended, a woman dancing waved an arm in the air.

"That's Carol," Gwen said, "my best friend, the yin to my yang."

"A philosopher, too?"

"Yes. She teaches aesthetics. Her husband, Serge, is an art historian. And the two young women dancing with them are from the environmental studies department. We attended their wedding last year."

Carol looked to be Gwen's age, attractive and full-figured with dyed black hair and crystal-blue eyes. There was something stylishly bohemian about the abundance of jewelry, the flowing floral skirt, the colorful scarf wrapped around the neck of her black, sleeveless top. Even if Samantha hadn't known she lived in Manhattan, she would have pegged her for someone from the city. A stack of bangle bracelets jangled on her wrist as she and Serge danced their way over, and Sam was quick to note the rings on her thumbs as she let go of her husband and took Samantha's hands in hers. With her brilliant smile and eyes that sparkled with intelligence and energy, Samantha imagined Carol easily capturing the attention of college students in a lecture hall.

Carol raised her voice over the music. "I was disappointed when this one here dumped me for you," she said, gesturing with her chin at Gwen, "but now I understand completely. I would have dumped me for you, too."

Samantha laughed at the compliment and squeezed her hands. "I'm sorry I became a game changer. It wasn't planned."

Serge stuck his hand out in greeting, and they let go of each other. He smelled faintly, and not unpleasantly, of expensive cologne and pipe tobacco, and his closely trimmed beard and long salt-and-pepper hair gave him a professorial, almost European flair. The couple from the environmental studies department was dancing their way closer, both sporting short blond hair and a healthy, outdoorsy look. Samantha pictured them hiking on the weekends in search of precious life forms that went unnoticed under the feet of reckless families traipsing through the woods. And not far behind were Liz and Phillip and Isabel and Carlos, talking and laughing more than they were dancing.

"Liz says Rosa's son is gay," Samantha whispered to Gwen.

"Ya think?"

"Ha! That's just what Liz said."

"But we don't mention *anything* to Rosa. God forbid. She has it in her head that Carlos will open a veterinary practice close to home and marry a nice Latina girl who will run the office and make plenty of grandchildren," she said as the DJ lowered the volume and asked everyone to start moving to their dinner tables.

As the dance floor cleared, Gwen stared at her adoringly. I don't know where you came from, Samantha Weller, or who sent you, but you do to me what no one's *ever* done. The first day we met, you said life was like a game of connect the dots. I wonder whether it's chance or fate that connects them."

"Well, one thing is for sure, it was Bertha who connected them. She saved my life…and now she's led me to the love of my life."

Gwen's smile faded and she swallowed hard. "You touch me in a deep place when you say these things."

"I want to touch all your deep places…and I'm hoping it takes at least twenty years to discover them all."

Gwen responded with a kiss, the feel of her soft lips stirring vivid memories of their lovemaking and filling her with a sudden and unbearable desire as they left the dance floor hand in hand and made their way into the dining tent.

The air of festivity inside was wonderful. Thousands of tiny white lights wrapped the frame of the tent. Chinese lanterns in an assortment of colors hung over the flowers adorning each table, and dozens of balloons had been set free, their waving ribbons dangling overhead.

It had been thoughtful, not to mention intuitive, of Isabel to seat Liz and Samantha at the family table. Rosa sat at the next table with Eugene, Carlos and Phillip, and four of the Laraway cousins who'd flown in from Florida. Rosa seemed out of character, though—tentative, almost wary as she politely introduced her son and her boyfriend to Samantha. Carlos was a handsome young man, as sweet and soft-spoken as Isabel. Eugene, however, was quite gregarious.

"*Buenos!*" he said, and took Samantha's hand in both of his. He was about Rosa's height and width, bald, with a thick mustache that took on a spidery life of its own when he spoke. He was Spanish-dominant, she quickly realized, but his animated face and mime-like gesticulations made words unnecessary.

Isabel, who was being the perfect hostess, checking on guests and getting them seated, finally collapsed into a chair next to Liz. Gwen kissed the top of Isabel's head, sat down next to her, and patted the chair beside her. But just as Samantha was just about to sit, a woman next to the environmental studies professors stood up and waved to her. "Sam Weller?"

Samantha stared at the familiar face, trying to place it as the woman came toward her. She was about her age, with similarly short, dark hair and eyes. Suddenly, a vision of the same woman with long hair came to her. "Jen?"

"Yes! Oh my gosh, Sam. What's it been, fifteen years?"

"At least. How are you?"

"Good. I can't believe you know the Laraways."

"And I can't believe you're in academia. Last I remember you were earning your MBA."

"I did. I work in the administration at the university." Jen gave a broad smile. "How about you? Still hanging around with dead people? Man, I remember those gruesome stories you used to tell us."

"Actually, I left forensics to pursue a writing career."

"That's awesome. What do you write?"

"Gruesome stories."

Jen laughed. "And you live here in the Berkshires?"

"No. I live alone in Westchester. Are you still on Long Island with…what was her name, Debbie?"

"Debra. Geez. I haven't thought about her in years. We broke up a long time ago—many girlfriends ago. I'm currently single and living near the university."

Samantha realized they were in the way of the staff bringing out salads. "Let's talk more later."

"Are you ever in the city?" Jen asked.

"Frequently."

"How about meeting for lunch or dinner? I'd love to catch up." She looked Samantha up and down. "Do you have a business card?"

"Not on me." Samantha patted her empty pockets.

"I'll give you mine after dinner, and I'll get your number."

"Okay," said Sam.

"All right then." Jen looked at her sideways, made a finger gun, and pointed it at her. "Catch you later, Detective."

Samantha sat down to salad and what seemed an ongoing academic conversation.

"So then what's the difference," Liz was saying to Carol, "between something being *beautiful* and something being *sublime*?"

Gwen leaned into Sam and whispered, "Now's your chance to run. You can stay and participate in the philosophical musings of professors or escape to another table and enjoy a normal conversation about sports, the weather, and how you're spending your summer vacation."

"Considering what I write about, I think I'm at the right table." Sam looked at her, undressing her with her eyes. "Besides, I'm next to you, so I must be in the right seat."

"Well," Carol explained, "beauty and sublimity are both aesthetic concepts, of course, but beauty is bound by its object, whereas the sublime is boundless. It's a quality of astounding greatness, perfection beyond measure, an experience that elevates us to a heightened state of awareness." She paused. "Take the most prized vase in Gwen's pottery collection. If I went in the house and broke it, its beauty would be lost because, as I said, beauty is bound by the object.

"But Gwen's *experience* of its beauty is sublime. Whether it's her expert knowledge that allowed her to recognize the creative brilliance and unmatched artistry of that pottery—or who knows, maybe the fact that something so exquisite originated from the soil, from the earth itself—something about it stirred in her a sense of incalculable awe…a feeling of beauty beyond beauty. *That* is the sublime!"

"Okay, trick question," Liz said. "Does this mean that a connoisseur of wine or cuisines can *taste* the sublime?"

"Ah!" Gwen said. "What a good philosophy student you would be. And that's a *yes*. The sublime can be found in the physical, the metaphysical, the artistic, spiritual…even technology can be sublime. But to experience it requires higher-level thinking, and one's senses must be cultivated. For example, I'm not much of a wine drinker, so I probably couldn't distinguish mediocrity from sublimity. But the wine connoisseur would."

"And don't forget nature," Serge said. "We might climb a mountain and see many forms of beauty on our way up, but when we reach the summit and look down, the scene before us might be so majestic, so awe-inspiring, that at that moment we become aware of an unsurpassed greatness…something greater than ourselves. That's what the Romantic painters tried to capture on canvas."

Bill had finished his salad. He was sitting back with his elbow propped on the chair, the back of his fingers pressed to his mouth in a thoughtful pose. "Maybe that's why people climb Mount Everest—to experience the sublime."

Samantha nodded. "I think you're right."

"And maybe the sublime is so powerful," he added, "that once it's experienced, the person wants to feel it again. Maybe that's why high-risk adventurers become addicted to their sport."

"Interesting point," said Carol. "I'll have to use that in class."

Sheila cocked her head. "I get what you're all saying…the sublime is something that lifts us to a *higher* level of consciousness, to an increased awareness above the normal scope of emotion…but in the field of advertising, we often rely on subliminal seduction, which is to say we appeal to consumers on a *lower*, subconscious level. If I want to sell a man an expensive sports car he can't afford, I'll make sure the ad features a beautiful woman in the passenger seat so that, subliminally, he associates buying the car with attracting a beautiful woman."

"It worked for me," Bill said. "The first time I asked Sheila out she was standing in the parking lot of my office. I was late getting back from another appointment that afternoon and late for my meeting with her. I pulled up in a Porsche, apologized for being late, and asked if we could have our meeting over dinner. She looked my car up and down and said yes. Next thing I knew, I had a beautiful woman in the passenger seat."

Everyone laughed. "That's not *exactly* how it happened," Sheila said, but she laughed along with the others. "What I'm wondering, though, is why the *sublime* refers to a heightened awareness, while the *subliminal* refers to a decreased awareness?"

Serge cleared his throat. "Let the historian answer that, if I may," he said. "It's a boring story that goes back to the first century, but suffice it to say that both words come from *limen*, Latin for *lintel*, which is actually the beam over a doorway that supports the structure above it. So it represents a threshold…and anything at, or above, or below that threshold…in this case, the threshold of consciousness."

"Hmm…" Sheila steepled her fingers. "Thank you for that, Serge." She winked at the others and looked at her husband. "And if you must know the truth, Bill…the Porsche did work. Once I saw that car I couldn't wait to get my hands on your stick shift."

Cocktail hour had lowered the inhibitions of everyone at the table, and they all laughed out loud—except for Isabel. The sexual innuendo caused her to visibly shrivel in her seat.

"Can't books be sublime?" she blurted out, as if to move the conversation comfortably along. "I find poetry to be sublime."

"Yes," Carol said. "Many of the old philosophers believed the sublime could be achieved through rhetoric—through dialogue and the exchange of higher-level thoughts. Have you ever read a book you just couldn't get into, and at another point in your life you pick up that same book and connect with it on such a deep level that it leaves you somehow transformed?"

All of them, except Bill, who wasn't much of a reader, shook their heads in agreement.

"And as Isabel points out," Carol added, "poetry is indeed the rhetoric of passion. When that spark rises from the poet's soul and ignites the reader's soul, the result is a sublime union, a spiritual communion between minds at a distance."

Samantha, who had been listening, finally spoke up. "But like the yin-yang of everything else, doesn't the sublime have a flip side? Can't something horrific—a vision or experience that catapults us to a higher level awareness of death, mortality, atrocities—be equally sublime?"

"The terrifying sublime!" Carol and Gwen said in unison.

Gwen smiled over at Samantha, obviously pleased with her contribution. "Kant distinguished between the *splendid sublime*, which we've been talking about, and the *terrifying sublime*."

"And not just philosophers," Serge said, "but many artists think that witnessing death is the ultimate in the terrifying sublime. In fact, a European one has publicly staged animal sacrifices to illustrate the terrifying sublime in the name of art."

Bill made a face. "Wouldn't that be the bullfight?"

"Stop." Isabel put her hands to her ears. "I don't want to know."

"Me neither," Carol said. "Let's just imagine Bill's mountaineer approaching the summit of Mount Everest when he loses his lifeline or his bearings in a blizzard and realizes he'll never reach the summit and never find his way back to camp. Likely, he'll experience the terrifying sublime."

Sheila had a long, polished fingernail between her teeth and was studying Samantha intensely. "I get the feeling you've experienced the terrifying sublime, Samantha."

"Ha. On a regular basis for many years, usually with my morning coffee," she answered.

"Before Samantha began writing," Gwen explained, "she had a career in forensics."

Both Sheila and Carol put a hand to their chest. "So you saw… murder victims?" Shelia asked.

"I did. And I will say there's something terrifying about witnessing the aftermath of a heinous crime…of being greeted by the still-shocked eyes of a victim, even though you know they're vacant."

They all gave quiet gasps, but Bill scratched his forehead. "Yet so many people seem to seek out the terrifying sublime—vicariously, at least. Look at all the violence in shows and video games."

"Well," Sam said, "I suspect there's something counterphobic in all that. We like to peek at things that terrify us, and horror movies allow us to do it safely from behind a bowl of popcorn."

Bill chuckled. "And what about ghosts? Sheila says you write a lot about ghosts. I would think seeing one of those would qualify as the terrifying sublime."

Samantha nodded. "Or it could be the splendid sublime, don't you think?"

Bill shrugged. "Casper the friendly ghost might be splendid, but not a poltergeist."

Sheila gazed at Samantha again. "Considering what you write, and considering your past experience around the newly deceased… have you ever…you know, seen or felt a real-life ghost?"

Sam glanced at Gwen and back to Sheila. "Not to speak of," she lied.

The mood lightened as dinner was served, and conversation moved to everyone's plans for the rest of the summer: vacations, new restaurants, must-see exhibits, Liz and Isabel's cottage renovation, and Bill's new boat. Everyone at the table was invited out on it. And no sooner had dinner finished than the Latin music began. Eugene, who'd been doing shots of tequila, jumped up and clapped his hands. "*Bailemos!* Let's dance!" he shouted, and grabbed Rosa by the hand.

Carlos pulled Isabel along to the dance floor, Phillip came for Liz, and Bill offered Gwen a hand. "May I have this dance, birthday girl?"

"Why, of course," she said.

The rest of the Latin-dance-loving people followed, while others were content to remain at their tables, mingle at the bar, or take a stroll. The sun was setting now, and the staff was lighting torches along the path to the water. Liz and Samantha made their way for drinks and settled for being momentary spectators.

"Gwen's a great dancer," Liz said as they watched. "So is Bill."

"He is. You wouldn't think it. He looks like a former football player, but he's so light on his feet."

"And look at this one," Liz said, as she watched Isabel move to the driving rhythm and pulsating beats of salsa music. "Those Brazilian women are smooth, aren't they?"

Samantha saw Gwen let Sheila cut in to dance with Bill and then lost sight of Gwen. "Judging from the way Isabel moves…all I can say is that when she finally lets go…she's going to make you a very happy woman."

"You think so?" Liz frowned. "I don't think it's ever going to happen. I don't think Isabel is feeling me. Not that way," she said, gesturing at the way she danced with Carlos. "I can't even stand to watch her body move like that. It's making me want her even more…and making me think she's a closet heterosexual."

"That's funny. A closet—" Gwen had sneaked up on Samantha from behind with a martini in hand.

She sandwiched herself between Liz and Samantha. "I don't mean to eavesdrop," she said, putting an arm around Liz's waist, "but Isabel does *not* like men, of this I can assure you. Carlos is her brother from another mother, as they say nowadays. And she's able to let go with him because, one, he's safe, and two, because she's half Brazilian." Gwen gave Liz's side a little squeeze. "I know Isabel is frustrating. Sometimes I want to shake her. But I do know that she has feelings for you, and the sexual attraction has her scared half to death. So don't give up just yet. I promise you, she's worth the wait."

"Thanks for the reassurance, but I just don't know, Gwen…I don't get any vibes from her. None whatsoever." Liz ran her fingers through her hair. "Your niece is such a paradox. I mean, there's this incredible physicality about her. She loves fast cars, loud music, Latin dancing, swimming, running and playing with the dogs. But when it comes to getting physical with a person she's—"

"Overly concerned with sexual propriety? Go on, you can say it—Isabel's a fucking prude."

Liz and Samantha both stared in astonishment.

"Whoops." Gwen raised her brow in self-surprise and glanced between them. "Did I just say that?" Her eyes dropped to the empty glass in her hand. "I do believe I've had one too many olives!" she said with tipsy politeness. "And if you'll excuse me, it's my birthday and I plan to have one more."

Liz cracked up as they watched her walk to the bar. "Gwen's a hoot when she's buzzed. I like her like that." Liz was still laughing when she turned back to see Isabel leaving Carlos and coming straight for her.

Isabel extended a hand to her. "You said you wanted me to teach you how to salsa."

Liz smiled coyly. "Are you asking me to dance, Ms. Laraway?"

"I am."

Liz took her hand and looked back at Samantha with a glimmer of hope as Isabel led her onto the dance floor. And as they went, Jen came out of nowhere and grabbed Samantha's hand. "Dance with me," she said with a big smile.

They moved next to Liz and Isabel, and while Samantha danced with Jen she tried to overhear and take instruction from Isabel. "Count to eight, but hold on four and hold on eight," she told Liz. "Ready? One, two, three…five, six, seven…And stop looking at your feet," Samantha heard Isabel say. "Just let go and feel my body…feel the rhythm."

It appeared as though Isabel's alter ego had emerged on the dance floor. Her body was working itself into a vertical slither, so fluid and mesmerizing as she took control of Liz.

And Liz, a quick study, was obviously in paradise. She caught on fast, and within minutes she and Isabel were moving as one. Of course, Samantha knew Liz was an expert at moving in rhythm with women's bodies—with or without music—and she certainly didn't need any instruction when the music changed to a merengue. Their hips and ribs rose and fell naturally, as though they were slinking up a staircase. Samantha tried to copy them, deciding that she herself could master those moves with the help of a studied partner. But Jen's hips and whole body were swinging all over the place.

The music changed to a cha-cha while Eugene's *bateria* took their places onstage. The DJ faded out then, handing the evening over to the samba band.

Eugene gave a shout out to Gwen. "*Feliz cumpleaños!*" he said, and then the samba band began with what sounded like a very slow salsa. It seemed Jen would have happily moved closer had Gwen not cut in.

Samantha saw something disapproving in Gwen's smile. "Bossa nova dancing comes from Brazilian samba," she explained, her tone was soft and sultry as they began to move. "It's a much slower dance…

more intimate, romantic…and so you should have *me* in your arms, darling…not her."

Samantha grinned, mildly amused by the idea that Gwen might be a tad jealous. "Point taken, Mistress. I was hoping you'd show up when you did."

"Good. Now follow me and loosen those knees so you get some bounce action."

Gwen was an excellent teacher, and Samantha had never felt so in sync with someone. "You're an incredible dancer," she said.

Gwen smiled. "Not bad for a white girl, huh?"

"Oh, you're better than bad." Samantha murmured. Bodies pressed together, they moved in a slow circle, and as they did, Samantha saw Isabel stop and awkwardly withdraw from Liz. Sheila had left the floor to talk to someone, and Isabel turned away and went straight into her father's arms.

Liz's shoulders drooped, the joy draining from her face, and she quickly turned and left the dance floor. Samantha watched her pick up her drink and a cocktail napkin and hurriedly wander out across the lawn.

"I saw that," Gwen said before Samantha could say anything. "Isabel was a little too close for comfort and got scared, but I could wring her neck for doing what she just did." She kissed Samantha's cheek and let go of her. "Go check on Liz."

Liz was standing in the middle of the lawn facing the trees, her glass in one hand, her other arm wrapped around herself.

Samantha came up beside her. "Hey, you…"

Liz glanced back at her and looked away. "What a slap in the face that was, huh? She just leaves me standing there in the middle of a slow dance and runs into her father's arms? Even he looked embarrassed for me."

"She didn't mean it, Liz."

"She's hopeless, Sam. And so am I. I can't do this."

"You heard what Gwen said…give her time to come around. After all, you haven't really known her all that long."

"You haven't known Gwen that long either. But you two had chemistry right from the beginning. And even though she rejected you at first, you knew she had feelings for you. It's not that way with Isabel. I've been around her long enough to know she does not look at me that way. Tonight will be the sixth night we've shared the same bed and—oh, just forget it, Sam. It doesn't matter." She set her drink on the ground and played with the napkin in her hands. "I wish I didn't have to sleep with her tonight. If I wasn't drinking, I'd drive home right now."

"Just take a deep breath."

"What I need to do is take a step back."

"A step back from what? You love being in her company. The two of you became instant best friends. Doesn't that mean something?"

"It means the world to me. That's the whole point, Sam, don't you get it? My friendship with Isabel will probably be the most significant one of my life. I just need a couple of weeks away from her…I need time to regroup, figure out a way to put my feelings back where they belong, because when I'm with her I can't even think straight."

"Aw, give me a hug." Samantha opened her arms, but Liz put up a hand and turned away.

"I don't want to hug you, Sam. If I do I'll fall apart. I don't want my mascara to run." She sniffled, dabbed the corners of her eyes with a napkin, and laughed at herself. "Look at me. How ridiculous am I?"

"You're not ridiculous. You're in love."

"Oh! Is that what it is?" She turned to Samantha with a sour face. "Everyone always talks about how one day I'll meet that special person and know how wonderful it is to fall in love. Well, guess what?" She shook her head and raked her fingers through her hair. "I did fall in love. And you know what? So far it sucks. Love fucking sucks. Big-time!"

Chapter Twenty-Eight

People always lingered at Laraway parties, and tonight was no exception. It was well after cake and coffee and after ten before they filed out. The DJ and the caterer and her staff were soon gone, and the party planners would be back in the morning to dismantle tents and floors, collect furniture, and clean up the colorful mess. Overnight guests were winding down in the house. Two cousins were catching up over a nightcap at the indoor bar, Eugene was helping Rosa put food away in the kitchen, and the rest had retired to the upstairs bedrooms, including Liz, who'd taken the dogs up with her.

Gwen had seen each of her guests out. All were thrilled to have met Sam and more than happy to see Gwen in love again, they said. Some gave her congratulatory hugs, some eyebrow waggles or sly smirks, and a few of her closest friends were curious to know Sam's age. Their impression, of course, was that Sam was younger, and Gwen knew she might have to get used to people assuming that.

When she finally went into the house alone, she realized she hadn't seen Sam in over an hour. She went upstairs, half expecting to find her passed out on the bed, but she wasn't there, so she went back down to see Isabel headed down the hall. "Honey? Have you seen Sam?"

Isabel stopped. "She was in the living room with Carlos and Phillip a while ago, but then I think I saw her go into the gallery. If she's not there she might be at the bar with the others."

"Come here a second." Gwen gave Isabel a big hug, a tight squeeze, and thanked her again for pulling off a perfect birthday gala. No matter the project, when Isabel took charge, every detail was given attention. She left no stone unturned—only the one in her head. And Gwen was determined to turn it over for her.

"Happy birthday, Aunt Gwen." Isabel hugged and held on to her. "I love you, and I'm glad you had a good party."

"I love you, too." Gwen stepped back and placed her hands firmly on Isabel's shoulders. "And I think someone else is beginning to love you. You know I rarely interfere, Isabel, but what you did to Liz on the dance floor was immature and very hurtful." She gave her the stern look that always made Isabel wince with worry. "I'm going to give you one piece of advice. If for one minute you think you might be falling in love with her, too, you better wake up fast. Otherwise, you're going to lose her."

Isabel gulped and just stared at her, speechless. Gwen didn't expect her to respond. "Now, if you'll excuse me, I want to find Sam." And with that she kissed Isabel's forehead and left her standing there.

Gwen opened the front door and checked the porch first. Then she looked in the living room, peeked in the empty gallery, and followed the sounds of laughter to the bar in the ballroom. "Has anyone seen Sam?"

"She was here drinking with us a little while ago," said her cousin, Margaret.

The other cousin, Henry, pointed to the back door. "I think she might have gone out to the gardens."

Gwen went to the windows. The torches outside had all been extinguished, but there in the moonlight, beyond the flower gardens, Sam was standing by the water. Gwen went out to her, studying her from behind as she did. She'd been stealing glances at Sam's back all evening long, waiting to see Alley and wondering if Rosa might be losing her mind.

"Still looking for ghosts?" she said.

"Hey there." Sam turned and smiled and put an arm around her waist. "Did you see the last of your guests out?"

"Uh-huh. I'm beyond exhausted. I can't wait to get out of these shoes and this dress."

"If you need help with that zipper, I'd be happy to assist."

"I could get used to having someone around to unzip my dress." Gwen laughed softly, and they stood enjoying the peaceful silence for a minute. Moonlight glistened on the water, and fireflies lit up all around them.

"Actually, I wandered out to admire your flower gardens in the moonlight. No one but my mother ever had so many flowers growing all at once."

"The florist and Sunday-school teacher…"

"Yeah." Sam gave a wistful smile. "Then I wandered down here, looking for Alley…and started wondering where they all are, where they all go."

"Who?"

"Everyone who has died. People, animals—all spirits. I wonder if they're all around us right now, watching from a place we can't see…just like there are sounds, vibrations all around us right now that we can't hear because they're outside the range of human hearing. And Alley…I missed seeing her tonight. I wonder where exactly she is in hyperspace."

"Sam, I'm so tired and drunk right now that I feel like *I'm* in hyperspace."

Sam didn't respond. She was staring out at the water, pensive, and so Gwen let her keep talking.

"You know," Sam said, "I keep thinking about your article and your reference to some thoughts on superstring theory, especially the idea that at another point in time, very early in the universe, all ten or more dimensions were unified, forced together—coerced, as they call it—so that we may have existed in all of them at once."

"Well, the thinking is that we may still exist in all of them, but because our senses are limited, we perceive ourselves in only three of those dimensions."

"But according to that theory," Sam said, "at one time we may have actually experienced and existed in harmony in all of them at once…until something happened, and we were cut off from the others, de-coerced…cast out."

"Cast out? Hmm…interesting choice of words. That hints at the idea of the Garden of Eden having been in hyperspace."

Sam laughed. "That's how my mother would have interpreted it."

"Don't think I haven't given that some thought." Gwen rubbed her back affectionately. "Darling, this is all interesting, but I imagine you're as drunk and exhausted as me. Let's go to bed and continue this conversation when I can think straight."

Sam nodded, but she didn't move. She seemed to have something else on her mind, and Gwen waited.

"Do you ice-skate out here in winter?"

Standing here on this summer night, the question took Gwen by surprise. "Isabel and I used to ice-skate all the time. It was always such a glorious winter wonderland…until Alley's accident. After that I…I just couldn't. It wasn't a happy place anymore." She heaved a sigh, warding off the awful memories. "It's a terrible thing when something you've always associated with fun and pleasure suddenly becomes a source of pain and anguish."

Sam nodded. "You had a white cat," she said matter-of-factly.

The statement came out of left field. "We did. Crystal. She died earlier this year at the age of twenty-one." Gwen glanced at Sam's profile. "Was Isabel talking about her?"

Sam shook her head. "No. I saw her in a dream. I was standing right here. It was winter, and the white cat went through the ice. That's how Alley drowned…trying to get out to her."

Gwen's heart skipped a beat. "Sam! How could you know that? No one knows what happened that day. Once winter sets in up here, that ice grows thick and stays safe well past the end of February. But that particular winter the weather was crazy. We'd plunge into a deep freeze one week, and then the temperature would rise and we'd see a thaw. All that melting and refreezing weakens the ice. Alley didn't know it was unsafe."

"Yes, she did. She knew. Dogs know those things. Apparently, the cat didn't." Sam kept her eyes on the water as if watching the scenario play out. "Did the white cat come home soaking wet that day?"

Gwen looked at her incredulously. "I don't know, Sam. It snowed all day, a wet and heavy snow. Everyone was wet. Once I realized what had happened and called the fire department, everything…everything became a blur." She ran her fingers across her forehead, nervously wiping the sweat beading on her brow, and felt her hand begin to shake. "What's going on, Sam? Are you saying you saw Alley's memories in your dream or something?"

"Or something…It's as if she wants to tell me her story." Sam took a deep breath. "I have to tell you something. But promise you won't get mad."

"Look at me." Gwen turned to her, brushed the hair away from Sam's forehead. "What have you done?"

Sam's mouth tightened, and she hesitated for a moment. "I touched her. That day I came to visit, I think I might have touched her then, just her chin, before you screamed at me not to. And then that night, after we were dancing, and she appeared on the patio…" Sam stopped.

"Go on. Tell me what you did."

"Something woke me up that night. I told you the owls were

hooting outside the window, but really it was a dog's whining. It's like she was calling me."

"And…?"

"I went downstairs to see if she was still on the patio. And she was there, waiting for me."

"That's why you were outside."

Sam nodded. "I knelt beside her, put my arm around her, and took a picture. I wanted to know if she'd show up in a photograph. But then you were there, and I realized you couldn't see her anymore."

"You're scaring me, Sam."

"Don't be scared, sweetheart. She means no harm. Really. What if all our deceased loved ones come to us from time to time, just to pay a visit? What if they stand right in our faces, waving, yelling, jumping up and down to get our attention, and we treat them like nothing because…well, because they *are* nothing anymore. Not in this world, at least. How heartbreaking must it be for those spirits to realize they have become so insubstantial that they can't even catch our attention."

The more Sam spoke, the more incredulous Gwen became. "This is all very upsetting, Sam. I don't know what to make of it. I pleaded with you not to touch her. I told you that I acknowledge her, but I've *never* reached out to touch her because…" She gave a sigh of reproach and frustration. "She's pure energy, Sam. We don't know what it is, where it comes from, or what it can do. I'm afraid it might have hurt you somehow."

"Hey." Sam took both her hands. "No one's hurting anyone," she said, her soft smile reassuring. "I'm sorry I went against your wishes. I was wrong. But that ghost has done nothing but project her memories somehow. That first day, when I watched her in that storm, I could feel her absolute despair. It was horrible to watch. And then when I went out to her that night we danced, she seemed less depressed, perkier."

"Perkier?"

"Yeah. I think she likes me."

Gwen made a fist and pressed it against her lips as Rosa's words filled her head. *That espíritu cares nothing for that woman…she's using her to get to you.* "Sam, I'm asking you right now to stay away from her! Next time you see that ghost, don't even *look* at her. Do you hear me?"

"Okay, sweetheart. I promise. It'll be hard to ignore her though, especially since she came to me in a dream. We're sort of bonded now."

"Bonded?"

"Yeah, you know, emotionally attuned to each other."

"That's what Rosa thinks. And she's convinced Alley's ghost has bonded to you in more ways than one. The way she's talking makes me think Alley's attached herself to you like something out of your stories—like that Mr. Minerva's ghost attaching itself to his wife's mistress."

"What…?" It was dark out, but the moonlight was enough to see Sam's face pale.

"You mean like…an auric attachment?" She gave a nervous laugh that seemed to catch in her throat. "Is that why Rosa wants nothing to do with me? She thinks the ghost is, what, feeding off my energy? Is Rosa crazy?"

"Let's hope so, Sam. Because if that ghost is feeding off you, it's only going to make her stronger."

❖

Gwen hadn't been asleep long when a strange noise stirred her, and she opened her eyes to see a light shining through the louvered doors of her walk-in closet. She reached over and patted the bed. It was empty. She'd been so worried she didn't think she could sleep, but the three martinis had won out in the end. She listened for a minute, then very quietly threw back the covers and got up, nervously pulling her nightshirt down over her hips as she slowly tiptoed across the carpet. The doors were open a few inches, and she stopped just before she reached them, listening to the sounds—papers being shuffled, boxes tumbling. Another few steps and she cautiously peeked between the doors. There was Sam, busily rummaging through her belongings on the shelves that lined the back wall.

"Sam…?" Slowly she took hold of the handles, pulled the doors open, and stared in disbelief. Several shoeboxes were strewn about Sam's bare feet, the lids off, shoes toppling out, as though they'd been carelessly knocked off the top shelf.

"Sam?" she said again, louder this time, but Sam was unresponsive. She kept digging around in the closet, and it struck Gwen then that she might be sleepwalking. She watched, paralyzed for the moment and suddenly afraid of Sam. She'd never witnessed a somnambulist, but she'd read somewhere that startling a sleepwalker was never a good idea, so she just stood there, frozen with fear, as Sam finally seemed to find what she was looking for—a bigger box, a keepsake box, filled with old family pictures, letters, sentimental trinkets. It was taped shut, but Sam peeled away the packing tape and opened the flaps as though she were wide awake. She began stirring her hand around inside the box, and when Gwen heard the jingling, she held a hand to her mouth to silence her gasp. She knew what it was before she even saw it—Alley's old orange collar and tags.

Gwen's hands trembled as she put them together and pressed her fingers against her lips.

Sam turned around then and stared right at her but showed no recognition. Her expression was dim, her eyes glazed over. She pushed right past Gwen then, bumping her shoulder as she went by, and made a straight line back to her side of the bed.

Speechless, Gwen waited, giving her plenty of space, and when Sam sat, she quietly made her way over to her. Sam remained in an altered state of consciousness for another minute, but slowly she seemed to become vaguely aware of Gwen, enough that she gave a confused but happy smile.

They'd all had a little too much to drink tonight, but Sam certainly wasn't anywhere near sloppy drunk. Not drunk enough to be in this kind of stupor. "Sam, darling? What…what's happened to you?"

Sam opened her mouth, but nothing came out at first. Dazedly, she handed Gwen the collar. "Let's walk," she said, and then, as if she were awake, she slipped under the covers, closed her eyes, and was sound asleep again.

Gwen got back into bed, curled up facing her, and laid a hand across Sam's stomach, so that if she sleepwalked again Gwen would be sure to wake up. But she couldn't fall back to sleep. For an hour or more she lay there, angry and afraid, furious with fear. Sam had touched that ghost and in doing so had set some force in motion. Sure, that had been Sam's body in her closet, but something was in there with her, instructing her, using her like a puppet.

Maybe it was her imagination, but suddenly she felt as though they weren't in bed alone, and she thought about the spirit Sam had felt at the Waldorf. "Alley? Are you here with me?" she whispered into the darkness. And then she choked on her emotions and the tears came. "I'm so sorry I couldn't save you, my sweet baby," she whispered into the night. "I'm *so* very sorry that had to happen to you…but it did. It's done. I can't bring you back." Crying, she reached and felt for the tissue box on the night table. "And I can't be with you now, Alley…it's not my time yet, baby. But if you go find heaven and wait there for me…I promise I'll find you one day. I promise," she said and began to sob.

She could have sworn she heard the collar she'd left beside the tissue box jingle ever so slightly, unless her mind was playing tricks. She'd never been this scared—scared that Sam had set in motion a force that might bring harm to both of them, all because she'd done the one thing Gwen had asked her never to do—touch a ghost. And as she lay there, fear begot fear, and her thoughts began racing.

She'd learned a lot about Sam these past two days. For one, Sam had broken her trust. Granted, reaching and possibly touching Alley that first time might have been accidental. After all, Sam had thought she was alive. But then after a strict warning she'd deliberately sneaked outside, put her arms around the ghost, and taken selfies, for God's sake! Even worse, she'd lied about it. Over the past day or two Sam had demonstrated that she was quite adept at lying. And why shouldn't she be? She made up stories, created literary illusions, basically lied for a living, didn't she? Look how easy it had been for her to help pull off the surprise party.

Gwen reached for another tissue. Her head was starting to swim with questions, and she began to doubt Sam. Sam with the big brown eyes: curious, sexy, honest…beguiling, too. Sam, who could keep a perfect poker face. The more she thought about it, the more she decided that Sam's conversation with Jen wasn't sitting well with her either. Gwen didn't know why it bothered her, but it did. She hadn't meant to eavesdrop, but the two had been standing right next to her chair. And it bothered her that when Jen asked if Sam lived here with Gwen, Sam answered that she lived alone in Westchester. Why couldn't she have just said that she lived in Westchester? Why did she make a point of saying she lived *alone*? Jen and everyone else at the party knew she and Sam were a couple, but Sam saying she lived alone seemed to suggest that she and Gwen were merely dating and not exclusive. Not that she expected a commitment just because they'd made love, but…

Gwen sat up and blew her nose. Sam and Jen would probably reconnect, and that was fine—she would never oppose Sam enjoying individual friendships—but she didn't entirely trust Jen. And now she didn't know if she could trust Sam. The two were close in age and would probably have fun together in the city, having dinner, maybe going to a gay bar. Or maybe Sam would invite her over. And that bothered her, too. Sam's bedroom didn't sit well with her.

Seeing where Sam lived had afforded Gwen a glimpse into the

private life of the mysterious mystery writer she'd fallen for, but that bedroom seemed decorated with seduction in mind. All that red gave the room a warm and romantic aspect, but, seriously, what single middle-aged woman who denied all interest in casual sex had wireless speakers and way too many candles in her bedroom? Who had body butter at the ready? And why did she have such practiced skill in giving sensual massages?

Maybe that was Sam's mode of operation. Maybe that was how she charmed and put women under her spell—by pretending to be the lonely writer, the perfect catch, single for so long in her search for true love. And Gwen did truly love her. She'd told Sam today that she was falling in love, but really, she had loved her at first sight. And she'd made a tough decision to trust her instincts. Now she wasn't sure it had been the right one.

It was time to apologize to Rosa and heed her warning. Gwen would need to distance herself, keep Sam away, if only to keep her safe. The *espíritu*, she finally understood, had immediately sensed the intense emotional connection between her and Sam. And then that spirit had summoned Sam to do its bidding. Maybe if Gwen pretended to lose interest in Sam, Alley would lose interest in her as well.

Laden with conflicting emotions, she curled next to Sam again and watched her sleep. More devastating than the thought of Sam not really loving her was the thought of Sam coming to harm. She'd waited a lifetime for someone like this, and ever so gently she touched the sleeping face of this woman who had come into her life so unexpectedly and turned her world upside down.

❖

It was a warm and beautiful day in the dream, an early summer morning. After breakfast she jumped up against the wall and knocked her orange leash and collar from the hook on which it always hung. And then she dragged it into the kitchen and dropped it at Gwen's feet.

"All right... all right," Gwen said from behind her newspaper. And soon they were off. She picked up a Frisbee at the end of the driveway and carried it in her mouth, all the way up the country road that few cars traveled, until they veered off on a path that led up a hill to a sunlit meadow, still damp with morning dew.

Gwen turned her loose, snatched the Frisbee from her, and flung it. It sailed through the air and she sped after it, jumping as high as

Gwen was tall, to claim it in midair—a magnificent catch that received claps of applause. They did this over and over, until she decided not to give it back to Gwen. "Ooh, you better give me that Frisbee!" They both crouched, faced off, and then their usual chase ensued.

She took off then, Gwen running behind her until she could run no more and collapsed in the grass, laughing and catching her breath. Dropping the Frisbee, she flopped down beside her and rolled on her back, content to listen to Gwen's breathing, her own panting. What a perfect day! Birds chattered and sang in the background, and when she looked up at the blue sky, the bright sun made her shut her eyes, but still she saw its orange brightness through her lids.

And when she opened her eyes again, Gwen and Liz were sitting beside her on the bed.

Gwen smiled tenderly. "Good morning, darling." She sat holding something in her hand that jingled—a familiar jingle.

"Hey, how's my out-law?" Liz asked. "You feeling okay?"

Samantha looked around. A steaming cup of coffee sat on the table beside her. "I'm fine…I think. Why do I feel like Dorothy waking up back in Kansas? What's the matter?"

Gwen and Liz exchanged glances, and Sam had a feeling they'd just had a private discussion.

"How'd you sleep?" Gwen asked.

"I slept well. Why?" Samantha sat up and looked between them. "Did something happen?"

Gwen handed her coffee. "Have you ever sleepwalked, Sam?"

"What? No. Never." She scooted up into a sitting position, sipped the proffered coffee, and looked at them both. "Why are you asking me this?"

Gwen let the collar dangle from her finger and held it up for Sam to see. "Do you remember taking this out of a box in the closet during the night?"

"No," she said, but she recognized the collar now. "I, uh…I think I might have seen it in my dream." She took another sip of coffee, put the cup down, and rubbed her face.

Liz looked at Gwen, and Gwen looked at Samantha. "What did you dream about?"

"I dreamed that you and I…I mean, that you and Alley took a walk to go play Frisbee. It was in a meadow…on top of a hill…right down the road from here."

Gwen pinched the bridge of her nose as though she'd developed a sudden headache. She quickly stood up, turning away from Samantha, and when she turned back, she did so with what seemed a forced smile. "I'm going to leave you two alone. Irene's back to help Rosa with a buffet breakfast, and everyone's starting to wake up, so let me check on things," she said.

When she left the room, Liz looked at her strangely. "Are you sure you're okay?"

"I'm fine, Liz, really."

Liz let out a deep breath, sat beside her, and patted her thigh. "Listen. I'm not going to hang around today. I think I'll get dressed, have something to eat, and hit the road. Are you staying?"

"No. I thought I'd give Gwen time alone to visit with her relatives before they fly out tomorrow. Besides, I'm driving to DC on Wednesday for a three-day book tour. I need to pack and prepare."

"Do you want to leave together? I'd feel better if I followed you… just in case you don't feel well."

"I feel fine, but sure. We can do that if you want."

"Good." Liz kissed her cheek and got up. "I'll meet you downstairs in about fifteen minutes."

"How's Isabel?" Samantha asked as Liz headed out.

She stopped in the doorway and turned back with a shrug of resignation. "Isabel is Isabel. What more can I say?" she said and closed the door on her way out.

Samantha got out of bed and stretched. She felt more than okay, actually. She felt like she'd just had a good workout, but the vibes she'd gotten from Gwen made her uneasy. Something wasn't right between them. As she headed for the master bathroom, she saw the orange collar and picked it up. Yep, that was the collar from her dream, all right, but it felt strange in her hands now, and she couldn't remember having touched it last night.

She laid it on the bed. "What do you want me to do for you, Alley?" she said into thin air. The dog-dreams she didn't mind, but the thought of sleepwalking sent a wave of nausea through her. Samantha was glad she didn't recall it; not remembering allowed her to pretend that it hadn't happened, that maybe the whole sleepwalking incident had all been part of Gwen's own dreams last night.

CHAPTER TWENTY-NINE

Between recent nights in Maine and at the Laraway estate, Liz didn't know where she was when she first opened her eyes Monday morning. It took her a minute to realize she was staring at her own ceiling. And when she did, she cringed. She didn't need to look at the arm resting across her stomach or the face on the pillow beside her to know whose it was.

Skyler. Cute little Skyler with the sky-blue stripe in her wild blond hair; Skyler, the struggling artist who taught art classes and moonlighted as a barista at the coffeehouse next door to her shop. They weren't exactly friends with benefits, more like acquaintances with benefits. Sometimes they'd meet up at the Cubbyhole, and they'd slept together twice, maybe three times. Liz couldn't remember which.

She wasn't prone to regret when it came to women, but her heart was filled with it right now. Never mix tequila and self-pity, she told herself. It was a poor combination that led to poorer behavior. Bringing Skyler home had seemed a good idea last night, a way of getting Isabel off her mind, but it hadn't worked. Liz found herself going through the motions, wanting it to be over. Come to think of it, she might have fallen asleep before it was. The only good thing about it had been closing her eyes and pretending Isabel was touching her. That part had been sort of exciting. She raked her fingers through her hair and sighed heavily.

"Good morning, gorgeous..." Skyler stirred beside her, but Liz kept staring at the ceiling. "Where are you?"

Liz turned her head on her pillow and smiled halfheartedly. "I'm right here."

"You weren't even here last night—not the Liz I know."

"Sorry, Sky...I'll make it up to you with breakfast."

Skyler reached for her phone. "Holy crap, how'd it get to be nine o'clock? I gotta get home for a quick shower and clean clothes. I teach class at eleven. Coffee would be great, though."

Liz was relieved she couldn't stay. She wanted time alone to wallow before meeting a client at noon. "Coffee coming up." She gave her a peck on the lips, slipped into an oversized denim shirt that she didn't bother to button, and pulled a pair of panties from a drawer. In the kitchen she left a pot of coffee to brew, went to brush her teeth, and when she came back Skyler was pouring coffee. Liz fixed herself a cup and joined her in the living room, but no sooner did she curl up in a chair opposite Skyler than the doorbell rang.

"Uh-oh. You're about to meet the illustrious Ms. Peterson," Liz said. If it were an outside visitor Ben would have buzzed her from downstairs, unless he'd left the door unattended to run across the street for coffee, as he sometimes did.

Ms. Peterson was her elderly neighbor who had enjoyed a long career in theater. At eighty-five, she still dressed stylishly, maintained her dancer's figure, and had perfect posture. Ms. Peterson adored Liz and sometimes stopped in for coffee or tea, enchanting her with stories of Broadway. And although she wasn't a lesbian, she always made a prideful point of recounting her one "brief experience" with a woman and making sure Liz knew about her many other "opportunities" along the way.

Liz set her cup down, got up, and went to the door, but when she looked out the peep hole, it wasn't Ms. Peterson. Isabel was standing there with the dogs.

"Fuck!" Liz grabbed her head with both hands and started spinning in a frantic circle. Of all days for Isabel to show up unannounced, it had to be while she had a woman in her apartment! What to do? She had few options. She could pretend she wasn't home, but that wouldn't be nice, and really, there was no one she wanted to see more. She took a deep breath, put on her best smile, and opened the door. Propped against the wall was a large flat package wrapped in brown paper. It looked like something framed. And in between the package and Isabel stood the dogs. They looked worried, as if they suspected this place might be a veterinarian's office, but once they looked up and saw Liz, tails started wagging.

"Isabel!" Liz happily greeted her, then looked at the dogs. "Hi, Blue. Hey, Loosey Goosey. What a nice surprise."

Isabel looked away, trying not to stare at Liz's open shirt. "I woke you. I'm so sorry."

Liz looked down at her partially exposed breasts and quickly clutched the two sides of her shirt with a hand. "Come in. I just made coffee."

"Okay." Isabel started to slide the package in. "I really just wanted to bring this to you…and um…apologize for my behavior the other—" Her jaw dropped at the sight of Skyler peeking over Liz's shoulder, and when Liz saw her almost stagger back, she knew things weren't going to turn out well.

"Morning," said Skyler.

"Oh…I'm…I…I didn't mean to intrude," Isabel stammered. "Forgive me. I shouldn't have come without calling. Here. I just…I wanted to drop this off," she said, without making contact. Her hands trembled as she pushed the package and leaned it in the doorway. Then she spun around and hurried away, pulling the dogs along with her. They followed Isabel, but they kept their heads turned back, looking at Liz confusedly as they tripped into each other.

"Isabel, wait!" Liz called, but Isabel only picked up speed until she was running down the long hall for the elevator. Liz took off after her, trying to button her shirt as she did, but she couldn't find the buttonholes as she ran and gave up. "Wait, Isabel. I can explain," she said, then realized how inane that sounded.

Isabel reached the elevator doors and pounded on the button.

"Please don't go," Liz pleaded when she caught up with her.

But Isabel wouldn't even look at her. She stood with her face to the elevator door, her nose almost touching it. "How could you betray me like this? How could you do this to me—how *could* you!" She started jabbing the button again.

Liz put a hand on her shoulder, but Isabel recoiled from her touch. "Isabel, what have I done wrong? I haven't betrayed you. We're good friends, right? We're friends and—"

"Oh, is that what we are, good friends? Thanks for clarifying that point for me. I must have missed something."

Missed something? Liz was dumbfounded, but then it struck her—Isabel thought they were together, a couple!—and, strangely, this jealous rage overjoyed her. She fought to keep from smiling.

"Isabel, you're not being reasonable. Please, come back inside and talk to me."

But Isabel wasn't having any of it. The bell finally dinged and the elevator door opened. Desperate to keep her, and before Isabel could even move, Liz snatched both leashes from behind and quickly stepped back with the dogs.

With an indignant toss of her head, Isabel stepped into the elevator anyway and held her hand out to keep the doors from closing. "Give me my dogs."

"No. Not until you talk to me."

"Give me the dogs and go back to your girlfriend."

"She's not my girlfriend. She crashed here last night," Liz lied. There was no sense in letting the truth worsen things. Liz doubted Isabel would feel much sympathy knowing she'd engaged in meaningless sex just to get her mind off her. "She's a friend, Isabel."

"So that explains why you're half-naked?"

"I'm not half-naked, I..." But she was. She felt horrible standing there barefoot in panties and an oversized shirt that had fallen open again.

Flustered, Isabel tore her eyes away from Liz's breasts and, withdrew her hand from the door. It started closing.

Holding the dogs back, Liz quickly slapped the elevator button, and the door opened again. "Get out of the elevator. Right now."

"No!" Her bottom lip quivered and her eyes filled with tears.

Liz stared at her helplessly as the door began closing again. "Don't you know how fucking in love I am with you?" she yelled.

Isabel's eyes widened, the door shut, and Liz gave it a swift kick with her bare foot. "Dammit, Isabel!" she shouted, and when she realized she'd frightened the dogs, she dropped to her knees, raised her voice an octave, and spoke in her best baby voice. "Aww, I'm sorry, Blue. It's okay, Goose." She ruffled their fur. "It's just that your mommy's driving me insane. Yeah, she is," she cheerfully cooed. "Hey, are you girls hungry? Let's go see what I've got for you."

Before Liz could stand up Ms. Peterson's door opened, and she poked her head out. "Oh my! Liz, is that you? Are you okay, dear?"

"I'm fine, Ms. Peterson. Everything's fine." And when she realized Ms. Peterson was looking at her bare breasts, she grabbed her shirt, buttoned it lopsided, and stood up. "Sorry for the commotion," she said, and trotted down the hall, pulling the tail of her shirt down over her panties and cursing under her breath the whole way. "Fuck! Fuck, fuck, fuck."

Skyler was standing in the doorway, ready to leave as the dogs walked in. "A pit bull and a...Scottie? Who are they?"

Liz frowned and shook her head. "My stepkids, if I play my cards right."

Skyler gave an understanding nod. "That explains where your head was last night."

"I'm sorry, sweetie," Liz said, and kissed her on the cheek, "but I've got to go make things right."

"It's all good. We'll catch up whenever."

"Thanks, Sky." Liz hugged her, and when she closed the door she dropped the dogs' leashes. They followed her panting into the kitchen.

"It's hot today, I know. If I'd known you two were coming I would have had biscuits and treats waiting." She opened the fridge. "Let's see…hmm…can I interest you girls in chicken cutlets? I think so." Liz cut up two, served them on paper plates, and left the dogs with a bowl of ice water while she took the fastest shower ever.

The buzzer rang just as she got out, and Liz rushed to the intercom in a towel. "Isabel?"

"Please bring Blue and Loosey down to the lobby."

"They're eating chicken right now. They said you should come up and get them."

"I'm not coming up there."

"There's no one here. She's gone."

"I know. She passed me on her way out. Thank you for humiliating me."

"Oh, Isabel…" Liz felt terrible. Her voice softened. "Please come up here and talk to me. You're not being fair."

"I'm not coming up there, Liz. Don't ask me again."

God, could she any more stubborn? Liz suspected that stubbornness might have come from the Waspy side of the family, but that fire in Isabel was all Brazilian. "Okay, okay." Liz thought for a minute. "I'll bring the dogs down under one condition. Have breakfast with me. Two blocks to your right is the Barking Dog. The outside patio allows pets. Go get us a table, and I'll meet you there in ten minutes."

There was silence on the other end. "Isabel?" Liz called through the intercom.

"Oh…all right," she finally said, but didn't sound too happy.

Liz threw on a tank top and cropped pants and ran some hair gel through her damp russet waves. Earrings, a little lipstick, eyeliner, and she was ready. But the package Isabel had delivered stirred her curiosity, and she couldn't resist opening it. She carried it over to the dining-room table and laid it flat, carefully unwrapping it and almost crying when she saw what it was—the Icart *Martini* print she'd seen for auction at Sotheby's. Had Isabel been the silent bidder? That explained what she'd been doing on her cell phone that evening. "Oh, baby..." What a special gift, a beautiful surprise. And she'd ruined it for Isabel.

Liz grabbed her bag and the dogs, and when she reached the café saw Isabel sitting at a table, just beyond the flower boxes that hung on the wrought-iron fence. A painful lump rose in her throat. She felt so ashamed of having had a woman in her bed last night, that Isabel had walked into the aftermath of all that—angry that she was ashamed because, really, she'd done nothing wrong. Isabel had treated her as no more than a friend, so why should it have mattered what woman or how many of them she slept with?

Liz walked through the gateway, and the dogs greeted Isabel like they hadn't seen her in hours. She put the loops of their leashes under the leg on her chair and looked up at Liz. The fury had passed. Now she just looked sad, heartbroken, and Liz wished she could hold her tight.

"Oh, Isabel...I opened your gift. It's so amazing...incredibly special...completely unexpected. I don't know what to say, except... thank you."

"You're welcome," Isabel said as the waitress brought coffee. Neither of them was especially hungry, not after what had just transpired, but Liz ordered French toast, and Isabel ordered the same. "I knew you loved it," Isabel said when the waitress left, "and I...I decided you should have it." She looked at Liz with regret. "I'm sorry I reacted the way I did. I had no right to think we were committed."

"Committed?" Liz was beyond perplexed. Her mouth dropped open, and she shook her head in confusion. Would she ever figure Isabel out? "I don't understand, Isabel. I mean, what were you thinking—that we were going steady?" She'd meant it as a joke, but when Isabel gave a nervous little shrug and tucked her hair behind her ear, Liz realized that was exactly what she'd thought. "We've spent a total of six nights sleeping in the same bed, Isabel...and we've never so much as kissed. I've had more physical contact with Blue and the Goose than I've had with you," she said. "How was I to ever know you thought we were more than friends? I told you I was gay the day we met. You changed the subject and never brought it up again."

"I thought you knew how I felt. I thought you just didn't want to rush into—oh, I don't know what I was thinking, Liz, except that...I thought I meant something to you."

"You do! You mean *everything* to me, Isabel. I think about you all day and dream about you all night. And I would never stray from you if for one minute I thought you were mine."

"I am…I mean, I want to be, but I…I don't know how. Isabel propped her elbow on the table and buried her face in her hand. "God, I'm such a mess."

"Mine? You want to be *mine*?" It all sounded too good to be true. Liz smiled affectionately, this desire she'd never known before filling every part of her. "Really?"

Isabel looked at her and nodded. "Yeah…really."

Breakfast came, and Liz waited before reaching across for Isabel's hand. "I'm so sorry for hurting and upsetting you, but…" she let out a heavy sigh, "you have to give me a break here. I'm not a mind reader, you know."

"And what about her?"

"There is no *her*. There's only you. Please believe me."

They managed to eat half their breakfast, and Liz checked the time as she watched Isabel feed the rest to the dogs." I have an important appointment with a client at my shop. Would you want to hang out with the dogs at my place and wait for me? I won't be more than two hours."

Isabel shook her head. "I'm not going back to your apartment. Not today."

As though it were the scene of a crime, Liz thought. But she understood. "Fair enough. Do you want to drive me downtown and see the shop?"

"I'd love to see it. Can the dogs come?"

"Of course. And then…" Liz thought before she spoke. "Would you be able to make it back into the city again tomorrow?"

"Actually, I'm taking the morning off. The animal shelter has a dog transport coming up from Tennessee. They're expecting eighteen animals to arrive by six in the morning. I promised to help walk and feed and get them settled in the kennels. Then I figured I'd go home to shower and change and make it into the office for a few hours."

"You have such a kind heart, Isabel. I love that you volunteer your time. If the shelter ever needs an extra hand for something like that in the future, let me know. I'd enjoy helping."

"They always need help."

"Good." Liz smiled. "So…about tomorrow, then…how about driving down after you leave the office? I'll make dinner—an official date—and we can continue this conversation, maybe even enjoy a first kiss."

Isabel blushed and looked away. "Okay," she finally said.

Okay? Wow. So she and Isabel Laraway were going steady. Liz smiled, but inside she felt the bubbling joy of a kid being told the carnival was coming to town. She wanted to jump out of her seat and sing and dance around the café.

One thing for sure, her new girlfriend had more than just a kiss coming tomorrow night, but Liz would wait until Isabel was in her apartment to spring the rest on her.

CHAPTER THIRTY

Liz had spent the afternoon shopping, cooking, and preparing for a romantic dinner. She half expected Isabel to cancel at the last minute, but she hadn't. She'd called Liz at noon to say she'd just gotten home from the shelter and would need to shower and stop by the office for a couple of hours. She told Liz to expect her by five, and no sooner had Liz finished dressing than Isabel arrived right on time, wearing a business pantsuit fit for summer and holding two bottles of wine: a Barolo, which she said would be perfect with the pasta dish Liz had prepared, and a nice port to enjoy after dinner.

They finished eating with a second glass of wine, and Liz suspected Isabel would need another just to keep her anticipatory anxiety at a tolerable level. She'd seemed awkward at first, as though wondering when that first kiss would catch her off guard, but once Liz got her talking about the arrival of the dogs that morning, she relaxed and ended up eating a second helping.

"You're a wonderful cook," she said. And when she noticed Liz just sitting back and smiling at her, she nervously picked up the bottle of wine and found it empty.

"I'll tell you what. Why don't you open that port for us and we can relax in the living room," Liz said, although she wasn't planning on spending much time with Isabel on the sofa.

Isabel helped her clear the table, and after Liz loaded the dishwasher she left Isabel to open the bottle. "I just have to make a really quick business call," she said. "Why don't you pour that and bring our glasses into the living room." And with that, Liz grabbed her cell phone, slipped into the bedroom, and dialed Sam's number. They'd spoken earlier in the day about yesterday's drama with Isabel, and Liz knew Sam intended to see Gwen tonight. She stood by the air conditioner so Isabel wouldn't overhear her conversation. "Hey, are you at Gwen's?" she said when Sam answered.

"Nope. Change of plans. I'm in Red Hook, waiting in the parking lot of a supposedly popular farm-to-table restaurant, and—in fact, here she comes now, her car just pulled in," Sam said. "She seemed hesitant about me going there for some reason, so I offered to make dinner at my place, but she suggested we meet halfway." After a pause, Sam added, "Gwen says she wants to talk. You know 'a talk' is never good. I know she's scared, and I know I screwed up with this…this ghost situation… but I'm hoping to put her mind at ease."

"So she's not spending the night with you?"

"Doesn't look that way."

"I'm guessing she knows Isabel came here for dinner?"

"That she does. And she's walking over to my car now."

"Would you ask her if it's okay if I keep Isabel with me tonight? Tell her Isabel's on her second bottle of wine and I don't want her driving."

"Ah…so the lioness finally has Isabel in her lair." Sam snickered. "Hold on a sec."

Liz heard Sam open her car door and listened to the sound of muffled voices, and then Sam came back on the phone. "Gwen says thank you for not letting her drive and to keep her overnight, or for as long as you like. She'll take care of the dogs and have Rosa feed all the cats." She closed her car door again. "So go have fun seducing your prey. It took a long time to lure her in, and I'm sure the lioness is quite hungry," she whispered. "Just don't eat her alive."

"That I can't promise. I'm starving for her, as you well know." Liz laughed. "Hey, tell Gwen thank you…and tell her I love her. I love you, too. We'll talk tomorrow."

Liz hung up and smiled with deep satisfaction. *Game, set, match!* Isabel was hers tonight. All night. She shut off the air conditioner, turned the ceiling fan on low, and lit a few big candles: one on each night table and one on the dresser beside the mixed bouquet of fresh flowers she'd picked up today. She could smell the freesia in the bouquet. It mixed well with the light scent of lavender that laced the fresh sheets. She stopped in the doorway and gave the room a sweeping glance. Perfect.

Isabel was looking through some CDs when Liz came out. "Put on whatever you like," she said. She took her glass, drew her legs underneath her, and sat waiting for Isabel with her arm stretched along the back of the sofa.

"I like what's playing—'Pretty Thoughts,' right?"

"I'm surprised you know it." She and Isabel had such different personalities, yet they couldn't have had more in common.

"I love Alina Baraz. I have a lot of her music," Isabel said as she wandered around the room and glanced at the wall over the sofa. She smiled up at the Icart print hanging there. "I saw that when I came in. That's a perfect place for it."

"I've been waiting for you to notice." Liz patted the cushion beside her and grinned. "And this is the perfect place for *you*, so stop pacing and come here to me."

Isabel sat down with her glass, and Liz shifted so she could face her. She stretched her arm out along the back of the couch, just behind Isabel. "Are you okay, comfortable being here with me?"

Isabel nodded and sipped her port.

She was absolutely beautiful, Liz decided. Maybe not the flashy type of beautiful that turns heads at a distance. Isabel's was a quiet, breathtaking beauty best savored up close. Every feature was fine, perfectly sculpted, and that dark hair fell so straight and shiny along the smooth skin of her high cheekbones. Her lips were perfectly shaped, her pretty little nose was just the slightest bit upturned, and the color of those sexy eyes reminded Liz of a bottle of dark tequila held up to the sunlight.

Liz took the port from Isabel's hand and set both glasses on the coffee table. How many women had she seduced? She'd lost count. But it didn't matter. This was the one that mattered, and she found it almost amusing that she herself was feeling a little nervous. She took Isabel's chin and turned her face. "So about that long-overdue kiss…"

Isabel just stared at her, her lips parted the slightest bit as Liz coaxed them to her mouth. They were soft, supple, sweetened with wine. But, God, was she tense, her mouth so tight. Liz moved in, softly trailing the tip of her tongue between those lips, nibbling the upper one, sucking the bottom one and trying to gently pry Isabel's mouth open with her own. She stopped, let her lips roam over to Isabel's cheek and up to her temple. "Now kiss me back…and kiss like you mean it."

Liz returned to her mouth, applying more pressure, until Isabel finally surrendered. Her mouth relaxed then, and she responded by awkwardly mirroring Liz's moves. Little by little a curious tongue came out to daintily explore Liz's mouth.

"That's more like it," Liz whispered against Isabel's teeth, and leaned even closer to deepen their kiss. She felt Isabel's pulse quicken, and when she heard a soft moan come from Isabel's throat, she knew it was time. If she left things up to Isabel they'd be sitting here in kissing-kindergarten all night. Liz pulled back and looked at her. She'd never wanted someone so much.

Isabel was too self-conscious to hold her gaze. She blinked a few times, looked down, and tucked her hair around her ear, but it only fell forward and covered her face.

Liz got up and held out a hand. "Come on…let's go relax in the bedroom."

Mention of the bedroom made Isabel's eyes widen. "Oh, I…I can't, Liz, not tonight."

"Why not?"

"I have to get home. I haven't even taken care of the cats in the barn and I—"

"Rosa's taking care of them. I already spoke to Sam."

Isabel began to flounder. "But there's the dogs and…"

"It's all taken care of. Gwen said not to worry. And she said for you to spend the night with me. You're drinking and she doesn't want you driving."

"I'll be fine in a little while. I'd like to stay, really, but I…I promised a TNR group I'd help set traps for some feral…" Isabel's voice dwindled out. She was fresh out of excuses.

Liz wanted to laugh, but she didn't. Instead, she waited patiently for Isabel to take her hand. "Come with me…I have a cat for you to trap. It's in the bedroom."

Isabel downed half her port, almost choking on the big gulp, and stared at the floor.

"Come on…bring your glass with you." Liz waited with an outstretched hand, but Isabel just sat there, looking up with eyes filled with both fear and desire.

"Isabel…come on. You're mine tonight. There's nothing to worry about. I don't bite," she reassured her, but then she grinned. "Actually, I take that back, I do bite. But not hard. I promise."

Isabel took her glass and stood, her head hung in resignation. Finally she grasped Liz's hand and stiffly followed her, as if being led off to the gallows. But when she saw the bedroom her eyes lit up. Liz took the glass from her hand and set it on the night table beside her own.

"It's beautiful in here," Isabel commented, then moseyed across to the lit candles and vase of freesia, daisies, and roses. "I love the flowers," she said, trying to make small talk.

"Good. I got them for you while I was out today." While Isabel smelled them, probably stalling for time, Liz quickly removed the throw pillows from the bed, turned back the covers, and came up behind her. She pushed Isabel's hair to one side, placing soft kisses along her neck.

Isabel scrunched her shoulders, as if the caresses tickled her. She turned in Liz's arms and tried to smile, but her lips only quivered. She was scared, clearly out of her element, and Liz felt bad for her. But not bad enough to stop. If she let Isabel leave tonight, she couldn't imagine how long it would be before Isabel agreed to come back. She took her hands and slowly walked backward, drawing Isabel with her until they stood against the side of the bed. "Have you been with *anyone*?"

"No."

Has anything bad ever happened that you didn't want to?"

Isabel shook her head. "I…I just never had feelings for anyone…not the feelings I have for you." She reached with tentative fingers and touched the hollow of Liz's neck, fiddled nervously with the gold chain that hung from it. "I know. You think something's wrong with me."

"Because you're a virgin?"

"Well…technically I'm not. I think I lost my virginity when I crashed and hit myself on the bar of a boy's bike when I was six."

"Ouch."

"I'll say." Isabel gave a comic snort. "When I went home and saw blood I was too afraid to tell anyone. But then Rosa was doing laundry and got hysterical. She knew I was too young to get my period. Gwen tried to take me to the doctor, but I refused to get in the car. I was too embarrassed to let anyone examine me down there…except for my aunt. She couldn't find anything wrong, no cuts or anything, so she decided I'd just…"

"Popped your cherry?"

Isabel nodded and Liz laughed. "Oh, Isabel," she said and cupped her cheek. "Nothing's wrong with you. Everything about you is so right."

"But you're experienced, and I…"

"Just like you're an experienced dancer and I'm not. I didn't know how to samba…but you taught me, didn't you?"

"You caught on fast."

"You will, too." She put her arms around Isabel's waist, moving slowly to the music wafting in from the living room. "Making love is just like dancing…and you're a wonderful dancer. You'll catch on as fast as I did."

Isabel looked at her with almost pleading eyes, and in them was a potent mixture of emotion that stirred in Liz an adoration and tenderness deeper than anything she'd ever felt for a woman. The initial panic had disappeared from Isabel's face, and heated desire burned in those tequila eyes.

"I'm afraid I wouldn't know…" Isabel stopped and swallowed. "I don't know what I'm supposed to do," she said in a timid voice that Liz could barely hear.

Liz softly kissed the side of her mouth, trailed her lips up to her ear. "You can start by undressing me," she whispered, and brought both of Isabel's hands to her blouse. Student drivers didn't learn to drive by sitting in the passenger seat, did they? They got behind the wheel, and that's where she intended to put Isabel—in the driver's seat.

Isabel did as she was told, opening the first button and then the next. And when she was done she pushed the blouse over Liz's shoulders just enough that gravity took it from there, and the silky fabric slid to the floor.

"That wasn't too hard, was it?" Liz lifted her chin and gave an encouraging smile. There was something so fragile, yet so magical about her.

"No…" Isabel said, her breathing now rapid.

Liz placed Isabel's hands on her breasts, delighting in the feel of Isabel moving them against the fabric of her pale blue bra. And under Liz's skillful hands and expert maneuvers, Isabel's clothes were gone before Isabel even realized she was naked. She smoothed her own hands over Isabel's small, firm breasts, ran them down her stomach, around to her back, exploring her petite form that was well-toned from wrestling shelter dogs and all those other outdoor activities she enjoyed.

Liz slowly wriggled out of the rest of her own clothes then, gently kissing her as pulled Isabel into bed and on top of her. The initial feel of Isabel's naked body aligned with her was exquisite, and she took a few minutes to luxuriate in that first moment of contact. Any other woman and she wouldn't have wasted time. Quick, fun, casual, and it would've been over, with Liz hoping the woman wouldn't hang around for long. But she wanted to take her time with Isabel, hold her for an eternity if she could. And if Isabel suddenly had a change of heart, Liz decided she'd be content to just lie with her like this, naked and kissing. But Isabel was ready. When Liz slid her hand between their bodies and moved it between Isabel's legs, her fingers slipped right in. She stroked her a few times. "Does that feel good?"

"Uh-huh," Isabel said, her breathing heavy, her eyes half-closed and glazing over.

Desire gushed from Liz's body. She wanted to flip Isabel over, taste her, take her. Instead, she took her hand away and guided Isabel's hand between her own legs.

Isabel drew in a sharp breath as her fingers slipped into the familiar yet strangely unfamiliar labyrinth of another woman. Her hand navigated tentatively at first, then stopped and rested over Liz's engorged sex. "What should I…how do you want me to touch you?"

"Touch me like you touch yourself," Liz whispered. She lifted herself to Isabel's hand. "A little harder…yeah…just like that, baby… that feels so good."

Despite Isabel's lack of experience and somewhat amateurish moves, she had surprisingly talented hands. Liz had waited so long to feel them that she could have climaxed right away. She held back though, wanting to build Isabel's confidence, wanting Isabel to see and hear and feel the pleasure she was giving. "I love how you touch me. If you keep doing that you're going to make me come," she murmured.

Liz felt Isabel's pulse quicken in response, her breathing becoming heavy. That was all Liz needed to know that her own arousal was exciting Isabel. Their kiss in the living room had evidently improved Isabel's prowess, because now her mouth was full on Liz's, claiming it with wild urgency. Liz writhed under the weight of her, loving the feel of Isabel's hot body pinning, melting into her. She couldn't hold back any longer. Withdrawing her mouth, she ran her fingers through that dark, silky hair, grabbed a fistful, and gently tilted Isabel's head back just enough to drunkenly stare into those tequila-brown eyes as she let go. "Now, Isabel…make me come for you."

Isabel inhaled sharply at her words and held Liz's gaze, seemingly amazed, bewitched, transfixed by Liz's sudden climax. "Oh…" she groaned as Liz let out a cry of ecstasy. She began moving herself on Liz's thigh, as though about to climax herself, but Liz wrapped her arms around Isabel and held her still.

"Oh, no, baby…not yet." Liz smiled. "I've got plans for you." She rested for a moment, and then with renewed energy she rolled Isabel onto her back and covered her with wild kisses and wet bites. When she parted and settled between her legs, Isabel gasped, arching her back. "Just relax…" Liz said, enjoying herself, loving Isabel slowly until she knew she was peaking. She slipped inside her, mouth and hands working in unison to create a perfect, pulsating rhythm that matched the changing cadence of Isabel's moans.

Isabel's hips moved smoothly, sensuously. Watching her dance the other night, Liz had known she would be a wonderful lover once she learned to trust and let go. Now finally she had let go, and they moved beautifully together. Liz gently rocked with her, attuned to the rise and fall of her hips as Isabel climaxed. She stayed with it, kept up with her, riding out Isabel's orgasm until waves of spasms subsided.

"You're so fucking incredible," Liz said as she kissed her way up Isabel's body.

Isabel grabbed Liz and held her tightly, burying a laugh, a muffled cry in Liz's neck. And just when Liz thought they might rest, Isabel was turning her over, teasing her nipples, kissing her stomach, working her way down.

"Isabel, if you're not ready you don't have to—"

"I want to" was all she said.

Liz was disinclined to refuse and in no position to argue.

"You're a wonderful lover," Liz said to her as they lay together quietly in a tangle of sheets. Liz was exhausted, hot, and happy to sprawl out on top of them, but Isabel modestly drew up the sheet to cover them both.

Liz ran a hand up and down her thigh. "Why are you hiding this beautiful body?"

Isabel shrugged on the pillow and drew closer to her.

The candles still burned, the Tiffany lamps casting colorful patches of soft light, and the scent of fresh flowers was heavenly. Liz felt as though she'd found her own heaven. "I'm so crazy for you," she said as they lay together quietly. I've been crazy for you since day one."

Isabel stroked her chest. "Really?"

"Really. The day Sam and I came for lunch and I saw you in that sexy, preppy blue skirt suit…oh, my God."

Isabel blew out a little laugh. "Hardly a sexy outfit."

"On you it was." Liz gently ran her fingers through Isabel's hair. "Then I saw your face…snuck a peek at those beautiful legs when you weren't looking…and when we spent the afternoon together I enjoyed your company so much. When I got home that night I knew I had met the woman of my dreams. Almost overnight you became my best friend…and then I found myself falling madly in love. I'm sorry it came out the way it did yesterday, but I do love you."

"I love you, too," Isabel whispered. "And I felt the same way the first day I met you."

"Oh, really?" Liz made an exaggerated frown. "You certainly did a bad job of showing it. You had me convinced you were just a very prudish straight girl."

Isabel cuddled close. "I didn't know how to show you. I was embarrassed that I'd never…you know…and I didn't think I could please you the way other woman do."

"Those other women have nothing on you, baby doll."

Isabel was silent for a minute. "Did you love her, that other one from yesterday?" she asked.

"Isabel, I told you, there is no *her*. There never has been. Don't you get it?"

"Then why…I mean, how could you make love with them?"

"I don't make love, Isabel. I mean, I haven't until now." Liz smiled at her. "So tonight was a first for me, too. All the other times were just…practice."

"I don't understand that. Yesterday was too upsetting for me. It made me jealous and I…I hated the thought of you being with anyone else…having sex for the sake of sex."

"Are you telling me I can't have any more casual sex?" Liz enjoyed teasing her.

"You can have all you want…but don't come back to me. I couldn't handle it…I could never accept that."

"Oooh! Laying down the rules already, huh?" Liz laughed, reached over, and started tickling her. "I'll play by your rules. In fact, I sort of liked seeing you jealous. It was the first time I thought you might actually want me. It turned me on."

Isabel seemed to be thinking and then, "I don't like this bed," she said, the statement coming out of nowhere.

Liz propped herself up on an elbow and looked at her with concern. "What's wrong, baby? You're not comfortable? It's a really good…" She stopped short, realizing what bothered Isabel about it—the other woman who'd been in it. "Oh, okay…I understand. I'll get us a new one if it's that important to you."

"I'll buy it for you," Isabel said. "Any bed you want."

The heiress had spoken. "You don't have to do that." Liz smiled and shook her head in wonder. "How about we pick out a bed together? Maybe I'll upgrade from a queen to king…something bigger so the dogs have room."

"That would be nice," Isabel said. "They'll like that." Liz lowered herself, and Isabel rested her head on Liz's chest, her long eyelashes tickling Liz's breast as they fluttered.

"Are you falling asleep on me?" Sex seemed to make everyone go to sleep, but it always woke Liz up. She could have sex, then get up and clean the whole house. She felt wired now, wonderfully alive.

"I'm just thinking how much I love being with you," Isabel said.

"Would you love being with me and dessert? I have Italian pastries for us."

"Yes!"

Liz laughed. "Is it too late for cappuccino?"

"Yes. But I don't mind staying up with you all night long."

"Good. We can have dessert and cappuccino in bed…and then some." Liz got up, put on a robe, and laid another out in case Isabel needed it. "Dessert coming right up." She paused in the doorway to look at the beautiful and amazing young woman in her bed. It was a good bed, and she'd miss it. But not as much as she'd miss not having Isabel in it.

Chapter Thirty-One

"Come away with me," Sam pleaded. They had finished dinner and stood in the parking lot by Gwen's car. "Why don't you just go home, grab a few things, and meet me at my place in the morning. We can spend an extra day in Philly, hit a museum, peruse the galleries and shops, and—"

"I can't, Sam. I have an appointment for a mammogram tomorrow."

"Are you all right?" Samantha swallowed against her sudden worry. "I'll go with you if you don't mind company. I can drive down to DC in the evening instead of the afternoon."

"I'm fine, Sam. Hopefully fine. It's just a six-month checkup. I'll probably meet Carol for lunch afterward. She can't wait to talk about the party." She rubbed Sam's chest with her hand. "Go in the daylight, Sam. I don't want you driving at night. I'll see you when you get back."

"See me where? You met me here because Rosa thinks I'm possessed and doesn't want me at the house. And you didn't want to come to my house because—what—you thought I'd want to be intimate, and you're having second thoughts about us, right?"

Gwen looked almost pained. She hugged Samantha, and Samantha held her tight. "Oh, Sam," she said into her neck. "Everything has happened so fast."

"Everything? You mean *us*?" And when Gwen didn't answer, Samantha grasped her arms firmly and pushed her back enough to see her face clearly. "What's going on?"

Gwen looked away and held her head up, as though looking up at the sky would keep the tears from rolling out of her eyes.

"Talk to me," Samantha said with growing impatience, and for the first time she understood Liz's frustration in getting Isabel to communicate. She supposed the apple didn't fall far…

"I'm so confused, Sam." Gwen dabbed the corner of one eye with a pinkie.

"I know I went against your wishes and lied to you. I'm sorry. Really I am, but…what can I say? I write ghost stories. I got carried away. Maybe it was the…the splendid sublime, the awe-inspiring sight of a real-life ghost that got the best of me. But I haven't lied about anything else, if that's what you're thinking." Samantha put a finger under her chin and forced Gwen to look at her. "Hey, Professor," she said, trying to make light of things, "don't I at least get a pass for correctly using the word *sublime* in a sentence?"

Smiling seemed to take some effort, but Gwen managed a small one. "I'll take that into consideration when giving you your final grade."

"I think you've already given me a final grade. And I feel like I somehow failed." She pulled her close again. "I love you," she said. It was the first time she'd said it aloud. But when Gwen didn't say it back, Samantha felt her heart begin to break and let go of her.

Gwen looked away again, fumbled through her bag for car keys. "Maybe when you get back we can think about seeing someone?"

"What?" Samantha knew where this was leading and frowned. "Who?"

"Maybe…maybe a team of paranormal re—"

"Like an exorcist?" Sam scoffed and stared at her. "If you're that frightened of being with me, you could have saved yourself a trip tonight and just broken up with me over the phone." She walked away, upset now and shaking her head as she went. She couldn't believe what she'd just heard. "An exorcist, huh? Nice, Gwen. Sounds like great fun. After that we can swing by the witch doctor's house. And if the witch isn't home we'll call Ghostbusters."

"Sam!" Gwen cried.

But Samantha didn't stop. When she reached her car, she opened the door and turned back. "Just tell me one thing. Is this just about the ghost, or does something have you questioning our age difference again?" And when Gwen didn't answer, Samantha waved a hand at her. "Fine. You know what? Take all the time and space you need. I'll call you in, say, a couple of months. How does that sound? Maybe by then you'll have come to your senses."

Samantha didn't wait for a response. She got in, slammed the door, and started the engine. She hadn't meant to be so sarcastic, but sometimes feeling angry was easier than feeling so deeply hurt. She had no idea what or who had gotten into Gwen's head, but she'd been unwavering, resolute, and Samantha suspected that Rosa had a hand in it. Damn that nutty woman's histrionics!

By the time Samantha got home, an odd feeling of malaise fell upon her. Packing could wait until morning. She made a cup of lemongrass tea, carried it up to the bedroom, and face-planted on the bed. Her sheets still smelled of Gwen's perfume, of her body, their blended bodies, and it made Samantha crazy. They'd made love here just three days ago. Would they ever be together again? To think they might not was so upsetting that when the phone rang she couldn't even speak. She waited for the answering machine pick up.

"Sam...I...I should have said I love you...because I do, and... Sam, are you there? Please pick up..."

But Samantha didn't. Everyone was entitled to a little pouting and self-pity every now and then. When Gwen hung up, Samantha moped into her study, pulled a box from an oak file cabinet, and started flipping through an assortment of blank greeting cards she kept. Finding one of an English garden she liked, a thatched cottage surrounded by flower gardens, she put it aside and pulled out one more—a murder of crows gathered in a tree, silhouetted against a sunset. She slipped that one into her computer case and took the other one back to her bed with a pen and paper on a clipboard. After some thinking, sighing, and scribbling a draft on paper, she opened the card and wrote:

If the age difference is still part of what's worrying you, I have only this to say on the subject, and I'm saying it in a poem because I promised at the Waldorf that I'd write you one.

Lovers' garden sown by fate
The lilac blooms, the aster waits
One born too soon, the other late
'til ivy creeps and tangles seasons
Fragrance wafting past all reason
To carry far the lilac's call
So that spring might know the fall

She addressed, stamped it, and on her way out of town the next day dropped it at the post office and headed straight for Washington DC. She had arranged to start at the farthest point, two hundred and fifty miles away, then work her way back to Baltimore, Philly, and straight home.

Four hours later she was in Maryland. Miserable the whole way, she had listened to music, thought about the readings she'd give, and kept a recorder handy so she could narrate the book she was finishing, but she couldn't concentrate on anything except Gwen. And just as she crossed into Washington, a deep apprehension rose in her without warning, and her heart began to pound.

Samantha had never had a panic attack, but out of nowhere one assaulted her with such intensity that she almost jumped out of the car right there on the thruway. Spotting a rest area up ahead, a sign for Starbucks, she struggled to contain herself until she could veer off and come to a quick stop near a grassy area. An escalating sense of imminent disaster gripped her chest and brain, as she nearly rolled out of the SUV, and for a moment she felt she'd either go completely insane or simply drop dead—right there in the grass, smack in front of Starbucks. Feelings of depersonalization overtook her. Her hands, her whole body felt as though they weren't her own. Even her thoughts seemed strange. *Where are you taking us? Where is this place? Why so far? Too far. We need to get back. Gotta get back!*

Back to Gwen… Samantha held her head and walked in circles, trying not to hyperventilate, until the unexplained dread passed as quickly as it had descended on her. It left her drained, shaky. When her breathing returned to normal and she felt she wouldn't pass out, she went inside for a bottle of water and settled on self-soothing with a venti mocha Frappuccino.

She drank it in the car while blasting the AC and intermittently holding the cold water bottle to her neck and forehead. This book tour couldn't end soon enough, and she fought the pressing need to turn back as she continued on her trip. Relief finally came when she reached the Four Seasons Hotel. She'd rest for a while. And then maybe relaxing with an early dinner would help her regain both her physical strength and mental stability.

That evening she sat alone in the hotel's restaurant, pushing the food around on her plate mostly, and when a call came in from Liz, she motioned for the check and walked to the lobby. Liz was in la-la land over the turn of events with Isabel, and Samantha wasn't about to spoil her joy with a woe-is-me story. When Liz asked how things were, Samantha assured her that everything would turn out fine.

"You don't seem fine," Liz said. "You sound depressed."

"Just tired. And you sound like you're on top of the world."

"Yep. I am. On top of the world, on top of Isabel…same difference."

"So love doesn't suck after all," Samantha said, although she herself was beginning to think it did.

They chatted a few more minutes, and as they were hanging up Liz had a sudden revelation. "I was just thinking…if we both end up marrying Laraway women, you and I will be twice-related by marriage. How about that?"

Liz's zany thinking made her laugh. "Let's make that our goal," she told her.

In the time she'd been on the phone, two text messages had arrived from Gwen, the first asking where she was and what she was doing, the next asking how she was feeling.

I miss you was all Samantha texted back. There seemed nothing else to say. Besides, Gwen should have known how miserable Samantha was. A minute later came Gwen's reply: *I miss you, too, Sam. So much.*

After getting her clothes ready for the next day, Samantha settled at the desk in the room with a glass of wine and the other greeting card she'd brought along. If she mailed it from the hotel early in the morning, Gwen would get it by Saturday and know that she was alive and well. Well, maybe not *well*, but alive. She missed her more than so much; this sense of separation, of loss, was excruciating, and she tried to express the sentiment in another poem:

In riddles and rhymes,
Over oceans of time,
My spirit birds wait tethered.

Quill dipped in red wine,
Signature signed,
I free them to fly you this letter.

They circle the moon,
Deliver by noon,
I touch you with their feathers.

Oh, could hands become wings,
This plume would then sing,
My whispers would serve you much better.

Being in bookstores the next day was the only thing that made her feel herself. Speaking, reading, and joining a group of readers at a local coffeehouse in the late afternoon was a welcome distraction. By the time she backtracked to Maryland for Friday's signing in Baltimore, her feeling of malaise seemed to lift a little. And when she left Baltimore on Friday evening to continue up to Philly, it lifted even more. It seemed the closer she got on the map to Gwen, the better, more steady she felt.

Samantha grabbed dinner on the road, and when she checked into the Hilton Philadelphia at Penn's Landing, she passed the pool. It was dinnertime and not a soul was in sight. She had packed her bathing suit, as she always did, and decided a few laps would do her good. Writing two books at once had kept her sedentary this past month. Aside from dancing and, well, sex, she hadn't enjoyed her usual aerobics.

Samantha loved the water. The heated pool felt wonderful, and having it to herself was relaxing. She did three laps without pause, then floated in the deep end for a while. It was quiet, except for the sound of water rippling around her hands, and she started thinking how nice it would have been to have Gwen with her. She hoped her doctor's appointment had gone well. If something went wrong, if Gwen got sick again…she couldn't bear to think of it. She closed her eyes, imagined swimming with her, laughing, holding her wet body, kissing her wet lips…making love to her right here in this warm and private ocean. Her mind drifted with her body, and soon she felt as though she could fall asleep floating…just floating. But out of nowhere that sick uneasiness descended on her again. Without warning it gripped her chest with such force that she panicked and started sinking. Frantically, she flipped over and swam to the steps, coughing up the mouth full of water she'd swallowed and struggling to breathe.

The sensation was physically unnerving, something she'd never felt before in the water, and she quickly got out. Something wanted her out. The pool that had been so inviting seemed suddenly dangerous, a death trap. She'd never feared drowning, but she did now, and she grabbed a towel and hurried back to her room.

In her sleep later that night, she did drown. In the dream she did.

After that first crack in the ice, she knew it was too late with the same certainty as anyone who has made a fatal mistake and, in that final moment before death, knows the mistake cannot be corrected. The terrifying sublime…

Her legs were splayed, her belly frozen on the ice, and though she tried with all her might to bring her legs together, to stand, to push herself away from the hole, her efforts failed. She heard another crack then, deep and resounding, petrifying, and then the ice groaned like a sleeping monster woken from its winter slumber. Her body shook violently as its dark and petrifying mouth opened and in one gulp swallowed her whole.

The frigid water took her breath away, stole her strength, but she fought—fought to keep her eye on the circle of light. It was her only way out. She gasped, breathed in lungs full of water the way a hooked fish fights to breathe the air. As she pawed at the ice, she shifted and lost direction, lost the light. In one last effort to surface in the dark, her head missed the mark and only bumped against the frozen ceiling of the pond.

Samantha woke up tangled in the sheets, flailing, hyperventilating, fighting for her life. And when she sat up the dog was standing on the bed, looking down at her. Alley looked like she had that night on the patio, outside the ballroom—a photographic negative.

Disoriented in the unfamiliar hotel room, she stumbled out of bed, groped in the dark for the lamp switch. When it came on the apparition was still there, drenched, solidifying, taking on the lifelike colors it had shown her weeks ago. The soaking-wet dog shivered, its eyes pleading, full of terror, and so was Samantha. Slowly she backed up until she hit the wall by the door. She saw no point in opening it and running; after all, their energies, their particles, seemed entangled now, didn't they? If she ran the ghost would only follow. She slid down the wall, drew her knees up, and wrapped her arms around them.

And then she cried—cried in fear, cried in sympathy for the kind and gentle dog who had died this cruel and suffocating death. She cried for disobeying Gwen, for ever thinking she could touch a ghost without consequence. When she wiped her eyes with the back of her hand and looked up, the apparition had dissolved into thin air. Samantha slowly stood and walked back to the bed, expecting the covers to be soaked, but they were dry. The whole watery mess was gone. But not Alley. Invisible, yes, but ever-present. Samantha knew that now. She'd been forced to take this road trip with Samantha, to hitch a ride, and as sure as hell she'd be hitching a ride back.

Samantha couldn't say if she fell asleep again or not. One minute she was lying there with the light on, and then hours had passed and it was morning. The last thing she remembered was changing her mind about seeing a paranormal expert. An exorcist, a witch doctor, she'd agree to anything Gwen thought was necessary. What she needed was a real-life version of Detective Crowley.

She was physically exhausted, emotionally drained. How she'd pull off her gig in Philly without collapsing she didn't know. But she did. She stopped in a coffeehouse afterward, grabbed a hot vanilla latte for the road, and checked her messages. Four missed calls from Gwen. She decided to call her as she drove.

Gwen didn't even say hello. "I've been worried sick, Sam."

"I'm sorry. I'm in Jersey now, heading home."

"I received your cards…I love your poems, Sam…they're very special."

"Inspired by you, my new and very special muse. How was your doctor's appointment?"

"Great. Everything looks good."

Samantha sighed in relief. "I'm so glad. I've been worried, you know."

"I know. And how are you? You sound exhausted."

"I am. I think I'm getting sick…a cold maybe."

"Oh, Sam, just…just come straight here and let me take care of you. I hate that you're not feeling well and driving alone. I should have gone with you. I don't know what's wrong with me. I feel like such an ass for—"

"I'm the ass." Samantha didn't want to go into detail and worry her even more, but she had to say something. "She's here with me, Gwen."

"She who?"

"Alley."

There was a pause on the other end. "My God, Sam…are you sure?"

"Uh-huh. I'll do whatever you want. I'll go see anyone you think can help."

"Where are you now?"

"Jersey."

"How far from the bridge?"

"Oh, I don't know…maybe ten miles as the crow flies. Of course, crows aren't subject to Saturday traffic heading into Manhattan."

"Drive here to me, Sam. Just bring her back and we'll figure out what to do."

"I don't think that's a good idea."

"Well, if you don't want to come here, I'll come to you. I can meet you at the house."

"No. Don't. It's better this way. She's desperate to get to you, Gwen. Maybe when she realizes that I won't bring her back, she'll let go of me, try to find her way back to you, and hopefully get lost and find the light instead."

"And what if she can't separate from you? I should never have left you alone with this…this burden. Never."

"Gwen…I can't think now. I'm trying to stay awake. I feel like the life's being sucked out of me. I just want to get home and take a nap."

"Okay." Gwen was quiet for a moment, and then she said, "I do love—"

"Don't…you don't have to say it."

"But I do love you, Sam. Please know that."

"We can slow things down and see what happens Whatever you want. Let's get through this ghost thing first…okay?"

Gwen sounded as though she might cry. "Promise you'll call me the minute you get in the door?"

"Sure." The call ended. Samantha gripped the steering wheel and drove on, but a few minutes later, before she approached the bridge, she was filled with an overwhelming desire to see Gwen. Right now. The sudden compulsion seemed to automatically override her previous decision. Her finger, as if pulled by a puppet string, reached for the GPS, tapped the screen, tapped Gwen's address, and off she went on a mindless change of course.

❖

Gwen spent the next three hours on the porch with her laptop, searching documents, looking up contacts. Pete Russo, an anesthesiologist she'd once interviewed, was particularly interested in NDEs, near-death experiences. He wholeheartedly believed in them and was well respected by people in the field of paranormal research. Maybe he'd be able to recommend someone. She found contact numbers for a few others whose brains she had picked while writing her own papers.

If all else failed, she'd speak with the minister at the United Church of Christ. It was the family's church and she knew him. Not that anyone there would believe any of this. Or maybe Rosa could sneak home holy water from the Catholic church—a gallon or so might do the trick. It was worth a try. Who knew. Maybe dousing Sam would dislodge

Alley's spirit. If it did, Alley might still be here, earthbound, but she'd return to the parameters of the pond. And Sam, having learned a hard lesson, would know better than to ever attempt physical contact.

Whatever she had to do, she would make things right. It was *her* dog, her dog's ghost that was haunting Sam. She'd find a way to fix this. And when it was over, she'd make things right between the two of them, unless Sam herself was having second thoughts. After pushing her away, she couldn't very well blame Sam for not wanting to come around anymore. She'd probably send Liz to collect her crow and belongings and become nothing more than a memory—the memory of the most wonderful affair with the most wonderful woman she'd ever known.

Gwen picked up Sam's cards on the table, read the poems again, and smoothed her fingertips over Sam's handwriting. The first card had arrived yesterday, and when she received the second one in today's post, she'd broken down. Yes, whispers would serve her much better. Hearing those whispers, feeling the brush of Sam's lips against her ear, was all she wanted right now.

Everyone else on the property was happy today, and the joyous sounds of that happiness were beginning to grate on her nerves. Rosa was in the kitchen, making salsa and talking to Eugene on speakerphone. Every few minutes the two of them laughed their heads off over something apparently funny and spoken in Spanish, and Loosey was happily barking in the distance. Gwen guessed she was in the cottage where Isabel and Liz were working. They had music playing, and every once in a while, laughter erupted from there as well. Happy sounds. Normally she would have been elated to hear the happiness, but right now it was aggravating her no end. She wanted to think and suffer in silence. And when she couldn't take the joyous noises anymore, she looked down at Blue sitting beneath the table. The Scottie looked as solemn as she felt. "You and me, kiddo. How about getting out of here and taking a walk?" she asked.

Blue's ears perked up. She stood and shook herself in the affirmative.

"I thought so. Let's go." Gwen went into the house, came out with a leash, and they were off for a long trek down the road. Walking always calmed and helped her think clearly.

CHAPTER THIRTY-TWO

Around five in the afternoon, Samantha passed the apple orchards and had just turned onto Gwen's road when she noticed a curling wisp of smoke circle her head. She glanced up and around, then looked in the rearview mirror and shrieked at the ghostly dog staring at her. In one seamless move, she threw the car into park, unbuckled her seat belt, and jumped out. "JESUS CHRIST!" she screamed and flung open the back door. "GET OUT. GO! LEAVE ME ALONE!"

She should have been used to the ghost popping up without warning. They'd shared a bed last night, and who knew how many nights before that, so why should seeing her in the car be any more shocking? But it was. It reminded her of those horror movies where the poor guy makes it to the car and locks the doors, thinking he's safe from the monster, only to glance in his rearview mirror and see it sitting there in the back seat.

Samantha bent over, rested trembling hands on her thighs, and stayed that way until she caught her breath. The soothing sound of running water came from a nearby creek. She'd spent the last three days on tour, in one city after the next, and the quiet peacefulness here seemed magnified. Then it struck her. She straightened and looked all around in a daze. One side of the road was wooded, trees tall and looming, and across from them was an open field, an orange sun hanging low in the western sky.

What the heck was she even doing here? Gwen wasn't expecting her, and she hadn't intended to come. The plan had been to head straight home, and she couldn't remember exactly when or why she'd decided to detour. Leaving the ghost in the car and walking the quarter mile came to mind, but she knew it would only follow. Besides, she was too exhausted to walk, so tired that she felt like stretching out in that sun-warmed field and sleeping for a while.

Samantha looked again at Alley, shouted at her, but the ghost-dog seemed impervious to her ranting. She wouldn't even glance at Samantha. She was standing on all fours, perfectly materialized in Technicolor, fixated on the road ahead and panting a smile like a lost dog who'd finally found its way home.

"Jesus, help me…" Samantha got back in, put the car in drive, and looked in the rearview mirror. Alley was destabilizing now, coming undone, turning white and losing clarity. As the image dissipated, its energy filled Samantha with an immediate and intense joy—no, not filled her, it swathed her. It enveloped the whole car. Slowly, she continued.

A figure appeared in the distance, too far away to know if it was a man or a woman. A little farther, and Samantha saw something moving low to the ground beside the figure. A dog, she decided. A person walking a dog. Another hundred yards and both figures gained distinction. The person was a woman. She could see the blond hair in the afternoon sunlight, the stocky black dog. Gwen and Blue? It must have been, because a deafening shriek issued from inside the car, an ear-piercing cry of thrilled anticipation. It intensified to such a high pitch that she feared her eardrums might rupture. Alley was home. And she'd spotted Gwen.

Cringing, Samantha stepped on the brake, took her hands off the wheel to cover her ears. The screeching stopped and everything was quiet, still for a moment, until the ghost's heavy presence began to creep forward, pushing itself between the front seats, forcing its way into her lap with the undulating rhythm of a serpent.

"Get off me!" she yelled, jabbing wildly at it with an elbow.

Stronger than she was now, it kept coming, wedging itself between her chest and the steering wheel. She tried to push it away, but its energy seemed only to expand, putting enormous pressure on her chest and a paralyzing weight on her legs as it worked its way down to the floor. She kept her foot on the brake, struggling to free herself, to throw the car into park and jump the hell out. But before she could she heard a deep rumble, a guttural and threatening growl of warning that shook both the car and Samantha intensely. She felt the lash of invisible teeth against her face and scalp, felt her foot being lifted off the brake, placed on the gas pedal.

The SUV took off then, the jolt of sudden acceleration causing Samantha's head to fall back against the seat. The speedometer needle climbed to forty within seconds. Up ahead, she saw Gwen rush to the shoulder of the road with her dog, as though wondering what maniac was speeding out of control along this quiet back road. Samantha tried to lift her foot from the pedal, but it felt heavy as lead. She held tight to the steering wheel, trying to keep the car straight, but it was being pulled to the right, aimed directly for Gwen.

Gwen's eyes widened as the distance quickly closed and she seemed to realize it was Samantha coming at her. The two of them exchanged looks of horror. Gwen froze in place, but Blue bolted into the woods, yanking Gwen's arm so hard when she reached the end of her leash that Gwen lost her balance.

Samantha wrestled with the wheel, using every muscle in her body to turn it to the left. She'd rather run off the road, hit a tree, lose her own life, than let Alley kill Gwen. "I won't let you have her!" she screamed at the force that had both her and the wheel in its grip.

With every bit of energy, with every ounce of strength she had, Samantha pushed against the entity in her lap, hugged the wheel, and with all her might she managed to swerve just before the car plowed into Gwen. The car turned sharply, the sideview mirror whacking Gwen just as Blue's forceful yank made her topple back into the safety of the brush. Time seemed to slow as the SUV flipped and slid down the road on its roof. The last thing Samantha saw from the window was the upside-down tree just before she crashed into it. She heard the sickening thud, heard the airbags deploy. *Bang, bang, bang!* They fired off like gunshots, salting the air with a fine white powder that obscured her vision. Metal crunched. Glass shattered.

A sudden darkness took Samantha. She felt herself passing out, but a moment later she was conscious again. Everything stopped and a quiet stillness engulfed her. She waited for the excruciating pain, preferring it to the numbing paralysis of a severed spine, perhaps. And the pain did come as she struggled to untwist and orient herself. Confused, caught in the tangle of airbags, she struggled to right herself, not sure which direction was up. But her leg was trapped. She reached blindly for it, grabbing it with both hands and pulling, but quickly let go when she felt a searing pain. Her hands came back dripping blood. Her pants were soaked. Everything was wet with blood. She lay back, feeling it pumping from her leg.

Suddenly Gwen was there at eye level, on her knees in the road, pounding on the window and shouting at her. Then Gwen was up, trying to open the mangled upside-down door. Gwen screamed something to her then and ran away, but Samantha couldn't hear any of it. Sounds were fading, her vision blurring. Gwen was alive, though…Gwen would be okay. And then that thought faded along with all the other thoughts in her head, and she slipped back into darkness.

Music wafted from the cottage. Isabel and Liz had been in there working since breakfast, and since having sex up against the wall. Now they were trying out paint samples on it. The flooring Liz had ordered a week ago would be delivered tomorrow, and they needed to decide on paint colors. They both held brushes, but when Camila Cabello's "Havana" came on the radio, Isabel stopped painting and danced up behind Liz. Her hips gyrated, slow and smoothly, as only Isabel's hips could move. Liz felt the rhythm against her back, felt those hips softly grinding her ass. Over the past several days it appeared Isabel had embarked on a long-overdue quest of sexual discovery. She'd become extremely curious, unexpectedly assertive, and Liz was loving every minute of it.

"Ms. Laraway…my, my, my…" Liz turned around, the paintbrush in her hand, and narrowed her eyes seductively. "What have I unleashed?"

Isabel played coy, as if surprised by her own behavior. She smiled that demure and tantalizing smile of hers, then hid her face in Liz's neck, as though suddenly shy. "Am I too much? Are you complaining?"

"No! Never! Absolutely not!" Liz laughed, luxuriating in the feel of Isabel's hot lips as she kissed and nibbled and trailed her tongue down Liz's throat. Liz held her head back, giving Isabel full access. "Baby, you can take me anytime, anyplace, anywhere, anyhow."

Isabel pulled back and gazed into her eyes with wonderment, as if thoroughly amazed by how wonderful it was to let go—to love, to desire someone so much. Liz covered Isabel's mouth with her own then, and the two of them melted into a deep kiss until a raucous sound louder than the music came through the open cottage door.

They pulled back from each other and listened. "What's going on out there?" Liz said, but before either of them could look, Bertha flew in. Cawing frantically, she landed, looked at them, ran out the door, and took off again. They stared at each other, dropped their paintbrushes, and dashed after the crow.

"Where's Loosey?" Isabel asked as she took the lead, racing from the back of the property.

"I don't know. Rosa must have let her in." Liz ran behind her along the side of the house. When they reached the front, they stopped and gazed around. Bertha stood in the driveway, waiting for them. She squawked again and then was back in flight, headed down the driveway. Isabel started to run again, scanning the property as she did, but suddenly she stopped, and Liz almost bumped into her.

Isabel pointed to the pond. "I didn't know Sam was here…and who's that…that dog?" The moment the words came out, she covered her mouth and gasped at the sight of the obviously familiar canine who'd died seven years ago. "My God…it can't be. That looks like… like…oh, Alley…"

"I thought you couldn't see her ghost." Liz didn't see any of what Isabel saw, but she felt that presence. And it didn't feel good today. It exuded something ominous and oppressive. And Sam? She couldn't see Sam either. "Come on, let's go," she said and started running again. But here came Gwen, running up the driveway. She was frantic, breathless.

"Call 911! Call 911!" she screamed. "Hurry! Sam's had an accident. Tell them she's trapped inside and losing blood. Someone get me a towel and a hammer—*now*!"

Isabel looked at her with an open mouth, obviously bewildered, and she pointed to the pond. "But…but Sam's fine. She's right there… walking with…with…"

Gwen followed Isabel's finger and began to sway dizzily. "NO!" she cried out. "Oh no…no, no, no, Sam. Please don't leave me!" And when Sam smiled and waved at her, she staggered back and forth and then collapsed.

Clearly confused, Isabel dropped to her knees beside Gwen. "What's going on here? Aunt Gwen?" She slapped her cheek. "Aunt Gwen!"

Liz didn't waste a moment. She spun around and raced to the phone in house. It was closer than the cottage. A minute later she was back, zooming past Isabel with towels under her arm. And running right behind her was Rosa, holding a hammer and something rope-like.

"Is Gwen breathing?" Rosa asked Isabel without stopping.

"Yes."

"Then leave her. *Vamos*, let's go," she ordered.

Liz was in the lead, dreading what she would find when she reached the road. If Sam died she didn't know what she would do. She didn't think she'd be able to live through it.

Bertha's frantic call cut through the sweet summer air, and in the near distance she heard the approaching sound of several sirens.

Samantha didn't feel half bad. The pain had subsided, and she wasn't bleeding anymore. How she'd gotten out of her car she didn't know. She remembered Gwen pounding on the window, then going for help, and the next thing Alley was licking her face—probably in apology for attacking her, wrecking her Range Rover, and nearly killing Gwen. Walking up the driveway would have made more sense, but she was following Alley through the woods. She called out to Gwen then, but for some reason couldn't hear herself. Her voice was strangely muted. She hollered again, louder this time. Nothing. The whole world seemed eerily silent.

Without much effort Samantha moved through the thicket, strolling through the woods and up around the pond without really moving her feet. She felt different, weightless. Even the water, the trees, the sky looked different. Something about the entire landscape had changed. It was almost colorless. She saw the white house ahead, felt herself passing by, and as she did she saw Gwen, Isabel, and Liz. They were standing together looking at her from the far distance. She waved to them, wanted to go to them, but she didn't know how to stop this force that had set her in motion. It felt like the hose of a giant vacuum was stuck to her chest, and although the suction wasn't too strong, it kept her moving forward. She couldn't stop it.

Two crows landed in a tree in front of her. One watched while the other appeared to be calling to her. Bertha. It had been almost a week since she'd seen her. Her beak opened and closed, and Samantha thought she could almost hear her, but the sounds were weak and muffled, as though Samantha were hearing them from underwater. From one tree to the next they flew, following her, keeping up with her, until suddenly that suction on her chest strengthened, and she began moving faster than the crows could fly. She heard a humming all around her then, a sound she remembered hearing once while standing in the field of a power station—the hum of electrical energy. When she looked back, both the crows and the white house seemed miles away. The present faded into the past, far away and long ago. The humming grew louder, like a plane on takeoff, and she began to vibrate. Everything around her shimmered and vibrated. She felt the weight of something piggyback her, and with a sudden jolt she was sucked into that vacuum at the speed of light.

So many images and memories, colors and sounds passed her in rapid succession. It was a disorienting ordeal, though not entirely unpleasant, and she didn't feel scared. She was moving too fast to feel anything as she traveled, pulled through this cosmic thread in time, until everything stopped and she stood alone someplace in a heavy mist. It was thick as fog, but golden rays of sunlight burned through in places.

She felt something lift from her then. That energy that had swathed her like a heavy coat in the car suddenly slipped away, fell from her, and Alley was by her side. The dog shook herself and looked up at Samantha. She patted the dog's head. She would have been justified in hating Alley, but she was alone now and oddly grateful for the company. She ran her fingers through the dog's warm, thick fur. It caught the rays of light, and Samantha was struck by its rich beauty.

Something caught the dog's attention just then, and she lowered her head, staring straight ahead. Samantha squinted, struggled to focus as a pair of gray eyes peered out at them. They seemed to float in the mist, low to the ground, as smoky as the fog. Alley's ears perked up, tail wagging, and she stepped forward. The eyes moved forward, too, and Samantha watched as the silvery body of a Weimaraner emerged.

Even after all these years she'd have recognized that goofy, tongue-lolling smile anywhere. "Arthur? Is that you?"

Sam! he seemed to say. He did a wild tap dance, spun in happy circles, but when Samantha tried to touch him, he dodged her.

He rushed to Alley. Side by side, nose to tail, they greeted each other. Then their bodies stiffened, heads held high, each waiting for the other to make the next move. Alley crouched. Arthur crouched, a playful catch-me-if-you-can gleam of mischief in his smoky eyes. He dodged her as he had Samantha, broke into a full run, and disappeared in the mist. Alley took off in pursuit.

Samantha felt like she was on a stage, backstage, trying to find her way out from behind a big curtain. She parted the fog, pushed her way through until the sun lit a brilliant and unexpected landscape. She'd never been able to see this far before. For miles and miles stretched endless expanses, lush and green, rolling hills dotted with what looked like cottages and blooming gardens in an array of unearthly colors. And on the horizon, where the green met the blue of the sky, a herd of white horses galloped by. But it all looked so far away.

She took a step. That one step moved her ten steps, and she fell forward on her hands, wobbly with a sense of motion sickness. Parts of her body felt inflated with helium, no longer subject to gravity. Other parts felt filled with lead. Her perspective was off, too, her vision as unreliable as her motor skills. Like the telescopic lens of a camera, her eyes zoomed in and out with each step her feet took. Did she even have eyes and feet anymore, or was she simply experiencing memories of having them?

Another unsteady step. The landscape wavered and shifted, and suddenly she was standing in the middle of a flower garden that had seemed far away a moment ago. The seasons appeared confused as well. Spring-blooming wisteria, lilacs and tulips blossomed along with summer sunflowers and fall-loving asters and mums, golden rod and yuletide camellia. How strange this beauty. A beauty beyond beauty. The splendid sublime. She wished Gwen were here to see it all. But then, no, Samantha hadn't wanted Gwen to come here; she'd made the ultimate sacrifice and come in her place, hadn't she?

Out of nowhere, a woman in a loose white dress, her golden-brown hair pulled back, stood waist-high in the flowers. Without really seeing her face, Samantha knew it was her mother. She stared at her profile, steadying herself and trying to focus.

"Mom?"

Her mother looked at her, seemingly unfazed by her presence, and seeing those hazel eyes she hadn't seen in fifteen years made Samantha want to cry. She was beautiful, the way she was before she'd gotten sick and lost her hair. Even more beautiful than that, really. She looked like the young mother she remembered as a child. Samantha had often thought what it might be like to meet a loved one in the afterlife, and it wasn't the emotional encounter she'd imagined.

Her mother didn't seem especially surprised or excited to see her. She was more focused on her flowers. Samantha watched as she shook her head in displeasure, her lips tightening into a thin line. "I just don't know about these hollyhocks, Sam. How do they look to you?"

Samantha was the wrong person to ask. She couldn't even see straight. "They look great," she squeaked. This was definitely *not* the kind of tear-jerking reunion she'd expected. It felt too ordinary, like just another day during her college years, when she'd stop by after classes to help out in the greenhouses. Even Arthur had been more excited to see her after all these years.

"Am I dead, Mom?"

"Now these red velvet dahlias here…spectacular, aren't they? I'm very proud of them. I'm thinking of surprising Henry and his hives by planting some around the apiary—particularly these red velvets. They're bee magnets, you know." Just then a bumblebee landed in the yellow center of the velvety red petals, and her mother laughed. "See what I mean?"

"Mom? Am I dead?"

She didn't answer. She pointed instead to two dark specks moving across the hills at high speed. "Look at Arthur go! And look at that—who does he have with him?"

Samantha shielded her eyes from the sun, trying to track the two racing dots. How her mother could even tell they were dogs she didn't know. Samantha would have needed a telescope to make out the animals. Up over one slope and down another the dots sped. They had to be a mile away. But in the blink of an eye they were right there, Arthur and Alley, charging full speed and ready to plow right through her mother's flowers. Samantha cringed as they trampled the blooms, but her mother only laughed. The flowers sprang right back up, and all was well.

"And who do we have here?" her mother asked Arthur.

"Alley," Samantha answered. "Her name is Alley."

"Alley…" Her mother smiled. "She must be new."

"Yes. She came with me. She belongs to Gwen, a woman I…I once knew," she said, forcing those awful words past the despair of knowing she'd never be present with Gwen again.

"Gwen…yes, the woman you *know*," her mother said, as if correcting her. "That makes me happy. And your brother…he's going to be a father…"

"Where'd you hear that?"

She didn't answer. She was too busy smiling at the dogs. "Alley, what a sweetheart you are." She bent over, kissed her head, and laughed as Alley licked her face. "Well, Arthur," she said with a pleasant and satisfied sigh, "I do believe you've got yourself a girlfriend. A match made in heaven, I'd say." She giggled to herself as though realizing the pun she'd just made. An inside joke, Samantha presumed.

Her mother turned away then and left her standing there. The dogs followed. "I think I'll head up to the hills to check on those olive trees," she said. Samantha made a move to follow, but her legs wouldn't cooperate, and she fell forward again.

"Mom, wait! Help me. I don't know where to go."

"You should go back, Sam," her mother said in a casual, singsong voice and without even looking back.

"Can I? Can I go back?"

"You should. Before it gets too dark."

But it wasn't dark. It felt like only morning. The day couldn't have been brighter. In a split second her mother and the dogs had traveled several acres, and Samantha feared being left alone in this fragile, destabilized state in which she found herself. She wished she had something to hold on to. Her mother's arm would have been nice. She made an attempt to follow before she lost sight of them, but one careful step forward brought her mother swiftly back again. Her face loomed above Samantha, gigantic, larger than life, her countenance threatening. "I SAID, IT'S GETTING DARK," her voice boomed. "YOU BETTER GO BACK NOW!"

The shock of it rattled Samantha, and she obeyed the command without question. She turned in fear, not knowing if her legs or even her eyes could find their way and take her back to the mist. But when she turned, that glistening gray curtain was right there, blackening. She felt as though she were on top of the world looking down at the night sky dappled with stars. Afraid she'd trip and fall if she tried to walk, she lunged, hurling herself into the inky fog. Something on the other side sucked her in and pulled her back through that thread in time.

CHAPTER THIRTY-THREE

Samantha awoke to the steady beeping of monitors and the sensation of someone's warm hand in hers. Her eyes fluttered open just long enough to see that she was in a hospital room and that Gwen was sitting in a chair beside the bed. The image was blurred, but she didn't need to see Gwen to know it was her. Her throat was dry and it was hard to speak, but she managed a husky whisper as she closed her eyes and squeezed Gwen's hand. "Mmm…I'd recognize that perfume anywhere."

"Sam? Oh, Sam, you're back!" Gwen was up in a flash, still holding her hand. She leaned across her, reaching to push the button for a nurse.

"Wait. Not yet," Samantha said. Her mouth was parched, her head was banging, and she couldn't bend her left leg. "How much damage did I do?"

"Don't try to sit up, darling." Gwen took a piece of crushed ice from a cup and pushed it between Samantha's lips. "You have a slight concussion, a couple of stitches in your head…and your leg is wrapped—sutures inside and out. You cut the popliteal artery behind your knee. You almost," she started to choke up, "almost bled to death."

"More ice, please," Sam said. Gwen gave her another piece. She sucked on it and spoke again. "I thought that mirror broke your arm."

"I'm fine, just bruised. It's nice that those mirrors bend," She attempted to laugh but looked as if she might break down.

"How many days have I been out?"

"Only a few hours, but…oh, God, Sam…I thought I'd lost you," She grabbed a tissue and wiped her eyes. "Let me get a doctor. I'll be right back."

"Just wait a minute." Samantha reached for her wrist as she turned to leave and held her there. "I went somewhere, Gwen."

"I know...I know you did. I saw you walking with Alley...and I thought you were gone...for good."

"I was with my mother...and my dog, Arthur...in a beautiful place. Alley went there with me, too."

"And...?" Gwen hesitated, as though afraid to ask the question. "Where is she now?"

Sam shook her head on the pillow. "She didn't come back with me."

"Good." Gwen nodded, sighed in relief, and held a tissue to her mouth. "That's good."

"Last I saw her she was running off with Arthur and my mother... to check on some olive trees."

"Olive trees?"

"Yeah." Sam smiled and gestured at the cup of ice again. "I know it sounds crazy. You probably think I was just dreaming, but—"

"I believe you, darling. If anyone would believe you, it's me. And I want to hear everything...but not until the doctors see you and you've rested, okay?" Gwen was standing over her now, and she brushed the hair off Samantha's forehead and gently kissed it. "I love you, Sam... so much," she said, and turned away, sniffling.

"You didn't call my family, did you?" Sam asked as Gwen left the room.

"Of course we did. Liz did."

"God, she didn't have to do that. I don't want my father to worry, and Jason doesn't need to come."

"Jason's here. He's downstairs getting coffee with Liz and Isabel and your sister-in-law."

"Oh, geez...they came all the way here from the city? Where am I, anyway?"

"Pittsfield Medical Center. About twenty miles from the house."

"I wish Liz hadn't called. I know they're busy with work and—"

"Stop. It's all taken care of. I'm putting them up at the house for the night...or for as long as they want to stay."

Just as Gwen headed out, her brother and sister in-law appeared in the doorway. Jason was tall like Sam, even taller, and looked just like her. They might even have passed for twins if he weren't eight years younger. And Lisa looked nothing like Liz. She was a younger version of her mother, Gina.

Jason came up to the bed. "Nice stunt you pulled there, sis," he said jokingly. He always masked his emotions with humor, but Samantha could tell he was beside himself. "Next time you get an urge to do a wheelie and flip your car, fasten your seat belt first."

"Did you call Dad?"

"Not yet. We didn't know what to tell him. I didn't want him jumping on a plane or having a heart attack until we knew if you were…" He rubbed his face and started again. "If you were going to be okay."

"I saw Mom," she said.

Jason patted her hand. "That's nice."

Samantha knew he was placating her, humoring her concussion. If she described her near-death experience, if she told him Lisa was pregnant, he'd only attribute it all to a loss of blood and a hit to the head, so why spoil the surprise of impending fatherhood? "Listen," she said. "Please don't worry Dad. I'll be all right. Let me call him myself. Maybe tomorrow, okay?"

He nodded as Isabel and Liz walked in. And then in came Rosa, the last person she expected to see. Everyone was beyond relieved to see her conscious and talking. Isabel put her hands together and shut her eyes as if in silent prayer. Rosa clutched her chest as if, deep down, she actually cared. A little. She walked over with a purse dangling from her elbow and that don't-say-I-didn't-warn-you look in her eyes and waggled a finger in Samantha's face. "Nobody ever listens to me. You two are both lucky to be alive…and I'm glad you are," she added with a frown. She paused then, as if trying to read the air, then patted Sam's good leg. "It's gone, the *espíritu*. We'll all be okay now."

Jason and Lisa both furrowed their bow and exchanged questioning looks, but before they could ask anything, two doctors came in and asked them all to leave the room.

Liz was the last to go. She came over, and Samantha could tell she'd been crying. Her eyes were red and puffy. So was her nose. "You look like crap," Samantha teased her.

"Ya think? And you know I *hate* looking like crap, especially when it's all your fault. And by the way, you look ten times worse than me." The two doctors cleared their throats behind her. Liz smiled back at them, held up a finger, then bent down and put her lips to Sam's ear. "You're the only out-law I have," she sweetly whispered. "If you ever pull something like this again, I'll beat the fucking shit out of you. Stick to the ghosts in your novels and leave the real ones alone. Understood?"

Sam wanted to laugh, but her scalp hurt too much. "Understood."

"Oh, one more thing," Liz said before taking her lips away. "I love you to the moon and back. Never forget it."

Samantha was moved out of ICU that night, and everyone went back to the house to eat and get some sleep. Except Gwen. She went out, brought dinner back for the two of them, and stayed by Sam's side all night. The more brain activity, the more stimulation and social engagement the better, she'd evidently decided. She listened to Sam recount her experience, watched her sleep on and off, engaged her with the story of how Bertha had saved her life yet again.

"I wasn't of much use after I saw your spirit walking away with Alley. I was sure you were dead and…they tell me I fainted." Her voice caught in her throat, and Sam stroked her arm. "If Bertha hadn't gone and got the girls, and if Rosa hadn't responded as fast as she did, you would have bled to death, Sam." Gwen sniffled and grabbed a tissue from the box. "And can you believe Isabel, of all people, saw you and Alley, too?" She laughed and cried at the same time. "I guess falling in love has opened her to a new level of spiritual awareness."

"It's amazing what sex can do, huh?" Sam said, and they both laughed.

Gwen sighed and blew her nose. "Anyway, Liz called 911, Rosa ran down with a hammer and the sash from her bathrobe. She and the girls were able to break a window, use the sash as a tourniquet, and keep pressure on that leg. Those extra minutes made all the difference. The doctors said so."

"I owe Rosa an apology. And a million thanks. But considering we're not family, I'm surprised the doctors discussed anything with you before my brother got here."

"Oh, we discussed everything all right. I told them I was your wife."

"Ah. I kind of like the sound of that." Sam grinned. "That was good thinking. Thanks for lying. I may be obliged to make an honest woman out of you."

Gwen laughed and slowly shook her head, as if amazed that Samantha was alive and here with her. "Oh, Sam…it's so good to have you back."

"So Bertha one-upped me and saved my life a second time, huh? She's incredible. And so smart. I love that darn crow. And don't tell her I feel this way, but I really hate her not living with me."

"That crow loves you, too, and she's as torn as you, Sam. She loves it here, loves that she's found a mate and a good bird's life, but she absolutely hates it when you go." Gwen gazed into her eyes, and Samantha saw the flood of emotion in them. "Maybe one day you won't."

"Are you proposing?"

"I'd like to propose a lot of things. But let's wait and see how well that leg heals. Before I make any commitments I need to make sure you can dance and keep up with an older woman."

Sam laughed. "Don't you worry, sweetheart. And don't ever underestimate me."

Gwen smiled. "Meanwhile, I have some good crow gossip to tell you," she said, "if you think this is a good time to break some news."

"Tell me."

"Well, Bertha and her mate have a nest in one of the locust trees."

"Really?" Sam felt as excited as an expectant grandparent. "Bertha's going to be a mother?"

"Not exactly." Gwen hesitated. "More like a father."

"A father? Are you sure?"

"I witnessed the dirty deed, and all I can say is that Bertha was… well…on top."

Sam frowned. "Bertha's a boy? Can that be?"

"Sam, you've had her for a few years. Female birds lay eggs from time to time, even without a male to fertilize them. Has Bertha ever laid an egg?"

Sam stared her blankly, then started heaving with quiet laughter. "Ouch, oh, that hurts!" She winced, holding an arm to her ribs, a hand to her head, but she still couldn't stop laughing.

Gwen laughed along with her. "I'm glad you're taking the news so well."

"He'll always be Bertha to me. And no, I'm not changing his name."

"I was thinking we really should give Bertha's mate a name… and start coming up with some baby names. At least one, if not two or three."

"Well, being that Bertha was named after a hurricane, I'd like to keep with that tradition."

"Hmm…I like that. We'll have to give it some thought."

❖

Another day, another visit from the neurologist and surgeon, and Sam was ready for discharge. Gwen was there for it all. Jason and Lisa, who were wonderful and expressed their gratitude, had returned home, and Rosa had called her at the hospital to say she would prepare dinner before leaving for the day. Gwen received a text from Isabel just then, letting her know that she and Liz would be at the house to get Sam settled in and join them for dinner.

The change in Isabel over the past week was truly remarkable. Gwen didn't know what Liz had her doing, but whatever it was, they were doing an awful lot of it, and it showed.

"I'm telling you right now," Gwen informed Sam later that night, after she'd helped her shower and made her comfortable in bed, "you're living here with me until you're better…at least until you're better… and then you can do whatever you want."

"Yes, ma'am."

"Tomorrow you'll make a list of things you can't do without. Isabel and Liz will go to your house, pack everything, and bring it here. After your sutures are out and physical therapy starts, you and I can make another trip for whatever else you'll need."

"Well, I'll definitely need any and all papers on my desk, some clothes, my laptop…and my bookends."

Gwen played coy. "Bookends? You mean the ones with those cascading Persian-rose flowers that tangle themselves around the feet of those omniscient Ming-blue rooks?"

"Yes, those." Sam laughed. "That one three-dollar bookend was the best investment I've ever made, the investment of a lifetime. I'm glad it found its mate. And I'm so glad I found mine. In fact, I think you and I are rather like bookends."

"Oh, really?" Gwen looked at her flirtatiously.

"Really. Come here, and let's see how perfectly we fit together," Sam said, and pulled Gwen on top of her.

Gwen resisted. "Are you sure? I'm afraid I'll hurt your leg, Sam."

"The only thing you hurt are my feelings when you doubt me."

"I'm so sorry I did."

"Does that mean you're done with this nonsense about me eventually leaving you for a younger woman?"

"Not completely, but I've decided to take my chances and thoroughly enjoy every minute until you do."

Sam frowned. "I love and adore you. You're my twin flame. We're entangled, you and I—spiritually, emotionally, and in a few minutes physically, if you let me have my way with you." She ran her fingers through Gwen's hair. "I'm in this for the long haul, Professor, whether you think so or not. We're both women of a certain age…we've both had relationships. I like to think we've saved the best for last."

Gwen shifted and settled her weight on Sam's body, careful not to put pressure on her leg. "It is by far the best, my darling, and the last as far as I'm concerned. I'd grown content being single…until you came along and made me realize what I was missing." She gazed into Sam's eyes, stroked her cheek. "But I'm telling you right now, if it's not you, Sam, it won't be anyone else."

"Well then…" Samantha turned her head on the pillow and gestured at Gwen's wineglass. "If you'll hand me that glass, I'd like to make a toast to us."

"No wine. You just took a painkiller."

"Oh…right. Well, I'll make a toast anyway."

Gwen lost herself in those rich-brown bedroom eyes that were looking especially sexy right now and marveled over the woman beneath her.

Samantha smiled up and drew Gwen's face to hers. "Here's to the last and the best," she whispered against her lips. "May they last a *very* long time."

Epilogue

It was Valentine's Day, and a light snow fell as Gwen and Samantha got out of the car. Liz and Isabel had slept in, and the two of them had managed to sneak away for a cozy brunch at the inn, where they exchanged gifts. Gwen was wearing a beautiful ruby bracelet, and Samantha couldn't wait to put on the diamond earrings Gwen had just given her. Tonight, the four of them were heading into the city for an opera. That was Gwen's gift to everyone—that and a night at the Hilton.

Isabel and Liz were sitting on the porch wearing jackets, lacing up their ice skates as Gwen and Samantha came up the steps. Isabel had bought them all a pair for Christmas, and for the first time in seven years Gwen was skating again. Alley had moved on. Just knowing she'd found a paradise, a place to wait until they one day met again, had helped heal Gwen's heart, and a bittersweet joy had returned to this winter wonderland. Samantha would never get the hang of ice-skating, she decided, but she enjoyed having Gwen pull her around and sometimes enjoyed pulling Gwen down when she slipped and fell.

"You ladies better watch the time," Gwen warned them. "If we want to catch the 4:20 train we have to leave here in exactly three hours."

"We'll be ready," Isabel promised her.

Liz's phone beeped, and she let out a groan as she read a text. "It's my mother asking about Lisa's baby shower again. Why am I in charge of everything?"

Samantha paused on the steps. "Because it's your sister and our nephew, and the shower has to be in New York."

"Don't worry," Isabel said as Liz stuffed her phone into her pocket. "Sam and I will help you coordinate things and get invitations out."

The renovation of the cottage was complete, and Isabel and Liz were now dividing their time between the Berkshires and the city. Samantha, on the other hand, was undivided. She'd given up her rental after the new year began to live here with Gwen, and with Bertha, her soul-bird and favorite muse.

When Samantha reached the top step and looked at Liz, she put her hand out in front of her face, pretending to shield her eyes from the diamond on her finger. "Should I go back to the car and get my sunglasses? That rock is absolutely blinding. I can't even see. Could you at least show a little consideration for others and keep it turned around or maybe just take it off and keep it in your pocket?"

"Not happening, Sam." Liz's smile was almost as blinding as her engagement ring. She leaned into Isabel and held her arm out to admire it. She'd received it along with a marriage proposal just last night. "You better go get those sunglasses because it's never coming off."

"Look what Sam gave *me*," Gwen said and showed off her new ruby bracelet.

"We saw it when she first bought it," Isabel said.

"Well!" Gwen feigned indignation.

Samantha smiled and looked out at the snow. She knew there'd be a wedding reception on this property, maybe next summer. And, who knew, maybe another one soon after that.

Isabel pointed to the front door. "The UPS truck just delivered a box for you, Sam."

"Yeah?" Samantha got excited when she saw the box and rushed to it. "Don't anyone go anywhere," she said as Isabel reached for her gloves and Liz worked a mitten over her big diamond. "I have a gift for each of you—a paranormal romance."

"A romance?" Gwen asked. "What could be more appropriate on the occasion of Valentine's Day?"

Samantha put the box on the table and peeled off a piece of tape, but before she could finish, the crows flew in, all four of them—Bertha, Sandy, and their two kids, Harvey and Irma. They all stared at the can of peanuts and cracked corn on the porch. "You birds will have to wait one minute," she said, and returned her attention to the box. She peeled off another piece of tape, opened the flaps, and pulled out a book.

"Oh, Sam." Gwen's face lit up. "Your new book?"

"One of them."

"What's that on the cover?" Isabel asked. "A crow?"

"Mm-hm."

Liz was losing patience. "Come on already. Let's see it."

"Hold on." Samantha dug into the box for two more. "One for each of you," she said and handed them out.

They all gasped at the cover. It clearly startled Gwen. "*As the Crow Flies*? It's Bertha and…our *house*?" She turned the book over and read the back cover. "I don't know what to say, Sam. Is this…"

"Our story," Samantha said.

Gwen held the book to her chest and stared at her, speechless.

Liz hugged her copy and jumped up and down.

"We all know what we'll be reading on the train," Isabel said. Nothing excited her like a new book.

"But just tell me now, Sam, because I need to know," Liz said. "Does my character get the girl in the end?"

Samantha grinned at Liz as she took Gwen in her arms. "Of course." Samantha winked at her over Gwen's shoulder. "Everyone gets their girl in the end. If they didn't, it would be a story of unrequited love. And that would be a tragedy, don't you think, and not a romance at all."

About the Author

Karen Williams is a writer, psychotherapist, and licensed wildlife rehabilitator who holds degrees in communication arts, philosophy, and clinical social work. In addition to her novels and short stories, she has published articles on nature and the human-animal bond, and was awarded the Maxwell Medallion by the Dog Writers Association of America. Her most recent novella, *Meeting Ms. Roman*, was a Goldie finalist.

She loves music, dancing, romantic comedies, and speculative conversation, but most of all loves communing with nature, exploring the woods with her canine buddies, and howling with the coyotes who share her property.

Books Available From Bold Strokes Books

All of Me by Emily Smith. When chief surgical resident Galen Burgess meets her new intern, Rowan Duncan, she may finally discover that doing what you've always done will only give you what you've always had. (978-1-163555-321-5)

As the Crow Flies by Karen F. Williams. Romance seems to be blooming all around, but problems arise when a restless ghost emerges from the ether to roam the dark corners of this haunting tale. (978-1-163555-285-0)

Both Ways by Ileandra Young. SPEAR agent Danika Karson races to protect the city from a supernatural threat and must rely on the woman she's trained to despise: Rayne, an achingly beautiful vampire. (978-1-163555-298-0)

Calendar Girl by Georgia Beers. Forced to work together, Addison Fairchild and Kate Cooper discover that opposites really do attract. (978-1-163555-333-8)

Cash and the Sorority Girl by Ashley Bartlett. Cash Braddock doesn't want to deal with morality, drugs, or people. Unfortunately, she's going to have to. (978-1-163555-310-9)

Lovebirds by Lisa Moreau. Two women from different worlds collide in a small California mountain town, each with a mission that doesn't include falling in love. (978-1-163555-213-3)

Media Darling by Fiona Riley. Can Hollywood bad girl Emerson and reluctant celebrity gossip reporter Hayley work together to make each other's dreams come true? Or will Emerson's secrets ruin not one career, but two? (978-1-163555-278-2)

Stroke of Fate by Renee Roman. Can Sean Moore live up to her reputation and save Jade Rivers from the stalker determined to end Jade's career and, ultimately, her life? (978-1-163555-162-4)

The Rise of the Resistance by Jackie D. The soul of America has been lost for almost a century. A few people may be the difference between a phoenix rising to save the masses or permanent destruction. (978-1-163555-259-1)

The Sex Therapist Next Door by Meghan O'Brien. At the intersection of sex and intimacy, anything is possible. Even love. (978-1-163555-296-6)

Unexpected Lightning by Cass Sellars. Lightning strikes once more when Sydney and Parker fight a dangerous stranger who threatens the peace they both desperately want. (978-1-163555-276-8)

Unforgettable by Elle Spencer. When one night changes a lifetime… Two romance novellas from best-selling author Elle Spencer. (978-1-63555-429-8)

Against All Odds by Kris Bryant, Maggie Cummings, and M. Ullrich. Peyton and Tory escaped death once, but will they survive when Bradley's determined to make his kill rate 100 percent? (978-1-163555-193-8)

Autumn's Light by Aurora Rey. Casual hookups aren't supposed to include romantic dinners and meeting the family. Can Mat Pero see beyond the heartbreak that led her to keep her worlds so separate, and will Graham Connor be waiting if she does? (978-1-163555-272-0)

Breaking the Rules by Larkin Rose. When Virginia and Carmen are thrown together by an embarrassing mistake, they find out their stubborn determination isn't so heroic after all. (978-1-163555-261-4)

Broad Awakening by Mickey Brent. In the sequel to *Underwater Vibes*, Hélène and Sylvie find ruts in their road to eternal bliss. (978-1-163555-270-6)

Broken Vows by MJ Williamz. Sister Mary Margaret must reconcile her divided heart or risk losing a love that just might be heaven sent. (978-1-163555-022-1)

Flesh and Gold by Ann Aptaker. Havana, 1952, where art thief and smuggler Cantor Gold dodges gangland bullets and mobsters' schemes while she searches Havana's steamy red light district for her kidnapped love. (978-1-163555-153-2)

Bold Strokes Books
Quality and Diversity in LGBTQ Literature